THE MEDUSA
PROPOSITION
BY
CINDY DEES

AND

RISKY
ENGAGEMENT
BY
MERLINE LOVELACE

Dear Reader,

I always look forward to starting a new Medusa book because they're personal favorites of mine. But I have to say this one was extra special fun, because it marks the beginning of a whole new Medusa team! Never fear, though. All of your favorite original Medusas will still show up from time to time to help save the world and show the boys how it's done.

The Medusa Proposition launches the stories of another feisty and talented group of ladies out to kick butt and make the world a better place…oh, and maybe find themselves a smokin' hot hunk along the way. This set of Medusas brings a broad array of skills to the game that will make the capabilities of the Medusa Project just that much more exciting.

We begin with Paige Ellis who's looking to take her life in a new direction. And boy does she ever when she bumps into Thomas Rowe. These two are gasoline and fire from the moment they meet. So buckle your seat belt and get ready for a wild ride as the Medusas storm back into action bigger and better than ever!

Happy reading,

Cindy Dees

THE MEDUSA PROPOSITION

BY
CINDY DEES

All the characters in this book have no existence outside the imagination of
the author, and have no relation whatsoever to anyone bearing the same name
or names. They are not even distantly inspired by any individual known or
unknown to the author, and all the incidents are pure invention.

First published in Great Britain 2011
by Mills & Boon, an imprint of Harlequin (UK) Limited,
Eton House, 18-24 Paradise Road, Richmond, Surrey TW9 1SR

© Cynthia Dees 2010

ISBN: 978 0 263 88532 3

46-0611

Harlequin (UK) policy is to use papers that are natural, renewable and
recyclable products and made from wood grown in sustainable forests. The
logging and manufacturing processes conform to the legal environmental
regulations of the country of origin.

Printed and bound in Spain
by Blackprint CPI, Barcelona

Cindy Dees started flying aeroplanes while sitting in her dad's lap at the age of three and got a pilot's license before she got a driver's license. At age fifteen, she dropped out of high school and left the horse farm in Michigan where she grew up to attend the University of Michigan.

After earning a degree in Russian and East European Studies, she joined the US Air Force and became the youngest female pilot in its history. She flew supersonic jets, VIP airlift and the C-5 Galaxy, the world's largest airplane. She also worked part-time gathering intelligence. During her military career, she traveled to forty countries on five continents, was detained by the KGB and East German secret police, got shot at, flew in the first Gulf War, met her husband and amassed a lifetime's worth of war stories.

Her hobbies include professional Middle Eastern dancing, Japanese gardening and medieval re-enacting. She started writing on a one-dollar bet with her mother and was thrilled to win that bet with the publication of her first book in 2001. She loves to hear from readers and can be contacted at www.cindydees.com.

Chapter 1

Paige Ellis stared grimly at the gray turmoil of the ocean below. How was it the sea always so accurately reflected her mood? The weathered Adirondack chair beneath her was cold and hard, and somehow that was fitting, too. No comfort for her, no, sir.

Guilt writhed in her gut like a serpent, eating at her from the inside out. Not many television news journalists could lay claim to having single-handedly gotten their cameraman/best buddy/sometimes lover killed. Oh, sure, she hadn't technically come right out and asked him to try to track down that extremist group to set up an interview for her. But she'd darn well hinted around that it would mean the world to her if he could pull it off. She might not have killed Jerry outright, but his blood was on her hands, nonetheless.

Other people had argued that he should've known better, that he knew what he'd been getting into, that he was too much of a risk taker, and it had finally caught up with him. But her sense of responsibility was too deeply ingrained for her to let it go that easily.

She ought to throw herself over the cliff into the icy embrace of the sea and just let it take her. Except the fall was probably only about fifty feet and she doubted it would kill her. And even if it did, a cold, quick death was better than she deserved—

"Paige! Phone!"

Her father's voice jerked her out of her dark thoughts. "I'm not taking any calls!"

Uh-oh. He was striding across the backyard with that Ellis jaw-jut going full force. "You need to take this one." He shoved the handset at her.

"Who is it?" She didn't reach for the phone. She wasn't kidding. She really didn't want to talk to anyone. Not to nosy reporters trying to find out how one of their own died, not to her boss at the TV network, and most certainly not to anyone who would attempt to talk her out of her self-recriminations yet again.

"Find out for yourself." Her father dropped the phone in her lap and stalked off.

Sheesh. What had his knickers in such a twist? She picked up the phone cautiously. "Hello?"

"Hello, Paige. My name's Vanessa Blake."

"Do I know you?"

"Not yet. But I'd like to meet you. I have a proposition for you. One you're going to find very interesting if I haven't misjudged you."

"Is this a *sales* call?" She was going to kill her father. "I'm *so* not interested in a time-share, or an overseas investment opportunity or in opening a mutual-fund account."

The woman at the other end of the line laughed in what sounded like genuine amusement. "Good. Neither am I. I work for the U.S. government. What I want to talk with you about is classified. Highly classified. Is there somewhere we can meet? I'll come to Maine if you'd like, or you can come to North Carolina to see me. Or, of course, we can meet halfway, say in Washington, D.C.? Neutral ground for both of us?"

Interest flared in Paige's gut. She smelled a juicy story. Particularly when this woman very smoothly wasn't taking no for an answer. Paige knew the technique well. She used it all the time herself to wrangle interviews out of people. A little flustered at being on the receiving end of her own bulldozer tactics, she belatedly answered, "I'd rather go to D.C."

Her parents' beach house was sacred. It was her final sanctuary, her last line of retreat from everything and everyone. Besides, if she was going to take control of the meeting with this Blake person, she might as well put the woman at ease. Let her think she was safe, get her to let her guard down.

Ms. Blake was speaking again. "I'll have a plane waiting for you in Bangor in four hours. I'll arrange your hotel in Washington tonight, and we can meet first thing tomorrow morning. Oh, and bring your passport. I'll take care of everything else."

The line went dead.

Paige stared in disbelief. That woman wasn't a bulldozer. She was an industrial-size steamroller! And four hours? It was nearly a three-hour drive to Bangor, and she'd still need to pack. Paige jumped to her feet and hurried to the house.

The plane turned out to be an unmarked Learjet that whisked her down the coast to Dulles International Airport. Dusk was falling on the nation's capitol as a similarly innocuous SUV met her at the plane and drove her to an understated hotel in Alexandria's Old Town neighborhood. It was the kind of place high-profile politicians might use to meet their mistresses or maybe meet a journalist on the sly. After all, the fine art of the news leak was alive and well in this city.

Who was Vanessa Blake?

In the last few minutes before she'd had to leave for Bangor International Airport, Paige had frantically researched her on the Internet and came up with absolutely nothing. In some ways, that was more telling than finding out the woman's life history. As far as Paige could tell after Net surfing high and low, nobody anywhere believed a Vanessa Blake in government service in North Carolina existed. Either the name was an alias or this woman worked in the intelligence community. Deep inside the intelligence community.

Paige's interest was piqued. How could it not be? To quote Crocodile Dundee, she was a reporter and a woman, and that made her the nosiest person on the planet.

A call from the hotel phone on the nightstand woke her up the next morning, and no surprise, the caller was Vanessa Blake. "Good morning, Paige. I hope I didn't wake you up."

"No, of course not." God, she hoped she didn't sound half-asleep.

"I'll be downstairs in Private Dining Room B in a half hour. How do you like your eggs?"

"Uh, sunny-side up with a side of bacon. Toast and grapefruit juice while you're at it, please."

"I'll see you in thirty minutes."

In spite of herself, Paige was a little intimidated. She didn't want to be late and put herself at an even bigger disadvantage. She hustled through a shower, grateful that her strawberry-blond hair needed only a quick hit from the blow-dryer to be wavy and lush around her face. She tossed on a little makeup and leaped into clothes with two minutes to spare. Thankfully, she didn't have to wait long for an elevator and strolled into the private dining room exactly on time per Vanessa's phone call, looking as cool and composed as could be.

Vanessa Blake looked to be in her mid-thirties. She was pretty, but not someone who would turn heads in a crowd. In fact, intuition told Paige that this woman worked to underplay her good looks most of the time. She didn't carry herself like a law-enforcement type. Not FBI, then. CIA, maybe? Paige's pulse jumped a little. When news stories came out of Langley, they were usually juicy.

Her quiet hostess seemed content to let Paige eat in peace, and the meal passed without any stunning revelations. Finally, Vanessa laid down her fork and linen napkin. *Showtime.* Paige leaned back casually, as if her every sense wasn't on the high alert that it was.

"For the record, Paige, I have an electronic jamming device in my purse that will prevent all listening devices from penetrating this room. It also will scramble any recording you try to make of this conversation."

That sent Paige's brows skyward. She replied, "If we're going to speak strictly off the record, then what is the point of this meeting? I have to be allowed to report the story."

Vanessa smiled. "I'm not speaking to you in your capacity as a journalist. I'm interested in you for another purpose altogether."

Okay, now she was confused. Where was this woman taking this? Was she being recruited to work for the CIA? *Holy cow.* Time to take the offensive. Aloud she asked, "Why me?"

"You fit my criteria…and very, very few women in this country achieve that," her cryptic companion replied.

Paige frowned. "I beg your pardon? What criteria?"

"You're smart. You're resourceful. You're an outside-the-box thinker. You're reasonably physically fit—although I'll improve on that quite a bit before it's all said and done. Your career puts you in a position to be extraordinarily useful to me because you can plausibly go places that most people aren't allowed to go."

Uh-huh. Recruiting me to be a spy.

Vanessa leaned forward and looked Paige square in the eye. "But most of all, you're motivated. You have a powerful and personal reason for accepting the offer I'm about to make you."

"And what is that reason?" Paige asked, vaguely alarmed now. Did this woman actually think she could blackmail a high-profile journalist into working for her?

"Jerry Sprague. Your cameraman, and if I don't miss my guess, significant other."

Paige involuntarily lurched back from the table.

Vanessa's gaze held hers forcefully, but her quiet voice continued inexorably. "The real story of what happened to Jerry Sprague. Not the sanitized one that was fed to the public, and to his family for that matter."

It was Paige's turn to stare aggressively. "How exactly do *you* know the real story?"

Vanessa didn't answer directly. But what she did say stunned Paige into frozen horror.

"Please allow me to express my condolences on your loss. Sprague was a good man, and that was an awful way for him to die. If I don't miss my guess a second time, you're hauling around a nearly unbearable burden of guilt at the moment." She paused and then added lightly, "I thought you might be interested in getting a little payback against the forces that did something like that to a friend and lover."

How on God's green Earth did this woman know she and Jerry had been occasional lovers? They'd been extremely discreet about their off-camera relationship. The network didn't even have any idea of it. Paige blurted, "Who are you to presume to know how I feel about Jerry's death?"

An infinite well of sadness and knowing filled Vanessa's gaze. Paige's anger dissolved abruptly in the face of this woman's compassion. Vanessa murmured, "You're not the only person in the world who's been touched by evil. Who's seen death. The only difference between you and me, Paige, is that you point cameras at it and I do something about it. Today, I'm offering you the chance to quit being merely an observer and take action."

"Who *are* you?" Paige demanded. She was startled to register something already unfolding in her gut in response to this woman's words. Whether it was yearning for redemption or simple hope that it was possible to act against the badness in the world, she couldn't tell. She just knew that all of a sudden, this woman had her complete, undivided attention.

"Let me properly introduce myself. I am Major Vanessa Blake of the U.S. Army, Team Leader of the Medusa Project."

"Never heard of it."

"Good. If you had, I'd have to shoot you."

Paige blinked. From the deadpan way the major said that, she wasn't entirely sure the woman was kidding.

"I have a proposition for you, Miss Ellis."

Chapter 2

Two years later

Breathing deeply, Paige lengthened her stride to a full-out run. Funny how running so often hurt so much, but every now and then it was like this. Exhilarating. Powerful. Free. The beach sand had just the right give beneath her bare feet, and the waves crashing beside her were as wild and untamed as she felt. The jungle on her other side was thick and mysterious in the pale light of dawn.

Maybe it was because she was so wrapped up in her runner's high that she didn't spot the dark lump on the shore ahead of her until she was nearly on top of it. Her initial impulse was to swerve and continue around it. But something about the size and shape of the sodden canvas bag set off warning bells in the back of her mind. If she'd learned anything in her long months of Special Forces training with the all-female team of soldiers known as the Medusas, it was to listen to her gut. And her gut said something wasn't right about that sack.

She slowed. Walked cautiously the last few paces to the bag. It was big, easily four feet long, and stuffed with something bulky and irregular. The drawstring that held it shut was swollen and stiff with salt water in addition to being heavily knotted. Paige pulled her switchblade out of the concealed sheath sewn into her running shorts and sawed at the tough rope until it popped free. Good thing it was Medusa policy never to go anywhere completely unarmed.

Her nose twitched. The rotting seaweed smell rising from the bag held another subtle note…something foul that made her gut roil ominously. Carefully, she pulled the neck of the sack open. Peeked inside.

She spun away as vomit hurled up and out of her throat explosively. She fell to all fours on the sand beside the bag, her back arched like a cat's, and emptied her gut. Remnants of bile burned like acid in the back of her throat, tasting so terrible that she retched again. But there was nothing left to heave this time.

Sonofa—

It was one thing to see a dead body. Lord knew she'd done enough of that in her years as a foreign war correspondent. But it was another thing entirely to see the dismembered, partially decomposed remains of someone you knew. She knew that one firsthand, too.

Shaking off the memory of her old cameraman's mutilated corpse in a military morgue, Paige glanced down at the canvas bag at her feet. It smelled of salt and seaweed—and rotten death. She knew that smell, too, thanks to Jerry.

Nobody'd blamed her when she'd decided to take extra time off and drop out of sight after Jerry's death. There'd been some murmurs about the nearly two years she was gone. But her cameraman's death had been a shock, after all, and rumors persisted that she'd been involved in it somehow. Thankfully, the worst of the rumors had been long forgotten by the time she finally showed up on her old network's doorstep again, leaner and noticeably fitter with an imminently more self-contained look in her eyes than before, asking to go back to work—the more dangerous the locale, the better.

A cold wave washed over her ankles, startling her into jumping back hard. The canvas bag containing the dead man rocked as the water receded. She grabbed the sack and dragged it higher up the beach.

The dead man had a name. Takashi Ando. He'd gone missing forty-eight hours ago, although the Japanese government was downplaying it, claiming he'd gone on a short vacation before the economic summit formally commenced. He was a ridiculously wealthy businessman, and it was fully possible he'd jetted off for a day or two of fun in the sun before attending this important global economic conference. Officially, Paige was here as a journalist to cover the meetings.

Unofficially—well, that was another story.

Paige reached reluctantly for the cell phone in her hip pocket. Her fingers paused over the numbers. Who to call? Greer Carson, her boss at the news network? Or her other bosses? The secret ones nobody knew about?

She'd get all kinds of attention for breaking the big story of the summit. Two years ago, she'd have made the call to the newsroom in a heartbeat. But now…

…now she was less interested in fame. Much more interested in the larger consequences of the news she covered. The network execs would splash the death of the Japanese delegation chief all over the news, and it would rock the core of the summit, if not cause various key parties to withdraw their delegations and go home. Exactly the kind of reaction her other bosses were hoping to avoid.

She sighed. Vanessa had warned her that she would face constant conflicts of interest if she tried to be both a credible journalist and a Medusa. And she'd naively vowed that there was no conflict. That her loyalties were clear. The Medusas first. Her career second.

After all, she'd had plenty of opportunity to expose the Medusa Project to the world and she hadn't. Even she had to admit she'd probably get a Pulitzer if she wrote the story of women in the Special Forces. But puh-lease. No way would she go through the rigors of army basic training, continue to work her butt off for another year, then sweat, claw and bleed her way through Medusa indoctrination, just to get a story. Nobody was that big of a masochist.

Paige stared down at the bag at her feet. She'd spent her entire career standing back from events like this, detached and objective, merely observing the casual atrocities taking place around her. But she'd never done a damned thing. Oh, sure, she'd felt her share of moral outrage along the way. But she'd never acted on it.

Not until now.

Now she was a soldier. A Special Forces operator with the capacity and duty to respond to the murder of a famous, important man. Shockingly, she realized that her careless detachment was gone. Gone, too, was her reporter's jaded eye. This was *her* turf. *Her* summit to protect. And someone had died on her watch. It felt good to be angry, good to know she could act to right this wrong. And in the meantime, she'd show them all that she belonged in the Medusa Project.

Resolutely, she dialed her phone. "Viper, it's Fire Ant." The original Medusa squad all took nicknames of dangerous snakes. Her training group of Medusas had elected to give themselves field handles of dangerous insects. Vanessa Blake was Viper, and Paige had been dubbed Fire Ant in honor of her reporter's sharp bite. Her reddish blond hair probably had something to do with it, too.

"What's up?" Vanessa asked briskly.

She thought she detected sleep in Vanessa's voice, but phone calls at weird hours came with the job. She took a deep breath. "I found Takashi Ando."

"That's great!"

"Not great. He's dead."

Silence greeted that announcement. Then, a terse, "What happened?"

"It's bad. We're gonna have to call in the local authorities."

"Our orders are to keep this summit on track, and the way I see it, Ando's death has potential to derail the whole thing. Do you concur?"

Paige sighed. "Yes, I concur. The North Koreans are only here because the Chinese twisted their arms. They're looking for any excuse to pull out. And if any of the South Asian rim nations take their new offshore oil finds and go home, the whole purpose of the summit evaporates."

"So why do you want to bring in the police?"

Paige winced, but answered evenly enough. "To catch Ando's killer, maybe? He was murdered."

A long silence greeted that announcement. Paige was always fascinated to hear what Vanessa came up with when she started thinking hard. But in this case, her commander's eventual response was only a bland question. "How did he die?"

"Don't know. I found his body washed up on the beach in a bag. In pieces."

Another long silence. "Where are you?"

"I'm on the west shore of the island about four miles north of the hotel strip." The summit was being held on Beau Mer, a resort island smack-dab in the middle of French Polynesia. Neutral territory for all the interested parties. She glanced down at the bag on the sand. Not so neutral after all.

Vanessa announced, "I'm calling in some backup for you."

Paige's impulse was to protest. To argue that she didn't need help. That she could handle this alone. Except, it would be a lie. A dismembered corpse lay at her feet. And she frankly didn't know what to do next. A niggling feeling that she was missing something important plagued her. It was the same feeling she got when a big story was breaking under her nose and she hadn't spotted it yet. But what? What was she missing?

Vanessa's voice interrupted her turbulent thoughts. "The guy I'm going to send you will answer to the name Wolf. Stay put and don't move Ando."

Paige snorted. "Takashi isn't going anywhere."

"Report to me in an hour."

Paige disconnected the call and stared glumly down at the gray-green bag. She became aware of fine tremors passing through her body, like aftershocks of a major earthquake. "Who did this to you, Mr. Ando? And why?"

You're an investigative reporter, Einstein. How would you investigate this thing?

She'd try to track his movements for the last few days of his life. Find out who he'd met with. Called. E-mailed. She'd poke into his past. Into his business dealings. Look for enemies who wanted to see Ando dead. She'd check out everyone who wanted to see this summit fail. Of course, that wasn't much of a stretch to figure out. Neither the North Koreans nor the Russians were thrilled to be here. And either group had the resources, resolve and mind-set to kill someone if that was what it took to put an end to the summit.

Paige started as the sound of an engine disturbed the rhythmic whooshing of the waves. Far down the beach, a speck was racing toward her. She glanced around quickly. No time to hide the body. She could push it in the water but might risk losing it in the capricious tides. Subterfuge, then.

Quickly, she bent down and pulled shut the neck of the sodden canvas bag. Scuba gear. She'd claim it was diving equipment in her bag and she was waiting for a friend to pick her up.

She was surprised when her nerves calmed and her body fell into a state of relaxed readiness. Wow. All that training from the Medusas must have worked. Certainty that she could handle whatever happened in the next few minutes flowed through her. She'd feel better if she had an assault rifle in her back pocket, though. She made a mental note to carry a firearm from now on when she went for her morning runs.

The speck resolved itself into a blob of yellow, and then into a four-wheeled, all-terrain vehicle. Driven by a man. A holy-moly, *ay Chihuahua,* gorgeous man. Although his hair was dark, slicked back like he'd been swimming recently, and his eyes were dark as well, he looked Caucasian. Just with a really good tan.

A pair of surfboards stood upright in the passenger seat beside him. He wore a baggy pair of swim trunks that did nothing to disguise the sculpted power of his legs and showed off a tanned, muscular chest that frankly made her want to fan herself. Even his bare feet were sexy as he grabbed the roll bar over his head and swung athletically out of the vehicle.

He frowned as he looked at her. "There must be some mistake. I'm supposed to meet a guy called Fire Ant out here this morning. But you're obviously not him."

Paige grinned. It was an honored Medusa tradition to mess with male operators and fail to mention that the Medusas were women. She replied cautiously. "You Wolf?"

"Who's asking?" he replied tersely, all traces of the casual surfer dude abruptly gone.

Ah, the joys of special operators dancing carefully around each other, afraid to blow their covers. She said quietly, "I'm Fire Ant."

His frown intensified. "Come again?"

"I'm Fire Ant."

"Sonofa—" He broke off. "Yeah, I'm Wolf." He nodded at the canvas bag. "That your gear?"

"No. That's the problem you're here to help me with."

"What's in it?"

"A dead man." She watched carefully to gauge his reaction to the announcement. Interestingly enough, his expression barely flickered. Was he used to being around dead people or was he just extraordinarily self-controlled?

"What do you want me to do with him?" Wolf asked.

"Help me hide him until the right people can come and claim his body."

He took that news calmly enough. "Who is it?"

Interesting that he should assume she knew the dead man. But then, what other explanation was there for why she'd want to hide the body? She hesitated to tell this guy the dead man's identity. After all, she didn't have any idea who he really was.

She shrugged.

He studied her all too perceptively. If she read him right, he didn't buy for a minute the idea that she didn't know the dead man. For all she knew, he might suspect she'd been the one to off the victim.

Wolf asked casually, "Any sign of chains or weights in or on the bag?"

"I dunno. I didn't look yet." Not to mention she hadn't thought of it. She clamped down on the chagrin bubbling up in her gut.

"Help me check."

They squatted in the sand near the bag and examined its exterior surface for tears, holes or other signs of attempts to weigh it down. The smell was worse this close to it. Paige held her facial expression perfectly still, particularly after she caught Wolf's sidelong gaze on her.

She leaned back on her heels. "I don't see any signs from the outside."

"Me, neither. Let's open it up, then."

She clenched her jaw but held her position resolutely.

Her companion swore under his breath when he got his first look at the dead man and the condition he was in. Then he breathed, "Ando."

So. Wolf was familiar with the attendees at the upcoming summit...or else he was conversant with Japanese businessmen and could recognize them on sight, even while dead and starting to bloat.

He commented, "Doesn't look like any fish have been nibbling on him. Which means he was bagged before he went in the water."

Wolf reached into the bag and around in the various— appendages—while Paige's gaze slid away.

He rinsed his hand in the surf as he announced, "Nothing obvious in the bag with our guy. Odd. Who'd ditch a body and not weigh it down?"

Her gaze snapped back to him and she blurted, "Someone who wanted it found, obviously."

He stared at her speculatively for several seconds. "Grab the bag," he abruptly ordered.

She blinked. "I beg your pardon?"

"Help me lift your guy into my ATV."

Distastefully, she grabbed the wet canvas and, between the two of them, they heaved the wet sack onto the back of the vehicle. It landed with a sickening thud. Trying to hide her involuntary shudders, she helped Wolf lash the surfboards across the spare tire mounted on the back of the vehicle. The guy knew his way around ropes and knots. But then, so did she.

He swept his arm toward the passenger seat in invitation.

As she climbed in, she asked, "What do you suggest we do with him?"

"Put him on ice."

She frowned over at her companion as he started the engine. "Literally?"

"Yeah. Unless you want me to help you bury him. Can't leave a body out in this heat and humidity for more than a few hours for obvious reasons."

He flashed her a grin and her breath caught in surprise. Whoa. In the television business, that was known as flesh impact. Normal people might call him charismatic. She'd call him a walking advertisement for raw sex.

She mumbled, "The idea is to conceal his death until the summit is well underway. It starts tomorrow. We're only looking at a day or two. Just until someone can get here quietly to take his body home. His family deserves to get his remains."

"Where are you staying?" he asked.

"At the beach cottage of a friend. It's close to the resort the summit is being held at."

"Perfect. We'll keep him at your place."

"No way! I've got a refrigerator, but the freezer isn't close to big enough to hold our friend."

He shrugged. "So, we'll buy you a freezer."

"You can't just walk into a store and say, 'Excuse me, I need a freezer right away. Something big enough to hold a dead body for a few days."

"Sure you can."

"You're nuts."

He glanced over at her. "You got a better idea?"

She sighed. "No."

"Technically, he only needs to be refrigerated if we're looking at less than a week of storage."

Lovely. They bounced over a high berm of sand and turned onto a paved road, heading south. The ATV accelerated smoothly as she studied her companion surreptitiously. Who was this guy? He obviously worked for Uncle Sam, but in what capacity? And how did he know so much about storing dead bodies? She supposed she should leave it alone and just be grateful he'd come so quickly to help out. But she was too much the nosy journalist to let it go.

Of course, she couldn't ask him outright who he was. Special operators told you only what they wanted you to know, which was usually less than nothing about themselves. Everything else was off-limits. Case in point, she had no idea how much or how little Wolf knew about the Medusas. Just because Vanessa had sent him in to back her up didn't mean he was briefed on the Medusa Project. Paige memorized his face carefully. And the license plate of the ATV. And the fact that he surfed. It ought to be enough for her to get a name, at least.

"Any idea how he died?" he asked without warning.

She answered as emotionlessly as she could muster, "I didn't examine his body carefully, but I can tell you this. He was tortured before his death."

"How so?"

"His fingertips were black. He was electrocuted. That blood pooling would've had to happen before he died."

"Could be the corpse just beat against some rocks before it washed up here."

She replied shortly, "Trust me. I've seen the results of electrical torture before."

He didn't comment, and she had no desire to elaborate. Visions of Jerry's body threatened to steal her composure. She directed Wolf to turn onto the dirt road that led to her place.

The ATV pulled to a stop in front of the whitewashed stucco bungalow. A thick wall of trees blocked it from her neighbor's view to the south, and a large rock outcropping separated her from the neighbor to the north. She and Wolf carried the bag around to her back porch without incident.

She opened the door and Wolf followed her inside. The kitchen abruptly felt tinier than it already was. Contained within walls like this, her impromptu companion suddenly lived up to his nickname. His eyes were dark and fierce with a predatory intensity that warned her off in no uncertain terms. Not that she was interested in making a play for the guy while a dead man was lying on her back porch.

He opened her refrigerator, a boxy 1970s model, briskly ordering, "Help me empty this out."

He passed her what little food she had inside, some fresh fruit, a half pound of smooth Havarti cheese, a partial container of pâté and two bottles of wine. He stopped to read the labels of those. "Good choices. Although, that Merlot is too overpowering for a cheese as mild as the Havarti. You need an aged Stilton to hold up to a wine that robust."

She wrinkled her nose. "I hate blue cheeses."

He sighed, passing her a metal shelf he lifted out of the refrigerator. "Uneducated palate."

She scowled. "I don't need to be sledgehammered by the taste of my food. I appreciate subtle flavors. My palate is *refined,* thank you very much."

He grinned at her as he pulled out the last shelf. "There. That should do it. Let's get your boyfriend in here."

Jerry's dead face flashed through her mind. She snapped, "He's not my boyfriend."

Wolf threw up his hands. "I was just trying to lighten the mood a bit."

Her anger subsided, leaving her chagrined. "Sorry. Touchy subject."

"Why. Your boyfriend the kind who kicks butts and takes names?"

She snorted. "Like I've got time for a boyfriend with my work schedule?"

He closed the refrigerator door abruptly, leaving them standing face-to-face, no more than a foot apart. He was a lot more muscular than he looked at first glance. And lethal looking. Like her instructors back on the island. She thought she'd gotten over the whole fluttery female reaction to overwhelmingly alpha males in the past two years, but apparently not.

Belatedly, she realized she was staring at him. She turned abruptly on her heel and headed for the back porch. Wolf didn't comment, but she felt him smiling at her back as clearly as if she'd been looking at him. When she reached the door, she tossed a quick glance over her shoulder, but his features were perfectly straight. The smile still danced in his smoking hot gaze, though.

She rolled her eyes. Alpha males. All the same. They knew their effect on women and had the gall to be entertained by it. Just because some instinct left over from the Stone Age drew her to him, that didn't mean she had to act on it. Far from it. She'd learned long ago to run screaming from guys like him.

They lifted the bag and wrestled it through the kitchen door with a minimum of conversation. Getting the dead man into the refrigerator involved standing the bag upright and cramming it into the small space. But eventually the door closed and stayed shut on its own. They tied a rope around the unit to hold the door in place just in case, though.

"I wouldn't open that until you're ready to take him out."

"Ya think?" she asked dryly.

Grinning that thousand-watt smile of his, Wolf slipped out the back door. The screen slammed shut behind him.

"Thanks!" she called.

He touched a finger to his brow in a mock salute. And then he was gone. And her little cottage felt oddly empty—despite the fact there was now a dead man in her refrigerator. She headed for a hot shower to wash off the sweat of her run and the creepiness of handling a body bag.

Talk about two ships passing in the night. Too bad she was never going to see Wolf again. He was hot.

She finished her shower, got dressed and duly reported in to Viper. Vanessa told her that an American forensics team had already been dispatched to collect the body and perform an autopsy. They'd arrive on Beau Mer around midnight local time.

In the meantime, Vanessa told her to go on with her normal day and act like a reporter covering the upcoming summit.

Sure. No problem. Morning run. Check. Discover dead body. Check. Stow it in refrigerator. Check. Yep. Just another day at the office.

Paige gathered her laptop computer, a notebook and her car keys, and headed out for her nine o'clock interview with Thomas Rowe, the reclusive billionaire financial advisor to the American delegation at the summit. Apparently, he was some sort of genius regarding anything to do with money.

Getting this interview had been a coup. Rowe never gave interviews. He was barely ever photographed for that matter. As it was, he'd forbidden recordings of any kind during her interview with him. She got to do it the old-fashioned way. Shorthand. Good thing she could take dictation at well over one hundred words per minute and had nearly total audio recall. But what Rowe didn't know wouldn't hurt him. At least, not until she wrote her story.

She parked her rented MINI Cooper and walked into the plush Athenaeum Hotel at six minutes until nine. The past two years in the military had taught her that if she wasn't five minutes early, she was late. She stepped up to the concierge's desk.

"May I help you, mademoiselle?"

"I'm here to see Mr. Rowe. I have an appointment at nine."

"I'll ring his suite and buzz you into the elevator."

She looked around the marble interior of the hotel. It was decorated like a Greek temple, with stone columns and carved wall friezes, which could have been incredibly cheesy. But the decor was so tastefully interspersed with plush Aubusson carpets and luxurious furnishings that the overall effect was impossibly elegant.

"Mr. Rowe is not quite ready for you, but his assistant says you may come up now."

She stepped into the elevator the concierge indicated and pushed the button for the top floor. Of course Rowe had a penthouse suite. What else? She stepped out of the elevator into a small hallway and knocked on the last door on the right.

An obnoxiously gorgeous blonde wearing a tight business skirt and tailored silk blouse opened the door immediately. "Miss Ellis. Please come in. I'm Gretchen, Mr. Rowe's personal assistant."

Ha. She'd bet. With a body like that, it didn't take a genius to guess just how *personal* Gretchen meant. Paige followed the woman into a sunken living room decorated in stark white, with lots of chrome and crystal. But then she caught sight of the view out the floor-to-ceiling windows. The Pacific stretched before her in brilliant shades of turquoise, cobalt and sapphire that stole her breath away. White sailboats bobbed on the waves, and a few brightly painted fishing boats added quaintness to the otherwise surreal picture.

"May I get you a cup of coffee or some juice?"

Paige wasn't fond of the strong coffee favored in this part of the world. "I'd love a glass of water. No carbonation and with ice, if you have it."

"Of course. If you'd like to sit down, Mr. Rowe will be out shortly. He was held up with a private matter earlier and is running a little behind."

As Gretchen strolled away, Paige watched the woman's impossibly long legs. Three guesses as to what—or who—that private matter was, and the first two didn't count.

Instead of sitting, Paige went over to stand by the windows and gazed at the magnificent ocean below. She didn't like to meet powerful people from a seated position. It gave them too much subliminal control of the interview from the start.

She'd stood there for maybe two minutes when a door opened behind her. Paige turned around and said, "Thanks for the water, Gretch—"

Not Gretchen.

Wolf. He was clean shaven now, his hair dry and styled—not slicked back from his face—and wearing a tailored business suit that must've cost thousands, but there was no mistaking him. If only she'd been able to find a picture of the reclusive billionaire to have recognized him on the beach! The casual surfer dude was gone, and in his place stood this formidable businessman. But the eyes…the eyes were the same. Intense. Smoky. Mysterious.

"You? You and the surfer are the same pers—"

Another door opened and Gretchen stepped out, carrying a tray with coffee, croissants and a pitcher of water.

Wolf held out his hand quickly. "I'm Thomas Rowe. Pleasure to meet you, Miss Ellis."

Chapter 3

Tom watched his assistant impassively as she set down the tray on the coffee table in the living room. "That will be all, Gretchen."

She nodded and turned silently to leave. Good assistant. Didn't need or want pleasantries from him. Plus, she was the soul of discretion and *scary* efficient. He made a mental note to give her a raise. The door shut behind Gretchen and he turned to face the imminently less predictable woman still in the room with him. She'd moved again by the window and stood facing him, her posture defensive. Good. He liked reporters back on their heels. This one in particular after she'd shocked the hell out of him.

"*You're* Paige Ellis?" he demanded. "How in the hell do you know Vanessa Blake?"

"Gee, I was just about to ask you the same thing," she snapped.

He answered evasively, "We're old friends. You?"

"Ditto."

Riigghhtt. The obvious answer was that the woman in front of him was part of Vanessa's secret team—

He discarded the idea out of hand. No way was a well-known journalist like Paige Ellis part of the Medusa Project. It was laughable to even think about. Except she'd answered to the code name Fire Ant on the beach. A biting insect… hadn't Vanessa's husband said something a while back about the new Medusa team going for dangerous bugs instead of snakes for their names?

Surely not. She was a civilian for God's sake. A pampered media princess. No way did she have the stamina, the fortitude, the sheer guts to be a Medusa.

"So, tell me, Mr. Rowe. What is an important guy like you doing out at the crack of dawn surfing alone?"

"I like to surf. And I like my privacy."

"But it's dangerous. Too dangerous for a man of your stature."

He raised an amused brow. "What's wrong with my stature? Aren't I tall enough to surf?"

She rolled her eyes at him.

He studied her as she moved from the window to stand across the coffee table from him. Tension vibrated through her entire body, and something deep in his gut responded in kind. Damn her. He didn't like being off balance like this.

Although she was an attractive woman overall, the first thing a person noticed when they looked at her were those incredible electric blue eyes of hers. Bright and inquisitive, they looked right through a guy and made him feel a little naked in front of her. He jumped in before she could ask the next question burning in her glorious gaze. "And what were *you* doing on the beach at the crack of dawn, Miss Ellis?"

"Hauling dead men out of the surf, of course."

"Do you do that on a regular basis?" he asked dryly.

"At least twice a week. It's great aerobic exercise," she snapped.

Touchy, touchy. He asked more seriously, "What do you know about Takashi-san's death? His family will be devastated."

"You know the family?" she asked softly.

Careful to keep his expression smooth and give nothing away, he nodded. "His first wife died of cancer years ago. Wife number two is a former high-fashion model and quite the wild child. But he seems—seemed—happy with her. He's got a couple of grown kids from the first marriage."

"Any idea who'd want to kill him and then dispose of his body in such a fashion?"

"You're the reporter. You tell me."

She shrugged. "The North Koreans and the Russians have every reason to sabotage this summit and properly provoked, they're both capable of murder. Of course, it could be some business or personal enemy of Ando's, maybe the Yakuza—the Japanese mob is still pretty powerful. And then there's always the ubiquitous child who wants to collect an inheritance sooner rather than later."

Tom jerked, offended. "Not Ando's sons. They're both honorable men."

Paige shrugged. "Then we're left with enemies or politics."

"Who's coming to collect the body?"

Paige pursed her lips and looked prepared to be stubborn about answering. He added gently, "I can always call the local police and tip them off to check out your house. In this part of the world, they'd throw you in jail first and maybe get around to investigating the murder later. Or maybe they'd just lock you up and throw away the key."

She did an odd thing. Her eyes became preternaturally intense, and she became very still. Like she was readying herself to do violence. It was something he'd expect to see in a soldier, not a girly-girl TV journalist. For make no mistake about it, Paige Ellis was all girl. She wasn't a big thing, maybe five-foot-five. And slender. Not skinny, by any stretch, though. She looked fit. But feminine. And those eyes of hers…he was having trouble looking away from them. They were even brighter and bluer in person than on television.

She spoke quietly. "I don't take well to being threatened, Mr. Rowe."

That was more like it. Now she was the one on the defensive. He grinned and picked up a plate of croissants. "Snack, Miss Ellis?"

"No, thank you," she bit out.

He sat down on the couch facing the magnificent ocean view and poured himself a cup of coffee. Since he never took anything but coffee and croissants before noon, he assumed the water on the tray was for her. He poured some into a crystal glass already filled with ice. He set it on the low table in front of her without bothering to ask. She struck him as the kind of woman who'd answer no to anything he asked of her just to be obstinate.

He enjoyed watching her struggle to corral her temper as she sat down stiffly across from him. Slowly, she pulled out a notepad and a pen. And when she finally looked up at him, her face was calm. Pleasant even.

Impressive.

"So, Mr. Rowe. How did you get involved with this summit? Were you approached by our government, or did you approach them?"

Ah. Retreating into her reporter persona, was she? Surely she was aware of his reputation with journalists. He was known as the worst interview in America. He made no secret of the fact that he despised anyone poking into his personal life. He was even known for finding questions about his business matters offensive. But suddenly, he was finding it damned hard to be offended when he could hardly tear his gaze away from Paige's tanned and toned legs.

She asked him the usual questions about the global business climate, the outlook for the future, what recommendations he was planning to make at this summit of world business and political leaders. In return, he fed her his usual dodges. He was the master of answering a question with a question, sidetracking the conversation into clarifications of exactly what questions meant and, when she finally nailed him down with a direct question, blatantly not answering it and straying into vague politician-speak about hope for the future.

After about ten minutes of cat and mouse, she sighed and laid down her pad and pen. "Mr. Rowe. If you're not going to cooperate at all with this interview, why did you agree to it in the first place?"

He leaned back, grinning openly. "I give an uncooperative interview every few years just to make the point that I still don't talk to reporters. And when I heard you were coming back to television, I thought you'd enjoy the welcome back gift."

Chagrin flitted across her face. Uh-huh. She thought she'd landed the big catch that would launch her comeback. Sorry. He was nobody's trophy fish.

A cute little frown wrinkled her brow as she pressed. "Seriously. Why me?"

Now there was a loaded question. With more loaded answers to it than he cared to examine closely. His gaze narrowed. Two could play that game. "I wanted to see if your eyes were as blue in person as they are on TV."

Only the barest flutter of her eyelashes gave away that she was flustered by the innuendo in his voice. She was really very good at what she did. It was just that he knew her reporter's game all too well and had no intention of playing along. Women tried to use sex as a weapon against him all the time. He was rich, single, reasonably good looking and still in his thirties, which was to say, he was the Holy Grail to women like her.

"And are they?"

"Are they what, Miss Ellis?"

"As blue in person?"

It was his turn to hide his surprise. He got the distinct impression that was a personal question. Purely off the record. Was she flirting with him?

He studied her, letting his gaze range from head to toe and back until she squirmed once, ever so slightly. Then he answered casually, "Actually, I was more curious whether they're that blue in bed."

"In your bed?" she asked shortly.

He shrugged, a grin tugging at the corners of his mouth.

"That is something you'll never find out, Mr. Rowe. This interview is over. I shall, of course, be happy to make it known to my colleagues that you are still as stubborn and arrogant and obnoxious as ever."

His grin broke free. She was magnificent with her eyes snapping cobalt fire like that and her cheeks bright with color. She leaped to her feet in agitation as he rose casually to his. So. She'd turned down his fairly unusual offer to bed her, had she? A fascinating first.

"Give me a call the next time you find a dead guy on a beach and need help," he drawled at her ramrod stiff back.

She paused deliberately at the door and looked slowly over her shoulder. She said pleasantly, "Good Lord willing, Mr. Rowe, the next dead body I find on a beach will be yours."

He laughed heartily as the door slammed shut behind her. He was still chuckling a few minutes later when Gretchen stepped into the room, frowning.

"What's up, Gretch?"

She handed him a sheet of paper with an e-mail printed on it. "We received another threat against you, Mr. Rowe."

He sighed. "I get death threats all the time. Tell Nils. He knows what to do." Nils Olson was his chief of security and a former Swedish Special Forces commando. They'd met when they got caught in a blizzard, helicopter skiing on a mountain in Austria. The big Swede had found him snow-blind and half-frozen. They'd made it down that mountain together and been fast friends ever since.

"Here's your schedule for today, Mr. Rowe."

He'd tried for years to get Gretchen to call him Tom, but she'd never budged. He was the boss, and would forever remain Mr. Rowe to her. He knew everyone thought they were sleeping together. But he also knew that she was hopelessly in love with Nils, and Nils was hopelessly focused on his job, completely unaware of her feelings. Tom tried to respect her privacy as much as she respected his, however, and stayed out of the whole thing. And in the meantime, he had a great security chief and an equally great assistant.

He sighed and took the typed schedule. His day was packed with meeting various members of the sixty delegations at this summit, then he had an hour to work out, an hour to rest and shower, and last on the list, the opening ball this evening.

"Have my tuxedo steamed and my black dress shoes shined, will you, Gretchen?"

"Of course." She moved to the coffee table to collect the tray. "How did your interview with Miss Ellis go?"

"Actually, it went fantastic."

That made Gretchen look up. She knew as well as anyone how much he despised reporters.

He grinned. "She only lasted ten minutes before she stomped out in a huff."

"The last one made it nearly a half hour before she gave up."

"The last one was hoping to get me in the sack."

Gretchen tsked. "Still. Only ten minutes? You must have been particularly unpleasant today. Either that or this one wasn't the least bit patient."

"You're right. She's not the least bit patient, our Miss Ellis. Not patient at all."

* * *

Paige looked around the grand ballroom, scoping out who was present and if her light blue satin gown was too horribly out of fashion. It felt weird to be wearing high heels and jewelry and have her hair piled on top of her head like this. She'd spent so long crawling around in mud, wearing fatigues and toting an assault rifle that she'd almost forgotten what it felt like to get dolled up.

The crowd ranged in more or less concentric circles around the room, with the people growing progressively more financially important as she walked toward the heart of the party. Her gaze swept the innermost circles of power here tonight—a who's who of the world's most influential business leaders. Her stomach leaped at the sight of a familiar silhouette, a tall, athletic form she'd recognize whether dressed in surfing trunks or a designer tuxedo.

Of course, he had to choose that exact moment to look up. Their gazes locked. Damn him! He would have to catch her ogling him in a fancy tux that made him look like a cover model. He smirked at her and her palm got a sudden itch to swipe the expression off his face. But rather than give him the satisfaction of getting a rise out of her, she instead pasted on a pleasant smile as she veered away from him and his companions.

Paige snagged a flute of champagne from a strolling waiter and downed the thing in a single gulp. When the next waiter passed, she exchanged the empty glass for a full one and sipped this one a little more temperately. Although she'd been gone for two years, the faces were mostly the same. She had interviewed many of the dignitaries in the room and made polite small talk with them as she cruised the ball.

A number of her fellow journalists were clustered around a bar at the far end of the huge room, but she avoided them. They had an alarming tendency to reminisce about Jerry with her, and frankly, she avoided those memories whenever possible. She might have come to terms with her role in Jerry's death, but it didn't mean she wanted to wallow in her lingering guilt.

She felt eyes on her and glanced up, her gaze colliding with the dark, amused one of Thomas Rowe halfway across the room. Jerk. She looked away pointedly. But she couldn't resist peeking his direction a minute later. Dammit! He was still staring at her!

She yanked her gaze away, vowing to herself not to look at him again tonight. But then the darnedest thing started happening. She'd glance innocently at something or someone, and there he'd be, smack-dab in her line of sight. It was like he was trying to make her look at him. Surely he wasn't that juvenile.

And then he started moving in on her. Oh, it was a gradual thing, and to the innocent observer would undoubtedly be completely undetectable. But she was aware of every foot closer to her that he came. Was he *stalking* her? She actually had to curb an impulse to sidle away from him. Double jerk.

The annoying game was interrupted when she overheard his name mentioned among a group of women clustered just to her right. Paige recognized one of them as the wife of the American ambassador to China, a woman she'd interviewed before.

Paige moved in smoothly. "Mrs. Carrillo. You look fabulous! Tell me, are you still working with that international women's rights group?"

"Why, hello, Paige. Yes, I am. You're looking lovely yourself."

"You're too kind. I didn't mean to interrupt you ladies… please, don't stop on my account."

A woman Paige didn't know but who sported a thick European accent—French, maybe—laughed. "I was just telling them about Mimi Ando's rather sordid past."

Paige said winningly, "I'm sorry. I thought I overheard you mentioning Thomas Rowe."

The Frenchwoman replied, "You did. He and Mimi were quite an item a few years back. They had a scandalous relationship, even by Parisian standards."

Curbing her eyebrows, which seemed to want to sail upward, Paige encouraged the woman. "Do tell."

"Well, they partied their way across Europe and had spectacular fights in the most inappropriate places. And then she met Takashi and dumped Rowe cold. He hasn't dated another woman seriously since. Rumor has it that she broke his heart."

Indeed? A jilted lover, was he? Funny he hadn't shown more reaction to Ando's body this morning, then, even if to show a certain satisfaction at a rival's death. But he'd acted entirely unaffected. Not even surprised, come to think of it. Had he known what was in that bag? Was it possible? Had Thomas Rowe murdered Takashi Ando? Over a woman? Her instinct was to reject the notion as absurd. But her training, both in journalism and things military, demanded that she consider every possibility, no matter how outrageous.

She risked glancing around the room in an attempt to spot Rowe. There he was, speaking to a very tall brunette with the kind of body that made other women feel completely inadequate. "Who's that Rowe's talking with over there?" Paige asked.

The other women looked around and the Frenchwoman burst out laughing. "Speak of the devil. That's Mimi Ando."

Another woman murmured, "While the Takashi cat's away, the Mimi mouse will play...."

The Frenchwoman shrugged. "Maybe their romance isn't as dead as it seemed."

Paige flinched at the reference to death. Ando's body was still in her refrigerator, awaiting the American forensics team due in later tonight. A gruesome image of his remains flitted through her head. Surely Tom wouldn't say anything to Mimi about her husband's death before the American team had a chance to examine Takashi's remains. And even he wouldn't be so callous as to tell a woman in a public venue like this that her husband had died.

"If you'll excuse me, ladies, I could use another glass of champagne. Enjoy your evening."

"Look me up the next time you're in Beijing, dear," Mrs. Carillo called as Paige drifted away.

Paige stepped into the hotel lobby and paced the length of the cavernous space, troubled. Why would Vanessa Blake send a possible murderer to help her this morning? If Rowe was some sort of agent of the U.S. government, had he gone rogue? She opened her cell phone and dialed Vanessa's private line as she stepped outside into a lush garden in search of privacy.

"Hey, Viper."

"What's up?"

"Who was that you sent me this morning? I mean I know who he is. What capacity do you know him in?"

"A professional one. Why?"

Paige frowned. "Could you be a little more specific than that?"

"Mind me asking why?"

"Were you aware he had a torrid relationship with Mimi Ando she broke off so she could marry Ando?"

A long silence greeted that announcement. Finally, Vanessa said heavily, "I'm forced to acknowledge the relevance of that, but I'm having a hard time believing what you're suggesting. I've known Tom for years. He was on Jack's team."

Paige's jaw dropped. Vanessa's husband was Colonel Jack Scatalone, a longtime Special Forces officer and team leader. He was still one of the Medusas' primary instructors. And Rowe had worked for him?

"Are you telling me Thomas Rowe is…was…one of us?"

"He was. He's not an active operator anymore."

Paige asked grimly, "So, if he wanted to go off the reservation, he'd know how to do it?"

Vanessa sounded surprised. "You seriously think he's turned? That *he* killed Ando?"

"I think we can't rule it out."

"Jack's going to have a cow at the idea. He thinks the world of Tom."

"So don't tell him about it just yet. Let me poke around a little and see what I can find out."

Vanessa sighed. "That's not how Jack and I do business, but thanks for the offer. Call me if you learn anything new."

"Right, boss."

She lifted the phone away from her ear thoughtfully.

"And what are you poking into now?" a male voice asked from directly behind her.

Paige whirled, startled, and almost dropped her phone in her shock. Thomas Rowe. "That's none of your business, Mr. Rowe."

"Ah. So the journalist likes her secrets, too, does she? Are we being a hypocrite, perhaps?"

She scowled at him. "You wish. I'm just doing my job. What's your excuse?"

He laughed, a low masculine sound that scraped across her skin, leaving goose bumps in its wake. "You're missing all the fun, Miss Ellis. Come inside."

"Why?"

"Because I want to dance with you."

That made her stare. "What on earth for?"

"To start rumors and wreck your credibility should you attempt to do some sort of negative report on me."

"I thought you don't give a damn what the press says about you."

"I don't want them to say anything about me at all. That's entirely different."

"Dancing with me isn't going to shut me up."

He grinned. "I doubt much of anything could do that."

"And on that insulting note, Mr. Rowe, you can take your invitation to dance and shove it."

She turned and strode away from him with as much aplomb as she could muster. But she didn't count on him following her inside. Furthermore, she didn't count on him reaching out fast to wrap his arm around her waist tightly enough that it would take violence on her part to shake it off. Heads were already turning their way, and if she wasn't mistaken, eyebrows—and tongues—were wagging.

"Don't be a spoilsport," he murmured. "Dance with me. It's a waltz."

"And your point?"

Of course he ignored her question entirely and instead commented, "Did you know the waltz was declared scandalous when it was introduced? It was thought to be too sensual for proper ladies. So. Are you a proper lady or not, Miss Ellis?"

She opened her mouth to suggest as politely as she could that he remove his hand from her waist before she broke his fingers, but before she could, he spun her around him and onto the dance floor. Despite his dashingly lean appearance, the guy was shockingly strong.

And she was waltzing.

With Thomas Rowe.

Playboy. Billionaire. Bastard.

And all she could think about was how incredible sex with him would be.

Chapter 4

Tom grinned as the waltz shifted into a slow ballad, the kind where the guy pulls the girl as close as he thinks she'll let him without slugging him, and the dancing is actually just swaying and shuffling while checking out each other's bodies. Paige made to step back, but he tightened his arm around her waist to prevent the movement.

"What are you doing?" she whispered furiously.

Amused, he murmured back, "Your reputation isn't wrecked, yet. One dance with me could just be a polite thing after I granted you an interview. But two dances means there's something going on between us."

"You are such a jerk!"

"You're just now figuring that out? You mustn't have done your homework on me before our interview, Paige." Her entire body vibrated in his arms, almost like she was growling. He grinned down at her. "You're cute when you're mad."

Her eyes narrowed to distinctly feline slits. For just a moment, alarm resonated in his gut. If she'd been a man and looked at him like that, he'd have given second thoughts to provoking the guy any further. But as it was, she barely came up to his chin and couldn't weigh much more than half of his solidly muscled 220 pounds.

His left hand slid down the slinky satin of her gown, caressing the inward curve of her spine. Her body arched slightly away from the touch, which brought her belly very nicely into intimate contact with his groin. Blue lightning snapped and crackled in her eyes.

He probably ought to stop. But damned if he didn't want to see just what she'd do if she exploded on him. His hand slid lower. The pert bulge of her derriere filled his hand like it had been made for him. Her flesh was firm and resilient and, about as quickly as he registered its sexy texture, went rock hard under his palm.

Her gaze went black. Cold. Furious.

Oooh whee, she was pissed off. It was a sight to see. He had himself an armful of fireball, now....

Her gaze left his for a moment, focusing on something over his left shoulder. Alarm flashed in her eyes, at sharp odds with the fury pouring off her.

And then, without warning, she went limp in his arms, a hundred plus pounds of deadweight jerking him downward. It wasn't that he couldn't hold her weight. In fact, he did it easily. It was just that he had to adjust to the surprise of it.

A slight breeze whiffed over the top of his head. What the—

Something hooked behind his right ankle. Jerked sharply. Twin fists smashed into his shoulders. He flew backward, slamming onto his back at full length on the dance floor.

Something heavy landed on top of him. Breasts smashed into his face, and he smelled the most luscious combination of warm female and sexy perfume he'd ever encountered.

Holy cow. She was a hellion when she blew up. He mumbled against her chest, "I want you too, honey, but do you think this is the place for—

"Shut up and stay down," she snapped.

He froze. That was exactly the tone of voice one of his buddies on his old Special Forces team would have used when bad things hit the fan.

"What's up?" he bit out. Paige was vibrating again, but this time it was pure fight-or-flight adrenaline coursing through her. He could smell it on her skin.

Her breasts lifted away from his face far enough for him to breathe, but she continued to sprawl on top of him. And then it dawned on him—her stance was protective.

She spoke without glancing down at him. "Someone just shot at you. Stay here. I'm going after him."

And then her weight lifted away from him and she was racing across the room in a flash of ice blue satin. He leaped to his feet. People around him were staring, still frozen in that moment of initial shock before they began buzzing like bees. He hadn't experienced the time distortion of a hyper-adrenaline rush since his Special Ops days, but damned if everyone around him wasn't moving in slow motion now.

With preternatural strength, he bolted after Paige. She was already slipping onto the terrace and into the night. He put on an extra burst of speed. If she got to the gardens before he caught up with her, it'd be hell not to lose her in the thick tropical foliage and overhanging palm trees.

She dodged down a shadowed path between giant ferns and he followed suit, thankful for her pale dress in the blackness. Damn, she was fast! His legs churned as he chased after her. A branch whipped across his face and he ducked grimly, but pressed on.

Surely she was mistaken. They'd been on a crowded dance floor, for goodness' sake. There was no way of knowing who the shooter had been pointing at…assuming there even was a shooter. He wouldn't put it past Paige Ellis to have imagined the whole thing. She was a reporter, after all. She made her living sensationalizing things.

For all he knew, she was chasing nothing at all. But he couldn't in good conscience leave her alone to the vagaries of whomever might be in this isolated area late at night. Although the way she'd knocked him down in the ballroom, she probably could take perfectly fine care of herself. Okay, so he was out here tearing after her because she interested him. And very few women did that.

He stretched into a full run, arms pumping, breathing hard. There. Another glimpse of blue satin ahead. He ran even harder. Sweat popped out on his brow. The path turned sharply and his dress shoes slipped on the crushed granite. He flailed his arms and managed to catch himself, but Paige had pulled away again.

How big was this stupid garden anyway?

Yard by yard, he gradually closed the gap on her. How on Earth was she running in high heels? The foliage thinned slightly. He vaguely recalled hearing about a rose garden that this resort was known for.

And then he glimpsed something that made his blood run cold. A second fleeing figure not far ahead of Paige. Attired in all black and running like his life depended on it. Worse, she was almost on the guy. And what exactly was she planning to do with him once she caught him? The guy was obviously a pro. He'd break her neck in a heartbeat.

For the first time tonight, true panic speared through him. He'd been shot at plenty during his military career, and he'd had plenty of bullets wing past uncomfortably close to him before. But the idea of watching Paige get her head ripped off scared him like nobody's business. He dug deep and with supreme effort found an extra gear. Ten yards from Paige. Eight. Five.

A shot rang out and he flinched reflexively.

Rifle. High-powered, large caliber. Sniper rig, then.

The man fleeing before her went flying, tumbling head over heels and crashing into a bush. Paige hit the dirt beside the man and Tom slammed flat beside her. "You okay?" he bit out.

"Yeah. You?"

"Good. What about the other guy?"

Paige reached up awkwardly with one hand and felt the downed man's neck. "Dead. Sounded like a sniper rig."

He agreed with her assessment of the lone gunshot.

She muttered, "You need to get out of here. I can handle this on my own."

"Yeah, well, you're stuck with me."

"I mean it, Tom. Go back inside. You'll be safe there."

"I don't give a damn about safe. I want to know who just killed the guy who tried to kill me."

She glared at him in the darkness. Although she sounded pissed, she looked closer to panicked. "I won't have your death on my hands! You'll be safe inside, and I need you to get undercover right now."

"Not happening."

Her mental wheels were turning so hard he could almost see them as she tried to cook up some reason to make him go inside. Time for a little distraction. "You packing?" he muttered.

"Where in this dress am I going to stow a weapon?"

He grinned as his hard gaze scanned the area. Too much cover out here. They'd never spot the shooter. Besides, assuming the sniper had killed his intended target, the guy would have already left the area.

"How 'bout you?" she asked in turn, her head swiveling all around in search of the latest assassin. "You armed?"

"Nah. Hotel security forbade it," he answered in disgust.

She glanced at him in surprise. "And you actually followed the rules?"

He snorted. "I sure as hell won't from now on. Who's the dead guy?"

"Dunno. His name badge says he's conference security. Goes by Claude Dufresne. He looks European."

He raised a skeptical brow. "And how does a European look?"

She answered absently as she rummaged in the dead man's pockets. "Bad teeth covered with nicotine stains from unfiltered cigarettes."

Okay, he'd give her that one. A certain group of Europeans certainly fit that set of parameters.

She continued under her breath, "His credentials look legitimate. I think he actually was conference security."

"We'll have to verify that. If this meeting is compromised, we've got a big problem on our hands." A huge problem, in fact. "It'll be a mess if the conference has to be delayed or rescheduled—"

She interrupted his train of thought as he started to spin out the alarming possibilities if this economic summit failed. "Tom, you've got a bigger problem than that. Someone just tried to kill you."

"You don't know that for sure—"

She cut him off briskly. "I was looking directly down the bore of this guy's weapon. The back of your head was his target."

"I didn't hear a shot."

"He had a silencer on the weapon. I saw the sideways flash when he fired."

He frowned, still skeptical.

She added with scant patience, "The cops can recover the round and do a ballistics analysis to confirm it. But in the mean time, I've *got* to get you undercover. Have you spotted the second shooter?"

"Nope."

"We've got to assume he's still out there, then. Stay low and follow me."

He jolted. Follow *her?* She could follow *him*. He retorted, "I'll go first."

"You're the *target*. I'll go first."

"You're the girl—"

"Shut up, Rowe."

Well, okay then. He tried another tack. "You're not exactly dressed to crawl around out here."

"I'll survive. Let's go."

He watched in shock as she hiked up her ball gown around her hips and commenced scrabbling along in a shockingly efficient low crawl, her belly barely an inch off the ground. It took huge strength do that. Where in hell did Paige Ellis develop that kind of power? He knew male Special Forces soldiers who couldn't do it that well.

Shouting voices in the distance sounded like they were approaching. The cavalry coming to the rescue, no doubt. Paige stopped in front of him in the shadow of an overhanging banyan tree. He pulled up beside her, elbow to elbow. The length of her thigh pressed against his, strong and slender. And damned if she still didn't smell good.

She glanced sidelong at him, a glint of humor in her eyes. "Wanna stick around to talk to the authorities? The way I hear it, you like them about as much as you like journalists."

He snorted. "Snakes or lizards—take your pick. I suppose you're going to want to dust yourself off and jump in front of a news camera and cover this, aren't you?"

She frowned. "It'll be a hell of a breaking story. Unfortunately, I have somewhere else to be this evening."

He matched her scowl, inexplicably irritated. "You got a hot date or something?"

"Or something." She pushed up to her hands and knees and then to a standing crouch. "You have fun evading the cops, Tom."

"You're leaving me?"

"Now that every security guy on the island is converging on this garden, I expect you're about as safe as you're ever going to be. Our shooter is either bugging out right now or is already gone. He won't stick around for the entire French Polynesian police force to surround him."

She was right, but for some reason, he didn't like the idea of her leaving him. There was something electric about her presence. She stood upright and commenced dusting off her gown. "Need help with that?" he asked.

She glanced at him. "Lay a hand on me and you'll withdraw a bloody stump, buddy."

He snorted with laughter. "Big words from a little girl."

She turned and stalked off into the shadows. He glanced down, perplexed. Barefoot. Again. She'd been barefoot on the beach this morning, too. He'd noticed then that she had nice feet. High arches and pretty toes with sassy red nail polish. He jogged after her and caught up. "Where are you headed?"

"Back to my place. Thought I might clean out my refrigerator."

"Ah."

They walked quickly back toward the hotel, dodging the bulk of the security personnel streaming toward the source of the gunshot. Without warning, Paige grabbed his arm and yanked him off the path into a stand of bushes that had some sort of sharp, prickly frond.

He murmured under his breath, "I knew you were attracted to me, but I had no idea you were this desperate."

She glared at him and whispered, "They would spend all night questioning us, and meanwhile you wouldn't be getting any safer. I need to get a security perimeter set up around you."

A pair of police officers raced past them. Another pair. Lots of shouting erupted behind them in the vicinity of the dead man.

Paige stalked back out to the path and took off toward the hotel without waiting to see if he caught up with her. A security perimeter, huh? It kinda made a guy feel loved. This could turn out to be an interesting conference, after all. Not to mention, damn, she was fun to tease. She rose to the bait so easily for him.

They'd almost reached the brightly lit hotel before he broke the charged silence by asking, "Who's coming to collect Ando?" Maybe now that someone had tried to kill him, she'd be a little more forthcoming with him. And indeed, she was.

She answered, "An American forensics team. They'll try to determine cause of death and look for anything else on the body that might help catch the killer."

"This is going to make a hell of a story for you."

She threw him an exasperated look. "If I was going to break the story, I'd have done it this morning when I found that bag on the beach."

He countered, "There's nothing to stop you from breaking the story now."

"Yeah, except national security interests and the safety of everyone at this summit."

He stared. "Are you telling me you actually have a conscience and think about these things?"

She rolled her eyes and merely strode along faster.

He lengthened his stride to keep pace with her as the hotel loomed.

She muttered, "We shouldn't be seen together. I'll walk around to the front through the gardens. You can go inside here and kiss whoever's butt you need to."

He grinned. "They mostly kiss mine."

She retorted dryly, "Well, you enjoy that then."

It was his turn to roll his eyes. She veered away from the ballroom, which appeared to be in an uproar and was emptying quickly. He veered with her. The gardens in this area were crowded with guests and he murmured under his breath, "I'll give you a ride back to your place."

"That's not necessary."

"I never said it was. Nonetheless, the offer stands. My car's over there."

Although she glared at him when he took her by the elbow and steered her into the parking lot, she made no further protest. He escorted her to the passenger side of his Jeep and steadied her as she swung into the vehicle. Her ball gown hung up on the door and their hands collided as he reached for the satin to release it. His gaze snapped up to hers.

Her eyes were wide, her pupils dilated. And something flared in his gut in response. It was lust. Just lust. It had been quite a while since he'd been with a woman. Truth be told, until Paige showed up, he'd been cruising the party in search of a female who'd go for a little meaningless sex. Plenty of women at these affairs knew the score. A few nights of mutual pleasure, no strings attached, no promises. A nice piece of jewelry when it was over, and everyone went their own way. But here he was instead, driving away from the hotel with a virago who'd bite his head off if he even hinted at the idea of jumping into the sack with him. He sighed.

Thankfully, for a busybody, she was capable of keeping her mouth shut now and then. The short ride to her cottage was quiet.

He turned off the beach road and stopped abruptly, flipping off his headlights. "I see lights on at your place. How do you want to play this?"

She studied the pair of large, dark SUVs parked in front of her cottage for several seconds. "I'll take care of it. You head on back to the hotel. And thanks for the ride."

Did she seriously think he was just going to toss her to the sharks like this? Without comment, he watched her climb out of the Jeep and square her shoulders. Leaving the lights off, he backed up the vehicle and pulled away. But he only went to the beach road before he pulled over and tucked the Jeep behind a stand of palmettos. His tuxedo wasn't exactly ideal for sneaking around in the bushes, but it would have to do. After a mental apology to Giorgio Armani for ruining his tux, Tom plunged into the dense undergrowth.

With every light blazing in her little house, it was an easy matter to make his way unseen practically to her back door. Three coplike guys who sounded American were clustered in front of the open door of Paige's refrigerator examining the bag stuffed inside it.

Four more suited men, who sounded local, were standing by glaring and muttering among themselves. One of them turned to Paige and snapped, "Why were we not informed of this discovery immediately?"

"Monsieur Martine," she answered evenly, "I notified my government immediately. They deemed the security of the summit more vital than following the exact letter of police procedure."

"You have interfered with a police matter, madame. You face serious criminal charges."

Tom watched with interest as Paige's gaze went the temperature of an arctic glacier. She responded in that same measured tone of voice, "You face a much more serious problem than me, monsieur. When word gets out to the members of the summit that one of their own was murdered, you're going to have a wholesale flight of many of the delegates from the island. And how will you explain to your superiors that your failure to protect the delegates and or to keep a lid on this security breach caused the collapse of an important international summit? Not to mention the negative impact it'll have on tourism revenue to your island when I break this story. Every wire service in the world is going to pick it up. There will be a feeding frenzy over it."

The police inspector blustered and broke into angry French that required no translation. Paige crossed her arms to wait out the guy's tirade. Tom couldn't help but notice the spectacular things the pose did to her cleavage in that low-cut gown. The blue satin had seen better days after tonight's adventures, but the dress was still magnificent on her.

Paige finally interrupted Martine. "Which is it going to be? Am I breaking the story of Ando's murder on my network within the hour, or are we all going to be discreet and cooperative with one another about this?"

More grumbling from the inspector, but the guy was weakening.

Paige continued in a cool voice. "Inspector, unless you're planning to arrest me, I need to go to my news bureau. I have a story to file."

"And exactly what story will that be, madame?" the inspector demanded.

Paige shrugged. "For the record, I am under no obligation to answer your question. But as a courtesy, I will tell you that I do not plan to mention the tragic death of Mr. Ando just yet. His family should have a chance to be notified in private before they hear of it on the TV news. I do, however, plan to broadcast the story of tonight's attempted shooting of Thomas Rowe."

Tom jolted. He couldn't be splashed all over the news like that! If her network broke the story, the others would be crawling all over him before long. He had to stop her. At all costs. He couldn't afford any publicity. Not here. Not now. She'd ruin *everything.*

Chapter 5

Paige sailed out of the cottage and sagged against the porch railing as her bravado abruptly evaporated. She had no intention of publicizing Ando's death—her role in it was suspect for one, and secondly, it really could cause a panic at the summit. The United States was committed to seeing this economic conference come off without a hitch, and to that end, she wasn't about to rock the boat.

The shooting at Rowe, however, was an entirely different matter. He was a private citizen not attached to any delegation. He was also high-profile tabloid fodder. A shooting at him was the stuff of sensationalism, not necessarily serious news or a threat to the summit. She had no compunction about splashing him all over the news.

Who had the second shooter been? Was he or she a threat to the summit, too? Did she break the news story first or proceed with a military investigation of the shootings? Be a reporter or be a soldier?

Swearing under her breath, she headed for her car. Thank goodness she'd taken a cab to the ball earlier and her MINI Cooper had still been at her cottage. Pointing the tiny car back toward the hotel, she came to a decision. Report the story now while the police were still crawling all over the ballroom and the gardens. Later, when the excitement had cooled down, would be soon enough to go forth and do her Special Forces thing.

She turned her attention to composing her news story's lead off. "Shots taken at American billionaire on eve of summit." Or maybe she could get away with, "Billionaire bad boy shot at." That would get Rowe's goat. She grinned just imagining the expression on his face if she used that line. Unfortunately, she didn't have a lot of details on the dead shooter. She'd have to go with a simple breaking news angle. Admittedly it would open up the investigation of who'd shot at Tom to all the news media, and she hated to give up her current advantage over her fellow journalists. But better that another network solve the mystery of why someone had tried to kill Tom than have him end up dead.

She blinked. Stared at the road unfolding before her headlights in minor shock. Was she actually concerned about Thomas Rowe's well-being? When had *that* happened? She pulled into the hotel parking lot and hurried to the World News Network's temporary bureau in a conference room on the resort's ground floor. Her boss, Greer Carson, was in the room, a cell phone plastered to each ear as usual. How he held two conversations at once like that was an abiding mystery to Paige.

She sat down at the lighted table, yanking a brush through her hair, fixing her ruined makeup and cleaning up her dress as best she could. Her disheveled ball gown was a little low cut for a broadcast, but it would do for a short breaking-news segment.

In the mirror, she watched Greer hang up both phone lines. She talked fast as she applied powder to her face to knock down the glare of the camera lights on her skin. "Greer, you'll never guess what happened tonight. I was dancing with Tom Rowe when a sniper took a shot at him. Barely missed him. I can be ready to go with a breaking-news bit as soon as you have a live feed up to the network back home."

"Yeah. About that…" his voice trailed off.

She pivoted on her stool, alarmed. She *so* didn't like that tone of voice. "What? What's going on, Greer?"

"I gotta kill that story."

"Why?" she burst out. "It's huge. It'll be a scandal back in the States. He's one of the most eligible bachelors in America—heck, maybe in the whole world."

"Sorry, kid. Can't do it."

Paige stared at him in shock. Then she choked out, "Who got to you?"

Carson shook his head at her. "They played the *national security* card on me. Nothing I can do about it."

They. She hated *They.* Who was They, anyway? They never had a name but was responsible for just about everything that went wrong in the world, it seemed. Her gaze narrowed. In this case, though, she had a darned good idea just who They was. Or more accurately, "He."

She slammed the powder brush down on the makeup table. "Gee, Greer. Thanks so much for your underwhelming support. Since when did you lose your spine?"

And with that, she stormed out of the newsroom. She probably wasn't being entirely fair to Greer. After 9/11, the U.S. government had been granted broad powers to curtail the media in the name of security. It was possible that Rowe hadn't killed the story at all. *But not probable.* It made her furious to think that anyone was interfering with fair and unbiased reporting of the news.

A twist of guilt in her gut took her by surprise. It wasn't like she had any room to talk on that subject. She'd interfered just as badly with the reporting process when she'd stuffed Takashi Ando in her refrigerator and not broken the story. She'd *told* Vanessa Blake she would be a reporter and a Medusa simultaneously. But her boss had been right after all. On her very first assignment to wear both hats at the same time, the worst had happened. She'd been forced to choose.

She'd been a journalist for a long time. Was she ready to set aside her professional standards as if they didn't count for anything? Frowning, she slowed her reckless charge through the hotel lobby. She spotted a deep armchair in a quiet corner and headed for it. Could she do this Medusa thing after all?

She thought about it for a long time, weighing the pros and cons. She loved being back out in the field as a journalist. She loved chasing a story, trying to figure what was happening and why, the adrenaline and pressure of it all. But she loved being a Medusa, too. She'd gotten a rush out of chasing down the first shooter, knowing how to respond in a crisis, not panicking and freezing up in a life-or-death situation. No solutions were forthcoming, however, and fatigue weighed down her eyelids.

Paige must have dozed off because she blinked awake some time later. The lobby was quiet, mostly deserted. She glanced at her watch. Nearly five o'clock. She went into the newsroom and pulled out the bag of exercise gear she kept there and changed into running attire. Then she headed down to the beach and put in a hard six miles in the sand as the sun began to rise.

It burned off a little of her frustration at Greer but didn't scratch the surface of her fury at Thomas Rowe. How dare he interfere with her career like that? How dare he kill a great story in the name of not liking media attention? He could take his privacy and shove it!

Speaking of privacy, she bypassed the concierge and headed for the bank of elevators that would take her to the luxury suites at the top of the hotel. She got out one floor shy of Rowe's and made her way to a stairwell at the end of the hall. Taking note of the big red signs warning that opening the door would sound an alarm, she pulled out the fanny pack of emergency toys she'd grabbed while she was at home last night. A quick run around the edge of the door with the tip of a knife, a few strips of aluminum between electrical contacts, two wires and four electrical clips later, and the door opened without a peep.

She shook her head. Some security.

She ran up the stairs lightly, repeating the process of disarming the alarms on the next stairwell door. Twice while she was working on it, the shadow of footsteps interrupted the band of light passing under the door. She timed the third pass, shaking her head again. Somebody was patrolling the hall at even intervals of two-and-a-half minutes. Picturing the L-shaped hallway on the other side of the door, she timed forty-five seconds after the next guard pass and cracked open the door. She peeked out. The guard was about ten feet from turning the corner. The second he disappeared from sight, she slipped into the hall and sprinted to the end door on the right.

With a glance at her watch, she knocked on the panel. She had about twenty seconds to wait for an answer. Antsy, she knocked again, watching the seconds tick off on her watch. Dammit, the guard would be rounding that corner again any second! She couldn't wait any longer. She raced back to the stairwell and slipped into it just as a dark form rounded the corner. Rowe wasn't home. Perfect. She could let herself in and look around, see what she could learn about him.

She caught her breath while the guard finished his circuit of the hall and passed again, headed away from her. Plastic card wired to lock-picking gizmo in hand, she timed her stairwell escape again. Three. Two. One. Go!

Another light-footed run down the thickly carpeted hall to Rowe's door. This time she didn't bother knocking but immediately slipped her electronic pick into the lock. In no more than five seconds, a little green light flashed on above the door handle. Gripping tightly, she turned it. And opened the door.

She slipped inside and paused just at the door. The living room was dim, floor-to-ceiling panels of blackout blinds obscuring most of the early-morning light. She glanced around quickly. No movement. Four closed doors led off the sunken living area. She eased toward the one from which Rowe had emerged yesterday morning for their interview. Time to give the jerk a little wake-up call.

His bedroom door eased open silently under her hand. Crouching, she slipped inside low and slow, easing the door shut behind her once more. It was darker in here, and she paused for two full minutes to let her eyes adjust. A long lump in the bed would be Tom asleep, the covers pulled up high around his ears.

He was a big guy. Strong. She'd need to subdue him fast before he could fight back. She eased forward staying low, sticking to the deepest shadows along the walls, until she was no more than four feet from the bed. It was a big bed, and he was sleeping toward the middle.

In a single leap, she pounced, landing astraddle…

…a puffy set of feather pillows with no substance at all. As she crashed through the pile to the mattress, a single curse had time to pass through her mind before her training kicked in. She rolled hard and fast, flinging herself to the side, which turned out to be a good thing as a black-garbed figure landed where she'd been just a millisecond before.

Paige had rolled off the bed, landing in a crouch with her feet under her. She sprang up, reaching fast for the switchblade in her fanny pack. She flipped it open and settled it comfortably in her hand. The assailant wore a black stocking mask and rolled off the foot of the bed to face her.

"What have you done with Tom Rowe?" she snarled.

The man didn't answer, but advanced, hands low and in front of him in a trained fighter's stance.

"Tell me, dammit. If you've hurt him…so help me…"

She leaped, on the attack.

All Medusas were intensively trained not to be passive females, not to sit back and wait for the bad guy to attack. It was the fatal flaw of most women in violent situations. They let themselves be the victims and failed to take charge.

She slashed high with her knife, and when the man threw up his arms to block it, she swept low and fast with her foot, clocking the assailant in the ankle with the heel of her shoe. His leg collapsed from under him and he staggered against the bed, rolling across it and regaining his feet. Damn, this guy was hard to knock down!

She pressed her attack, flailing at him with fist and blade, darting in and out, always pushing forward, keeping him on the defensive. She spotted a splash of white on the floor behind him—the bed's satin sheets had been ripped off sometime during their fight. She redoubled her attacks, driving the guy back a step. Another. One more and then…

The guy jumped back from a particularly vicious stab of her knife at his gut. He landed on the slippery satin, and his feet shot out from under him. Before he'd even hit the floor, she pounced, landing on his chest, her knife blade at his throat.

She growled. "Talk. What have you done with Tom Rowe?"

The man beneath her shook.

"Answer me!"

Still nothing. Cautiously she sat up, still sitting on his chest, the knife still biting dangerously into his flesh. With her free hand she reached up and tore off the mask. A thin line of red sprang up under her blade and a trickle of blood ran down Tom Rowe's throat.

She hissed, "I should kill you where you lie."

He grinned up at her unrepentantly. "Why, Miss Ellis. I never knew you cared so much about me."

"Gah." She shoved off of him in disgust, planting her hand in his solar plexus as she pushed up.

He coughed hard and sat up slowly while she paced the room in agitation. Adrenaline flowed through her veins like wine, heady and intoxicating. She needed to *do* something. Hit something. Run a few miles.

Tom spoke from right behind her. "God, I feel great. We need to do that more often."

Paige didn't stop and think. She just reacted. She turned and buried her fist in his stomach as hard as she could.

But what she didn't count on was him being prepared for it. His stomach muscles were contracted into a steel washboard that her fist all but bounced off of. He grabbed her wrist and gave it a quick twist, and in the blink of an eye she was plastered against his chest, her arm twisted up to her shoulder blade, pinned high behind her back.

His eyes blazed down into hers, every bit as charged as she felt.

She swore at him, a stream of the worst invectives she could muster. And he laughed. She yanked against his grip and only earned a shooting pain through her shoulder joint. Wincing away from it, her body slammed into his full on. Belly to belly. Chest to chest. And, oh, God, groin to groin.

Her adrenaline surged anew, fueled this time by a powerful, if completely inexplicable, rush of lust. What the hell was wrong with her?

"Aah, aah, aah. Not so fast, hellcat. Why'd you break into my suite?"

"You killed my story, you jerk." Fury rolled through her all over again at that fact. It was her career, her reputation, he was wrecking if she didn't break the big story first.

He laughed down at her. "Yeah, and what are you planning to do about it?"

Her gaze narrowed. "You may have stopped me today, but I'll finish what I started and slit your throat one of these days. When you least expect it, I'll be there and there won't be a damned thing you can do about it."

She rode the wave of her anger, vaguely aware that she was reacting out of all proportion with the moment, but too high on adrenaline to care.

He laughed again. Darkly. "Try it, and I'll break your neck."

"Yeah, like you did such a great job of that a few minutes ago. I had you. My blade. Your neck."

"I took it easy on you in the fight. I wanted to see how mad you were. And what moves you had. Truly, you're not bad for a girl. I think Gretchen could take you one-on-one, but still. Not bad."

That did it. She snarled low in her throat and tore free, shoulder pain be damned. And oddly enough, he let her go. She stood a few feet from him, panting in her struggle to keep herself from clawing his eyes out.

"Why on earth were you masked and hiding in your own bedroom?" she demanded.

"Call it healthy paranoia. Someone just tried to kill me. If you were me, would you be sleeping in your own bed and just waiting for someone to come kill you?"

God, she hated it when superior logic made hurting someone moot. It was an effort, but she rolled up her emotions in a little ball and set them aside.

He laughed quietly. "Really, you're very good. Better self-control than I expected from you."

She wasn't *that* good. Her simmering fury broke free again. "I swear I'm going to hurt you—"

He cut her off. "You hungry? I gotta say, I've worked up quite an appetite."

He turned away from her and strolled toward the bathroom, tossing over his shoulder, "Order up some breakfast for us while I'm in the shower. I'll be out in ten."

And on that note, the door closed behind him.

The lock clicked.

She grinned at the door, her rage broken in an instant. Ha. She'd made him lock his door. Not bad for her first ever real fight. She spun and headed for the living room and the hotel phone. After all, she wasn't done giving him a piece of her mind about interfering with her job. And she was hungry. The man might as well buy her breakfast.

Hmm. Maybe they had hemlock on the menu. Or a little arsenic.

Oh, no. The two of them were far from finished.

Chapter 6

Tom emerged from his bathroom, toweling his hair dry, half-surprised that she hadn't picked the bathroom lock and attempted to murder him in the shower. So, Paige was worried about him, was she? Worried enough to go crazy and try to kill the guy she'd thought had hurt him? Warmth seeped through him at the memory of her rage on his behalf. It wasn't often that someone else went to bat for him like that. He was usually the guy who took care of people around him.

Wearing nothing more than a towel slung around his hips, he poked his head out into the living room. Sonofagun. She was still there. Standing in front of the windows, whose blinds she'd pulled back. Sunrise was pouring in, outlining her in a nimbus of rosy light that matched the color of her gloriously tangled hair. It would look that way if they'd made passionate love all night, he'd bet.

She spun to face him as he strolled into the room, her hands flashing up into a defensive position in front of her.

He tsked. "You've got to work on hiding that reflex. Once you finish your military training, the key is to hide all of it. Don't let your enemies know you've got it. But if your hands keep whipping up like that, you'll give yourself away to every bad guy in the room."

She scowled, but said nothing. Odd. Usually, she talked nonstop.

He asked, "You wanna take a shower? You're close in size to Gretchen. I can have her send up a change of clothes, if you want."

"I don't want," Paige snapped. "Let's get one thing straight right now. Don't mess with me or my work again. I'll stay away from you, and you stay away from me. Got it?"

He grinned lazily and threw the towel he'd been using on his hair around his neck. He walked over to the window, maybe eight feet away from her, and gazed out at the idyllic scene below. "Small problem with that. I have to attend the conference and you have to cover it."

She shrugged. "It's a big hotel. I'll just make sure to be where you're not."

He glanced at her, amused to catch her staring at the towel sagging low on his hips. She turned her head away sharply, and if he wasn't mistaken, that was a blush climbing her averted cheek.

"So tell me, Paige. May I call you Paige? After all, you've jumped into my bed and we've had our hands all over each other now."

She didn't deign to reply, so he pressed on. "Tell me. Why did you go ballistic when you thought I was some assassin who'd killed me?"

"I didn't go ballistic," she retorted indignantly.

"Really?" he drawled. "I'd hate to see you really lose it, then."

She glared and again retreated into silence.

"Not gonna answer, huh? Guess that means I get to draw my own conclusions." He grinned and leaned a shoulder against the thin aluminum post between a bank of windows, facing her full-on. "How very interesting."

She rolled her eyes.

Man, she really was working hard not to rise to the bait. Must've shaken herself up with the violence of her first combat adrenaline rush. It had been all he could do not to act upon his own and throw her down on the bed and have his way with her. She would never know how hard it had been to walk away from all that crackling energy and the blatant invitation for sex that had been clinging to her in a red-hot haze. He hadn't locked the door to keep her out of his shower. He'd locked it to keep himself in.

Her spine stiffened in sudden resolve. "I think we understand each other, Mr. Rowe. I think it might be best if I leave now."

"Don't go," he blurted. "Stay. Eat breakfast."

Her gaze snapped up to his, as surprised at the request as he was at having made it.

He continued, feeling lame and more than a little desperate. "I'm serious. Go take a shower and I'll have Gretchen send up some clothes. And then we'll eat." She looked unconvinced and he reluctantly added a word he rarely used. "Please?"

She stared at him doubtfully for a moment more, weighing his request. She must have heard some sincerity in it because her posture wilted abruptly. She mumbled, "Tell Gretchen I've got spare clothes in the World News Network bureau."

He exhaled hard, inexplicably relieved that she'd acceded to his request. "Will do. There are clean towels in the cupboard to the left of the shower."

She nodded jerkily, still not entirely unwound from her snit.

When Gretchen showed up with clothes, he snatched them and hung them on the bathroom doorknob then forced himself to retreat to the living room once more. He unceremoniously kicked Gretchen out—shocking his assistant mightily—when she would have fussed over the bruise starting to form on his left cheek and the suspicious swelling of his lower lip. Frankly, the worst of it was his ribs. In keeping the blade away from his face, he'd taken a couple of well-placed body blows from Paige. He had to hand it to her. The girl could fight.

But then, all of Vanessa Blake's girls could. He remembered Viper telling him once it was the single most common way men underestimated the Medusas. They mistakenly assumed the Medusas couldn't handle themselves in a straight up, hand-to-hand brawl.

He fingered his tender lip. But for Paige to have gotten in two good blows to the face on him like that—he was getting out of practice. He resolved to make a trip back to Timbalo Island and put in a few weeks of training with the guys there from his old unit.

Damned if he didn't resort to pacing as his impatience for her to join him grew. Odd. He never waited around on women like this. They always waited on his pleasure, hanging on his every word and working only to please him. Although he had to snort at the idea of Paige Ellis waiting on him hand and foot. She'd just as soon slit his throat as be caught doing that. A woman of many firsts for him, she was.

He prowled the living room as restlessly as a caged lion, glaring at the closed bedroom door about every fifteen seconds until he caught himself doing it. In disgust, he turned to the window wall, planted his feet and crossed him arms resolutely to wait her out. Hell, knowing her, she was in there taking her sweet time because she knew it would drive him crazy.

Breakfast had arrived and still there was no sign of her. When he was about an inch from barging into the bedroom, pounding on the bathroom door and demanding to know when she was coming out, he heard a door open behind him. He turned, and his breath caught.

Paige was dressed in a charcoal gray suit. Just a suit, but on her, it looked cool and polished and professional. She was beautiful: her makeup perfect, her hair lying in sculpted waves around her face, her expression impossibly remote. Where had the knife-wielding hellion disappeared to?

A pang of disappointment coursed through him. Now she looked just like all of the other wedding-seeking socialites who threw themselves at him endlessly.

"Is breakfast here yet?" she asked with perfect composure.

He gestured at the linen-covered table in the far corner. "Whenever you're ready we can eat."

She moved over to the table for two without comment and without looking at him slid into the seat he held for her. She smelled good. Like fresh cut flowers, tangy green notes mingling with sweet fragrance. He stepped away from her chair and stared at the back of her head in shock for a second before moving around to his chair. He never analyzed women's perfume, thank you very much.

He sat down and offered her coffee, which she declined, and then poured himself a cup. He took his customary croissant while she reached for a half grapefruit and two slices of toast.

"Didn't you work up any more of an appetite than that?" he asked. "I guess next time I'll have to let go with you a little more, won't I?"

Her gaze raked across him with a hint of the old fire. "There won't be a next time, Mr. Rowe. I'm done with you."

The words sliced through him painfully, and he frowned, startled at the sensation. If he had anything to say about it, there would be a next time. Even if it meant he had to call her boss and offer up a no-kidding interview where he actually answered questions and cooperated with her.

The thought made him shudder. But it did give him an idea. He leaned forward. "Have lunch with me today."

She glanced up at him, startled. "You're kidding, right?"

"Not at all. Come as my guest. I'm dining with Jeremy Smythe."

"Smythe? *The* J. Smythe of Smythe Industries?" she exclaimed.

Ha. That had gotten her attention. "The very same."

Conflict raged in her eyes. Smythe was a far sight more reclusive even than Tom—the man never made public appearances and all but never left his sprawling Sussex estate in England. It had been a huge coup when the planners of this conference had convinced Smythe to attend and lend his financial expertise to the proceedings.

And Tom had just offered Paige a chance to talk to the guy. At length. In private. It would be the scoop of the year...if she got over being mad at him and accepted his offer. Aah. Pride or professional success. It was a terrible dilemma.

He enjoyed watching her wrestle through the decision as it danced through her expressive eyes. He could look into those baby blues all day long and never get bored.

And then, finally, they narrowed at him in irritation. "This is blackmail, you know."

"Of course it is. If you want access to Smythe, you've got to spend more time with me."

She leaned back in her chair, folded her napkin and laid it beside her plate. Deliberately, she stood up. He rose to his feet, as well. "I'm sorry, Mr. Rowe, but neither I nor my career are for sale. Have a nice lunch with Mr. Smythe, and do send him my regrets."

And with that, she walked with silent, athletic grace to the door, picked up her bag of running clothes and toiletries and let herself out.

He stared, flummoxed, at the closed door. "Sonofa— She can't possibly walk away from lunch with Smythe!"

"I beg your pardon, Mr. Rowe?" Gretchen stepped through the office just then.

If she was startled by his rare outburst, she kept it to herself and said smoothly, "Shall I contact Mr. Smythe's assistant and have him add Miss Ellis to your lunch itinerary?"

He exploded up out of his chair with a curse and flung down his napkin. "No, dammit!"

Gretchen did stare at him then in mild shock. Yeah. He knew exactly how she felt. No woman had turned him down flat like that in…hell, ever. He'd offered Paige the one thing she wanted more than to hate him, and she'd *walked away* from it. From *him!*

He stormed out of the room, swearing, without bothering to take his neatly printed daily itinerary from Gretchen.

Paige took the exquisitely fragile porcelain cup of perfectly prepared Earl Grey tea and carefully lifted it to her lips. "Thank you so much for speaking with me, Mr. Smythe. I must say, this has been a delightful conversation. You're every bit as brilliant and charming as I'd heard."

The silver-haired octogenarian seated in a wheelchair opposite her laughed gaily. "Oh, no, Miss Ellis. It has been my pleasure, indeed. When Henry Stanforth called and asked me to take a meeting with you, how could I resist? Any young lady who can muster a former U.S. president to make her appointments I have to meet. And you have not disappointed. No, indeed, not."

She smiled over at him warmly. It probably hadn't been exactly sporting of her to take blatant advantage of her Medusa contacts to wrangle this short-notice interview with the great J. Smythe himself, but darned if she was going to let Thomas Rowe get the best of her.

The elderly man chortled. "Our young Mr. Rowe should be along any minute. Do you have any further questions for me before he arrives, Miss Ellis?"

"No questions. But if I may speak to you off the record for a moment?"

The piercing intelligence that had made him one of the richest men in the world flashed in Smythe's gaze. "Methinks we come to the real purpose of your visit today, young lady."

Yep. A smart cookie, he was. "I have some information for you, sir. And a warning."

"Do tell."

"It is not public knowledge yet, and his family is probably only just now being informed of it, but Takashi Ando has been murdered."

Smythe jolted. "How do you know this?" he demanded.

"Let us be frank. You know who I work with, do you not?"

He nodded. "I have a good idea. Your…sisters…have been most helpful to me on a prior occasion."

"Then trust me, sir. I saw his body myself. Ando is dead, and he did not die by natural means. Furthermore, there was an attempt on Thomas Rowe's life last night. Sadly, it failed."

Symthe's mouth twitched momentarily. "You're here, then, to warn me to be careful? As the only other private businessman invited to this summit you think my life is in danger? Is that it?"

"Pretty much."

"I thank you for your concern, Miss Ellis. I assure you, though, that my security team is of the very highest caliber."

Vanessa had mentioned in the call earlier—when Paige had asked her boss to pull strings and get her a meeting with Smythe—that his security team were all former SAS men— British Special Forces.

Paige's reporter side kicked in again. "Do you have any idea who might want to eliminate you, Mr. Rowe and Mr. Ando?"

Smythe leaned back, assessing her alertly. He knew something. Her reporter's instinct smelled it. She leaned forward, staring directly into his eyes. "We're still speaking off the record. You know who I am. Who I represent. If you know something, I need to hear it so I can do my job. My real job."

"A reporter and a special operator," Smythe mused. "I'd like to know how you manage to juggle both."

"It's not easy," she muttered.

"All right then. Here's the thing," he announced in a sudden decision. "I was contacted a few weeks ago. Offered the deal of a lifetime. What amounts to an entire country is being sold off by its leader for pennies on the pound. Tens of billions of dollars' worth of assets liquidated at fire-sale prices. The seller is going to be at the summit. Said he'd give me the full details here."

Paige frowned. "I'm sorry, but what does that have to do with Takashi-san's death and Mr. Rowe's near death?"

"Don't you see? They were likely offered the same deal I was. Maybe even other players here, too. Perhaps someone doesn't want to enter into a bidding war for the whole kit and kaboodle and has decided to kill off the competition."

"Who's the seller?"

"I have no idea. More than a few emerging nations have overstretched themselves financially over the past few years or decades. Any one of them could be looking for a quick infusion of cash to prevent economic collapse."

"So they're selling their country?"

Smythe shook his head. "Not officially. Technically, it's merely controlling interest in the key production resources within the country. I haven't received the dossier of specific assets for sale yet. I expect to get it any day, though."

Well, then. That explained a lot. Too bad Tom Rowe hadn't seen fit to share the same information with her when he helped her fish Takashi Ando's body out of the Pacific Ocean. Or when she'd risked her life to catch the guy who'd tried to kill him. What a colossal jerk!

A neatly dressed man opened the double doors into the library and announced, "Mr. Rowe has arrived."

Smythe replied, "Right on time. This *is* going to be entertaining. Send him in, Chester."

Frantically, Paige tried to pull her scattered thoughts together. Tom hadn't acted the least bit surprised when he had seen Ando's body. He hadn't told her about the deal. Was *he* the one trying to eliminate the competition?

Tom strode into the room, all cheerful confidence and energy. "Hello there, Jeremy! Long time no—"

He broke off, staring at Paige.

She smiled icy daggers back at him. "So nice of you to join us, Mr. Rowe. We were just having a most informative conversation, Mr. Smythe and I."

"What are *you* doing here?" Tom burst out.

She answered lightly, "Why, my job, of course. And speaking of which, I think I'm finished. Thank you so much for your time and hospitality, Mr. Smythe. It has truly been an honor and a pleasure to meet you."

"Pleasure's all mine, my dear. All mine." The man's voiced wavered with unholy amusement as he glanced back and forth between her and Tom. She got the feeling the old geezer was seeing far more than she'd have liked him to in the sparks crackling between her and Tom.

She stood up to leave and moved over to Smythe's wheelchair to shake his hand. The papery claws were strong as he held her hand and forced her to meet his gaze. "Thank you for your kindness, Miss Ellis. And please do visit me again."

"I will, sir."

With a last smile for him as Smythe released her hand, she turned on her heel and headed for the door. Unfortunately, she had to brush right past Tom to get there.

"What are you up to?" he muttered as she drew near.

"Don't you wish you knew?" she replied breezily. "Have a nice lunch, gentlemen."

Wheezy laughter floated her way as she reached the doors. "Thomas, my boy, I think you've finally met your match. You two make a good pair. I must say, I envy you. Were I forty years younger, I'd give you a run for your money with her. Frankly, I'm not entirely sure you deserve her."

Paige's cheeks burst into flame as she pulled the heavy doors shut on Smythe's voice.

"Yes, indeed, boy. You're in for a hell of ride with that one, you are."

Chapter 7

"And we'll be back after the break with five tips on how to clean up your financial house this year." The teleprompter went blank, the camera's red light went off and Paige let the bright smile fade from her face.

"Sixty seconds," Greer announced from behind the cameraman, "and then we'll go to a live feed with Mitch and the American delegation head."

"Got it," she replied. She made an adjustment to her earbud and smoothed her hair.

A ruckus erupted by the door and she looked up in time to see Tom Rowe put a nifty wristlock on the lighting technician and shove the guy out of his way. Rowe growled, "Paige, you and I need to have a little talk. Now."

Ha. Must've just finished his lunch with Smythe. "Not now. I'm in the middle of a broadcast."

"Tough. Someone else can fill in." He strode onto the brightly lit set, squarely between her and the camera.

"No, they can't! I'm the on-air anchor and we are back in…"

"Thirty seconds," Greer announced sharply. In a loud voice aimed at Tom, he added, "Somebody get this guy out of here, dammit!"

"Anybody touches me, I'll rip their arm off," Tom snarled back.

Trepidation erupted in Paige. She'd seen him irritated before but never ready to completely lose it like this. He looked worse than furious. He looked downright deadly.

"Please, Tom," she murmured soothingly.

Greer said desperately, "You can have her in two minutes, Rowe. But she's got to throw the broadcast to a sound bite and then back to the New York office." Tom opened his mouth to protest, but Greer cut him off. "Swear to God. Two minutes. Now get out!"

A production assistant announced frantically, "We go live in five…four…three…"

Paige sent a pleading look in Tom's direction. He scowled blackly, but stepped out of camera range just as the red light over camera one illuminated.

"I'm Paige Ellis, reporting live from the site of the upcoming global economic summit. We take you now to Mitchell Cameron who's with the American delegation chief. Hi, Mitch. What can you tell us about American expectations for next week's meetings?"

The director pointed to a monitor, and the engineer switched feeds. The red light went off over camera one.

"What the hell are you doing here?" she snapped at Tom. "You can't just barge in on a live newscast! How'd you get in anyway? The door's locked."

Tom snorted. "Yeah. Just like the door to my suite."

She winced. Okay, so he could pick a lock as easily as she could. Still. "I'm at work, here."

"You mess with me, I mess with you. Seems fair, don't you think?"

Greer interjected, "We're coming back to you in twenty, Paige. Can you two lovebirds wrap up your spat so I can put on a newscast, here?"

She glared at her boss. Why did everyone assume she and Rowe were romantically involved, dammit? They were so *not* a pair.

"One minute," Greer pleaded with Rowe. "Stand over here by me and keep your mouth shut. And then I give you my blessing to haul her out of here and fight with her all you like."

Paige wasn't sure whose gaze narrowed more, hers or Tom's. But either way, he grudgingly did as he was asked and backed off the set once more. The teleprompter lit up and she dragged her attention to it, concentrating fiercely on the individual words, but unable to string meaning together from them in her own jumbled mind. She prayed that it had been typed in correctly because whatever scrolled past was exactly what she read.

Finally, an eternity later, the screen went dark, and Greer passed the broadcast back to the New York office. Paige surged up out of her seat, furious. "Rowe, you ever interrupt a taping of the news like that again, and you'll be the one with the broken arm!"

"I'd like to see you try."

She glared hotly but asked coolly, "That's a nasty scratch you've got on your neck. You need some shaving lessons, maybe? How'd you get that, anyway?"

He glared back. "Cat scratched me. Pesky vermin, cats."

"Jerk."

He lunged and she reflexively dodged backward, tripping as her heel caught on a row of electrical wires taped to the floor. Tom grabbed her so fast she barely had time to lose her balance before he righted her roughly by the elbow. He didn't let go of her arm once she was back on her feet. "Come with me, Miss Ellis. We need to have a word in private."

She tried to yank her elbow free, but his grip was like steel and had about as much give. Vaguely aware of the smirks of the crew as he dragged her out of the bureau by force, she continued to struggle against him as they approached the hotel lobby. He didn't let go, however, and continued to hustle her through the cavernous space.

"Let go of me, Rowe. You're creating a spectacle."
"Quit fighting me and there won't be a spectacle."

He was right, but that didn't mean she had to like it one bit. Scowling at him, she subsided purely to save what little reputation she had left as he all but goose-stepped her past the crowd of delegates milling about waiting for a scheduled press conference to begin.

He didn't stop until he'd pulled her into an elevator and the door slid closed. Only then did her let her go so he could slam in his key card for the top floor. Then he turned aggressively and planted a hand on either side of her head against the back wall of the elevator.

"What the hell were you doing talking to Jeremy Smythe?" he demanded.

"Why the hell didn't you tell me about the little side deal you've got brewing here?" she demanded in return.

"He told you about that?" Tom sounded surprised.

"Yeah. Funny how you didn't bother to bring it up when you were staring at your competition for the deal—dead in a bag."

Tom's voice rose in outrage. "You don't seriously think I had anything to do with Ando's death, do you?"

Not for a minute did she actually think he'd killed Ando. She may have considered the idea for a moment or two when Smythe first told her about the deal. But if she was honest with herself, she knew she could trust Tom. But in the name of investigating the murder, she needed to see how he reacted to the idea of being under suspicion. She shrugged, keeping her facial expression carefully stony. "Why not? What reason have you given me to trust you?"

He sputtered. "You'd question me? My trustworthiness?"

She pressed the point. "Yes, Tom. I would. I consider you a prime suspect in Ando's murder."

"What about the shooter last night? Someone's trying to kill me, too."

"Yeah, and he missed," she retorted. "You could've hired someone to take a potshot at you to throw suspicion."

"Oh, come on. If I wanted to kill someone, I damned well wouldn't leave a mutilated body lying around to wash up on a beach! I'm better than that."

"You're right. You *are* a trained killer." He still wasn't giving her an unguarded reaction. She pushed harder, asking with light sarcasm, "So you're telling me you're not physically capable of knocking off Ando?"

He stared down at her, and she was relieved to see he looked genuinely shocked. "I'm a billionaire. Several times over. Why would I *want* to kill anyone when I can buy absolutely everything I want in life for myself?"

She didn't like pushing him like this, but it had to be done. She answered coldly, "You can't buy everything, Tom. Or everyone."

His gaze raked down her derisively. "I can buy everyone I want."

She reeled at the insult in his voice. Okay, so she deserved the hit for pushing him like this. But it still hurt like hell. So. He didn't actually want her. All those sparks were exactly what they appeared to be, then. Irritation, plain and simple. Nothing more. Something inside her deflated. She'd thought… okay, so it had been stupid to think he might be interested in her. Still, it had been fun to imagine the bad boy billionaire falling for her. To be the one woman who could turn the head of a man like Thomas Rowe.

This entire conversation sucked. Really sucked. *C'mon, Tom. Gimme an honest, unguarded reaction so I can back off.*

She struck a cold tone of voice calculated to get a rise out of him. "It's not about the money with you. It's about winning. You'd do anything to be the one who lands the biggest fish. To be the guy who makes the deal of the century. I think it's entirely possible that you'd kill off your competition in order to win."

He stared at her a long time. And as he studied her searchingly, the fury slowly drained out of his eyes. "Do you seriously think that of me?"

Damn him. He still wasn't letting down his guard! She looked him dead in the eye and lied. "Yes. I do."

He pushed away from her. Turned his back to her, shoulders hunched with tension.

Thank God. That had been pure, unadulterated shock in his eyes before he turned away. Pain. Horror that she thought that of him. Nope, Tom Rowe absolutely couldn't be the killer. Not with a reaction like that. Relief coursed through her.

But hard on its heels, something else occurred to her. She'd just insulted everything he stood for. Mortally offended him, no doubt. She'd taken the one part of his life that he took very seriously and very personally and had attacked the hell out of it.

How on Earth was he going to forgive her for that? Why should he? She'd made cruel and hurtful accusations against him. Sure, it might have been part and parcel of the job. But still. She got the distinct feeling she'd just crossed a line with him that he was not going to forgive her for any time soon.

The elevator finally dinged to announce its arrival on Tom's floor. The door whooshed open. He started to step out, then put his hand against the open door to hold it and half turned to look at her. His gaze was as cold and distant as Neptune and his voice colder. "I thought you were better than that, Paige Ellis. I thought I might have finally found an honest woman. But I guess I was wrong."

And with that parting shot, he stepped off the elevator. The door slid closed and the conveyance lurched as it rushed downward, away from Tom. Away from what could have been. Away from something she had a sneaking feeling she was going to regret losing someday.

Damn this job! Pushing him *had* been the right thing to do. But had there been another way? She'd taken the opportunity that had presented itself and made the most of it just like she'd been trained to do. She'd done no more and no less than what had to be done.

But, God, the cost of it. A keen sense of loss speared through her. No wonder all her teammates warned against mixing the job and pleasure. This was the *pits*.

Had he seriously expected her to reveal her real thoughts to him? When was the last time any man had asked that of her? Sure, her instructors demanded it of all the women training to be Medusas. But that was different. Those men were in the business of stripping away the layers of personalities, forcing her and her teammates to learn to trust each other implicitly. It was easy to trust those women. Easy to bare her soul to them. The Special Forces world operated by a different set of rules.

Had Tom expected *that* of her?

But how could he? This was the civilian world. Nobody wore their true self on their sleeve in a gathering like this. Reporters jockeyed for a great sound bite, politicians manipulated the media to suit their ends, the network execs chased after ratings, and somewhere in there, the truth took a backseat. It wasn't that reporters and broadcasters didn't want to tell the truth. Far from it. They had a burning desire to do so. But the reality was so much less idealistic than that. Tom knew the score. He'd been a private businessman plenty long enough to know the rules of engagement for this world.

Tom had to understand that she lived in both worlds. It was unrealistic of him to expect her to operate solely as a soldier in this environment. If that was the condition of a relationship with him, it was probably just as well she'd found that out now. She wasn't about to let him inside her defenses like that.

It was too bad he wasn't willing to straddle both worlds. To have been with a man who could accept her—every part of her—just the way she was…that might have been nice.

She'd never really given any great thought to how being a Medusa might affect her personal life going forward, and her dating life more specifically. She'd just assumed it would be one more secret she'd keep to herself. Something private she didn't share with others. No big deal. It wasn't like she could blithely confess to all her dates that she was now a trained killer who served at the pleasure of the U.S. government whenever and wherever she was needed, and that her personal life would have to take a backseat to that.

What she hadn't counted on was being so very different, herself. On respecting something different. On wanting something—someone—different. Someone who could understand and embrace both sides of her. She swore under her breath. She had a sinking suspicion she'd just driven off a man who could've done exactly that—had he chosen to.

But there was more than one fish in the sea where Tom Rowe came from. There would be other men. Men who understood her and were like her. Right? She was an attractive, intelligent, interesting woman. Some great guy would want her enough to put up with the sudden absences and unanswered questions about what she did when she was gone.

Then why did it hurt so much that Tom had just walked out of this elevator and not looked back?

The elevator door opened, disgorging her into the lobby. Happy hour was in full swing, spilling out of the cocktail lounge into the main concourse. She dived into the crowd with a vengeance, flirting freely with all the reasonably young, non-trollish, apparently unmarried men she ran into.

And was bored out of her mind.

Granted, these guys were financial types, bankers and economists for the most part, but none of them...challenged her.

It didn't matter, dammit. She didn't have time for a man in her life, anyway.

To hell with Tom Rowe.

She ordered a martini, extra dry, and tossed it back with a flourish.

Her purse vibrated under her arm, and she briefly considered not answering it. But her innate sense of responsibility kicked in and she fished her cell phone out of her bag. The number on its face made her start. As she answered the phone, she made her way toward the edge of the crowd. She had faith this would need to be a private call.

Paige murmured, "Hi, Viper. What's up?"

Vanessa Blake answered tersely, "I've got some information for you. And an assignment. Let me know when you can talk."

All vestiges of the martini flew right out of Paige's head. She pushed open a heavy glass door and stepped onto a relatively deserted veranda. "Okay. I'm in the clear."

Vanessa got right to the point. "The guy who tried to shoot Thomas Rowe last night was, indeed, a security guard for the summit. Worst case, we have to assume he was not the only plant within the security team."

Great. "So, you're telling me the summit's security is breached?"

"Yep. People at a higher pay grade than you and me are negotiating bringing in an American security contingent to take over."

The logistics of an eleventh-hour handover of security on an event this big with so many world leaders present made her head spin. "Ouch," she muttered.

Vanessa chuckled. "No kidding. Thankfully, that's not the Medusas' problem."

"Amen, sister."

"But, we do have a problem of our own to take care of. And I need you to get on it right away while I send a team to help you."

A full-blown Medusa team was coming here? To back her up? Whoa. What the heck was going on to merit that?

"The President has asked me, as a personal favor, to see to the safety of Tom Rowe. And I said I'd do it."

Oh, no. No, no, no. She saw where this was going. No way. Paige burst out in alarm, "Unsay it! I don't want anything to do with that—"

"Lieutenant."

Her boss didn't need to say another word. She knew the score. She was in the military, now. Subject to orders. Not at liberty to turn down an assignment because it would force her to work with a man who'd just given her the coldest possible brush-off. She'd been given a job to do, and that was all there was to it. Still, she sighed.

"Understood, Viper. I'll get right on it."

"What's the problem? Tom's a pretty cool guy."

Yeah. Too cool. Too attractive. Too sexy. Too interesting. Too...everything, dammit. Paige answered wryly, "Let's just say he and I have had several differences of opinion."

Vanessa laughed. "Sparks are flying, eh? You gotta watch out for those sparks, Paige. They'll burn you alive."

Ha. Her boss didn't know the half of it. Deeply uncomfortable with the subject at hand, Paige changed topics. "When can I expect backup to arrive?"

"Best case, two days. Worst case, upwards of a week. An autopsy team the locals were willing to roll with. A team of armed commandos on their turf may be more of a problem for them."

"A *week?*" Seven days of round-the-clock contact with Tom Rowe? This was worse than a nightmare. It was hell on earth!

Vanessa was speaking. "—depends on how cooperative or uncooperative the local government decides to be."

Paige rolled her eyes. "If my contact with the local police is any indication, don't expect them to welcome the Medusas with open arms."

"All right. Thanks for the heads-up."

Paige asked, "Any word on the Ando autopsy? Cause of death? Time of death?"

"Yes, as a matter of fact. He died of blunt force trauma to the back of his head, three, maybe four, days ago. The lab folks estimate that he was tortured for no more than twenty-four hours, then killed, dismembered and thrown into the sea. He was in the water roughly two days. The powers that be would love it if we had his murder solved before the summit begins."

That would place Ando's death on Monday. It was Friday morning, now. And the summit started in three days. Not long to solve the guy's murder.

Paige asked, "What's my first priority? Investigating Ando's death or protecting Rowe?"

Vanessa didn't hesitate. "Rowe."

Drat. She'd been hoping for a loophole in her orders to distance herself from the guy. No such luck.

"And on that note, I'll let you get to work. Get to his side and stick to him like glue."

Desperate, Paige replied, "Have you considered the fact that Rowe may not want me guarding him?"

"Too bad. The President considers him a national asset and we've been assigned to protect him. He can get over it."

"I doubt he'll see it that way," Paige responded doubtfully.

"So stalk him if you have to. Just stay on him and keep him safe."

Lovely. And wasn't trailing along behind Tom Rowe everywhere he went going to just do wonders for her reputation? People were already gossiping about the two of them after he made her dance with him last night and then they ran out together after the shooting attempt. Not to mention the "lovers' quarrel" her coworkers had witnessed earlier today. Her return to the newsroom would be wrecked before her career barely got moving again. And it was all his fault!

At least she'd get the satisfaction of knowing that this security arrangement would bother him at least as much as it bothered her. Heck, if she was lucky, it would drive the guy completely nuts.

Chapter 8

When even Gretchen retreated and took cover, Tom knew he was in a truly foul mood. He managed to hold it together through his first afternoon meeting with a doddering old fool from a tiny Baltic bank with visions of grandeur. Tom barely resisted an urge to remind the guy sharply that his little blip on the map was no longer part of a mighty, and long defunct, Soviet empire and nobody gave a damn about his bank.

But when the fellow tottered out of the hotel suite, leaving Tom blessedly alone, an urge to pick up something heavy and breakable and heave it through one of the floor-to-ceiling windows persisted.

She'd really had him going there, for a while. That whole roaring to his defense business, and her sassy mouth and combat moves...he'd thought he might have found a one-of-a-kind woman.

And then she had to go and accuse him of killing Ando. Of all the nerve.

Him? He had a whole lot more medals for valor and honor and service to his country than she'd ever dream of pinning on. And she questioned his ethics? His morals? Hell, his basic integrity?

His jaw clenched so hard it ached until he loosed it enough to mutter a few choice words for Miss High-and-Mighty. Who the hell was she to take some morally superior stand with him? She was the one who stuffed Ando in her refrigerator and called neither the police nor her news network! Sure, he understood the security reasons behind her decision, and they were sound. But it wasn't like her hands were entirely clean here, either. They were both in the business of doing the right thing, not necessarily the legal thing or the socially acceptable thing.

His mental tirade screeched to a halt when a quiet knock sounded on the door to his suite. Gretchen would get that—oh, wait, he'd chased Gretchen out of here, snarling over nothing at her earlier.

He swore under his breath and headed for the door. Wasn't the concierge supposed to ring the room and announce anyone before they came up here? Must be housekeeping.

He flung the door open for the maid—

—and stopped in his tracks, staring.

"What are *you* doing here?" he burst out, throwing his hands up in disgust.

Paige had the strangest look on her face. Strange enough that he did a double take. He expected contrition. Preparedness, maybe even determination, to beg. But what he saw was… reluctance? What the hell was that about?

"We…I…need to speak with you," she said.

"Well, I don't need to speak with you. How'd you get a key card to get up here, anyway?"

"Gretchen."

"Ahh."

He started to close the door, but she stuck her hand out and stopped the panel from slamming shut in her face. "I'm sorry, Tom. But it's business."

Dammit! He swore long and hard under his breath. He hadn't for a second missed the implication of how she'd said that word. *Business.* Not journalism and economic summits or financial transactions. Nope, she meant another business. The secret one they both were involved in. *That* business.

It was a dirty, rotten trick to invoke it. She knew darned well that he wouldn't—couldn't—say no to that.

He spun away from the gaping door and stormed across the room. "Make it fast."

The door clicked shut quietly behind him. "I got a call from my boss a little while ago. It seems that the President of the United States has decided that you need a bodyguard. And, uh, well—"

Tom frowned and looked up at her. "Spit it out, woman."

Her spine stiffened. "He's appointed me to the job."

What the—

She continued in a rush, "Well, not me exactly, but the Medusas, and they can't get here for a couple of days. So, Viper has assigned me to the job until the rest of them arrive."

"Son of—" he exploded. *Paige* was supposed to be his bodyguard? No. Way.

Paige smiled weakly. "I thought you might feel that way. I did my best to talk her out of it, but no go. I was hoping you might call your, uh, contacts to see if you have any better luck talking them out of this plan."

He jammed a hand through his hair. "Hell, I'd have to call the President himself to get this one overturned."

Paige's eyes widened. "Can you do that?"

He replied grimly, "Only one way to find out."

He picked up the telephone receiver on the desk in the corner and punched a button. "Gretchen, get me the White House. Tell the operator I'd like to speak to the President."

"Directly to him or to one of his aides?" Gretchen replied. How she managed not to sound surprised, he had no idea. The woman was made of steel.

"To the man himself. As soon as possible."

"I'll get to work on it, sir."

Tom put down the receiver with more force than was strictly necessary. Now what the hell was he supposed to do? Twiddle his thumbs while he waited for the President to call back and unground him like some contrite teenager who'd done his time without the car keys?

Paige, across the room, was drawing thin gauze blinds over the windows.

"What are you doing?" he snapped irritably. "I happen to like the view."

"Until you pull your fancy strings, I'm your bodyguard, and you and I both know these giant windows are a sniper's dream."

"This is such a load of bull," he burst out. "How many favors did you have to call in to arrange this farce? I have to give you credit, I didn't see this one coming."

Paige whirled and stared at him in shock that quickly morphed to fury. "You think I *want* to spend time with you? That I'd volunteer to spend a single second more than absolutely necessary in the same room with you?"

He arched a skeptical eyebrow. "Don't you?"

"Hell, no!" she all but shouted.

His own fury spiraled upward in response to hers. He was the injured party, here. Why were her knickers in such an all-fired twist?

She spoke more calmly. "Look, Tom. Neither of us is happy about this situation. But we don't have any choice in the matter. The guy who shot at you last night was a member of the summit security team, as we originally suspected. Which means the conference's security is breached. We have no way of knowing if any more infiltrators have managed to get hired on for the conference. The American delegation has its own security guys, but they already have their hands full and you're a private citizen. For better or worse, the President determined that you are a national asset in need of protection."

"Hence, you."

"Hence, the Medusas," she retorted. "And I happen to be the only one here at the moment. When my teammates arrive, I'll be happy to go as far away as possible from you and never darken your doorstep again."

And for some reason, that statement sent him over the edge. She'd be happy never to see him again? He stalked toward her in a towering rage. "Happy?" he ground out. "Never to see me again?"

She took an alarmed step backward. Another. But he kept on moving forward. "Uh, yeah. Sure."

He grabbed her by both shoulders and shoved her against the wall at her back none too gently. "I swear, if you ever lie to me again, I'll rip your head off."

Lightning all but shot from her blazing blue eyes. "What do you want me to say, Tom? That it'll kill me to leave you? That I'm going to regret driving you away from me for the rest of my life? That it makes me sick to my stomach to think about what we might have had if I hadn't had to accuse you of killing Ando to see how you reacted?"

He stared. She'd accused him to see how he—what the hell? She'd *played* him? He wasn't some random civilian she could manipulate and use like that. He was a soldier, dammit. His honor had no business being brought into question. How dare she?

Belatedly, the other stuff she'd said registered. Kill her to leave him…regret driving him away…what they might have had…

How was he supposed to react to that? At some level, was that what he'd wanted her to say? Was he glad to hear her admit she had feelings for him? Or did it just piss him off that she would admit to manipulating him in one breath and claim to like him in the next? He was so jumbled up inside he didn't know what to feel.

"Well, you can forget hearing any of that out of me, Tom Rowe. I'm not going to say any of it to you. You want the truth? Here's a little truth for you. You're arrogant. And spoiled. And you treat women like dirt. And you think because you're so good-looking and so smart and so rich that you're better than everyone else. Well, you're not. You're no better than anyone else."

He snorted. Nothing she was telling him was news to him. But the fact that she was glaring up at him and spitting out the damning words like she was passing some sort of judgment on him did it. He cracked.

He took another step forward and swept her into his arms, crushing her against him and kissing her with all the pent-up anger in his gut. Her fists pounded on his chest until they grasped at the lapels of his suit coat, dragging him closer.

Their bodies vibrated against one another, out of sync, jangling his nerves until all he could think about was throwing her down, tearing off her clothes and making love to her until she shut up and admitted she wanted him as badly as he wanted her.

She sucked at his lower lip, biting it, drawing it into her mouth and laving it with her tongue at the very same time her hands shoved at his chest and she struggled against the power of his arms. Which was it? Did she want him or hate him?

Maybe it was both.

He knew the feeling.

Finally unleashed, his passion was shocking. Every civilized rule of behavior flew right out of his head. He tore the top of her shirt open, exposing her creamy shoulder. He bit his way down her neck, burying his hand in her hair to pull her head back and expose more of her entirely edible flesh to him.

She made a sound of distress like he was hurting her, but frankly, he didn't much care. She was a soldier. A Special Forces operator. If she wanted to play with fire, then she could damn well put up with getting a little bit burned. But he did ease up the pressure of his teeth slightly.

That earned him another sound, though, and this time a raw groan of pleasure and need ripped from her throat. Better. He released her hair, his hand sliding down the sexy inward curve of her back to her buttocks. Through the scratchy wool of her skirt he gripped her pert, firm behind and dragged her up against him. She arched eagerly, not needing the encouragement to plaster herself tighter to him. And then she had him by the tie, dragging his mouth to hers. Her hands plunged into his hair and she hung on like she was never going to let him go. The thought galvanized him.

He wanted this woman like a fire craved oxygen. He fed on her. Inhaled her. Burned alive wherever she touched him. And that was pretty much everywhere.

Her right leg came up to wrap around his waist, and her skirt slid up her thighs until—holy Mother of·God, the vixen was wearing thigh-high stockings and garters.

With deft fingers he flicked the fasteners loose, relishing the juicy little popping sound of each one giving way. He swept his hand around behind her and encountered bare, silky flesh.

And a thong?

Who'd have guessed that beneath her gray suit the commando was such a wanton hussy? Fire and ice, she was. All cool and calm and poised on the outside, and a born-again hellion wearing naughty lingerie on the inside. Lord, this was a woman he'd enjoy plundering. So many layers to strip away. No telling how many more surprises she had in store for him. And he'd find and reveal every last one of them before he was done with her. Oh, yes. This woman was going to make for a most enjoyable conference.

He reached for the zipper of her skirt. The damned thing was snug enough he wouldn't get it off her any other way. Her white silk blouse slithered free of the skirt, spilling out all over his hands, as warm and sensuous as the woman beneath.

He encountered a push-up bra so sheer it barely felt like she had one on. Of course. What else? Her flesh molded beneath his fingers, firm and throbbing at his touch.

His belt buckle rattled and his shirt melted away from his chest. And then her mouth was on his belly and rational thought deserted him. His hips rocked forward, seeking her heat, his erection so hard it was painful. Now. He would have her now.

The phone rang once loudly and they both started violently. Paige straightened abruptly and broke free of his arms. She leaped in front of him, placing her body between him and the door protectively. The sight was comical. A five-foot-five, half-naked mama bear, her hackles up and claws at the ready to protect her six-foot-two cub made of solid muscle, towering behind her.

He laughed. "You better hope they shoot at my knees and not my head, pip-squeak, because that's about all of me you can cover. And chill out. That was just the phone."

She spun and glared at him. He had to hand it to her. What she lacked for in size, she made up for in speed. "Height isn't the only requirement for a good bodyguard, you know."

He snorted as he walked across the room toward the phone on the desk, his unbuttoned shirt flapping. "Yeah, but it doesn't hurt. Maybe I should just be your bodyguard until your friends get here." He picked up the phone before she could reply. "Hello. Oh, hi, Gretchen."

"The President sends his regrets that he is too busy to speak with you today. However he sent a brief message."

"And that is?"

"You're welcome."

Tom scowled at the phone and slammed it down without bothering to say any more. He hadn't been calling to thank him, dammit! He spun away from the desk and caught sight of Paige, her hair disheveled, her lips red and swollen from their violent kiss, staring at him hopefully.

"Sorry, babe. The President can't talk to me today. Looks like we're stuck together until I can convince him to take my call."

"How long's that going to take?" she asked in dismay.

He grimaced. "At least a day."

She sank down onto the edge of the couch. "Great," she mumbled. "Just great."

He knew the feeling. Oh, how he knew the feeling. How was he ever going to explain having a beautiful, hot journalist tagging around with him everywhere he went? Nobody on the planet would buy the idea of him allowing a reporter to cover his entire day. He put up a fuss when one of them took his picture, let alone actually talked to him. There was no help for it. He was going to have to convince everyone at the conference that he was sleeping with Paige Ellis.

He eyed her speculatively. He could do a whole lot worse. She was definitely enough of a sexpot to pass for the sort of casual arm fluff he was known to wear from time to time. But for some reason, casting her in that light didn't sit right with him. No help for it, though.

"We've got to get you cleaned up," he announced.

"Why's that?" She eyed him in deep suspicion. Smart girl. Looked like she was getting to know him a little, after all.

"Because if you're going to be my girlfriend, you will have to look the part."

Chapter 9

His *girlfriend?* Oh, she didn't think so. "You wish," she spluttered.

He grinned, pure shark. "Then you tell me how you plan to explain tagging around with me, plastered to my side, everywhere I go for the next few days."

She stared, thinking hard. There had to be some other explanation. "How about I've convinced you to let me film your life? I can snag a cameraman from the network to follow us around."

"Already thought of that. Thing is, I have a bit of a reputation when it comes to reporters."

"Yeah, well, maybe I'm the reporter who changed all that."

"Which brings us back to my conclusion that you're going to have to pose as my girlfriend."

She felt like growling. Or maybe stomping her foot. Talk about reputations—hers was going to be shredded after this little episode. She darn well hoped the Medusas appreciated what she was about to sacrifice for them. It had taken her years to establish credibility as a tough, fair, aggressive reporter who didn't use her looks to get a story. Worse than that, though, was the annoying fact that he was right.

She huffed. "Fine. If anyone asks, I'm the girlfriend."

A grin lit up Tom's face. "Oh, when I'm done with you, they'll ask, all right."

Alarm blossomed in her stomach. Exactly what did he mean by that? "Look, Tom. I know we haven't exactly gotten off on the right foot. But I have a career, here. And I need it to come out of this week intact if I'm going to be of any use to my…other…employers. Could you go just a little easy on me?"

"Honey, I'm a lot of things, but easy on my women is not one of them."

She scowled, ignoring the flutter of interest in her gut at what it would be like to be his girlfriend for real and to experience the full broadside of his attention.

He interrupted her speculations abruptly. "I need to leave for a formal dinner meeting in less than an hour. Can you be spectacular by then?"

Less than an hour? Formal? Spectacular? Holy cow. Where was she going to get a decent dress in that amount of time? Last night's ruined blue number was the only truly formal dress she'd brought with her on this assignment.

She must have hesitated too long because Tom groaned. "Don't tell me you're one of those women who takes four hours to get ready to go out."

Her gaze narrowed. "I *can* take four hours, but I certainly don't *need* four hours. My problem tonight is proper clothing."

"Ah. Buy yourself something in the boutique downstairs and charge it to my room. Knock yourself out. But be ready to go in forty-five minutes."

She narrowed her gaze and gave him a few orders of her own. "Don't leave the suite while I'm gone. And don't let anyone in until I get back. Got it?"

He grinned unrepentantly. "Honey, I was pulling personal security assignments before you knew what a bodyguard was. I know the drill."

"Knowing it and following it are two different matters. Promise you won't do anything stupid until I get back."

His grin widened. "Roger. Hold the stupidity until you return. Got it."

Thankfully, she was a decisive shopper and narrowed down her choices to two dresses in about five minutes. And then she simply bought the most expensive one. An off-the-rack Valentino, it was red and smashing, a sleeveless sheath slashing downward asymmetrically to a flared skirt that frothed around her legs, revealing glimpses of tanned limbs through its many-layered silk folds. Best of all, it would conceal a thigh holster without leaving any telltale bumps. And from now on, she was traveling armed at all times—not only because of would-be killers, but also because she wanted to be prepared to shoot the man she was supposed to protect.

The *pièce de résistance* of her outfit was a pair of red evening gloves that extended above her elbows, and the wide Cartier bracelet, encrusted with diamonds, that went over the right glove. Its price tag approached a year's salary for her. Gleefully, she charged that to Tom's room, as well.

Outfit in hand, she raced down to the temporary news bureau to use the makeup kit there. She didn't have time to do anything elaborate with her hair, so she merely pulled it back into a sleek ponytail and ran a flat iron through it. The austere style went nicely with the lines of the dress, and the garment's brilliant color brought out the red highlights in her hair. She slipped her feet into barely there stiletto sandals with five minutes to spare, her Glock service pistol neatly tucked against her thigh along with a few other critical gadgets no girl commando should leave home without. Her gear had been smuggled in via a diplomatic pouch, which meant she had little by way of explosives and limited ammunition. Still, it was better than not being armed at all.

She knocked on Tom's door exactly forty-five minutes after she had left to get ready. She was tempted to wait a minute just to get his goat but decided that being on time would ultimately annoy him more.

The door swung open. Gretchen answered it, and Paige's eyebrows sailed up. So much for Tom following her instructions not to let anyone in.

His assistant smiled warmly. "You look marvelous, Miss Ellis. I'll let him know you're here."

"Thanks."

Pacing wasn't really an option in these shoes, so she practiced kicking them off a few times in case she needed to get rid of them fast. She was just bending over to slip the strap back over her heel when the bedroom door opened. She straightened. And stared. There was no help for it. Tome Rowe in a tuxedo was one of those sights in life a woman just had to stare at.

His gaze raked down over her hot and fast, then back up slowly to her face. "The lady knows how to dress," he murmured approvingly.

"Thank you," she mumbled back, startled by the compliment.

He gestured toward the door. "Shall we? The hotel rang a few minutes ago to let me know my limo's waiting."

She nodded, and managed to beat him to the hallway door by about a foot. "I hate to break it to you, big guy, but I get to go first."

His jaw tightened, but he made no comment as she stepped into the hall and looked it up and down. Deserted. She shot him the military hand signal for all clear and he joined her. They walked the short distance to the elevator, and he moved to one side without her having to tell him. If a gunman were inside when its doors opened, Tom's position kept the shooter from having an immediate line of fire on him.

A bell rang and the doors slid open. Empty. Paige stepped inside and nodded at Tom. He stood beside her in silence, and they rode down to the lobby, each staring straight ahead, lost in their own thoughts.

As for her, two conversations were running in her head simultaneously. The first one was a quick review of security procedures, mapping the route through the hotel lobby in her head and considering possible hiding locations for an attacker as she moved Tom through the space.

The other conversation ran something along the lines of, "Breathe… Act like you do this sort of thing every day…. You always wear designer gowns and jewelry worth more than your house…. He is such a hunk…. Please, God, let him not figure out that I think so…. If only my teammates were here to do this security thing with me, then I wouldn't be so jumpy…. Well, okay, I'd be this jumpy, just for different reasons…. Lord, he's gorgeous in that tux…."

The combination of the two conversations kept her blessedly distracted enough not to register anyone staring at her as she and Tom strolled through the lobby. Her gaze roved back and forth in a steady sweep for threats.

"Keep looking around like that and you'll get a reputation for being a jealous woman," Tom murmured.

"So be it if I keep you alive," she muttered back.

He stared for a moment and then broke into a grin. "Having you for a girlfriend is going to be interesting."

"Enjoy the fantasy while it lasts," she mumbled.

"I might say the same for you," he retorted.

Regret knifed through her. Another time, another place, who knew what might have happened between them? It was a rotten shame, really.

They made it to the limo without any threats popping up, and she was relieved to slide into the spacious vehicle after him and close the bulletproof door. She needed a few minutes to rest. Just that short walk through the lobby had been intensely stressful. She was trained to work in teams of no less than four and more often teams of a dozen when it came to personal security. Doing solo duty was tantamount to having to think and act like several people all at once.

The limo ride was short, a few blocks down the beach to another resort fully as swanky as theirs, where a European delegation was hosting a meal for the key movers and shakers at the summit. Tom went over the guest list with her quickly in the car, and she couldn't help but be impressed. If a bomb went off at this evening's soiree and killed everyone there, the global economy wouldn't recover for years.

When they arrived, if anyone raised their eyebrows at Tom's dinner date for the evening, they did it behind Paige's back. Still, there was a tangible undercurrent of other guests savoring the juicy gossip item they had suddenly become. Tom was right. By tomorrow morning, everyone on the island would be asking questions about the two of them. Dammit.

Of course it didn't help that his hand kept straying to the small of her back, his fingers stroking down her arm, and God help her, his hand coming to rest lightly on the back of her neck. That one about had her leaping out of her skin with nervousness. The intimacy of it staggered her. She suspected her face was as scarlet as her dress by the time his hand finally drifted down her spine, leaving a trail of destruction in its wake.

The pair of suited security men stationed just outside the French doors leading to the beach were the only people present who didn't act startled to see her with Tom. But they certainly were startled when she sidled up to them and asked for status reports on the security procedures at this hotel.

According to the guards, the place was locked down as tightly as the conference hotel, and this venue in specific had been thoroughly swept just an hour before the party. If the Medusas were here, they'd have conducted their own security sweep. But no such luck. For now, she'd have to rely on strangers to cover her and Tom's backs.

Dinner was rich but blessedly served slowly enough so she could enjoy some of all the courses without fearing for the seams of her dress. The leisurely meal gave her plenty of time to study Tom in his native environment. The conversation over the meal was highly technical in nature and ranged across the spectrum of financial issues. Tom was fluent in them all and offered a number of sharp and insightful comments that the other financiers at the table listened to with respect. And considering the host of experts seated around the long table, that was no mean feat.

As coffee was poured all around and a course of sherbet served to cleanse palates before dessert, Tom leaned back in his chair and smiled at her. "Bored to tears yet?" he murmured.

"Actually, no. I'm finding the discussion fascinating. Although you do surprise me with some of the viewpoints you take. I'd love to hear more about why you think some of the things you do." That sent one of his dark eyebrows upward. She continued, "Frankly, I expected you to be more worried about protecting your own best interests."

That sent his other eyebrow up. "I have more than enough money for ten lifetimes. Why would I be greedy at this point in my career?"

"In my experience, the richer people are, the more interested they are in protecting their wealth."

He grinned. "Some would argue that their concern with money is why they have a lot of it."

She shrugged. "I'm still surprised. I had you pegged for a crusty old fart in the making."

He laughed. "Honey, I'm a long way from that. But then, you haven't been in bed with me—yet—so I won't hold you responsible for not knowing."

He just had to get in the jab at her, didn't he? She shot him a look laced with irritation. "Good luck with that."

His eyebrows climbed even higher. "Are you challenging me to get you into bed? What's the bet?"

"I wouldn't gamble with you to save my life, and I certainly wouldn't take a bet over something like that."

"Chicken," he murmured silkily.

She smiled blandly. "You know, a couple of years ago I might have risen to that bait. But I know full well who and what I am these days." And God bless her Medusa instructors for imparting that lesson to her. Although she doubted they'd ever intended to have it applied in exactly this scenario.

He leaned close, throwing his arm over the back of her chair, and whispered in her ear. "You and I both know you're afraid to sleep with me. And I don't need a bet to find the challenge irresistible."

She turned her head and all but put her lips on his ear. "You hold on to your delusions because that's all you're ever going to get from me."

He laughed low and husky, drawing the attention of several people around them. She suddenly found herself intently studying the napkin in her lap. She'd lay odds he'd engineered that little scene to make it look like they were flirting with each other. Although, come to think of it, she supposed they actually had been flirting. In their own rather bizarre, backward way.

After the meal, the men retreated to a smoking lounge to drink brandy and sample cigars, but Tom declined the invitation to join them. Which was nice of him. She would have hated to make a stink in front of all these people about not being separated from him. Instead, he suggested a walk on the beach.

Paige snorted. "Like that's a better security option than you in a generally safe room full of your colleagues without me?"

He shrugged. "If there's someone after me, I'd just as soon draw him out and take him down than hang around waiting for him to attack."

It occurred to her that he must trust her training at least a little if he was willing to bet his life that she could stop whoever was out to get him. She probably didn't deserve that much confidence. After all, this was her first time out in the field, and by herself, no less. Aloud, she asked, "Jeez. Am I that bad a girlfriend? You'd rather try to get yourself killed than spend a few days with me?"

He grinned and opened one of the French doors for her. She stepped into the sultry humidity of the night, relishing the darkness and the smell of the ocean.

"In truth, you're a great deal more interesting than most of the women I go out with."

She replied lightly, "That's what you get for dating empty-headed supermodels."

"Actually, some of them are highly intelligent. Good businesswomen. Nonetheless, I swore off supermodels for good after Mimi."

"Mimi Ando?" she asked.

He paused at the end of the veranda and leaned down to untie his shoes. She followed suit and kicked off her heels. "Yeah. You know her?"

Paige answered, "I know of her. What's she like?"

"Imagine a great white shark, but skinny and tall. And selfish. And childish. Oh, and mean." He strode out into the sand.

Wow. A wee bit bitter, was he? After all this time? Mimi must have really done a number on him. Paige caught up to him, looking around for threats and begging her eyes frantically to adjust to the dark. "And you dated her why?"

He snorted. "I'd just made my first billion. I thought it was what I was supposed to do. You know. Get rich, get a famous, gorgeous girlfriend who puts you on the front pages of the tabloids."

"How did things work out?"

He glanced at her as the sound of the ocean grew louder. "Not so great. I guess she didn't want to wait around for me to die so she could get her hands on all my dough. She dumped me for another billionaire who was forty years older than me. She married him."

"Did she make Takashi happy?"

"She didn't speak a word of Japanese, and his French was barely adequate to order a meal in a restaurant. That was probably the key to their success at standing one another for as long as they did. I heard a few months back that there was trouble in paradise, but I don't really follow such things. There are always rumors."

"I really don't like having you out in the open like this, Tom. You're making me nervous. Can we please get you undercover?"

He shook his head. "How can you be a Medusa and not like to live dangerously?"

"There's a difference between danger and stupidity, and this is the latter."

He laughed. "You're calling me stupid?"

"Yes. And reckless."

"Well, then. What do you suggest I do, great mother hen?" He kicked at a seashell with a toe, examining it.

"Let's go back inside. We'll order a nice armored limo to take us back to the hotel where I can tuck you into—"

Bang.

She dived on him before a curse could even form in her head. She knew that sound. High-powered rifle. Had Tom not bent down just then to pick up a shell, he'd likely be minus his face right now.

"Into the water," she bit out. "Stay low. I'll be on top of you."

Cursing under his breath, he rolled beneath her to face her. Under other circumstances she might have gotten a thrill out of lying on top of Tom Rowe. But as it was, she was merely scared. And mad. She'd warned him.

"Let's go get him," Tom argued up at her.

"No. Absolutely not. Into the water now. No arguments, Tom. I'm the bodyguard."

He stared at her for a long moment, and she waited, holding her breath. At the end of the day, she couldn't force him to do anything. He would have to cede authority to her voluntarily.

He exhaled hard. "Okay, okay." Then he added, "But as soon as we're in the water, I want to try to spot him."

"Fine. Just move," she retorted, exasperated. Every second they delayed here on the beach gave the sniper more time to reload and zero in on them.

She did a push-up, and Tom rolled beneath her once more. It was awkward crab-walking above him as he crawled into the surf, but he was taking bigger facefuls of salt water than she was. Finally, the water became deep enough for him to swim out from under her and for her to push off the bottom and swim against the tide, as well.

She followed Tom away from shore until they were both bobbing on the waves several dozen yards out.

"See anything?" he asked.

She fumbled in her sodden dress, thankful that the light silk was not yards and yards of heavy cloth dragging her down and tangling in her legs. She unzipped her thigh pouch and felt around for the fist-size cylinder inside. She found it and pulled it out.

Treading water, she raised the spotter's scope to her eye and scanned the shore. The optical device was used to help snipers find targets and zero in on the exact distance to them. And it worked great in a pinch as a small telescope.

"Color me impressed," Tom commented from beside her. "You had a scope under that skirt?"

"Mmm hmm." Odds were the sniper was sitting in the jungle just to the north of the hotel. Speaking of which, she saw a group of armed security men moving fast out of the hotel garden toward the trees she was scanning.

She reported to Tom, "Hotel security's heading for that stand of jungle. Our shooter's bugging out by now."

"Let's swim north and see if we can get ahead of him."

She glanced over at Tom. "We're swimming. He's running. No way will we outpace him."

"We will if he's having to move stealthily."

"Maybe," she replied unconvinced. "But then there's the little problem of actually getting in front of him and putting you squarely into his sights again. Sorry. No can do."

"Dammit, Paige. He's right over there. If we can catch him, the threat to me is eliminated for good."

"I disagree."

He looked over at her, startled. "How's that?"

"The shooter's a hired gun. Somebody is bankrolling him. We catch this shooter and another one will be hired to replace him. The key to making you safe is to figure out who wants you dead."

Tom was silent at that, which she took for tacit admission that she was right. Then he said, "If we catch the shooter, maybe he'll tell us who hired him."

"C'mon, Tom. Think. The shooter won't talk unless we torture him, and even then, he probably won't know who hired him. The deal will have been done by intermediaries who never met face-to-face."

She thought she heard a sigh drift across the water. Then he murmured, "Vanessa Blake does pick smart women to work for her."

Bang.

They both flinched hard and she shoved him reflexively under the water as she ducked under herself. She bobbed up first, and when Tom emerged, she bit out, "You hit?"

"No, but that was close. I felt the bullet go by." He sounded distinctly more tense than before. Good. Maybe he was finally taking the threat to his life seriously.

"How far can you swim?" she asked, weighing her options for getting him back under safe cover. She'd met him with a surfboard in hand. Please let that mean he was a strong swimmer.

He grunted. "As far as you need me to, boss."

Thank goodness. And thank goodness he was finally feeling cooperative, too. "Your resort's about a mile down the beach from here—"

Bang.

She swore mentally as she ducked underwater again. That shot had passed right between her and Tom. And they weren't more than two feet apart. She swam off to the south, tugging on Tom's shirt to indicate that he should go with her.

When they both surfaced she panted, "Head south and stay under except for breathing!"

Tom moved in the direction she indicated and she followed close behind. They swam in tense silence, each concentrating on keeping a low profile. And she suspected Tom was praying just like she was that the sniper didn't get another decent shot at him. That last one had been way too close for comfort. She placed herself between Tom and the shore, trying to time surfacing to breathe with his bobs to the surface. It wasn't much by way of protecting him, but it was the best she could do out here.

The shooter took another shot at them, but it sprayed well wide. Thankfully, water changed the trajectory of bullets enough that she wasn't worried about getting hit as long as she and Tom stayed mostly under the surface. But as they swam, her thoughts churned. Was there more than one shooter? Surely the guy parked just north of the hotel had been chased away by that squad of hotel security men. The thought of a team of hit men coming after Tom made her sick to her stomach.

After about thirty minutes of swimming with no more shots fired, she felt fairly certain the sniper or snipers had abandoned the idea of shooting at them again this evening. Still, she didn't relish bringing Tom ashore and exposing both of them at the water's edge. She didn't want to endanger him more than she absolutely had to. She needed a stretch of beach where the water was deep right up to the shoreline, and with plenty of cover once they got ashore.

And she knew just the spot.

She tapped Tom's foot and he surfaced, treading water. She asked between pants, "Have you got another mile or so of swimming in you?"

"Yeah. You?"

She was gratified to hear him breathing hard. "Me? I'm fine. You see that rock promontory sticking out into the water a ways ahead?" When he nodded, she continued. "We're headed for a spot just beyond that."

"Then what?" he replied.

"Then you and I go to ground."

Chapter 10

As he passed through fatigue into that dogged state of perseverance special operators could maintain indefinitely, Tom became aware of something else.

Fear. It was one thing to be in a firefight armed to the teeth and able to shoot back. At least a guy felt like he had an even chance of surviving then. But this. Bobbing along in the ocean with no cover except the water itself gave new meaning to the phrase *sitting duck*.

He kicked off his tuxedo, abandoning the heavy clinging cloth to the embrace of the ocean, stripping all the way down to his spandex undershorts. They could pass for a pair of biking shorts or a swimsuit in a pinch. Thankfully, the Pacific in this part of the world was reasonably warm year-round, particularly close to shore in shallow waters like these.

As a half hour stretched into an hour with no more shots fired at them, he finally began to relax. Which wasn't necessarily any great blessing because his survival adrenaline drained away, leaving only the insidious drag of the water, the darkness and an interminable swim in painful silence.

He wasn't about to complain, though. If Paige could do this without whining about it, he damned well could, too.

Eventually, she murmured from behind him, "There. You see that little beach just beyond that big outcropping? That's where we're headed. To the rocks on the far side of the sand."

"Got it," he managed to grit out without sounding like he was panting too badly.

He dragged himself ashore behind Paige, immensely relieved to be done swimming for the night. His arms felt like lead, and his entire body was heavy with exhaustion. Frankly, he couldn't believe Paige had survived that grueling swim without crying *uncle* a long while ago. Every time he thought he knew what the Medusas were capable of, they went and surprised him again.

Sometimes he regretted having left active duty before he got a chance to work with the all-female team. The way he heard it, they were making quite a name for themselves in the Special Forces community. And he could see why. If Paige Ellis was only an adjunct member of the team, he'd hate to see the full-timers at work.

"You got a little crawling left in those arms?" Paige muttered.

"Have you?"

Her smile flashed white in the darkness. "I'm a Medusa."

And he supposed that said it all.

She hand-signaled to him to follow her, and he signaled back an acknowledgment. She'd picked a good spot to come ashore. They'd been able to swim right up to a jumble of boulders and creep behind their plentiful cover. Thick foliage loomed only a few yards ahead. They gained the cover of the heavy underbrush, and then she turned south, skirting the edge of the jungle. He followed, grateful for the cautious pace she was setting. And then he rounded a palmetto bush and spied their destination. He grinned. Clever. Paige's borrowed cottage. The local police knew she was staying here, but no one else knew. Whoever was trying to kill him wouldn't have been able to give this address to a hit man.

She dug a door key out of that magic pouch under her skirt. They both rose to a crouch and slipped inside the back door low and fast, leaving the lights off. She motioned for him to sit down on the kitchen floor, and he leaned against a cabinet while she moved off in the dark to do a quick security sweep of the house. He had to give her credit for being thorough.

It felt weird having someone look out for him like this. Under less threatening circumstances, he might even have enjoyed it. She really was cute when she went all fierce and protective on him. Although, after the last two hours, his reaction was turning more into admiration than amusement.

"The house is clear," she murmured from the kitchen doorway. "Let's keep the lights out, however. No sense advertising our presence."

He nodded. That made sense. Besides, his vision adjusted well enough to the dark not to need any more than the thin stripes of moonlight filtering through the window blinds for illumination.

"Why don't you jump into the shower and get warmed up?" she suggested. "I'm afraid I don't have any clothes that will fit you, but I can offer you a clean sheet." She added slyly, "You'll look great in a toga."

He grinned at her. "I'd rather go commando, thanks."

"Go take your shower."

"Ladies first."

"Sorry. I'm not a lady at the moment. I'm a Medusa. And we don't tolerate preferential treatment based on our gender."

"Right. I forgot. You Medusas have got to be more macho than the guys."

She answered surprisingly mildly, "Not at all. We've never tried to be like the men. And we've certainly never pretended to be as strong as our male counterparts. But in an operational situation, there's no time for niceties. We have to be just another soldier to the operators around us."

"And the guys you work with manage to treat you that way?" he asked in disbelief.

"It usually takes them a few field exercises to get over babying us because we're girls. And sometimes we have to help them…overcome…their preconceived notions. But most of them get the hang of it eventually."

He heard humor in her words. He'd bet there were a few good war stories of the Medusas humiliating their male colleagues behind that dry comment of hers.

"Go. Shower," she ordered.

He grinned. "Yes, ma'am."

Hot water sluiced across his body, rinsing the salt off his skin and out of his hair, but it didn't do a damned thing to combat the shivers that set in partway through his shower. He recognized it: post-mission reaction. Be as cool as a cucumber when the bullets were flying, and save the emotional stuff for later. Most special operators only let go of the adrenaline rush afterward. When they were alone. When the rest of the team wasn't there to witness what a mess a guy was behind that calm, collected facade. And if a guy was lucky, someday the facade became the real thing.

Time was when he could get shot at and not think twice about it. But it hit him hard tonight. Yep, he'd been out of the field too long. Gone soft.

Was Paige having this reaction right now, as well? Was she huddled in a corner in the dark, sweating bullets over how close a couple of those shots had come to taking both of them out?

The thought of her scared and alone drove him to race through the rest of his shower. A compulsion to comfort her, to tell her everything was all right had him toweling off at light speed and ripping back the shower curtain hastily.

He stopped. Looked carefully around the bathroom. Where in the hell were his shorts?

They were gone.

Had Paige taken them away to wash, or was this some kind of joke? He noted wryly the neatly folded white sheet on the toilet lid. Great. She hadn't been kidding about the toga. At least she's been thoughtful enough to leave a belt for him. He folded the sheet in half and cinched it around his waist in a skirt that he preferred to think of as a rather manly kilt.

He stepped out of the bathroom.

"Cute," Paige commented cheerfully. "I never noticed what nice knees you have."

Dammit. No crying, trembling female to comfort. He scowled at her. "I'm sorry now that I saved you some hot water."

Laughing, she disappeared into the bathroom.

Her shower was quick, too. Maybe she'd waited like him to let go of the nerves in there. Maybe now she was having her private breakdown, standing naked under a jet of hot water....

Whoa. Not exactly the appropriate image to have in his head with only a flimsy sheet between his male response to that mental picture and acute embarrassment.

Why did he feel so protective of her, anyway? She'd made it perfectly clear that she was entirely capable of taking care of herself. But still the urge persisted to gather her close, smell her skin, wrap her up in his embrace and never let her go.

He sat down on the floor of the living room out of sight of the windows in case the sniper had somehow managed to follow them here. A jolt of alarm hit him at the idea. It figured. For all those years when he didn't particularly care if he lived or died, nobody ever seriously tried to off him. Now that he finally had something great going, the bullets started to fly—

Something great? What was so different about his life right now than it had been two days ago, before anyone tried to shoot him?

The answer was obvious, but he shied away from acknowledging what—or who—had come into his life so suddenly. She was just a temporary thing. He buried his head in his hands. Lord, he was a wreck.

"Hey. You okay?" a soft voice murmured out of the shadows.

He glanced at her bleakly, and she moved to his side immediately, sitting down so close to him that their knees practically touched. Her sleeveless T-shirt and shorts distracted him plenty, but not enough to totally erase the fact that someone was trying to kill him.

Her murmur sounded genuinely sympathetic. "Is it hitting you that someone tried to kill you tonight?"

He shrugged, but somehow, that seemed like a cop-out. "Yeah," he muttered. "I guess so."

"It's okay, you know. You're allowed to be a little freaked out by that. You don't have to be Mr. Macho for me. I work with girls, remember? We don't run screaming from letting our emotions show now and then."

A wry grin quirked his mouth momentarily. "I shudder to imagine a whole team of girl operators emoting together."

Paige's smile flashed in a patch of moonlight. "It's not that bad. What stinks is when six or eight of us PMS at the same time. Now that can be a challenge to maintain professional relations around."

He laughed. "I tremble at the thought. Armed crazy women."

Her hand came to rest lightly on his shoulder but froze there as she frowned abruptly. "You're wicked tense, Tom. If this weren't the middle of an op, I'd offer to work out some of those knots for you."

He surveyed the darkened room. "I don't see any imminent threats." He added casually, "And I'm known to pay good masseuses outrageously well."

"How outrageously?" she asked lightly, and perhaps a tiny bit breathlessly.

He glanced to her and replied low, "Try me and find out."

And suddenly, it was incredibly important that she take him up on his romantic offer. For that was exactly what it was. He ventured a look at her and her expression was inscrutable.

"What are you thinking?" he finally mumbled. "I can't read your eyes."

"Good," she replied. "I'd hate to think you could tell what I'm thinking right now."

He half turned to her. He wanted to pull her into his arms, but she hadn't invited him to, and with a woman like her, he sensed that the invitation was extremely important. "Tell me what you're thinking."

A wistful look entered her wide, dark gaze. "I was thinking about how nice it would be to take you up on your offer."

"Then do it." The words were out of his mouth before he could reconsider them, before he could call them back.

The hand on his shoulder drifted up to his neck. Her fingers threaded into his hair. "That sniper really did a number on you, didn't he?"

His throat was too tight to answer. His own hand drifted up to the half-dry waves of strawberry blond framing her face. He pushed a strand back and tucked it behind her ear. A fine shudder passed through her and sharp need surged in his gut.

He murmured, "You're beautiful."

"You're blinded by the salt water in your eyes."

"Don't be modest, Paige. You're stunning. Not many women are truly beautiful with wet hair and no makeup, but you are."

"It's pitch-black in here. You can't see a thing."

"Didn't they teach you Medusas how to take a compliment?"

She sighed then, a gentle thing, maybe even a sound of surrender. He traced the rim of her ear with one finger and trailed it down the corner of her jaw, along the slender line of her neck and across the faint hollow above her shoulder blade. It didn't feel like she had a bra on under that sleeveless muscle shirt.

"We shouldn't…" she started.

She was right, of course. "But that doesn't mean it's not going to happen," he replied easily.

That elicited a faint smile out of her. "I think this is the part where I'm supposed to exercise discipline and keep my hands off you."

"To hell with discipline," he growled.

That got a faint laugh out of her. "You're not helping here."

"I almost died tonight. I'm a little messed up in the head. And right now I want you so badly I can't see past the end of my own nose."

"I wouldn't have let you die."

"What, you'd have flung yourself in front of me and caught the bullet meant for me?"

"Absolutely."

Her answer was firm, certain, without a hint of hesitation. He retorted incredulously, "Seriously, you'd die for me?"

"In a heartbeat, Tom."

He stared, flummoxed. Yeah, sure, he knew it was her job. But to have a woman like her look him in the eye and say it out loud did something funny to his gut. Something that twisted and tightened it in a shockingly pleasant way.

"Come here." He opened his arms but made no move toward her. This had to be her choice.

She hesitated for an endless, heart-wrenching moment, and then she slid closer. Her arms closed around his waist and her head went to his bare chest. It felt like she was falling into him, and he into her. The room actually spun a little as sensations flooded him. Her breasts were soft against his chest, her arms surprisingly strong around his waist, her hair cool and silken against his neck. Soft and hard, sleek and strong, she was a mixture of contrasts that somehow managed to be all woman.

"You smell amazing," she murmured.

"Mmm. The intoxicating scent of seaweed."

She raised her head to laugh at him. "Now who can't take a compliment?"

"Touché."

"Too bad we can't dance, right now. But we can't risk giving anyone that silhouette in the window."

"No law says dancing has to be fully vertical," he replied. He swayed back and forth with her in his arms a few times and then rolled over her and took her down to the floor. "Or if you prefer," he said, rounding onto his back and pulling her on top of him, "you may lead."

She smiled down at him. "That's one of the things I like best about you. You're secure enough in your masculinity not to be afraid of letting me be in charge now and then."

"Or maybe I'm just lazy and let the girl do all the work."

"You're a lot of things, Tom Rowe, but lazy is not one of them."

"Thanks, I think." He grinned up at her. He couldn't remember the last time a woman had made him feel this good. "What else am I?"

"The possibilities in answer to that boggle my mind. I'd better pass."

He might have been worried had her voice not vibrated with humor. Nonetheless, he answered seriously, "Then let me tell you what you are."

She gazed down at him questioningly.

"You're a woman who makes me forget about everything else when I'm with her. You're a woman who makes me laugh. You make me think about ice-cream sundaes."

"Ice-cream sundaes?" she exclaimed.

"Mmm hmm. Slathered in warm chocolate sauce and covered in whipped cream, every last bit of it in need of licking off."

"Oh," she rasped, then breathed, "Oh, my."

"You're a woman who makes me want to put that breathless note in your voice all the time. I want to make you gasp in delight and cry out in pleasure. I want to see wonder in your eyes when we make love."

She blinked several times fast, her eyes bigger and bluer than ever in the scant moonlight. "Wow. All of that?"

"And more." He couldn't wait any longer. He slipped his hand under the weight of her hair and drew her down to him by slow degrees. He never broke the lock of their gazes and reveled in the dawning desire unfolding in her eyes. Her body undulated faintly against his as if she strained toward him but fought to hold herself away.

"Let go, Paige. Come with me."

"Where are we going?" she asked.

"How about I show you instead?"

Their lips touched. It was exactly as he remembered. Lights exploded behind his eyelids and lust surged so powerfully in his gut that he missed a breath. She lurched forward, her tongue plunging into his mouth eagerly. He sucked it into his own mouth, laving it with his tongue, tantalizing her with quick thrusts and slow strokes against her hot, wet flesh.

She groaned. "You don't fight fair."

"We already established that."

"Lord, I want you."

"Then have me."

Her hand stole between them, reaching for his belt. The buckle gave way beneath her fingers and cool air wafted across his naked body. "Now what's wrong with this picture?" he murmured.

He sat up, taking her with him, and reached for the hem of her shirt. As he'd guessed, she wore no bra. Her breasts were firm and high and swelled perfectly to fill his hands. He leaned down and took a nipple in his mouth and rolled his tongue around it, then stroked it hard enough to draw a little gasp from her. He resumed sipping at her flesh, but she arched forward, pushing more of herself into his mouth.

"Do that again," she gasped.

Ah. The lady liked a little danger. He would never hurt her, but she clearly was turned on by the thought of him pushing her a little beyond comfort. A compulsion to push her way beyond comfortable overcame him. He carried her down to the floor and swept her shorts and panties off in one fast movement.

He used his knees to move her thighs apart and captured her wrists and drew them wide, pressing her down to the floor. "Will you let me do whatever I want to you tonight?" Even he heard the dark edge in his voice now.

She hesitated a moment. "I trust you."

"Is that a yes?"

Her answer was more sigh than speech, but it shot like an arrow straight through him. "Yes. Anything."

Fierce desire ripped through him.

"But—" she started.

He froze.

"—the next time I get to do whatever I want to you."

He laughed. "If that's what you want after tonight, I'll agree to it."

And then he let go of the pent-up demons within him, all the lust and fear and adrenaline that had been pounding through him. He drew her hands together over her head, grabbed her discarded T-shirt and wrapped it around her wrists expertly. A quick lift of the corner of the sofa to loop the armholes of the shirt around the leg of the couch, and she was partially immobilized. She could wedge a shoulder under the couch and free herself any time, but she'd given him her word. Tonight she was his.

He took his time exploring her body, relishing how she, by turns, moaned with pleasure and begged for more. Her body went fluid and pulsing, blood throbbing beneath her skin as he explored every inch of her with hands and mouth. He left nothing to privacy. He wanted to know every contour of her, every bit of skin, every ticklish spot, every sensitive spot. He wanted to plunder the very depths of her soul.

And plunder her he did, denying his own stone-hard flesh, in ways she'd never been taken before. He could tell it in her sudden tension, her gasps of surprise, the way she arched up eagerly into him for more and then drew back, self-conscious. But he tolerated no such modesty from her. He drove her past modesty, past shyness, past anything but raving need for more and yet more of what he did to her. And when she was literally in tears, begging for him to take her, he finally plunged to the hilt inside her.

She climaxed immediately, crying out sharply, her internal muscles shuddering violently around him. He grabbed her ankles and spread her wide, opening her up to him completely as he drove into her relentlessly, seeking and finding such intense pleasure he thought he might perish.

"Look at me," he ground out.

Her eyes fluttered open, glazed and unfocused, awash in such pleasure that he couldn't help but smile. He continued to rock against her, stronger now, deeper. She tensed again, took a short, hitching breath and cried out again, a long, keening moan this time that went on and on around him.

Unable to stand it anymore, he let go of the last shreds of his restraint. Gazing deep into her magnificently expressive eyes, he opened up his soul and poured everything he was into the very core of her. Her cries were hoarse this time, raw with her final release. A groan of his own tore free from his chest to meet hers as they shuddered together in the aftermath of their lovemaking.

Time passed.

There were no words for it. What they had between them went beyond syllables and meaning. It reached into some primal place within him he'd heretofore had no idea existed and loosed something inside him he could not name. It was more than need, more than possession, more than mind-blowing sex.

He knew one thing, though. He wanted more of that. Much, much more.

It was a long time before either of them spoke. Her body had gone soft and relaxed around him, and he was nearly recovered enough to move. He gathered his strength and rolled to her side, releasing her hands from the sofa leg.

She untangled her shirt and pulled it down over her head. As she reached for her shorts where they'd landed on the windowsill, he noticed for the first time just how sculpted her arm and shoulder muscles were. The Medusa in her was showing through. The way he heard it, the training regimen the Medusas followed was at least as rigorous as that of any male Special Forces team.

She smiled down at him, disbelief still prominent in her eyes. "Hungry?" she asked.

"As a matter of fact, I did work up an appetite swimming earlier."

She laughed. "Right. Swimming."

"How about you?" he responded, relaxed and lazy all of a sudden.

"I don't have much around here to eat, particularly since I had to empty out my refrigerator yesterday, but you're welcome to it."

"As I recall, you had a couple of nice bottles of wine."

She grinned. "Just what I need to do to cap off this night. Get snockered on duty. Viper would love that."

"Any sniper worth his salt would've taken advantage of our, uh, distraction, and shot us already if he was planning to. We're probably safe for the rest of the night. You can let down your hair a little."

"Sorry. That's not how I'm trained to operate."

He sighed. It wasn't how he was trained, either. He was still having a little trouble equating this gorgeous, sexy, mesmerizing female with a special operator, though. He couldn't blame her for her sense of duty, but he would've enjoyed seeing her relaxed and a little drunk. He made a mental note that, as soon as reinforcements arrived, he'd drink a bottle of wine with her.

Snagging the sheet and tucking it around his hips, he followed her to the kitchen. She laid out an array of crackers, some tuna fish, several cans of stew, a can of baked beans and a bag of chocolate-chip cookies. He grinned at the latter. "Emergency chocolate rations?"

Paige reached for the bag of cookies. "Oh, yeah. I'm a born-again chocoholic."

"Duly noted," he murmured. *Note to self: add feeding her outrageously expensive chocolate to that bottle of wine.* "Any other vices I should know about?"

She grinned. "Like I'd arm you with that kind of ammunition? I think not."

"I'll tell you one of my secret vices if you'll tell me one of yours."

She considered him thoughtfully. "Deal. You go first."

"I like to read comic books. I have since I was a kid, and I still do. I have Gretchen buy them for me and put them in my briefcase. When I'm bored at a meeting, I'll slip one into the papers on my desk and read it."

Paige laughed. "I bet you're a Batman guy, aren't you?"

"Why do you say that?"

"Reclusive billionaire who fights crime and thinks he can save the world. It's a no-brainer."

"I don't think I can save the world."

"Ha. But that won't keep you from trying."

He quirked a brow at her and reached for the tuna and crackers. "Like you're one to talk. Why did you become a Medusa anyway? That seems like a strange choice for someone as…high profile…as you."

"You mean why would I do something that gets no public recognition like work with the Medusas when I'm such a glory-hound reporter the rest of the time?"

"I wouldn't put it quite so baldly, but I guess that's the gist of what I'm asking."

He wished there was more light to see the play of emotions across her face. As it was, he thought he caught a glimpse of wistfulness. Regret, even. But then her shadowed features hardened.

"I got sick of standing on the sidelines. I watched tragedies and injustice and indignities taking place, and I never did anything about them. A person can only stand that for so long."

"I thought reporters believe their role in life is to expose these things."

She was silent a long time, her gaze turbulent as she stared at nothing. Then she turned to him and said simply, "Sometimes they get personal."

Now, that was revealing. What on Earth could've driven a woman like her to do something as extreme as become a Medusa? He almost didn't want to know, except that burning curiosity to know everything about her was apparently still at work. He asked, "What happened, kiddo? What made you join the Medusa Project?"

A shrug was all he got from her. Okay, then. He'd take that as confirmation that a hell of a trauma had pushed her to it. He cast back in his memory a few years. He didn't remember anything hitting the news about something happening to World News's star reporter. He prodded gently, "You know that whatever you tell me stays between us, right?"

Another long pause. Then, she said, "It's no big secret. I lost my cameraman. His name was Jerry. Jerry Sprague. He was…my friend."

And from that loaded pause, Tom inferred that the guy had also been her lover. When she didn't continue, he prompted, "And?"

"And he was trying to land me an interview I wanted when he was kidnapped. You know the drill. Extremist group tortured him, put grisly footage of him on the Internet and then killed him."

And she'd been overcome by guilt and grief. Felt responsible for his death. And decided to become a Medusa. Wow. She'd either really loved the guy, or she was really committed to standing up for what she believed in. He asked as casually as he could manage it, which wasn't a whole lot, "Did you love him?"

She didn't hesitate. "We were friends mostly. Don't get me wrong. I loved him in my own way, but not like that. He and I traveled together into every life-threatening hellhole we could find. And…he was there. It probably sounds awful to say that he was convenient. But we were two Americans, alone, facing death on a daily basis. I really did care for him." She showed none of the telltale signs of a lie. He didn't know whether to be relieved or perplexed. "Why the Medusas?"

"Why not? Don't you ever get a hankering to fix the things you see on the news? You see an obvious and simple solution and can't understand why everyone else doesn't see it?"

"Yeah, I still get that feeling sometimes. I've been to a few war zones myself, remember?"

"It wasn't an entirely selfish thing for me with Jerry. I really did like him. We just didn't have magic."

The same kind of magic the two of them had just made? He frowned. He didn't know how to answer that one himself, and he definitely wasn't ready to hear how she would answer it. He spoke hastily to distract her. "I have to admit that if there would have been a woman on my Spec Ops team, I'd have slept with her now and then just to remind us both that we were alive."

Paige looked at him directly for the first time since this conversation began. "That's it, exactly. It's about knowing you're alive."

They shared a look of mutual understanding. And then it dawned on him what had just happened. He'd found a woman who understood that part of his life. The most important part of him. The hidden part that most of the world never saw and didn't even know existed. Other people saw a spoiled rich boy who'd gotten lucky in the financial markets. But Paige, she saw the soldier within him.

And damned if he didn't see the soldier in her. It was a weird combination to be sure—a beautiful woman and a special operator inhabiting the same body. But it was probably no weirder than him. Batman, indeed.

"Come here." He held out his arm to her.

She looked startled. "I'm not looking for a pity party."

"And I'm not offering one. Come here," he ordered gently.

He held his breath. Would she accept the gesture in the light it was offered, or would she reject it? Reject him?

Chapter 11

Paige studied him intently, his open arms, his unreadable expression. Was he offering her more than post-mission sex, here? Something genuine between them? Something deeper? She sincerely hoped their lovemaking had been more than simple adrenaline sex for him. It had been a life-altering experience for her.

She didn't sense any ulterior motive in him, just an offer for simple comfort. A hug in the small hours of the night, some human warmth shared.

She stepped forward.

And yet, it seemed like so much more than a hug as he wrapped his strong arms around her and her head drifted to his shoulder. It was as if they shared a tacit agreement that they had passed beyond client and bodyguard, past friendship, past casual sex partners.

She hadn't known exactly what to expect on this mission, but this sure as shootin' was not it.

Tom murmured, "I'll take the watch if you want to get a little shut-eye."

"I'm supposed to be watching you!"

"Look, Paige, I was a special operator for a long time. I'm perfectly capable of standing watch, and you've got to get a little sleep sometime. If you want to play bodyguard while I'm out in public, that's fine with me. I can use the extra set of eyes looking out for my back. But let me at least pull my weight here."

She sighed. He had a point. She'd used go pills before and they were capable of keeping an operator alert and functional for up to sixty hours, but the crash afterward was horrendous.

He led her into the living room, where he pulled the sofa cushions down onto the floor and presented them to her with a flourish. "Your bed, mademoiselle."

Thankfully, she didn't have to explain to him the danger of using the bed in the actual bedroom. It was the first place an intruder would look for them. She stretched out, the night's activities catching up with her all at once.

"You want my pistol?" she asked sleepily.

His grin flashed in the dark. "Ah, now there's a line I never expected to hear a beautiful woman use on me. Sure. I'll take it. Got a spare clip while you're at it?"

"They're in the top drawer of the bureau just inside the bedroom door and to the left."

"Let me guess. Under your lingerie."

She cracked one eye open to glare up at him. "You'd be surprised how many bad guys stop searching for guns and ammo when they hit black lace."

"Black lace, eh? This I've got to see. Model it for me?"

She was sinking fast. "Tomorrow."

"Sweet dreams, pip-squeak."

She sighed, "'Night, Tom."

And that was the last thing she remembered before sunlight streaming into the room woke her up the next morning. That and the smell of something delicious cooking in the kitchen. She frowned. There wasn't anything in the house to cook that would smell like that. What had he gone and done?

Paige surged to her feet. She'd been asleep for nearly six hours! He was supposed to let her catch a power nap while he stood guard and then trade off with her.

"Tom—" she started. She stopped cold as she crossed the kitchen threshold. He was just laying out an enormous breakfast, complete with fried eggs and bacon, orange juice, steaming coffee and stacks of pancakes.

"Haven't lost my touch in the kitchen, have I?" he announced cheerfully. "Not bad for pushing five years since I cooked anything."

"Yeah? And where did this *anything* come from?"

He shrugged. "I ran down to that little market on the main road and picked up a few things."

She didn't say anything to him. She just glared. And waited.

It didn't take long for him to look away, squirming. "Okay, so I probably should have woken you up and taken you along. But we consumed everything edible in the house last night and I was hungry. I figured you'd be hungry, too, after all of our, um, exertions."

That put a quick flush of heat in her cheeks. Enough to distract her momentarily from her disbelief that Tom would do something as stupid as venturing out alone.

"Look," he said cajolingly. "Our sniper was out running around for most of the night, too. What are the odds that he stuck around after sunrise this morning? You and I both know he called it a night and went home to get some sleep and figure out how to get me the next time."

"Maybe," she retorted. "But maybe he's professional enough to stick with the job until he finishes it. I would be. And maybe there's more than one sniper out there. Which means they could work in shifts and have you in their sights around the clock."

"You're a Medusa," he retorted. "You're trained to be paranoid."

Okay, so that warmed the cockles of her heart a little bit. How cool was it that he thought she rose to the level of a real, live Medusa? Which was a hell of a compliment at the end of the day. And not too shabby a distraction tactic from him. She forced her mind back to the problem at hand: controlling her protectee without inciting open rebellion from him. "Just don't go anywhere without me again, Tom. Okay?"

He sighed. "Oh, all right." A short pause. "Syrup with those pancakes?"

"Duh."

He grinned and passed her the maple syrup.

She dug in, as hungry as he'd guessed she'd be. "So. What's on your agenda for today?"

He grinned. "No idea. That's what Gretchen's for. I know there's a session this afternoon with all of the summit attendees that should run until nearly supper. I think I have a meeting with the American delegation some time this morning. First order of business will be to get back to the hotel and get some clothes, though."

"Speaking of which…" She got up, went to her bedroom and returned carrying something dark blue. "This is my biggest T-shirt. It'll be snug on you, but you've got the pecs to pull it off. And it'll be better than strolling back into the hotel in just your shorts."

He grinned widely and pulled the navy blue T-shirt over his head.

Oh my. He did tight cotton very nicely, indeed.

"I'll do the dishes while you get dressed," he murmured.

Okay, he was officially a perfect man. He made her scream with pleasure *and* fed her *and* did the dishes the morning after.

Her car was still at the hotel so Tom called for a taxi. They met it out at the main road, several driveways down from her own.

The drive was not long, and they made it back to the hotel with no problems. She ordered Tom to wait for her to come around to the passenger side of the cab to let him out and thought he might mutiny at that. Fortunately, by the time he unfolded himself from the backseat, she'd already made it around to the passenger side of the car.

"You're really carrying this bodyguard thing too far," he muttered as he levered himself awkwardly out of the tuna-can-size vehicle. "I don't need you opening doors for me."

"Get over it," she replied cheerfully. "I'm the big, bad bodyguard and you're the lowly principal."

"At least walk next to me like you're my girlfriend or something," he groused.

She laughed as he looped his arm over her shoulder and strode past the pair of doormen who swept the doors open for them.

Without warning, an explosion of shouts and flashing lights assaulted them.

She lurched and barely stopped herself from flinging Tom to the ground with her on top of him. *Jeez-o-peet.* The entire press corps was arrayed before them, pointing video and still cameras at them. Which meant that at any second…yep, here came the attack of the microphones.

"Where were you last night, Mr. Rowe? Were you kidnapped? Rumor had it you were shot. Are you hurt?"

The questions flew at them one on top of another, so thick and fast she could barely make out words, let alone meaning. Good Lord. Is that what the press looked like from the other side of the lens? No wonder Tom hated reporters.

She squinted into the blinding glare of the camera lights unable to make out a darned thing beyond them. She cursed under her breath. "Let us through!" she called out as she pushed forward.

No dice. The press wanted a statement and they weren't budging until they got it.

Tom tried shouting, "I'll have my people issue a statement if you'll let me through so I can brief them!"

Nada. The bristling phalanx of microphone-armed reporters only pressed in closer. And then someone got the bright idea to change tactics. A reporter shouted out, "Are you two an item? Has America's most eligible bachelor been landed at last?"

In the time it took Paige to flinch, all the other journalists took up the line of questioning. Tom's jaw went rock hard, rippling with intense irritation.

"C'mon, guys," she tried. "Let us through. It has been a long night and he said he'll make a statement to you in a little while."

"How'd you do it, Paige? How'd you catch the uncatchable man?" A cluster of microphones blossomed under her nose.

A breeze hit her from behind as the lobby's double doors swung open, and she turned quickly to assess the threat. Shock rendered her still for a moment, and then she grinned widely. Vanessa Blake must have pulled every string in the book to get the Medusas here so fast. God bless that woman.

She leaned close to Tom and called loud enough for him to hear over the din, "The cavalry's come to rescue us."

Aleesha Gautier, aka Mamba and one of the original Medusas, led a team of a half-dozen women forward, bodily throwing aside the journalists unfortunate enough to be standing between them and their goal.

Affecting a rich Jamaican accent, Aleesha spoke loudly enough for her voice to roll out across the entire crowd. "'Ey now, boys 'n' girls. Don't get your knickers all in a twist, 'ere. Back off and den meybee you gets to talk wit' de mon."

The other Medusas closed ranks around Paige and Tom, unceremoniously elbowing aside anyone and everyone in their way.

"Man, am I glad to see you!" Paige exclaimed to her teammates.

One of the pushiest reporters, a woman Paige recognized from a news show that was more about gossip than actual hard news, shouted shrilly, "If you don't give me a statement, Mr. Rowe, I'm going to report that you and Paige Ellis are involved and flaunting your relationship, and that her objectivity is hopelessly compromised as a journalist."

That jerked Tom's head to the side to find the source of it. Paige reached out to touch his elbow, to tell him not to rise to the bait, that she would have a quiet word with the obnoxious woman later, upon whom she happened to have blackmail material that would nix the report. But Paige was too late.

Tom's back went rigid. "You report that and I'll sue you for slander. I'll not only bury you, but I'll take your entire show off the air, lady."

Oh, God. Now he'd gone and done it. The first rule of dealing with the media was never, ever, pick a fight with them.

Sure enough, the sharks pounced. "Oh ho! So now you're defending Ms. Ellis's honor, are you? How long have you two been going out? Does your network know about this liaison, Paige? Aren't you afraid you'll lose your job by not revealing this personal bias?"

Paige pressed her lips together. She was so not getting into a pissing contest with this crowd.

Tom growled, "Paige Ellis and I are *not* dating. We are *not* an item, and I resent your insinuations."

Paige stared. What was he doing? They'd agreed that she would pose as his girlfriend to explain her hanging around him while she looked out for his safety.

Tom continued forcefully, "Unfortunate circumstances threw us together last night. Nothing more."

Paige staggered like he'd just kicked her feet out from under her. Nothing more? Was that all last night had been to him? Unfortunate circumstances?

He leaned into the nearest mike and stared frankly into the cameras. "Paige Ellis and I happened to be at the same dinner and happened to end up hiding together after a gunman fired shots. For you people to make something more out of that is just plain ridiculous. I mean, come on. You all know how I feel about reporters. Can you seriously see me dating one?"

That got a snicker out of the crowd. And it was a dagger straight to her heart. Who was she kidding? She of all people knew how he felt about reporters. He hated them with a purple passion. Of course last night had been a onetime thing. He'd even said so. And she'd acknowledged it. For her to have some giant crush on Tom was beyond stupid.

Tom pressed the crack he'd created in the journalists' hostility. "For ten years I've stonewalled even the most basic of interviews, and you think I'd arm any reporter with that kind of ammunition?" He laughed. "You think I'd get naked with one of you guys?"

That did it. The media frenzy was broken. Laughter and ribald jokes flew back and forth between Tom and the reporters. The Medusas, reading the situation correctly, let the jocularity flow for just long enough to relax the crowd, and then they resumed pushing through the crowd, apologizing pleasantly as they basically bulldozed an opening for Tom to escape.

Paige would have followed along in their wake, but a familiar voice barked her name above the general din. Her boss, Greer Carson. Oh, Lord.

She turned and made her way to him, waving off the avalanche of questions still being hurled at her.

"In here." Greer held open the door to their temporary broadcast bureau for her. She slipped past him and sighed in relief as Greer shut out the din in the lobby.

"You okay?" he asked.

She shrugged. "Yeah. Fine." Truth be told, she was reeling and felt like she'd just taken a few good body blows.

"Anything happen between you and Rowe last night?"

"Nothing that's anyone's business."

"Are you compromised for reporting on him and the summit?"

"No!" She blurted it out automatically, but a twinge in her gut made her wonder if she was telling the truth.

"Good. Now then, we've got some damage control to do. Rowe did his part to quiet the rumors, but now you've got to do your part."

"Fair enough. What have you got in mind, boss?"

"Something about Rowe. Hard-hitting. Tough. Something that'll shut up the critics who say you two have got a thing going on."

Her innards twisted. Tom would be furious with her. He'd accuse her of taking unfair advantage of their personal relationship to pillory him. And he'd be right. She opened her mouth to protest Greer's instructions, but reason kicked in, stopping her. Tom had just stated unequivocally, for all the world to hear, that she and he *had* no personal relationship.

She closed her mouth. Nodded. Then said, "I've got just the angle. It's huge. I wasn't sure about going public with it, but I think it's time. Are you aware that Takashi Ando is dead?"

"Whaaat?" Greer squawked. "Are you kidding me?"

"Nope. Interesting that two attempts have been made on Tom Rowe's life, as well, eh?"

"Why isn't this the biggest news of the entire conference? Why the hell didn't you say something about it before now?"

"The local police asked me to hold off reporting it to give them time to notify Mimi Ando and Takashi's sons. But I'd say it's safe to go public now."

"Get me documentation. I'd hate to be wrong on this one."

"And when I've got it?"

"Hell, I'll break you in to the live broadcast stateside. This will be a sensation! What a scoop!"

She didn't exactly share his jubilation, but she did share his determination to break the story before anyone else. She went to one of the telephones arrayed on a table in the corner and picked up the handset. An operator came on the line.

"I need to speak to the police," Paige said.

In about two minutes, she had her confirmation that Ando's family had been notified, and that the Japanese tycoon's death had been ruled questionable. The officer on the other end of the line didn't sound thrilled that she knew about Ando. They must still be trying to keep it under wraps. Too bad for them. She rolled her chair down the table to a computer and banged out a fast story. As long as she didn't tie the shootings to the summit, it should be okay to report them. The trick would be to spin the story as a lurid love triangle gone wrong. She hit the print button and headed for her makeup table.

"Check the copy while I do my face, Carson."

Her boss was doing the two-phones-at-once thing again, but he had enough spare attention to shoot her a thumbs-up and move toward the printer.

Before she could second-guess herself, before she had time to think better of it, she found herself seated before a camera. Its red light went on. Her last thought before the teleprompter started to scroll was that Tom was going to kill her.

"This is Paige Ellis reporting from the Global Economic Summit with breaking news. Amid rumors of a massive feud between billionaires over a former high-fashion model's affections, it has been confirmed this morning that Takashi Ando has died. Police are investigating the suspicious nature of the Japanese billionaire's death. Meanwhile, American billionaire Tom Rowe has twice evaded gunmen's attempts to kill him in as many days. Ando was married to French model Mimi Anoux, and Rowe was romantically involved with her for several years prior to Mimi's marriage to Ando. Officials wonder if there is a link between Ando's death and Rowe's near-death. When asked to comment upon it, British billionaire Jeremy Smythe, a close associate of both Ando and Rowe, was not available. Sex, scandal, shootings—this story will be one we definitely continue to follow as it unfolds."

The red light went off and she pushed back from the desk.

There. Let's see what Tom makes of that.

Chapter 12

Within two minutes of her story hitting the airwaves, Paige's cell phone rang. She pulled it out—Aleesha Gautier's number. "Hi, Mamba. What's up?" Paige asked.

A male—and outraged—voice exploded in her ear. "What in the hell do you think you're doing?"

Not Mamba. Tom. He must have borrowed her teammate's cell phone to call Paige. Her jaw tightened. "If you have a comment about a story my network runs, you'll need to speak to my producer. Here. Let me pass you to him."

"I don't want to talk to—"

She lifted the phone away from her ear and handed it to Greer. "It's Rowe. He's not a happy camper."

Her boss shrugged. "He's never a happy camper if his name appears on the air."

She suspected Tom was a little beyond unhappy, but Carson would figure that out soon enough. "I've got someplace to go. I'll stop by in a while to pick up my cell phone. Enjoy chatting with Mr. Rowe."

Carson lifted the phone to his ear, and then jerked it away as Tom commenced expressing his opinion—loudly—of the breaking news piece World News had just run.

Paige grinned and ducked out before she could get roped back into the fracas. "Toodles," she called over her shoulder as she all but ran from the bureau.

She made for a house phone and called Casey Chandler, a former FBI agent and one of the Medusas who'd come on this mission. "Hey, Scorpion. It's Fire Ant."

Casey answered, "Ah, the prodigal child herself. You've got Rowe pretty riled up. His assistant called him a few minutes ago to tell him about your little story, and he's been yelling ever since."

"Yeah, well, he can get over it. Where are you guys right now?"

"Aleesha, Alex, Monica and Cho have just taken him to a meeting with the American delegation. The rest of us will be waiting in his suite, hoping you'll take time out from your busy broadcast schedule to give us an in-briefing."

"How long is Tom going to be tied up at that meeting?"

"Just a sec." Casey went off the line for a moment. "Gretchen says it's scheduled to run at least an hour. She suggests you not be here when he gets back."

Paige laughed under her breath. It might almost be worth sticking around to see him apoplectic. "I'm on my way up."

When she stepped into Tom's suite, her three remaining teammates, Casey, Roxi and Naraya, were arrayed around the room, poking behind furniture and curtains, obviously doing a security sweep of the space.

Paige commented without elaborating, "I did this room yesterday. And Rowe's bedroom and bathroom."

The women looked up, speculative looks on their faces as they obviously pondered how she'd gotten access to Rowe's bedroom, but no one asked.

"Paige. You're looking good," Roxi Gianello commented.

Paige grinned at the fashion stylist turned commando. "You're just not used to seeing me wear makeup other than green grease paint."

"Really. You don't clean up half-bad," Roxi commented then laughed.

Coming from someone who'd dressed the stars for years, she'd take that as a compliment. "I assume Mamba's heading up this dog-and-pony show?"

Aleesha Gautier was one of the senior members of the Medusa Project. She would be the logical choice to lead the rookie squad of six women special operators she'd brought with her to the island.

The other women gathered around Paige as she sat down on one of the matching sofas. "That's affirmative," Casey answered. "Mamba brought us all to get our feet wet in the field."

Paige grinned. "So, the gang's all here. How cool is that?" It felt good to be reunited with her teammates of the past two years. They'd been to hell and back together en route to becoming full-fledged Medusas.

Roxi leaned forward. "What's going on around here? You say some Japanese billionaire is dead and now someone's trying to kill Rowe?"

Paige nodded. "That's about it. An anonymous party has approached the three private citizen billionaires attending this conference, and who knows who else, and offered them a chance to bid on upwards of a hundred billion dollars' worth of assets for a few cents on the dollar. And now two of those buyers are dead or under fire, and a third potential buyer is hiding under heavy guard."

Naraya El Saad, the team's resident Ph.D. in mathematics and cryptography commented quietly, "It sounds like one of the possible buyers is trying to eliminate the competition."

Casey piped up. "Who has this deal been offered to?"

Paige sighed. "Tom doesn't know. Smythe speculated that several more people had been approached when I spoke to him yesterday."

"But neither man knows who the seller is," Casey guessed.

"That's correct," Paige answered.

Naraya leaned forward. "Can you get me all the particulars that Mr. Rowe does know about the assets being offered? Perhaps we can analyze the data and narrow down a list of possible sellers."

Paige turned to the brilliant woman. "And what good will that do us?"

"Well, the seller can't like having the bidders for his prize dying off. The less bidders, the less money he'll make. If we can figure out who he is, he might be willing to tell us everyone he made the offer to. Then, if nothing else, we'll have a list of targets around whom we can concentrate our attention."

As always, Naraya's logic was flawless.

Paige glanced over at Gretchen, who was sitting in the corner in front of a computer, ignoring Paige's existence. Loyal to her boss, apparently. "Hey, Gretchen. Any chance you can give us some information? It might help us catch the person or persons who are trying to kill Tom."

The woman thawed considerably at that. And, in a matter of minutes, Gretchen and Naraya were seated in front of the computer surfing the Internet to find entities whose holdings matched those offered in the sale.

Paige turned to her remaining colleagues. "What's the plan for guarding Tom?"

Casey answered, "We're alternating. Mamba, Alex, Monica and Cho with Roxi, Naraya and me. I'll be team lead on the second shift since I've got field experience with personal protection details. We'll run six-hour shifts. Off-duty team members take turns sleeping and doing perimeter checks.

Standard stuff. We'll run the op out of this room. This summit won't be too hard to cover. The conference security isn't great, but it does some of the work for us."

Paige let out the breath she'd been holding. "So I'm completely off the rotation?"

Casey's eyebrow arched. "Do you want into it?"

"No, no," Paige replied hastily. "I was just making sure."

Casey studied her closely. "What's going on between you and him?"

"Nothing. Nothing at all. We basically hate each other's guts. He's an arrogant, spoiled, billionaire bad boy, and I'm a television reporter. In his world, that puts me just shy of the Antichrist." And last night had been a complete anomaly. Nothing more than a temporary truce.

Casey laughed. "Got it. I knew I picked up on some tension between you two down at that press circus we walked into earlier."

Paige commented wryly, "That's putting it mildly."

The phone rang and Gretchen picked it up. She listened for a moment, then announced, "Miss Ellis, Mr. Rowe's meeting just adjourned. If you don't want to…encounter him…you might want to leave now."

Not. "Thanks, Gretchen." Paige stood to leave. "I'm going downstairs to retrieve my cell phone. In about five minutes, you'll be able to give me a call if you need anything."

"Will do," Casey replied cheerfully. "We've got things under control. You go do your reporter thing."

Paige grinned and made her exit. She really wasn't in any hurry to see Tom again. In fact, she could happily delay that moment for, oh, ten years or so. She stepped into the elevator, and it whisked her downward. In the moment of privacy, she let down her defenses enough for the hurt to seep into her awareness. He hadn't wasted a second dumping her. The very minute the Medusas showed up to take over guarding him, he'd run screaming from her. Well, figuratively, at least. He'd denied having anything personal to do with her with all the vehemence of a wrongly condemned man.

The elevator decelerated.

So be it.

She'd been an idiot to let herself fall for him. It was her mistake, not his. She'd go on with her life, lick her wounds in private, and do her damnedest not to dwell on what could have been between them. Although she had a sneaking suspicion this guy wasn't going to be that easy to get over. Oh, well. Too late now.

The elevator stopped, the door opened and she looked up.

Into the one face she really, really didn't want to see.

Tom.

Glaring at her.

He was surrounded by her teammates, and several American diplomats stood nearby. She greeted him evenly—she hoped. "Mr. Rowe."

Instead of speaking to her, he turned his head fractionally toward Monica. "I'll wait while you clear out the elevator and secure it from any riffraff."

Riffraff? Was that all she was to him now? Riffraff? Her gaze narrowed. She stepped forward, brushing past Aleesha on Tom's left. "Jerk," she said under her breath. She hoped he heard her.

Tom scowled at the elevator door as it slid closed between him and Paige. *What was wrong with her?* They'd spent such a fantastic night together. And he meant that above and beyond the best sex he'd had in years. And then this.

How could she have made that report? How could she have exposed the deal, knowing that it would endanger not only him, but also Smythe? It could drive both the seller and the would-be killer underground. The shooter could very well decide to bide his time and strike at a later date with less security than this conference and when the potential buyers were more vulnerable.

And breaking the story of Ando's death? How could she do that to Takashi's family? They had to be devastated, and she'd callously dragged their loss out into the public spotlight. He'd thought she was a better person than that, dammit. Sure, it would've hit the airways eventually, but why did it have to be *her* who did it?

He didn't know whether to be furious or deeply disappointed in her. As the elevator door slid shut on that familiar, feminine shape and confident stride moving away from him, he settled on disgusted.

"She give you any trouble before we got here?" Aleesha Gautier murmured from beside him.

Damned Medusas. Too perceptive for their own good, they were. "Not too much."

"She do anything to mess up the op?"

"Not until that news report she fired off an hour ago."

Thankfully the Medusa team leader was silent for the rest of the elevator ride and throughout the graceful dance that was moving a principal to a hotel room. But she didn't leave it alone when he was safely tucked into his suite.

"How did Paige's report mess up this op?" the Jamaican woman asked.

He was vividly aware of eight pairs of shrewd female eyes measuring him…for some reason, Gretchen had decided to join the Medusas in studying him like a bug under a microscope. Surly, he answered, "She brought a whole hell of a lot of attention down on me and Jeremy Smythe."

"Sometimes, having a bright light pointed at you makes you harder to kill," Aleesha commented reflectively.

He snorted. "I highly doubt Paige made that report in the interest of protecting my safety."

"Why did she do it, then?"

He stared at Aleesha. "You tell me. You're the damned Medusa."

That made the team leader stick a hip out, cross her arms and purse her lips. "You got a problem with female operators? Don't get me wrong. I don't care one way or the other. We've got a job to do and we're going to do it whether you like it or not. But it would be helpful to us to know if you're planning to be a hostile participant in this little exercise."

He frowned. "I don't have a problem with female operators. But I have a huge problem with female operators who are also big-mouthed television news journalists."

Smiles threatened on several lips around him. Casey Something-or-other—he remembered she was a former FBI agent—piped up. "Yeah, we had that problem with her at first, too. But I gotta tell ya, Mr. Rowe. She sweated and suffered and gutted her way through training just like the rest of us. And with all due respect, she's got a real fire in her belly. She wanted to be an operator more than just about anybody here. And we all wanted it pretty bad."

He spun and closed on the former federal agent. "Then why did she potentially blow it all this morning?"

It was Aleesha who answered him, her eyes clear and level. "I don't know. You tell me."

"Why are you asking me?" he snapped.

"You're the one who's been with her for the past several days."

"You're saying I drove her to screw up this mission?"

The woman didn't answer. She just studied him dispassionately.

Swearing under his breath, he headed for his bedroom to change clothes and get ready for lunch. Damned women! Always peeling back the onion, looking for layers of emotions and reasons. Couldn't they just leave it alone? He took satisfaction in slamming the bedroom door on the lot of them.

But he was only granted a few moments' reprieve before Gretchen knocked. "Sir, there's a possible change to your itinerary."

"What?" he grumbled from inside a new undershirt.

"Mimi Ando is going to give a press conference in ten minutes and she asked that you be there."

"What the hell for?"

"Moral support."

He yanked the bedroom door open to stare at Gretchen. "She said that?"

"Yes, sir."

"That's a load of bull. She's got something up her sleeve."

"Shall I tell her assistant you'll be there or not?"

He weighed the pros and cons of it. Being seen with her so soon after her husband's death could start rumors about the two of them. But, on the other hand, if he didn't show up, he might look callous and uncaring. If nothing else, it might be interesting to see what Mimi had cooking. She was a world-class schemer. He yanked on a shirt and buttoned it jerkily.

"Fine. I'll go. But I can't stay for long. I don't want to be late to lunch."

"You'll have ten minutes at the press conference before you need to meet the British Finance Minister."

Tom tied his tie and brushed a speck of lint off his suit. "All right. That should be long enough to convey my sympathy without making it look like I'm moving in on the bereaved widow."

He strode out into the living room. "You Amazon princesses ready to go?"

There were grins all around as his security team took their places. It felt weird to be in the middle of such a phalanx. He was used to being on the perimeter, gaze roving, brain always assessing possible threats.

As he'd expected, the press conference was a zoo. Knowing Mimi, a lot of the chaos was her doing. Aleesha and company maneuvered him along the wall to one side of the room, conveniently next to a large pillar that cast him in deep shadow but where Mimi could spot him from the podium—if she actually needed him for moral support. Frankly, he doubted that. More likely, she'd just wanted him here to see the show. She'd always loved having an audience. This was a perfect spot from which to watch the show.

Three minutes before the press conference was scheduled to begin, he started at the sudden jolt of awareness flooding through him. *She* had just walked into the room.

He looked up and spotted a pair of brilliant blue eyes framed by wavy strawberry hair. Her curvaceous figure was shown off to perfection in a closely tailored suit, and confidence oozed from every pore of her flawless skin. He swore at himself. Why couldn't he have that reaction to some other woman? Why the one woman who drove him completely crazy and frustrated the living hell out of him?

If Paige spotted his presence, she didn't deign to glance his way. As for him, he couldn't keep his eyes off her. He watched her every move as she jockeyed through the crowd with her cameraman in tow, angling for the best shot of the podium. She was very good. She used a combination of feminine charm and old-fashioned sharp elbows to get just the spot she wanted.

Mimi was late. Not that it was any surprise to him. It had always been a source of contention between them. He was military trained to believe that punctuality was next to godliness. And Mimi was a firm believer that the world could wait for her.

Finally, the French model made her way into the room, dressed in a stunning black suit and large hat that matched her long, black hair and framed her tragically pale face. He'd lay odds she'd had to put on makeup to achieve that wan shade of ivory. She wouldn't be caught dead without a St. Tropez tan year-round.

Mimi swayed dramatically, but then a man moved forward on the dais to support her elbow. Who was he? Tom leaned over to Aleesha and murmured, "Do you know the guy holding her arm?"

"No."

"Get an ID on him, will you?"

The Medusa team leader was savvy enough not to question his request but merely nodded and murmured to one of her team members. A camera came out of a pocket, several pictures were snapped, and the tall, elegant Medusa called Monica slipped out of the room.

Mimi's assistant read a short statement expressing Mrs. Ando's deep grief and suffering at the loss of her husband and asked the press to please respect her privacy in this period of mourning.

Tom snorted mentally. Right. And that was why the bereaved widow was standing at a press conference in front of a hundred avid reporters. Because she wanted privacy.

Mimi moved up to the podium and answered a few predictable questions. When did her husband die? What were the police saying to her about it? Did she know the circumstances of his death? Tom was glad to see that Mimi genuinely didn't seem to know a thing about how Takashi's body was found or in what condition.

She wasn't a bad actress, but she wasn't great, either. To someone like Tom, who knew her very well, her grief was transparent. Sure, she was sad the old man had kicked off, but she fairly glowed when someone asked her if she was familiar with the contents of Takashi Ando's will. Of course, Mimi denied knowing what would happen to all of her late husband's billions. But Tom wasn't fooled. She must stand to inherit a ton of money from Takashi-san.

The tall, blond Medusa slipped past him and back into place as the press conference droned on. She murmured to him and Aleesha, "Harold Pinter. He's an African tycoon. Owns, among other things, a bunch of precious materials mines in East Africa, a ton of real estate in Dubai, a bank in Singapore. All but owns Meringa."

Bingo. Meringa was a small nation born out of a regional civil war a few years back. Loaded with natural resources, but thin on government and rife with corruption.

Monica continued, "Naraya says he's also her number one guess as to who's selling the private empire."

And he and Mimi were cozying up together? Didn't *that* just open up a whole new world of possibilities?

Aleesha went rigid beside him. "The seller is sucking up to the widow of one of the buyers? Ladies, the plot has just thickened."

Tom was still pondering the implications of that little twist when the Medusas whisked him out of the press conference a few minutes later. The British Finance Minister had a suite down the hall from his, and it was an easy matter for the Medusas to deliver him there on time. But the security guard who answered the door balked at the bevy of women accompanying him.

Tom explained, "They're my bodyguards."

"Right, mate. And I'm the Easter Bunny. We've got plenty of real security. You don't need your playmates in here."

Aleesha stepped forward and said silkily, "You seem like a nice boy. So I'm not going to break your nose right away. I hear Tim Smith is on this detail. Is he about?"

The guard looked bemused, but nodded. "One moment."

Another man returned with the first one. He took one look at Aleesha and stepped forward to wrap her in a bear hug with an exclamation of welcome. "Mamba! Your husband didn't tell me you were coming out here! Next time I see Michael, I'm gonna have to break his arm."

The Medusa laughed. "Your man here seems to think we're not real bodyguards, Tim. He doesn't want to let us in."

Tim turned to the first guard. "Didn't you ever hear of the Medusas when you were in the SAS? They're the American government's all-girl Special Forces team."

The first guard gaped at Tom's escorts. "No kidding? You're them?"

"In the flesh," Aleesha answered pleasantly.

"Son of a—come in!"

Tom grinned. Good thing he was secure enough not to be offended by his bodyguards being bigger rock stars than he was. Aleesha and Monica stepped into the suite first, had a good look around, and then waved him in. Alex and the quiet Chinese woman, Cho, brought up the rear.

"Tom! Good to see you again!" The British Finance Minister was in his forties and still as brilliant as his early rise to such a position indicated.

They shook hands, and in a matter of minutes were engrossed deep in conversation about future global economic prospects. Like good bodyguards, the Medusas faded into the background, practically becoming part of the furniture.

But then, near the end of the meal, a disturbance broke out in the corner. Tim Smith exclaimed in surprise and pulled a cell phone away from his ear. The security man stepped forward. "Gentlemen, I'm sorry to interrupt, but I'm afraid I have news."

Tom looked up in alarm. Clearly it was bad.

"Jeremy Smythe is dead."

Chapter 13

Paige all but fell into her chair when Greer Carson broke the news to her. Smythe had been found in his suite about fifteen minutes ago and ambulances had been called to the scene. But rumor had it the aged billionaire was dead. Cause of death unknown.

Except she thought she might know the cause of death. Her. She'd killed the poor, sweet old man. She'd had to be stubborn and do that report, and it had gotten an innocent man killed.

She'd done it again.

First Jerry Sprague. And now Jeremy Smythe.

She'd gotten so caught up in her work, in proving a point to someone, that she'd failed to stop and consider the possible consequences of her actions. She'd thought that by becoming a Medusa she'd fixed that fatal flaw in herself. That tendency to leap before she looked. To hurt others in her selfishness and ambition. Or in this case, in her pique at Tom Rowe.

"You okay, Paige? We need to tape a segment ASAP. All the networks will be breaking this one in the next two minutes."

Tape. Right. Something inside her curled up in a little ball and shut down. Good thing Tom had dumped her before she got him hurt, too. Or worse.

Greer sat down at the computer and typed furiously. He called over his shoulder, "Get your face on while I throw together some copy. We'll go on as soon as you're ready."

She'd never be ready to tell this story. To put on a straight face and pretend she didn't know exactly how Jeremy Smythe had died. How in the hell was she going to look into the camera and not completely lose it?

"Paige!" Greer barked. "Let's go! We've got a story to break."

She was afraid this one might break her.

But it didn't. Somehow she got through reading the report. Woodenly, perhaps. And maybe with a strange undertone of shock. But viewers would probably put it down to the fact that she'd just met with the dead man a few days ago—a fact that Greer had seen fit to include in the story.

She dug deep and set everything aside but the words scrolling across the screen in front of her. She didn't try to comprehend their meaning. She just read them aloud. At least her Medusa training had turned out to be good for something in the journalism business. She made it through the report and sagged in relief when the red light over the camera blinked off.

"I've got to go, Carson."

She didn't wait for his permission. She just burst up from of her chair and rushed out of the bureau. Out of the hotel. Out of her mind.

Tom paced his suite restlessly, waiting for news to come in regarding how Smythe had died. He'd been waiting all afternoon. The place was crowded. Aleesha had all the Medusas on duty and on high alert around him at the moment. Personally, he figured the killer would take the rest of the day off after killing Smythe and come after him tomorrow. But he wasn't in charge of the security detail and it wasn't his call.

Aleesha had been on the phone continuously to H.O.T. Watch, which was apparently the Medusas' operational headquarters, since the news of Smythe's death had come in. But, the intelligence gathering unit had no information for them yet. He watched the senior Medusa hang up her phone yet again and send him a negative shake of the head. She dialed another number and he turned away.

For the next half hour, it was more of the same. Call to H.O.T. Watch. Nothing. Call to some other number that didn't seem to be answering. Nothing. Frustrated look on Aleesha's face. Lather, rinse and repeat.

Finally, as he stood well back from the big windows staring out at the deep, unfathomable blue of the ocean, Aleesha's reflection in the glass approached him from behind. Without turning, he murmured, "What can I do for you, Mamba?"

"Tell me what on God's little green earth is going on between thee and me girlie." The Jamaican accent was thick, which he'd already deduced meant she was either joking or defusing stress. He'd bet it was the latter at the moment.

He glanced over at her as she parked beside him, staring out at the ocean. "Why do you ask?"

"Because I've known Paige Ellis for two years, and not once have I ever known her to do something irresponsible."

"And?"

"And she has disappeared. She's not at the news bureau, she's not in the building according to hotel security, and she's not answering her phone."

That made him turn his head fully to stare at the woman beside him. No special operator would dream of ignoring the phone. Ever. Soldiers like them served at the pleasure of the United States government, and their lives were not their own to pick and choose when they went to work. Theirs was a 24/7/365 profession.

"She's not answering her phone?" he echoed.

"Nope. And me'tinks you be de reason, boyo."

"Me? Why?"

The Jamaican accent abruptly disappeared. Aleesha answered him dead seriously. "I don't know. You tell me."

He sighed. He'd forgotten about this part of being a special operator—the complete and utter lack of privacy. Every aspect of your life, even the most embarrassing and intimate bits of it, were on display for all your teammates to see.

Reluctantly, he replied, murmuring low enough so the other women couldn't hear, "Paige and I, we have a bit of thing between us. I'm not sure exactly what it is, but it's something. Or at least it was. I don't know where in the hell her head is at now. After that report she made about me, your guess is as good as mine."

Aleesha stared out at the ocean for a long time, clearly thinking hard. Finally she said quietly, "Paige got hurt bad last time around with a guy. She's steered clear of men for a couple of years, now. I'm thinking maybe she fell hard for a smart, pretty boy like you. I'm guessing you charmed her socks off and she fell like a ton of bricks."

"I didn't set out to charm her," he protested. "I was a royal jerk to her when we officially met, in fact. She was trying to do an interview with me and I wouldn't cooperate."

"Were there sparks?" Aleesha asked.

He thought back. Hell, yes, there had been sparks. He couldn't tear his gaze off those eyes of hers, and when he did, his gaze landed on her legs and wouldn't budge. They might have argued, but there'd been real passion in it. He grumbled. "Affirmative on the sparks."

Aleesha nodded wisely. "And she fell for you. Fast forward to now. You've pushed the relationship quite a bit further than sparks if I read you right, yes?"

He winced. "Yeah."

"Okay. And was there a lover's spat?"

He wanted to blurt out that they weren't lovers. That it had been a onetime thing. A night of passion fueled by adrenaline and fear and the need to be with someone else. But not lovers. Except…the morning after, when they'd eaten breakfast and talked and laughed together…that hadn't been a "thanks for the hot sex, have a nice life" kind of conversation. For better or worse, they *were* lovers. And then she went and stabbed him in the back. "We didn't have a fight," he mumbled.

Aleesha continued her line of reasoning. "But you did something to upset her or she wouldn't have made that report she knew would make you mad. I know Paige, and she's not vindictive for the random hell of it. You did or said something to piss her off. So, what was it?"

"Do we really have to get into this?"

"I've got a missing operator. A rookie who's potentially in way over her head. I've got compromised security at a global summit, and I've got billionaires dropping like flies. Yes, we have to get into this."

He sighed. Aleesha was right. Dammit. "I have no idea what I said or did to make her mad."

"Men. You never think about how we'll react to the things you say. You just blurt out the first words that pop into your heads. You need filters on your mouths." She shook her head, and then added, "And sensitivity transplants."

"I don't walk around trying to be a jerk—" he started.

Aleesha glared at him from under lowered eyebrows. "Single, handsome, rich boy like you? Surrounded by beautiful women fishing for a ring? Sure, you walk around being a jerk all the time. Either you're getting rid of the groupies, or you're taking advantage of them. Either way, you're being a jerk."

He pressed his lips shut. How was a person supposed to argue against logic like that? It was the "have you stopped beating your wife yet" question.

Thankfully, Aleesha moved on in her reasoning. "Was there a moment or several minutes in which Paige's behavior changed toward you? Markedly? Like a one-hundred-eighty-degree change of attitude?"

He frowned. "She was cheerful at breakfast. Then she stuffed me in that ridiculous little car of hers and drove me over here. We laughed and joked for most of the ride. Then we walked into the hotel lobby and the press assaulted us. Then she left and made that damned report."

"What did you say to her during the press conference?" Aleesha prodded.

"Nothing. I only spoke to the reporters. Hell, I tried to fend them off of her. They were starting after her for biased journalism if she was dating me. I did my level best to protect her reputation!"

Aleesha frowned. "Are you referring to that bit where you denied having a relationship with her and that it was merely an accident that you ended up together last night?"

"Yes!"

"Ah." A long pregnant pause. "Yep, you men definitely need relationship-skills transplants."

He shoved a frustrated hand through his hair. "Care to explain?"

"Think about it from her perspective. You're crazy about this guy, you're spending romantic time together, there's a big vibe going between you. And then he stands up in front of God and the international press corps and declares that he's having nothing at all to do with you."

"But you Medusas had arrived! She didn't have to pretend to be my girlfriend anymore, and doing so was going to wreck her reputation. It was only logical that I deny our being involved. I wouldn't want to blow her cover. Nor do I want her reporter buddies invading our private relationship."

"And did you explain all that to her before you announced that you two had nothing going on between you?"

"There wasn't time! I had a dozen microphones shoved under my nose!"

Aleesha laughed. "And you can't figure out why she broke that story? How'd you get so rich being so stupid?"

He scowled. Stared out at the ocean. Was it really that simple? Had he hurt Paige's feelings? She always seemed so tough, so sure of herself. Had she really let him get that far under her skin? Whoa. What did it mean?

He sighed heavily. "I think maybe I know where she went."

Paige made the turn for home, panting hard as she lengthened her stride even more. This run on the beach had been just what the doctor ordered. Her head felt clearer than it had since that gruesome bag washed up on the beach several days ago and Tom Rowe had barged into her life.

She had to face it. They were over. Not that they'd ever had a chance to begin with. She would put him behind her, lick her wounds and move on eventually. And in the meantime, she had her day job and her work with the Medusas to keep her busy. And speaking of which, she had an idea. It was a hunch, really. Nothing concrete, just a niggling suspicion that wouldn't go away. She wanted to check it out before she said anything to anyone else about it, though.

Instead of stopping at her cottage, she ran right past it and headed for the conference hotel. Her press credentials and the tools she would need were in her fanny pack, and she had fresh clothes at the hotel. She'd shower there and then check out her theory.

Greer Carson was out of the news bureau when she got there. Too bad. She ought to catch up with her cell phone sooner or later. Truth be told, she felt more than a little naked without it. She'd been so rattled when she heard about Smythe's death she'd forgotten to ask Greer for her phone back. And goodness knew, Carson had had too much going on just then to think of it. She stepped into the private bath attached to the bureau and took a quick shower. A half hour later she'd dried her hair, changed into a pair of dress slacks and a tailored shirt and finished tossing on a little makeup. Time to go test her theory.

The first order of business was to find out where Mimi Ando was right now. Thankfully, Paige had chatted up the concierge the first few days she was here, and he was more than happy to tell her that she could find her good friend Mimi in the hotel's spa. A quick call to the spa revealed that Mimi would be there wrapped in towels and mud for the next hour. Perfect.

Time to take an extracurricular look around the grieving widow's digs.

It was a shockingly easy matter to stroll unseen right up to Mimi's door, insert an electronic lock pick into the card reader and let herself into the suite.

The concierge had mentioned that Mrs. Ando's assistant had a separate room attached to Mimi's. Listening hard, Paige thought she heard the guy moving around in his room. In deference to him, she glided around the suite quietly, in search of anything that would confirm or allay her suspicions.

Mimi's things were scattered haphazardly around the suite, although someone had clearly straightened them and imposed a modicum of order on what Paige suspected would otherwise have been a chaotic mess of clothing and possessions flung around the place. She eased open the bedroom door and slipped into the dim space. It was messier in here, smelling thickly of some sort of floral perfume. Jasmine, maybe.

She poked around tabletops and dresser drawers, opened purses and looked inside the luggage stored in the closet. Nothing. But Paige's gut said there had to be something. She just wasn't looking in the right place. She moved into the bathroom.

And there she spotted the mother lode: Mimi's cell phone lying on the bathroom counter. Paige picked it up quickly and hit the button to retrieve all of the woman's recent phone calls. Whipping out a notebook and pen, Paige quickly scribbled down all the phone numbers stored for the last several weeks. She checked Mimi's voice mail for any saved messages, but that was a bust. That really would've been too much to hope for, she supposed. Still, the list of phone numbers was a major coup.

She laid the phone back down exactly where she'd found it and turned to leave, but noise in the outer room made her stop cold. Voices. Two of them—one male and one female. Damn! She leaped over to the light switch and slapped it off. Then she raced over to the shower and slid inside, eased the door shut behind her, crouched in the back corner and thanked God that the shower had wavy glass that obscured her from sight.

Someone came into the bedroom, and the voices resolved themselves into two people speaking agitated French. Apparently, Mimi was upset about something that had happened at the spa. Paige's French didn't include extensive beauty terminology, and she didn't follow the details of the conversation.

The bathroom door opened and the lights flashed on. Yelling stridently now to the man outside, Mimi went to the restroom while Paige held her breath and pressed even lower against the cold marble at her back. The toilet flushed, the sink ran and the lights went out. The room plunged into darkness once more.

Paige let out a relieved breath. Now to get out of here and run down that list of phone numbers! Her watch said it was nearly five o'clock. If she was lucky, Mimi had some sort of late tea or early dinner engagement and would leave the suite shortly.

No such luck. One hour dragged into two before Paige heard the outer door close and the suite finally went quiet. She gave it a few minutes to make sure no one was in the main room, and then she crept cautiously out of the shower.

The bedroom was nearly dark now as the sun set outside. She had one last job to do before she left. She unscrewed the metal air vent cover high in the corner and planted a tiny transceiver inside the duct, wiring it to the metal to boost the device's tiny antenna. After checking that it was activated, she replaced the vent cover and eased over to the living room door. She pressed her ear to the wood panel. Silence. Cracking open the door slowly, she took a peek into the main room. Only a single small lamp illuminated the space and it was empty. She breathed a sigh of relief.

When she was sure the hallway was deserted, she slipped out of the suite. *Clear.* She'd made it. Her first successful breaking and entering. Well, her second if she wanted to count sneaking into Tom's suite. Except he'd caught her that time. She pushed the image of him out of her mind. Work. Her life was about work. No more men. At least not for a good long time.

She made her way to the news bureau and was relieved to find it deserted. World News had a secure Internet connection that she used to send H.O.T Watch the list of phone numbers with an urgent request to track all of them down. Knowing the intel specialists there and the scope of their computer resources, she imagined it wouldn't be more than a few hours until they'd nailed down the owner of every number.

Until then, she had some free time on her hands.

Thoughts of Tom crept into her awareness along with pain. Loss. Sorrow. Maybe it was for the best she discovered now instead of later that she'd been nothing more than a casual fling for him. But that didn't make the knowledge suck any less.

The last few nights of thin sleep were starting to catch up with her, and her eyelids drooped. Time to settle in for a bit of surveillance. She went to the front desk and asked for a room in the hotel. The assistant manager told her they were full, but if she was willing to take something without a working shower, he could at least give her a bed for the night. She took it.

Mimi would be out for a couple of hours at dinner, so Paige set her wrist alarm and lay down for a much needed power nap. Just in case, though, she put the speaker that went along with her planted bug right next to her ear and turned up the volume all the way.

Some time later, the blaring of Mimi's voice practically inside her head brought Paige bolt upright out of a dead sleep. It took her a disoriented moment to figure out that the harridan wasn't in Paige's room, but was actually transmitting over a radio.

Right. The bug.

"…don't care about your excuses. I need you to finish the job!" A pause, and then she seemed to cut off someone. "Stop. I don't care why. Just finish it. Now." Another pause. "I don't care what it costs!" Mimi's voice was rising shrilly. "Hire three men. Six. Ten! Just get rid of him *now!* Do you understand me?"

Paige grabbed for the volume control. Nothing like having Mimi Ando screaming in your ear to wake up a soul. Or wake a soul from the dead, as it were. Sheesh. She hit the replay button on the digital recorder built into the speaker setup and listened to Mimi once more. For all the world, it sounded like the woman was talking to a hit man and berating him for failing to kill his target.

Could her suspicions really be true? Was Mimi Ando the would-be killer?

Chapter 14

Paige frowned, thinking hard. Were the killings linked after all to the mysterious business deal the billionaire targets had been approached with, or was it something else entirely?

She could see why Mimi Ando might want to kill Tom Rowe. He definitely had that effect on a girl. But why the others? Why Jeremy Smythe, and why Mimi's own husband?

One thing was for certain. If Paige was interpreting what she'd heard correctly, the threat level to Tom was about to go sky-high. Instead of a single would-be killer, an entire team of them was about to go after him.

Think, Paige. Do the analysis the way you were taught. Okay. Mimi had just told someone to finish the job immediately and to hire as many people as needed to get it done. Where was someone on this isolated and super secure little island going to scrape up several assassins on short notice? And how would the hit squad lay their hands on weapons? At the moment, security on Beau Mer was ridiculous. The only way she'd gotten a sidearm onto the island was by someone at a much higher pay grade than hers—like White House level—okaying use of the American diplomatic pouch to smuggle one to her. The only people on the island with guns were conference security personnel and the police....

Her train of thought froze in its tracks.

Surely not. The police?

Why not? The conference security team had been compromised, and as soon as the local police got involved in Takashi Ando's death, all sorts of rumors had started, which could only mean the police had a leak. A corrupt leak. Someone willing to trade information for cash, most likely. In her experience as a journalist, she'd found that where there was petty corruption, there was almost always major corruption.

Okay. So, assuming Mimi's hit man would recruit help from within the island's police force, that was going to be a pain in the rear for the Medusas to deal with. How were they supposed to tell apart the legitimate police who would protect Tom and the corrupt ones who would hide behind their uniforms while trying to kill him?

He had to leave the island. Leave the summit. Now. Before this new threat got organized and came after him.

She reached for the telephone beside the bed out of reflex, but then stopped. If some of the local police were corrupt, some of the hotel staff were likely corrupt, too. And they might very well be engaging in dodgy activities like phone tapping. She had to assume the phone lines on the island were not secure. Which meant she needed her cell phone back if she was to contact the Medusas and warn them of the looming threat.

She made a quick call down to the World News bureau and hung up frustrated. Where in the hell was Greer Carson? The other guys in the news bureau had no idea where he'd gone. Out for dinner somewhere on the island. Not helpful. She didn't even know if he'd gone to a public place like a restaurant or whether he'd gone to a private dinner.

No help for it. She'd have to warn the Medusas in person... and see Tom again.

Cursing under her breath, she headed for the elevators and rode up to the top floor. She paused for a moment in front of Tom's door, steeling her nerve. She could do this. Just go in, state her business and get out. Do her job, and nothing more. Heck, if she was lucky, he'd be in the bedroom and she wouldn't have to see him at all before she delivered her warning and left.

She knocked upon the panel.

Gretchen opened the door. Paige frowned. That was weird. She'd have expected one of the Medusas on duty to have answered.

"Hi, Gretchen. I need to speak to my colleagues. May I come in?"

"You may come in, but they're not here."

Paige stepped inside quickly and closed the door behind her, alarm bells clanging wildly in her gut. She asked urgently, "Where are they?"

"I don't know. Out somewhere trying to find you, I gather. Miss Aleesha tried to call you for hours, then Mr. Rowe said he knew where you were, and they all left."

"How many of the others were with him?"

"All of them, Miss Ellis."

Not good. Her teammates should be well into an established rotation of rest and bodyguard duty already. But if Mamba had the whole team around Tom, she obviously believed something was very wrong.

Paige asked Tom's assistant, "Did they give you any indication where they might be going? Any hint? Did they say anything?"

"I'm sorry, ma'am. They just picked up their backpacks and charged out of here."

That was good news at least. It meant her teammates had ample weapons and ammunition with them, in addition to a wide array of nifty tools of the trade. It also meant they must have left the hotel. Which meant—

Her cottage.

"Thanks, Gretchen. You've been a great help. If any of them happen to contact you in the next few minutes, tell them I'm where Tom and I took cover last night."

"Where you…"

Paige raced out of the suite before Gretchen could finish her sentence and headed for her car. Aleesha was worried about something, and Paige trusted her colleague's instincts completely. Heck, her own instincts were shouting that trouble was coming. Soon. Very soon.

Tom searched the cottage himself, even after the Medusas had finished sweeping the place. He'd been so sure she'd be here! Where was she, dammit? Worry pecked at the back of his eyeballs, too insistent to ignore. It was shocking to realize that no matter how mad he was at her stunt with the news report, he still cared about her. How could that be? She was a reporter for God's sake. A mouthy, pushy female who in no way needed him. Although maybe, at the end of the day, that was the draw of her. She was more his equal than just about any woman he'd met in a very long time.

"Believe me now, boyo?" Aleesha asked as he emerged from Paige's bedroom.

He shrugged. "Yeah, I guess so. But she was here not too long ago."

Aleesha's eyebrows sailed up. "How do you figure that?"

"Her bathroom smells like her. The scent would have faded if the last time she was in there was early this morning."

One of the other women piped up, "And you know she was in there early this morning how?"

Aleesha intervened smoothly. "That's a good point. Would you recognize if any of her clothes were missing?"

"Not hardly. About all I can tell you about her wardrobe is she wears far too many mannish, ugly slacks and shirts."

Several of the Medusas looked back and forth between him and Aleesha, comprehension dawning on their faces. Nope, not slow on the uptake these snake ladies. They'd all figured out how he had personal knowledge of Paige's morning activities.

"Are her running shoes here?" he asked.

Aleesha gestured to one of the women to check it out.

In a moment the tall blond one came back. "No running shoes," she announced.

"Which direction would she run from here?" Aleesha asked.

He shrugged. "Either way from here, there are a couple of miles of hard-packed sand. It's a little more isolated to the north, and that direction would be my guess. She strikes me as the type to prefer solitude for her runs."

Aleesha looked at the others. "Would you agree with that?"

Nods all around from Paige's teammates.

"Go have a look down the beach, Casey."

The woman nodded briskly at Aleesha's order and left via the kitchen door. Tom resisted an urge to pace and instead sat down on the sofa and commenced trying to relax the tension across the back of his neck and shoulders. The exercise was a complete failure.

Casey couldn't have been outside more than three minutes before Tom jumped at the shadow suddenly standing in the living room doorway. The former FBI agent murmured, "No sign of Paige. But we have a bigger problem. Someone's hiding in the jungle on the south side of the cottage."

Everyone's gazes snapped to the windows, but nobody made any other sudden move. Good self-discipline these women had. Dusk was falling outside, which meant they'd be brightly lit in here to anyone looking in. Fish in a barrel.

"Casey, slide into the kitchen and turn out the light. Alex, give it a few minutes after that and then turn out the lamp beside you. Cho, a few seconds after that, kill the bedroom lights. It's too early for anyone to believe the occupant of this place is going to bed for the night, but let's not make it blindingly obvious that we've spotted whoever's out there by slamming off all the lights at once, eh?"

Logical. Without Aleesha having to tell him, Tom slid off the sofa to sit on the floor in front of it. Any sniper who wanted to see him now would have to climb a tree right next to the house and look down into the room. And even then it would be a tricky shot.

The cottage gradually went dark around him.

Aleesha gave quiet instructions deploying the Medusas to cover each of the doors and windows, and shadows glided past him, ghostlike, as the women moved into position.

"What can I do?" he asked in a low voice.

"Lie down and take a nap," Aleesha replied, distracted.

"I'm serious," he insisted. "There has to be something I can do to help."

Her featureless face turned his way. "There is. Stay out of our way and do what we tell you to without questions."

"Thanks, but I know the drill," he muttered.

"Yeah, but not from the protectee's end of things, you don't," Aleesha retorted. "Don't you go all commando on me and try to be a hero, got it? You're the important guy we're here to keep alive. You keep your head down and don't pull any cute stunts."

He huffed, not at all pleased with this state of affairs. But what choice did he have? Aleesha was right. He was little better than a sack of potatoes to them. An object. Something to be kept safe from all harm. Nevermind he happened to be a living, breathing sack of potatoes.

"I've got movement," Casey murmured from the front window. "I count at least three targets, arrayed at fifty-foot intervals. They're either cops or killers working as a team."

Great. Just what he needed. A whole *team* of assassins come to get him.

"My experience with the local police hasn't been stellar," he murmured. "My money's on those guys out there being hostiles."

"Duly noted," Aleesha replied. "But let the record show we'll be treating everyone and everything that moves out there as hostile until proven otherwise."

"Ooh-rah," one of the women murmured from the bedroom.

Aleesha added wryly, "No shooting until I green-light you, Monica."

That was the tall blonde. Bloodthirsty type, was she? Who'd have guessed? Beautiful and lethal—these Medusas were something else.

And then Cho murmured from the window beside the front door, "I've got one guy well back in the trees, and he's pointing a weapon at the house."

Well, then. That answered the question of friendlies or hostiles.

"Look sharp, ladies," Aleesha bit out. "I want the best head count you can give me."

Cho added grimly, "Another guy just moved. He's carrying a high-powered rifle. Telescopic sight. Doesn't look infrared."

That was good news, at least. It meant the sniper probably couldn't see—and shoot—their heat images right through the cottage's walls.

"Don't assume everyone's identically armed," Aleesha warned.

He winced. Great. Maybe someone else could see through the walls and pick him off like a bug on the sidewalk. Aleesha scooted over to sit close beside him. "Nothing personal," she murmured. "Just want to confuse the signatures if they're peeking through the walls."

He nodded grimly. "I sure as hell hope Paige doesn't decide to come home right now."

Paige glanced at her front door, then looked back at the sniper fixated on the closed portal. At least all the lights were out. If she was lucky, Tom and the Medusas had come and gone already in their hunt for her. But her gut said she hadn't been that fortunate. The sniper was on full alert, his attention riveted on the house. He certainly was convinced someone was in there. And she was inclined to believe him.

At a snail's pace, she crawled on her belly to her left toward the south side of the cottage. The underbrush came closest to the building on that side and offered the best close-in cover for anyone wanting to approach the place unseen.

Moving this slow was a trial to her taut nerves, but she corralled them as she'd been taught and eased through the shadows at one with the night. As her eyes continued to adjust to the darkness, she made out more details around her...and spotted another shooter. And another. And then she saw something that made her blood run cold. A fourth shooter wearing a police uniform. Her heart dropped to her feet. She'd been right. And if the Medusas called for any local help, they'd be completely unable to tell the good cops from the bad cops.

Mimi's hit man had successfully augmented his hit squad and isolated the Medusas.

Which meant Tom and the Medusas were out of options and trapped squarely in the center of the kill zone.

Chapter 15

Paige hunkered down, staring fixedly at the cottage. *Are you in there, Tom?* And what about her teammates? Were they inside, too, counting their ammo and trying frantically to figure out how to escape this death trap?

If only she had her cell phone! A quick conversation with the Medusas and they'd all be on the same page, working toward the same goal. Although, supposedly, by training together so intensively, she should be able to accurately anticipate what her colleagues would do in a situation exactly like this.

No doubt about it. If she were guarding Tom, she'd have him inside that cabin. It was a defensible position, away from busy public places, and would allow her to concentrate her forces around the protectee.

Okay. So she'd work on the assumption that Tom and company were in there. What next? She'd have him planted on the floor well away from any windows. And as for her teammates?

She'd have them stationed at every window hiding from sight but keeping close watch out for any movement out here.

She'd be trying to get an accurate head count of how many hostiles there were and how heavily armed they were. Then, she'd prepare a reconnaissance sortie and send out one or two of the Medusas to test the enemy perimeter and find a route to safety.

She might be able to help with some of that. She had freedom of movement out here, and as far as she could tell, she was behind the hostiles. So far, she'd spotted four. Time to finish her painfully slow circuit of the cottage and get a final head count. Maybe she could even spot a half-decent escape route out of there.

Of course, then she'd have to find a way to communicate with her teammates. But she'd cross that bridge when she came to it.

Thankfully, the underbrush was thick, and even more thankfully, she'd spent the past two years crawling around lush tropical jungles on Timbalo Island, where the Medusas made their training headquarters. She settled quickly into the rhythm of it, slithering along under ferns and vines, rolling over logs, moving and pausing arhythmically so as not to sound like a living creature walking through the woods. It was almost strange how familiar and comfortable this activity was.

Paige spotted four more hostiles for a total of eight. A hit squad that size should be kid stuff for the seven full-time Medusas plus her—and Tom if it came right down to it. He might not have held a weapon in a few years, but she had faith it would come back to him fast, especially if someone was shooting at him with intent to kill.

She'd made her way around to the rock-strewn shoreline and had just determined to her satisfaction that no one was hiding in the sea-tossed boulders when the back of her neck suddenly prickled.

It was sacred Medusa mantra never to ignore a sensation like that. She sank down slowly into the sketchy cover of the rocks, her every sense on high alert. Whatever had triggered her internal alarms was still some way away, south of here.

She eased to her right to see if she could spot what—or who—was out there. The feeling was definitely getting stronger, but she was surprised at how much ground she covered without encountering any hostiles. Were her senses really that finely tuned? Vanessa had said Paige's proximity awareness was as good as any she'd ever seen, but Paige had never believed her. Until now, that was.

About two hundred yards south of the cottage, beyond a heavy stand of jungle, Paige started hearing the distinctive crackle of radio static. What was up with that?

If possible, she went into even higher stealth mode as she crept closer. The sound of quiet voices broke the night's silence. She began to make out more details in the murmur of noise. Several male voices. Terse. Giving orders. More voices muttering in acknowledgment.

She pushed aside the broad fan of a palmetto and froze, staring. A small clearing opened up before her. A half-dozen police cars filled most of it, and milling police officers took up the rest of the space. She counted fast. Twelve cops. And as she'd feared: wearing exactly the same uniforms as the ones lurking around the cottage behind her. How were she and the Medusas supposed to have the faintest idea who was on their side and who was out to kill Tom?

The only choice was to pull Tom out of there right now...before this force closed in on him and the chaos was complete.

She turned and headed for the cottage as quickly as she could without giving herself away. It was an exercise in sheer frustration. With each careful step, her impulse was to break into a full sprint and run screaming to warn him.

She had plenty of time to reflect on the fact that the killers themselves had probably called the police to bring them out here. What better cover could the hit team have than a whole bunch of police wearing the same uniforms as them? She corrected herself. The *would-be* killers. No way was she letting them succeed. Not on her watch.

As she approached the cabin, she turned her thoughts to her next problem. To signal the Medusas, she'd need a spot where she'd be visible to the occupants of the cottage but sheltered from any other prying eyes. Quickly, she reviewed in her mind the layout of the surrounding terrain. Not far beyond the cottage's front door, a pair of tall palm trees towered side by side. They wouldn't be in the direct line of sight of any of the snipers. The trees would serve her purpose nicely.

She eased around the side of the house and made her way between the giant tree trunks into a swath of thick shadow. Her skin crawling at the unnaturalness of it, she rose by inches until she was standing up, fully exposed between the two trees, visible to the house, but blocked on each side by the looming tree trunks.

Down by her hip, she eased her fingers into a signal indicating eight hostile shooters close by. After a few seconds, she transitioned to the signal for incoming hostiles. Then she flashed the signal for twelve shooters and the direction they were coming from.

She'd just have to assume someone inside had seen it. That vaunted Medusa unity of thought would come through. It had to. If not, Tom, and potentially all of her teammates, were toast. They had to get out of the cottage, and soon.

And she knew just the thing to help make that happen.

"What the…" Casey exclaimed under her breath.

"What is it?" Tom and Aleesha responded simultaneously. He looked over at the Medusa team leader and shrugged. Great minds.

"I've got someone standing up and deliberately showing themselves out here!"

Tom lurched toward the window, but Aleesha put a restraining hand on his arm. He shook it off impatiently.

Then she murmured, "It could be a trap to lure you into showing yourself. You stay right here."

He cursed under his breath. He was really getting sick of this business of not putting himself in harm's way. He wasn't some sissy in need of coddling. He could handle himself, dammit! But at this rate, he wasn't ever going to get the chance to do that. He'd been relegated to the status of useless rich guy. And he was hating every last second of it.

"It's Paige," Cho announced from her perch by the window on the other side of the front door. "She's signaling. She confirms eight armed hostiles in the woods."

Tom closed his eyes tightly as his stomach dropped to the floor. Paige was out there crawling around in the woods with a bunch of assassins? Taking head counts of them, no less? She was going to get herself killed! His pulse spiked until his temples pounded with pain. His urge to lunge through the front door, grab her and throw her to the ground out of the line of fire was all but impossible to curb.

Then Cho swore. The whole team went still at that. Apparently, she wasn't usually one for big outbursts.

Casey clarified grimly, "Paige just signaled that there are twelve more hostiles incoming from the south, estimated time of arrival, five to seven minutes."

Jeez. No wonder Cho had sworn. Eight guys they could handle, no sweat. But twenty? Unless the twenty were armed with no more than BB guns, this was about to get ugly real damned soon.

"We've got to get the principal out of here," Aleesha announced.

"The principal's standing right here," he snapped. "You don't have to talk about me like I'm completely witless."

Aleesha's smile flashed in the shadows by the front door. "So noted."

Casey spoke up, "Most of the shooters and that incoming force are clustered on the south side of the property. It stands to reason that we'd break north and flee that way."

"You'll run into a rock outcropping about a hundred yards due north of here that will be nigh unto impassable," Tom interjected. "It's climbable with technical equipment, but I wouldn't want to try free-climbing it. We'd have to swim around it. With that many shooters out there, we'd be dead meat in the water without scuba gear. And I don't see any of that lying around here." He thought for a moment. "What about barging out the front door and heading east to the main road? We'd be running across the majority of the shooters' fields of fire, which will drop their accuracy by a bunch, and the road's not too far away in that direction."

"We don't have a car positioned up there," Monica pointed out.

He nodded. "True. But where's Paige's car? She didn't drive up to the front door, and no way did she walk here from the hotel."

Aleesha frowned. "You said she's got a MINI Cooper, right? It will only fit about four of us, particularly if we're having to shoot from inside it. But we could do a jogging phalanx à la Secret Service. We can stuff you inside with a driver and someone else to lie on top of you, and the rest of us can run alongside and form a human wall."

He frowned. "You'd be completely exposed. Somebody would get shot for sure."

Aleesha's retort was desert dry. "That's what bodyguards do, bro."

Yeah, but it didn't mean he had to like it.

"Paige is signaling again. She says to come to her position on her command," Casey piped up.

Ha. He'd been right. She was standing due east of the house. But then the rest of it sank in. She wanted them to join her out there? For what purpose? Tom frowned. "What is she up to?"

Aleesha frowned back. "No idea. Any guesses, anybody?"

Monica spoke up. "She knows we're in here or she wouldn't be showing herself like that and signaling to us. And, she knows we're about to be trapped and outgunned. She's telling us to get the hell out of Dodge. I'll bet she has something in mind to help us make a break for it."

"But what?" Tom replied tensely.

"Only one way to find out," Monica replied. "We run out the door when she says to and see what happens."

Tom accused, "I know her. She's planning to do something stupid. Are you going to just let her? She'll get herself killed!"

"She's Medusa trained," Aleesha replied soothingly. "She won't do anything stupid. Risky maybe. Heroic maybe. But not stupid."

"We Medusas don't die easily. She'll be okay," Casey added.

He frowned, deeply disturbed. Big words, but he highly doubted their truth. Paige darn well would do something suicidal, particularly if she felt responsible for him being in danger. It was one of her most lovable—and exasperating—traits.

Paige didn't stop to think about the insanity of what she was about to do. It was the only logical choice, really. Okay, so she stood a statistically high chance of being shot or killed. But that's what being a Medusa was about. And it was going to take something spectacular to turn the tide building rapidly against them.

It was anybody's guess what the shooters had told their police comrades. Probably something along the lines of armed and dangerous criminals being holed up in a cottage and prepared to go down shooting.

Vanessa Blake said it over and over: find a way to turn your greatest weakness into your greatest strength. The Medusas' greatest weakness right now was their inability to distinguish legitimate police from hired assassins wearing police uniforms.

But that could also work against the police themselves. If they commenced shooting at hostile targets in the woods, only to realize they were shooting at their fellow policemen, she suspected all of the police would freeze up and have no idea what to do.

She'd lay odds their radios would be jammed with men requesting instructions and clarifications, cease fire orders being frantically relayed, and if she was lucky, even more frantic reports of policemen down. And from her own experience working with a close-knit team of individuals who routinely put themselves in harm's way, that call of *men down* would reflexively strike terror into the hearts of every cop out there tonight—good guy and bad guy alike.

Yep, weakness into strength. Tom and the Medusas' best shot at escape was a major outbreak of chaos and confusion among the police.

Now. How to get them shooting at each other? She had a little bit of detonation cord in her pack, but she hadn't been allowed to bring any high explosives into the country. Not that it mattered. She didn't have enough time to set up a daisy chain of booby traps before the main police force would converge on the cottage. But she did have her Glock pistol and a half-dozen clips of ammo. It should be enough for her purposes.

She crept behind the first shooter, circling well wide of him in the woods. He was alert and wary, his head swiveling constantly, taking in everything around him. Drat. He wouldn't work for what she had in mind. Maybe the next guy would be sloppier.

He wasn't.

Paige moved on to the third would-be assassin. This one's gaze was riveted on the cottage, and he wasn't paying the slightest attention to possible threats from behind him. She tsked. Tunnel vision. Bad habit for a guy like him to get into. Good luck for her, though.

She moved on her belly like a snake, easing forward inch by careful inch. She really needed another ten minutes to get into position, but she highly doubted she'd have it. She moved as fast as she could, dragging herself along by the elbows. Brambles caught in her hair and tore at it, making her eyes water from the sting. Dirt got in her mouth and down her shirt, but she dared not stop to spit it out. One of her sleeves ripped, and her forearm beneath it got scraped up, but doggedly she continued on, praying the smell of her blood wouldn't attract any creatures more dangerous than the ones she already risked encountering up close and personal.

She raised her head slowly, looking for the third shooter. There he was, about twenty feet away, his back to her. How close did she dare get to him? She wanted to make it look as if he were shooting at his fellow policemen, but she needed to be far enough away from him that the return fire she was hoping to elicit wouldn't kill her. At least not right away.

She studied the lay of the land between them. About halfway to him, there appeared to be a faint depression in the ground. Probably a small runoff gully for rainwater. It would have to do.

The leaves littering this stretch of jungle floor were alarmingly dry. She had to slip her fingers under them one at a time, fluffing them lightly before easing them aside. The tiniest of breezes ruffled the foliage overhead just enough to mask the faint sounds of her relatively hasty passage. If she had a couple of hours, she could make it over to that gully in total silence. But she had two, maybe three, minutes at most.

Fluff and slither. Sixteen feet from the shooter. Fluff and slither. Fourteen feet.

The little gully dipped away just out of arm's reach when the shooter slid backward abruptly. He'd apparently been lying on a small rise, for he dropped down behind it and rolled onto his side, reaching for his calf.

Paige froze. One look in her direction from him. One twitch from her. That was all it would take for her to be dead meat.

The man massaged his leg vigorously, grimacing like he had a major charley horse. But after several moments, he rolled again to his belly and crawled back up the ridge.

Paige exhaled slowly. Whew. That had been close.

She thought she heard branches cracking and leaves rustling behind her. Damn. The main police force was on the move. She wiggled forward the last few feet, angling her body to lie lengthwise in the shallow depression, perpendicular to the shooter. Ideally, she would cover herself with leaves and dirt, but that amount of movement would surely alert the guy now only ten feet away from her. She wiggled in as best she could. The twigs and leaves and mud she'd accumulated in her crawl would have to suffice for camouflage.

She eased her shooting hand under her body and across her torso. Her elbow dug into her chest, and in a few seconds, her shoulder was protesting loudly But, when the police arrived, she would have to be on her side to shoot at them, and she would have at best a few tenths of a second to take the shots. She needed the weapon in position and ready to go.

She studied the jungle before her, straining to see as far into the black gloom as possible. It would be critical for her to spy the cops first before they spotted her. She figured she could get off three quick shots before the shooter turned around and took her out.

Neutralizing him would be a difficult shot. The soles of his feet were the most visible part of him at the moment. Hopefully, he would stand up to turn around and give her a bigger target. Otherwise, she was in for a tricky piece of shooting to stay alive. The good news was that any firefight between the two of them would be at very close range. And at the end of the day, she trusted the lightning fast reflexes the Medusas had trained into her.

A dark figure—a member of the larger police force closing in—moved in the blackness behind her. It wasn't much, but it was enough. From her prone position on her side, she took careful aim. And pulled the trigger.

The explosion of sound was deafening.

Her target dropped heavily—the distinctive collapse of a dead man rather than a controlled dive for cover.

She sprayed two more clusters of shots to either side of the now prone target, and prayed that sufficed to make everyone dive for cover. She rolled onto her back and over to her right side to face the shooter directly in front of her.

As she'd hoped, he'd leaped to his feet. His weapon was coming up to point at her. She squeezed off two quick shots so fast she wasn't even conscious of aiming. Twin red rosettes blossomed in the guy's forehead. A look of infinite surprise crossed his face, and then his legs collapsed like a marionette's when the puppet's lines went slack.

She jumped to her feet, whirling to fire at the mass of movement in the woods behind her. Damn! There were so many targets! She spotted at least eight men on the move. She sprinted to the east, crossing the field of fire and diving for cover behind a massive tree trunk.

Bullets sprayed around her, stripping chunks of bark off the tree. A rich smell of cinnamon permeated the air.

She dropped her empty bullet clip, slammed in a new one and sprinted toward the first shooter's position, dodging and weaving as she went.

He was waiting for her.

A dull glint of gunmetal swung her way. She shot, her pistol an extension of her hand, and her hand an extension of her thoughts. She was stunned when the guy fell over backward, his semiautomatic weapon spraying a wild fusillade of bullets up into the jungle canopy.

Dang. She'd had no idea all those hundreds of hours on the firing range had made her such a good shot.

She careened forward, diving to the ground beside the dead shooter. She wrenched the weapon from his lifeless hands and held the trigger down, raking a spray of lead across the jungle behind her.

The underbrush lit up with muzzle flashes returning fire from at least a dozen different points.

And then the thing she'd been waiting for happened behind her. Somebody fired back at the police squad from over her shoulder. The caliber of the weapon was too heavy for the Medusas, who were armed only with pistols tonight.

The muzzle flashes shifted toward this new target. Taking advantage of their momentary distraction, Paige took time to assume a sniper's stance, prone on her belly and sight down the barrel of her weapon. She waited for the next muzzle flash in her field of vision and then fired.

She double tapped the trigger, sending out two rounds in quick succession. A voice cried out, then was silent. She took aim at the next firing position. She worked her way down the line of police, one of Tom's would-be assassins also shooting at the same line of police.

Another weapon joined in firing from behind her at the police formation. Although the chaos before her probably no longer qualified as a formation. Men were running around like chickens with their heads cut off, diving for cover, popping up to shoot wildly at they knew-not-what and generally acting panicked.

Weakness into strength. Vanessa Blake was brilliant.

And then the shouting started—men screaming back and forth for identifications, yelling for help, more yelling for cease-fires. The radios must be completely useless by now if they'd resorted to shouting. Paige took aim at the locations of the voices and fired the last rounds out of the dead man's weapon. When the trigger clicked harmlessly, she flung the weapon aside, jumped up and took off running again. Time to reduce the number of would-be assassins a bit more.

She headed for the last location of the first shooter, the one parked at the southeast corner of the house whom she'd circled wide of in the first place. She was sprinting hard, heedless of any noise she might make in the midst of a deafening gunfight, when the dark figure rose up in front of her without warning.

She had no time to dive for cover. No time to dodge the muzzle of the weapon aimed directly at her gut. No time to do anything but register the black, cold gaze of a killer staring her dead in the eye.

Chapter 16

"**P**aige is retreating into the woods. I've lost visual on her," Casey announced.

"Signal her back!" Tom exclaimed. "Tell her to leave the area or call the police or take cover! Don't just leave her out there sneaking around on her own trying to be a one-man army!"

Casey glanced back at him sympathetically. "Make that a one-woman army. And she's already gone."

He swore long and hard, not bothering to keep it under his breath. Aleesha finally broke his string of invectives by chuckling.

"Ah, you gots it bad, boyo."

He scowled at her.

Aleesha's grin widened. Then she got back to business. "Okay. Everyone over here by the door. Cho, Casey, you hold your positions spotting. The rest of you cluster around Tom. Weapons at the ready. We'll move out in standard formation. Tom, be prepared to run like hell. You go as fast as you can. We'll stay in position around you."

The question popped out before he could think about it. "Shouldn't I take a little off my max speed so you can keep up?"

Silence fell.

It was Naraya, the quiet Middle Eastern woman, who eventually answered. "Can you run faster than a 4.7 second forty-yard dash?"

He considered briefly. "Not anymore. I probably can't break five seconds."

Naraya replied gently, "Then we won't have any trouble keeping up with you."

Holy smokes. "Well, okay then. Full-out sprint for the trees, it is."

Casey asked, "What are our fire orders?"

Aleesha considered for a moment. "You are green-lighted to return fire. You are also green-lighted to lay down suppression fire. Free fire only on my order."

Speaking of an all-out firefight… "Anyone got a spare firearm for me?" Tom asked. "I'm feeling kinda naked here."

Aleesha shook her head regretfully. "Sorry. We had trouble getting a lousy handgun for each one of us into the country. Your mission remains to keep your head down and make as small a target out of yourself as possible."

Okay, now he really was alarmed. He was supposed to run out there into the middle of a hail of lead completely unarmed? To simply trust his life to these women he barely knew? A whole new understanding for the paranoia and reluctance of his former subjects of personal protection roared through him.

A popping sound from outside made him jump violently. That was gunfire. It wasn't anywhere near as close as he'd expected, and it wasn't nearly loud enough to be incoming fire to this location. But still. Who on Earth was having a gunfight out there that didn't involve this cottage?

Paige.

"I'm guessing that's our signal," Aleesha bit out. "Let's go."

Cho and Casey collapsed in on the group as Monica opened the front door. Naraya led the way with dark-haired Alex right behind her. They fanned out, weapons drawn, scanning the area as the rest of the team—with Tom crammed in the middle of them—surged through the opening.

To their right, a barrage of gunfire erupted without warning. It was still too distant to be aimed at them, but the volume of shooting was alarming. And Paige was in the middle of that? Tom's brain threatened to vapor lock entirely. A visceral need to save her, to protect her, to make sure she came back to him safe and sound all but knocked him off his feet. Holy crap. Was this…

…love?

It sure as hell was something. And whatever it was, it was all but incapacitating him.

"C'mon, Tom! Pick up the pace!" Aleesha snapped.

He did automatically as she ordered. His body felt strangely disconnected from his brain, like one part of him was a robot following orders while the other part of him was flying through the trees, racing to join Paige wherever she was right now, wrapping her in a cocoon of invisibility and safety.

Come back to me alive, dammit.

Whether or not she heard his thought was anybody's guess. But he sent it out to her over and over in a continuous and fervent stream.

The Medusas were as fast as advertised, dragging him toward the same pair of trees Paige had stood between a few minutes before. The sounds of gunfire were louder now. Coming closer.

A spray of automatic weapons fire erupted and at least a dozen weapons banged out return fire. A second spray of automatic fire exploded, followed by more return fire.

*Please, God, let Paige not be caught in the middle of that.
Let her be hiding somewhere safe with plenty of cover, well
out of harm's way.*

Oh, wait. He was talking about Paige, here. She'd be in
the thick of it, taking ridiculous risks and acting like she was
completely bulletproof.

He amended his prayer. *Please, God, save Paige from
herself and bring her back to me safe and sound.*

And then the tenor of the shots changed. Someone out
there had spotted him and his bodyguards running across the
lawn. The next fusillade of shots were much, much louder and
definitely pointed this way.

And then a series of sharp pops erupted to his immediate
right. The Medusas were returning fire. How in the world
were they pulling off shots while running at this speed?

The trees loomed and Aleesha shouted, "Dive!"

He knew without having to ask that the command was
directed at him. He took a flying leap, sliding into a mass
of fallen leaves as slick as any major league baseball player
stealing second base. Something hot and painful grazed his
back. And then a heavy weight fell across him, smashing him
flat.

"Sorry," Casey grunted. "Just took one to the back and it
knocked me into you."

"You're hit?" he exclaimed.

"Vest. I'll live. Too bad we didn't have a vest big enough
to fit you."

Holy Mother of God. She'd just taken that bullet for him.
Bullet-resistant vest or no, the idea massively freaked him out.
He had to get away from these women who would die for him
if he let them. He had to find Paige. He had to do something
other than be deadweight out here!

"Start crawling," Aleesha ordered. "Head for the thick
stuff."

He knew exactly what she meant by that. He pulled himself along on his belly with his elbows, digging his toes in the dirt for extra purchase. *Paige! Where are you? Please be safe, please be safe, please be safe....*

Aleesha gave quiet orders from somewhere nearby for several of the Medusas to move ahead and scout the road while two more moved out to guard their flanks. He still wasn't clear on exactly which insect or snake name went with which woman. But he didn't suppose it mattered. They all seemed perfectly capable of handling anything that came at them.

A hail of gunfire exploded nearby, and Casey flattened herself on top of him again. That had been close. And then he heard the words every special operator most hated to hear.

"I'm hit."

It was Naraya, off to his right.

"How bad?" Aleesha called out low, already slithering in that direction.

He recalled hearing that Aleesha had been a trauma surgeon in her former life and was a hell of a field medic.

"You ambulatory?" Aleesha murmured. He couldn't hear the low reply, but Aleesha's next words were, "To me, ladies. We're gonna have to carry her out."

This was it. His opportunity to get away from them and go find Paige. If the Medusas were ever going to have a lag in attention on him, it would be in this burst of concern for their downed comrade. He knew. He'd lost men before, himself.

He eased away from the women a step. Another. And another. One more step and he'd reach a swath of deep shadow.

"You coming, Tom?" Casey murmured from well ahead of him now.

"Uh-huh," he replied.

Another step.

He'd made it to the shadows. It was tempting to turn and run for it, but that kind of movement would attract the attention of the Medusas, who were crouching now in a group ahead of him, no doubt around Naraya.

He took several more soundless steps, sliding behind a bush smothered in thick vines of some kind. He couldn't see the Medusas anymore. Which meant they couldn't see him, either. He turned and ran.

He headed for the gunfire to his left. It had to be where Paige was. That woman drew fireworks to herself like a magnet drew iron filings. Probably why she was such a good reporter. She had an instinct for where the action would be. But it was going to get her killed if she wasn't damned careful tonight. He'd been in dozens more firefights than she had. He knew how to live through one. He needed to find her. To make sure she didn't do anything stupid, or worse, suicidal.

He zigzagged through the trees, moving fast until the gunfire sounded like it was twenty or thirty yards away. Only then did he slow down, shifting into stealth mode.

Where are you, Paige? Don't die before I find you.

The man in front of her looked over her shoulder and abruptly turned and ran. What had he just seen? Cautiously, Paige looked back.

A rapid movement made her whirl and drop to her belly all in a single move. She whipped her weapon up into a firing position as a dark figure emerged from the trees at a dead run. She tracked the hostile's movement across her field of fire, made the adjustment to lead his movement and began the smooth squeeze through the trigger.

The figure froze.

Dammit. She released the trigger at the last moment before she blew the guy's head off. Where did he go? He'd just disappeared! Her blood ran cold. That had been the trick of an experienced warrior. Who was this new and highly skilled threat?

Without moving her head, Paige raked her gaze across the foliage, seeking better cover. She swore under her breath. None to be had. She was lying in the edge of a stand of tall, grassy weeds, an arm's length away from a dead bush. She could slither under the bush, but there was no wind here, and the movement of the weeds would be impossible to hide. She was stuck out here, relying on her ability to remain perfectly still for whatever camouflage it could provide. And then she just had to pray that the new shooter didn't have great eyesight and spot her lying out here just waiting to get picked off.

A shot flew well over her head. It had come from behind her and was traveling in the general direction of that now vanished figure. Maybe that was the recently fled assassin sending out a shot to see if it drew incoming fire. Not a bad ploy, actually. Her gaze roamed back and forth, searching for a reaction to the shot.

Nada.

Damn, this guy was good!

And she was caught between him and another shooter at her back. It was never good to be the stuffing in the Oreo cookie. It always got licked out first. Her best hope was that neither man would shoot at her in fear of killing his comrade in the cross fire.

If only the Medusas would engage in the fight and take some of the heat off her! Although as soon as the thought crossed her mind, she dismissed it. As long as they stayed out of this mess it meant they were moving Tom to safety and hadn't been spotted by the bad guys sent here to kill him.

Of course, it also meant she was probably going to die. It simply wasn't reasonable to expect to survive a dozen or more heavily armed shooters all firing at her while she had only a handgun and a few clips of ammo to defend herself with.

Oddly enough, she was at peace with that thought. If sacrificing herself meant that Tom would live, then her death was worth it.

Whoa. She was willing to *die* for him personally, not just for him as the subject to be kept alive? When had that happened? The only people she'd ever been willing to die for were her fellow Medusas. And she'd been through two grueling years of training with them designed to turn them into a unit so tight they were practically a single person. She loved her teammates like sisters.

Good grief. Did she love Tom?

No. Not possible.

Okay, possible.

More than possible.

Dammit, a done deal.

Now what the hell was she supposed to do?

As the bullet whizzed over his head, Tom swore yet again at his lack of a weapon with which to return fire. The shooter popped out from behind a tree a second time and sent another round in Tom's general direction, well wide to the left this time.

Although the ease with which he could pick the guy off if he had a gun registered on Tom's brain, the thing that captivated him was what the guy was wearing. That was a *cop* shooting at him. What in the *hell* were the local police doing trying to kill him? Or was that guy really a policeman at all? Was he using the uniform to mislead the real police? Or was he a mole, like the conference security guard who'd tried to take him out? Not that it mattered either way. The guy was armed and shooting at him. He was in need of killing.

Tom might not have a gun or even a knife, but he had his hands. And the hands of an American Special Forces soldier were lethal weapons in their own right. All he had to do now was get close enough to the guy to use them.

Gazing between himself and the spot where he'd seen the muzzle flash of the shooter's gun, he mapped a course that would give him the most cover. That open spot with nothing but tall weeds for protection would be tricky to cross, but not impossible. Grimly, Tom eased toward the shooter.

He'd been gliding ahead for two or three minutes when he reached the edge of the clear spot. He took a deep breath and eased a foot forward.

All of a sudden, something grabbed his ankle, wrapping around it powerfully and yanking it from underneath him.

Gunfire erupted, but whatever had his ankle had made him fall so fast and so hard that, before the bullets aimed at him could slam into him, he hit the ground. Panicked, he rolled and grabbed, with no idea if he was about to come up with an armful of python or something even more dangerous.

Paige lurched as something heavy and writhing landed on top of her, flailing wildly. Gunshots erupted around her and she rolled frantically. Anything to get into a different position before the shooter got a bead on her last location!

Something horrifically strong wrapped around her throat and she yanked at it with all her strength.

And then warmth registered beneath her hands. Skin. That was a human arm around her throat. Ah. That she knew how to deal with…assuming she didn't get shot in the next few seconds.

She rolled again, doing her damnedest to reach the cover of the bush so tantalizingly near. She had to get undercover *now* or she was going to die, assailant or no.

Strangely enough, the powerful entity attacking her didn't fight the roll. In fact, he accelerated the movement, flinging her across his body and then back beneath him once. Twice.

Shadows and branches engulfed them.

But that wasn't much of a relief. She couldn't breathe, and the arm now lying hard across her throat was terrifyingly

strong. She was having no luck budging it. She had only a
few more seconds to get this attacker off her before she'd lose
consciousness.

Paige jerked up her knee, aiming for a groin. The assailant
dodged to the side. He maintained his grip on her, but his
arm eased off for just long enough that she was able to draw
a partial gasp of air. It wasn't enough, but the spots dancing
behind her eyes retreated momentarily.

Long enough for her to see the face of the man trying to
kill her.

Long enough for her to go completely limp beneath him
in shock.

Tom was trying to choke her to death?

Before any reaction to that thought could process through
her stunned brain, his arm whipped off her neck and swearing
erupted in her ear.

"What in the hell are you doing out here?" he bit out under
the noise of the mess around them.

"Same thing you are. Trying not to die."

Bang. Bang.

A flurry of gunfire replied from behind them. The chaos
out here was unbelievable. It sounded like several more
shooters had converged on this area. Must've been drawn by
the earlier shots. The hot zone had just boiled over.

Tom's heart jumped exuberantly in his chest. She was alive.
Unhurt. His prayers had been answered. Now to get her out
of here in one piece.

But first…to hell with discipline. His arms snaked out and
he pulled Paige close to him as he'd been longing to do ever
since the shooting started, crushing her against his chest.

Her arms wrapped around his waist in a hug that was only
slightly less viselike than his. "Thank God you're alive," she
breathed against his chest.

"I was a jerk at that press conference," he blurted. "I was so worried that you'd die before I ever got to tell you I'm sorry and I wasn't thinking about how what I said would sound to you."

She laughed silently, her shoulders shaking in his arms. "A squad of assassins is trying to kill us and all you're worried about is having been a jerk?"

"You agree, then, that I was a jerk?"

"Indubitably."

"Forgive me?"

She raised her head and rolled her eyes at him. "Good Lord, yes, Tom."

"There's something else I want to tell you…" His arms tightened possessively about her, pulling her even closer against him, as if he could will her to feel the truth in the words hovering on the tip of his tongue.

She gasped, "A little air, here."

Another burst of gunfire erupted, but thankfully not overhead this time. He sighed, loosening his grip on her only fractionally. Now wasn't the time for it anyway. "Are you really okay?" he murmured. "No heretofore unnoticed gunshot wounds?"

"Nope. I'm fine. You?"

"Fine."

"Good, then can you let go of me so I can lead us out of here?"

He laughed under his breath. That was his Paige. Feisty, independent and totally focused on the job at hand. He'd loved that about her from the first moment they met and she demanded help getting Takashi Ando's body off the beach. Never mind that the poor man had been tortured and mutilated and she'd had to look at Ando's remains.

She popped up and shot at the guy behind them, then pivoted left and shot at the men closing in from the other direction. A new flurry of shots erupted. She dropped to a crouch.

"Stop that!" he exclaimed under his breath. The woman had planted herself between two hostile forces of shooters, and was shooting at both in order to provoke a firefight with herself squarely in the cross fire! Was she nuts? Oh, wait. It was Paige.

She grinned. "Follow me." She ran a dozen yards with him right on her heels, darting behind a huge tree and using it for momentary cover from the shooters. Tom flattened himself beside her.

"Jeez, Paige. What are you doing out here? Drawing down the whole damned police force on you?"

"Yes, as a matter of fact. Some of them are corrupt. Trying to kill you. Using their uniforms for cover. Gotta get them all shooting at each other."

Tom threw her a thunderstruck look. He'd been right. She *was* nuts. Another barrage of gunfire exploded nearby and the two of them flinched simultaneously.

He muttered, "Looks like you've succeeded at causing a complete mess. Let's get out of here."

"Easier said than done. There are cops everywhere. They're all shooting at anything that moves."

It was his turn to order. "Follow me."

He crawled to their right, perpendicular to what seemed to be the direction of most of the gunfire. Thankfully, Paige came along without argument. They moved for a minute or so. Two exchanges of fire took place behind them, but neither was close enough to make him sweat.

And then he spotted movement ahead. "Shooter. Eleven o'clock," he hand signaled.

He stopped and Paige eased up beside him, her pistol drawn. God, he envied her that weapon. "I need a gun," he breathed.

She threw him a wry look and mumbled, "Coming up."

Before he could open his mouth to tell her not to do whatever foolishness she was considering, Paige was on her feet, up and running…good Lord…directly at the shooter. What in the *hell* was she thinking? She'd left so fast he didn't stand a chance of tackling her before she was out of his range.

A barrage of lead pinned him down, and he cursed uselessly at his lack of a weapon to lay down covering fire for her. He could only lie there helplessly and watch as the woman he loved sprinted forward directly into the jaws of death.

"Nooooo!" he shouted.

Chapter 17

The shooter rose up out of a cluster of bushes and took aim at her as she charged him. Several things registered almost too fast for Paige to separate in her mind. The shooter was settling himself into a sniper's balanced stance. *Not* wearing a police uniform. But clearly hostile.

She leaped to the obvious conclusion. This, then, was the original shooter hired by Mimi Ando and not one of the second-string cops brought in to assist. Lastly, she registered that there was no way she could bring her weapon into a firing position and get off a shot before this guy buried a bunch of bullets in her.

The most fundamental of all Medusa mantras popped into her head. When you can't overwhelm them with brute force, outthink them. It was the Medusa way. As women, they often couldn't bring more strength and raw power to bear in a fight. But they always could be smarter than the other guy.

All of this passed through Paige's head in less than a blink of an eye. The other shooter's weapon adjusted slightly as his finger started a squeeze through the trigger.

"Wait!" she cried out. "I work for Mimi, too!"

The finger paused, midpull. A male voice called back gruffly, "Who're you?"

Right. Like she was going to answer that. "You and me, we're on the same team."

The man uttered a foul curse. "Why didn't she tell me that she had someone else on this job?"

Paige rolled her eyes and planted her pistol-toting hand casually on her hip. She eased her index finger through the trigger guard to rest on the thin metal tongue of the trigger. "It's Mimi. Of course she hired someone else. Have you ever met a more suspicious woman?"

The shooter snorted and gestured with his chin behind her. "What's going on back there? Is the target down?"

"Yes. The job's done." In a smooth, neat movement, she cocked her wrist and shot from the hip, Old West–style. It was a difficult stance from which to shoot with any kind of accuracy, but the Medusas fired dozens of rounds from all kinds of crazy positions on a daily basis. The shot barely took conscious thought on her part.

Her target staggered back as she continued firing, bringing the pistol up in front of her, cradling its butt in the palm of her left hand. One bullet was rarely enough to kill a man unless a person got lucky and scored a shot in one of a few tiny locations on the human body. And this guy was going down and *staying* down if she had anything to say about it.

Two more quick pulls of her trigger, and the assassin fell. She sprinted over to him and crouched, verifying that he was dead and frisking him fast. She grabbed his rifle, a large-caliber pistol and a pouch of ammo clips for the gun. But as importantly, she found the small rectangle of his cell phone. She snagged it and took off running as more bullets flew past her far too close for comfort.

She dived behind the tree where she'd left Tom, slamming herself against the trunk as the wood at her back shuddered, absorbing a hail of bullets.

She dropped the pistol and ammo pouch in front of Tom's nose.

"There," she said dryly. "Now you've got a gun."

* * *

Tom scooped up the weapon and popped to his feet beside Paige, livid. "If you ever do anything that stupid again, I'll shoot you myself!"

She grinned at him as she flung the shoulder strap of the semiautomatic weapon over her head. "C'mon. Now we can really cause some chaos to cover our retreat."

"Stop—" he started.

Too late. She was off and running again. And of course, she was headed toward the force of a dozen or more hostiles behind them.

He took off after her. When he caught her, he was definitely going to kill her.

Thankfully she stopped well short of the advancing police line and he met up with her, murder firmly on his mind. *Her* murder. But before he could reach out to throttle her, she stepped out from behind another tree and let loose a stream of gunfire across the jungle in front of them. Leaves and strips of bark exploded in every direction. She pivoted and sent a similar rain of lead toward the shooters closest to the cottage.

The sounds of men shouting and cursing filled the air, and wild gunfire ensued. Tom ducked along with Paige as mayhem cut loose around them. He gestured to their right, perpendicular to the field of fire. She nodded and took off that way. Dammit, he'd meant for her to follow him, not for her to leave him to trail along behind!

She was as fast as her teammates, even encumbered by a heavy, clumsy rifle, and he had to work hard to keep up with her. The sounds of combat grew slightly fainter as they sprinted away from the gun battle now in progress. No one shot at them as they fled through the jungle toward the main road.

Son of a gun. The two of them might yet live through this night to see another dawn. And if they did, she was dead meat.

* * *

Paige's heart slammed into her ribs painfully. The Medusas were out here somewhere moving east toward the main road. She had to make contact with them if she was going to get Tom to safety.

He *had* to make it out. He had to be okay. If he got hurt on her watch, she'd curl up and die. The thought panicked her so badly she started to hyperventilate. She was forced to slow to a walk, to order herself to breathe in, count to three, and breathe out. Count to three, breathe in. Count to three, breathe out. It took a few moments, but the panic attack passed.

She took off running again. How long they tore through the underbrush, she had no idea. Time had ceased to have any meaning from the moment she first thought Tom might die at the beginning of this whole mess. She spotted movement ahead and screeched to a halt. Tom slammed into her so hard he nearly knocked her over. He cursed under his breath. He sounded none too happy back there.

Raising her rifle and squinting to make out the figures ahead, she took a cautious step forward. *Oh, God.* Aleesha and Cho were carrying a third person between them.

She darted forward, calling out low, lest her teammates shoot at her and Tom inbound, "It's Fire Ant and Wolf."

The threesome in front of her halted immediately. "To me," Aleesha replied low during a burst of gunfire.

Paige gestured toward Naraya's limp form. "How bad is she?"

Aleesha replied, "Shattered femur. A lot of blood loss before I got a pressure balloon in the wound. Passed out."

Tom offered from behind Paige, "Need me to carry her?"

The other women both shook their heads in the negative. Aleesha murmured, "Fire Ant, take point. Lead us to your car. It is out here, isn't it?"

"Yes."

She ejected her nearly empty clip, pocketed it and replaced it with her last full clip of ammunition as she moved ahead of her teammates. She didn't need to turn and look for Tom. She felt him stalking just behind her, practically treading on her heels. He was sticking to her like glue. Which wasn't a bad thing. He was an experienced field operative and it was comforting to know he had her back. But more than that, it was a relief to be with him, to know he was safe and unharmed, to have a weapon in her hands and the wherewithal to protect him from danger.

The going was slow, hindered by heavy brush and Naraya's deadweight. But a few endless minutes later, Paige spotted a thinning in the trees ahead. The road. She signaled back to Tom, who relayed to Aleesha. In a moment, he pointed to the right and flashed her a hand signal to proceed with caution.

Duh. She hadn't come this far to get him killed now.

If she wasn't mistaken, her car was a hundred feet or so down the road from their current position.

Abruptly, ominous silence fell in the jungle behind them.

Crap. The police had finally sorted out who was shooting at whom, and her nifty diversion had just petered out. Which meant that the surviving hostile shooters were now free to come after Tom and the Medusas. They had to get out of here *now*.

Directly ahead of Tom, Casey pulled out a cell phone and dialed it quickly. He eavesdropped shamelessly.

"Ops, Scorpion here. I need full satellite surveillance of our position. All unidentified persons approaching us should be considered hostile. And could you please call the local police and tell them to quit shooting at us? We've got Tom Rowe, and I doubt the U.S. government would take kindly to it if the police charged with protecting him were to kill him."

Casey listened for a minute and then muttered a disgusted "Roger."

She stowed her cell phone.

"What's up?" Tom asked.

"Five to seven minutes to bring a high-resolution satellite to bear. Until then, we're on our own."

"Okay, then," Aleesha said briskly. "For the next five minutes we do our damnedest not to get into any gun battles."

That was a lifetime in Special Ops terms. Five to seven *seconds* wasn't an uncommon time frame in which to completely wipe out an enemy unit. And they were supposed to wait around out here for five to seven *minutes?*

It was *so* time to get out of Dodge. Tom murmured over his shoulder in Aleesha's general direction, "Let's put Naraya in the car and get her out of here before the jungle goes hot again."

"You, too, pretty boy," Aleesha muttered back.

And Paige was damned well coming with him. No way was he leaving her side now that he'd found her again. Especially not after the antics he'd seen her pull back there in the jungle.

Paige murmured, "The car should be just ahead. Under that stand of palmetto."

Handy thing about itty-bitty cars. They were easy to hide. Aleesha signaled the team to get down, and they all sank slowly into the scrub and tall weeds lining the road. Easing forward on their bellies, they approached the MINI Cooper's passenger door. Casey reached up and opened it. The click of the latch was deafening in the tense silence.

Aleesha and Cho glided forward, dragging Naraya between them. How they managed to maneuver her inert form into the backseat that quickly and silently, he had no idea. He kept forgetting how much stronger these women were than they looked.

"In you go, big guy," Aleesha muttered.

"Is Paige coming with us?" he replied.

"No. Cho's a medic and I need her. Naraya's tried to crash on us twice already, and it'll take both of us to get her to a hospital alive. With you that makes four, and that's all the car can hold. You're going to have to drive, in fact."

Aleesha must have spotted the beginnings of his ferocious scowl because she added hastily, "Besides, Paige knows this jungle better than the rest of us and already has eyes-on intel regarding who's out here. She's also one of the best combat shooters I've got. She stays."

"Then I stay, too," he said resolutely.

Aleesha glared at him. "This isn't a democracy, and I'm ordering you to go."

"Sorry. I'm a civilian. And I'm staying."

"Don't be a fool, Rowe—" Aleesha started.

Paige interrupted. "Go, Tom. I *need* you to be safe."

"Yeah, well, I need you to be safe, too. I'll go crazy if I leave you, not knowing if you've been hurt or worse." He barged on before anyone could come up with any more good reasons for him to go. "I can pull my weight out here."

Aleesha snapped, "I thought you're a civilian. I don't draft civilians into firefights."

He opened his mouth to make a hot retort, but just then most of the team went still, listening to something he couldn't hear. Probably a radio transmission across their headsets, he guessed.

Casey murmured, "H.O.T. Watch just came up on our frequency. They've got some initial imagery and report a large force moving rapidly in our direction."

He spoke tersely to Aleesha. "There's no time to argue. I'm an able-bodied operator and you've got a soldier down. Get her to a hospital and let me do what I know how to do with the others. You're not doing your mission to protect me any good by standing here arguing."

Aleesha glared at him for a moment and then cast an irritated glance in Paige's direction. The Jamaican woman grumbled, "How you put up with him is beyond me, girl."

Triumph surged in his gut as Aleesha continued grimly, "So help me, if you get yourself killed out here, I'll haunt you till the end of time."

Cho murmured urgently, "Her pulse is getting thready again. We've got to go."

As the two medics leaned over the car seats awkwardly to work on their patient, Paige ducked into the vehicle and groped at Naraya's utility belt. She came up with a cell phone. Ah. No doubt H.O.T. Watch could use its GPS locator function to identify her, and Paige could use it to keep in touch with her teammates.

Roxi was drafted to drive while Aleesha and Cho worked on Naraya. In a matter of a few seconds, the vehicle pulled away.

Tom turned to face the jungle. Now it was just him and the remaining Medusas against the threat lurking out there. Adrenaline surged through him and he savored the sensation. It had been a long time since he'd felt this alive. Too long. He tried to recall why it was he'd ever gotten out of the Special Ops field in the first place, and he came up blank.

Shouts erupted in the jungle behind them.

"Time to go," Paige bit out.

No kidding. Casey sent Alex and Monica across the road to lay down covering fire if necessary. Once the pair had dived onto their bellies on the far side of the asphalt, he, Paige, and Casey raced half-crouching across the open space. No one shot at them. But that didn't mean no one had seen them.

Tom plowed into the grass, and a scant second later, someone else pressed up hard against him. He instinctively recognized Paige's lithe form plastered to his. He would never forget the feel of her body. And even through the tension permeating them all, he still knew the scent of her instantly.

"Stealth or speed?" Casey whispered to Paige.

"Stealth until H.O.T. Watch says otherwise."

Casey nodded, and the group slid ghostlike back from the road and melted into the trees. Tom's muscles protested the exaggerated slowness of movement, but his mind fell into the pattern of it right away. And it felt *good*.

Lying under a giant fern beside him, Paige brought the cell phone to her ear and listened intently. She hand-signaled to him that their pursuers were doing some sort of tracking maneuver behind them.

Their little team moved out once more. It galled him to be kept in the center of the pack like a helpless old lady, but Paige and the others were having no part of any other marching order. Still, it was better than being back at the hotel sweating bullets over whether Paige was alive or dead.

He checked his watch. Three minutes until the live satellite surveillance would come online. An eternity.

He took twelve steps, which in full stealth mode worked out to about two minutes…one step approximately every ten seconds. He was so close to Paige he felt the faint vibration of Naraya's phone against his arm. She eased the instrument up to her ear, listened for a moment, and alarm burst across her face.

Urgently, she hand-signaled him by putting her index finger by her ear and twirling it around like a tornado.

Crap. That was the signal to run like hell.

The police must be across the road and coming fast. He and the remaining Medusas took off running. So much for stealth mode. And soon enough, the correctness of that decision became apparent as the woods erupted in shouts and the sounds of men crashing through trees behind them. The police were making no effort whatsoever to be quiet. Which meant...his brain hitched.

Which meant this was a herding operation.

"Are we...being driven...into a trap?" he gasped between heaving gulps of air.

Paige's gaze snapped over to him. And that was a mistake. She stumbled, and he decelerated hard to grab her arm and keep her from going down. A fall now would be certain disaster.

She regained her balance, nodded once in thanks, and the two of them accelerated again. But in the scant second the two of them had paused, the Medusas ahead of them had darted out of sight. He slowed, signaling Paige to ask if she knew where the others had gone. She shook her head in the negative.

He swore to himself. Just what they needed. To be separated from the team!

The noise was growing louder behind them by the second. They must be using some sort of motorcycles or all-terrain vehicles to be gaining on them like this. Paige signaled him frantically and peeled to her right. He followed, perplexed, as she led him in a wide half circle. She wanted to run right back into the thick of their pursuit?

But he didn't question her. So far tonight, her instincts had been spot-on.

He definitely picked up sounds of motorized vehicles now. Then he thought he made out movement in the trees ahead. What in the hell was Paige up to? As soon as the question crossed his mind, Paige dodged left and dived behind a rotting log. He followed, going airborne and slamming into the dirt beside her. She made a quick adjustment to the oversize leaves of some tropical plant above them, and they were completely encased in green. It was a good hiding spot.

They both froze, doing their best to become one with the forest floor. Except it felt more like he was becoming one with Paige. Their bodies fit together perfectly, melting into each other as naturally as breathing. It was strange and frustrating being in the middle of an op and being this aware of the special operator beside him as a sexy, desirable woman. Must be the adrenaline spiking sky-high through his system. It was a heady combination.

And then he became aware of…something…rolling off Paige. Something musky and sexual and hungry. He heard her breath catch in her throat. She must feel this thing between them, too.

How long he lay there like that, in a suspended state of terror and unadulterated lust, he had no idea. It felt like forever and back.

He heard an odd swishing sound and frowned, trying to identify it.

Machetes. Hacking through the dense foliage. The police must have set up a search line where the motorized vehicles couldn't go and where sweeping the jungle before them to flush out him and the Medusas. But which police? The good guys or the bad guys?

The line of machete-wielding men drew even with their position, and he held his breath in spite of himself. Paige's ribs went perfectly still beside him. Leaves went flying no more than three feet away from his head.

Swish. Whack. Pieces of shredded fern rained down on them. Somebody must have swung at the very plant they lay beneath. He listened for movement on their other flank and thought he heard someone hacking away no more than ten feet from them.

Wow. Paige had done a spectacular job of estimating how much of a gap they'd have for slipping between the police and where to hide.

A faint tremble passed through her, and he restrained an urge to throw an arm over her and draw her even nearer. He did lean fractionally closer, though, letting the weight of his shoulder settle more heavily against hers.

The sounds of motors and men beating the jungle retreated behind them. Paige risked pulling out Naraya's cell phone to whisper to H.O.T. Watch Ops, "Relay to Scorpion that Fire Ant and Wolf are safe and proceeding toward home base. Tell the Medusas to get out of here. Pursuit is using vehicles and machetes."

Tom was lying so close to her that he heard the faint reply. "Roger. Will do, Fire Ant. Be advised that we have full telemetry. All hostiles are tagged and identified. We will be vectoring the Medusas from our location."

Tom grinned. The police were toast. With satellites overhead monitoring their every movement and passing that information to the Medusas on the ground, there was no way the cops were ever going to catch anything but thin air and a bunch of frustration.

Relief surged through him. They'd done it. They'd avoided a large and dangerous hit squad and evaded a dozen or more unwitting police accomplices to the killers.

"You up for a hike?" Paige murmured.

"Sure. Why not? After all, you've already made me swim half the length of the island, I may as well walk the other half of it."

Paige popped to her feet gracefully and held down a slender hand to him. An impulse to grab her hand and yank her down on top of him nearly overcame Tom. But there were still armed men out here, and this was not the time or place for a gratuitous roll in the hay…or leaves and snakes, as it were.

Paige led the way, retracing their steps quickly toward the road. Occasionally Naraya's cell phone vibrated and she listened to some instruction from ops controllers watching them from above with high-tech spy satellites. Generally, it involved relaying a small course correction or status report on the police forces. Handy, those H.O.T. Watch guys.

After a few minutes, the wail of sirens announced the arrival of a cavalcade of ambulances. He didn't envy the medics having to clean up the destruction the Medusas, or more specifically, Paige, had left in her wake.

When they were well away from the scene of the gun battle, Paige stopped and pulled another cell phone out of her back pocket. She fiddled with it for a few moments, appeared to listen to a few voice-mail messages and then let out a sound of triumph.

Using Naraya's cell phone, she had a lengthy conversation with the folks at H.O.T. Watch. Tom listened, stunned, as she relayed the evidence she'd just pulled from the dead assassin's cell phone implicating Mimi Ando in masterminding tonight's attack on Tom.

When he disconnected the call, he stared at Paige incredulously. "Mimi?" And then it sank in—earlier she'd shouted to one of the shooters that she worked for Mimi, *too*. Oh my God. Mimi was behind Ando's murder and the attempted killings of him.

"One and the same," Paige replied grimly.

"Why?"

She shrugged. "As best as I can figure, she wanted all those billions for herself."

"But why kill her own husband?"

Paige turned and commenced walking. She walked for several long minutes before she answered. When she finally did speak, it was in a subdued, reflective tone. "My research on him indicates that Takashi Ando was a conservative and deeply cautious businessman. What if he decided not to bid? Mimi might have thought it was too good a deal to pass up and knocked him off to pursue it herself."

"But Takashi undoubtedly didn't leave her all of his money or complete control of his estate."

"He must have left her enough that she thought she could do the deal if you and Smythe were taken out of the picture as competing bidders to run up the price."

"So she tried to have us killed?"

"That's my guess. The guys at H.O.T. Watch said they'd relay my information to the chief of the summit's security. He'll take her into custody and question her."

Tom commented bitterly, "Tell him to appeal to her ego. She won't be able to resist bragging about her scheme if he acts suitably impressed."

"And you dated her?"

He winced. "What can I say? It's taken me a while to figure out what qualities truly appeal to me in a woman."

"Do tell," Paige murmured lightly.

He suppressed the grin flickering at the corners of his mouth. "Well, I like a woman who looks good in Valentino. And who's interesting to talk to. And who rocks my world in bed."

"Rocks your world, huh? That sounds like a tall order to fill."

"Mmm. It is. I also like a woman who—"

Naraya's phone vibrated and he broke off while Paige took the call.

Eventually she hung up and said, "They just picked up Mimi."

They walked a while more, and Naraya's phone rang again. This time Paige reported, "Mimi offered to trade immunity from prosecution in return for handing over the would-be assassins. H.O.T. Watch informed the summit security chief that the assassins have been neutralized and no deal is necessary. She was devastated by the news, apparently. They expect her to confess momentarily."

"She always did have a good feel for when to cut her losses and run."

Paige shrugged. "I don't think she'll be running from this one. She orchestrated murder."

Tom might have hated Mimi's guts for trying to kill him, but it still pained him to see how far she had fallen. Paige interrupted his troubled thoughts by asking abruptly, "Is it worth it?"

"Is what worth it?"

"The wealth? The fame? Is it worth killing for?"

He snorted. "Actually, it's a pain in the butt as often as it's a good thing. People treat you weird and are always trying to figure out ways to get a piece of your checkbook. You have to be suspicious of everyone you meet, and it's mostly just lonely. Sure, I have cool toys and get to do some great traveling, but all of that gets old after a while. Honestly, I've never been more bored in my life since I got rich."

"Is that why you came down to the beach when Vanessa Blake called and asked you to help me that morning?"

"That, and I was desperate to get my finger back into the Special Ops pie."

She waved over her shoulder. "You want back into all of that? The danger and death and chaos?"

"Yeah, actually."

She snorted.

"What? Like you don't love it? I saw the expression on your face when you went charging into that gunfight like Billy the Kid against that assassin. For which I'm planning to turn you over my knee later and paddle some sense into you, by the way."

She laughed. "You and what army?"

They walked a while longer in companionable silence. His adrenaline levels gradually decreased to something resembling normal, and he began to process all that had happened in the jungle earlier. It didn't take him long to glare over at her and burst out, "Are you nuts?"

"My tactic worked, didn't it? Vanessa says to make our greatest weakness into our greatest strength. We weren't going to be able to tell the good cops from the bad cops, so I made it impossible for them to tell each other apart, either."

He shook his head. "Insane."

"Effective."

"Too dangerous."

She glanced over at him, her gaze charged. "Worth the risk."

He was worth risking her life over? A burst of heat started low in his gut and spread outward rapidly. He stopped right there on the side of the road and pulled her into his arms. "You are the darnedest woman."

"Is that a good thing or a bad thing?"

He grinned down at her. "The jury's still out on that one."

"This from the guy who refused the ride to safety in favor of running around in the woods unarmed against a large and motivated force of possible killers?"

He shrugged. "What can I say? I've missed being shot at."

"Okay, now I know *you're* nuts."

"Aw, c'mon. You know you love my craziness. Admit it."

She stared up at him long and hard. And for some reason, he found himself holding his breath, butterflies leaping in the back of his throat. He leaned down slowly and his lips brushed against hers.

They'd done it. They'd escaped nearly certain death. And they were together and alive. He dragged her up against him, devouring her whole. Their tongues clashed and then found a rhythm, sliding and swirling together. Her body undulated against his, straining nearer, eagerness flowing off her. Craving erupted low in his gut. No matter how often he did this with her, he wanted more each time. She was an addiction, and he didn't think he'd ever want to break this habit. In fact, he knew he'd never get tired of this.

Paige's fingernails raked through his hair and she muttered, "If I didn't know the H.O.T. Watch satellites could see us, I'd tear your clothes off, throw you down and make wild, passionate love to you right here."

Satellites. Damn. They probably could already see this embrace. He loosened his grip on her reluctantly. "It's probably for the best. Wouldn't want to get poison ivy someplace unmentionable."

She chuckled and he forced his arms to let her go. But he vowed to himself it wouldn't be for long. Just until they could get undercover and away from the prying eyes of Big Brother. If she would have him, that was.

"Admit it," he murmured teasingly, doing his damnedest not to betray that his heart was stuck in his throat. "You can't get enough of me."

She looked up at him wide-eyed for a moment. Then a smile broke across her face and her magnificent eyes sparkled wickedly. "I might...repeat, *might*...occasionally find you mildly entertaining."

He grinned down at her. "That's not what you said on the floor of your living room last night. Or against the kitchen counter or in the shower—"

She pressed her fingers against his lips. "Enough, already, you arrogant man. Let's get you back to town and under guard."

They started walking again. He asked leadingly, "The Medusas can't guard me forever. Who do you suggest I recruit for the job if I happen to think Nils could use a little help?"

Her breath caught as if she sensed the broad hint behind the question. But she answered evenly enough, "Jeremy Smythe's security team is out of a job at the moment. They're all former SAS guys—a few of them have worked with the Medusas before, in fact. I can recommend them highly."

"Speaking of which," he commented, "Aleesha got a call while we were holed up in the cottage. Jeremy's death was caused by a massive stroke. He died of natural causes."

Paige sagged beside him. Uh-huh. As he'd thought. She'd been racked by guilt at the idea that her news report had somehow drawn the killer—Mimi, he corrected—to Jeremy. He loved that about Paige. She had an intense sense of responsibility. Of right and wrong. Of loyalty and honor. Yep, she was some woman.

He murmured, "You didn't have anything to do with his death. You can let go of that guilt."

"Thanks," she mumbled.

The sky was glowing ahead of them as they approached the cluster of brightly lit resorts lining the beach. He knew from experience that as soon as they got back to the hotel and Paige reported in to her Medusa superiors, she'd be tied up with debriefs and reports for the next several days.

It was now or never.

He stopped by the side of the road.

"Paige. There's something I have to discuss with you."

Chapter 18

Paige gulped. Tom sounded serious. What had she done now? Lord knew she'd screwed up plenty on this mission.

"Paige, had it not been for you, I might never have been exposed to the Special Forces community again. And for that, I owe you my thanks."

She frowned, but he plowed on as if determined to get through this as fast as possible.

"During these past few days with you, I've realized how much I've missed being out in the field. My life is boring, safe and bland, and I'm sick and tired of it. I've made a decision. I'm going back into the Special Ops community full-time. As soon as we get back to the hotel, I'm calling Jack Scatalone and telling him I want back in."

Paige's heart thudded to her feet. For a second there she'd thought he was going to ask her…oh, heck, it didn't matter. A guy like him would never go for a girl like her. It had all been a lovely fantasy while it lasted. But pure fantasy it unquestionably was.

She stammered, "Uh, I'm glad for you, Tom. It's obvious you're a highly experienced and really competent operator. Uncle Sam will be lucky to have you back. I wish you luck with it."

"Is that all you have to say?" he asked, his voice low and intense. "Good luck and Godspeed?"

She flared up at him. "What do you want me to say?"

"How about pleading with me not to go? Or telling me how dangerous it is and that you'll be worried sick about me? Or that you won't be able to stand the suspense of waiting around for me to come home after long and dangerous missions away from you?"

Okay, now she was confused. "Why would I say any of that?"

He burst out, frustrated, "Because maybe you care for me just a little? Because you were hoping to spend more time with me and not have me running off to the nearest war zone? Maybe because you give a damn whether I live or die?"

"Of course I care about that, Tom. But I hardly have any right to tell you any of that other—"

He cut her off abruptly. "Oh, for Pete's sake." His mouth swooped down and captured hers, and then his arms wrapped around her, sweeping her up against him in a kiss that would have melted a sterner woman than she.

He grasped the back of her head with one hand, cradling it so his tongue and lips could thoroughly plunder her mouth. His body pressed impatiently against hers, and answering desire exploded within her. It was all right there, the scalding heat, the desperate need, the unbridled lust. And along with it came wonder, astonishment even, that this incredible man found her remotely attractive.

"You have the right, dammit," he growled.

Her brain was too muddled with lust to follow what he meant. "Come again?" she mumbled.

"You have the right to worry about me and tell me not to go. I love you, you gorgeous, amazing idiot!"

Everything stopped. Her heart ceased beating. Time stood still. She was pretty sure the universe stopped expanding for a moment. Her mind went completely blank and she stared up at him in total incomprehension. "Love? Me?" she finally squeaked.

"Yes. You."

"Oh." A pause. "Oh!"

"Well?" he demanded.

"Well what?"

"You know, for a television news reporter, you're singularly bad at forming complete sentences."

"I…oh…well, then. It's not every day the man of your dreams tells you that he loves you."

Tom nodded firmly. "Better." Then he seemed to fetch up mentally himself. "Man of your dreams?" he repeated in what sounded like minor shock. "Does that mean you love me, too?"

"You know, for a successful businessman, you're not so good at making logical deductions."

He laughed aloud. "Touché." He tucked her under his arm and started walking once more. "Life with you's going to be one hell of an adventure."

"I thought you said you're running off to join the Special Forces again."

"I didn't say anything about running off. I figure you're going to need plenty of backup over the next few years. All I have to do is follow you around the world, and plenty of trouble's bound to come to you."

"Gee. Thanks."

"Sure. No problem. Just keeping it real."

"So you're proposing to become my Special Ops teammate?"

He stopped. Took her by both shoulders. Stared down at her in exasperation. "No, pip-squeak. I'm proposing to marry you."

"Oh." Another pause. "Oh!" Heat rushed to her cheeks and suddenly she felt more than a little light-headed. "Ohmigosh. Are you serious?"

"As a heart attack, kid. You and me. Whaddaya say?"

"I think it sounds like the craziest, most maddening, completely chaotic thing I've ever heard of."

"So that's a yes?" he asked.

"Of course, you big galoot. I love you!"

He grabbed her then, picking her up in his arms and swinging her around. He gave a hoot of joy and kissed her soundly before setting her back on her feet. "You've just made me the happiest man in the whole world!"

She grinned up at him. "You hang on to that thought the next time I do a solo recon and stroll into the middle of a firefight in the name of saving you."

"Don't even *think* about it. Not on my watch."

She laughed at him unrepentantly. "We'll see about that."

"This is exactly why I have to marry you and go operational with you. Who else is going to keep you from getting yourself killed?"

The smile faded from her face. "With you in my life, I've got every reason in the world to fight to live a very long time."

He plucked the canteen out of her utility belt and unscrewed the lid. "Here's to us. And to growing old together." He took a sip and passed it to her.

She laughed and took the canteen. "Mmm. Body-temperature, stale water. Somehow that's entirely appropriate to this ridiculous proposition. You and me married *and* teammates?" She shook her head but then lifted the container to him. "Here's to our future adventures together. Lots and lots of adventures."

He groaned as she tipped up the jug. "How about just enough adventures to keep life interesting and none that could get you killed?"

"Sorry. You've fallen in love with a Medusa. You're in for it now, big guy."

Their gazes met and they burst out laughing. Oh, yes. This was going to be a grand adventure, indeed.

* * * * *

RISKY
ENGAGEMENT

BY
MERLINE LOVELACE

First published in Great Britain 2011
by Mills & Boon, an imprint of Harlequin (UK) Limited,
Eton House, 18-24 Paradise Road, Richmond, Surrey TW9 1SR

© Merline Lovelace 2010

ISBN: 978 0 263 88532 3

46-0611

Harlequin (UK) policy is to use papers that are natural, renewable and
recyclable products and made from wood grown in sustainable forests. The
logging and manufacturing processes conform to the legal environmental
regulations of the country of origin.

Printed and bound in Spain
by Blackprint CPI, Barcelona

Dear Reader,

Have you ever planned the perfect vacation, only to have one disaster after another occur? That's what happened when we jaunted down to Cabo San Lucas with our best pals, Neta and Dave. But even disasters can turn into fun with the right attitude—and they make terrific fodder for books!

I hope you enjoy this, the latest in my *Code Name: Danger* series. And be sure to check my website at www.merlinelovelace.com for news, information, contests, and releases yet to come.

Merline Lovelace

A retired Air Force officer, **Merline Lovelace** served at bases all over the world, including tours in Taiwan, Vietnam and at the Pentagon. When she hung up her uniform for the last time, she decided to combine her love of adventure with a flair for storytelling, basing many of her tales on her experiences in the service.

Since then, she's produced more than eighty action-packed novels, many of which have made *USA TODAY* and Waldenbooks bestseller lists. More than ten million copies of her works are in print in thirty countries. Named Oklahoma's Writer of the Year and the Oklahoma Female Veteran of the Year, Merline is also a recipient of Romance Writers of America's prestigious RITA® Award.

Prologue

Sweat trickled down his temple, into his eye. Impatiently, Wolf blinked it away. He and his team had kept the hacienda perched atop a sun-baked cliff under surveillance for two days and two long nights now. From all indications, the bastard who owned it would make his move soon. And when he did, Wolf would take him down.

In the meantime, he was close to broiling under the afternoon sun. Summers in this corner of Mexico's Los Cabos Peninsula could be brutal. October wasn't much better. It didn't help that the azure sea shimmered in the distance, making a

mockery of the sweat plastering his camouflage
shirt to his back and—

"El Lobo!"

The low exclamation brought his gaze whipping
to the man stretched out a few feet away on the
dry, baked earth. He was one of Mexico's elite,
handpicked by Wolf's counterpart for this op. Like
Wolf, he was covered from head to toe in desert
fatigues and dripping in sweat.

"Someone comes," he whispered urgently. "A
woman. Not from here, I think."

He edged to one side so Wolf could take his
place at the high-powered scope. Tripod mounted
and over a foot long when fully extended, the
scope packed almost enough power to pick out
Neil Armstrong's footprints on the moon. More
than enough to display in startlingly precise
detail, the female trudging along the unpaved road
leading to the hacienda they were keeping under
surveillance.

His jaw locked, Wolf catalogued sweat-streaked,
honey-brown hair showing beneath a wide-brimmed
straw hat. Oversize designer sunglasses hid the
upper half her face, but the lower half showed a
mouth set in tight lines. A rumpled linen sundress
in a pale green color, bared shoulders showing the
first flush of sunburn.

"That's it," Wolf growled, when she paused at the gate cut into the high walls surrounding the hacienda's vast acreage and tipped her sun glasses to peer at the phone box beside the gate. "Com'on, *chica*. Take 'em off and give me a good target."

He centered the crosshairs on her face. Slowly, so slowly, she slid the glasses down an inch. Two. With a grunt of satisfaction, Wolf nailed her.

Chapter 1

Autumn had painted the chestnut trees lining the quiet side street in the heart of Washington D.C.'s embassy district with brilliant color. The blazing reds and oranges and golds lent a festive, almost carnival air to the stately town houses shaded by their branches.

There was nothing festive in the air inside the town house midway down the block, however. A bronze plaque beside the door identified the building as home to the offices of the President's Special Envoy. Most Washington insiders knew the special envoy was one of those meaningless titles given by various administrations over the years to wealthy campaign contributors who wanted to rub elbows with the country's movers and shakers.

Only a handful of key presidential advisors knew the special envoy's real job. The incumbent also doubled as Director of OMEGA, an agency so secret its operatives were activated as a last resort, and then at the personal direction of the president.

One of those operatives was in the field now. And the shot he'd taken just moments ago had sent everyone in the high-tech control center on the third floor of the town house into a frenzy of activity.

Nick Jensen, code name Lightning, had served as OMEGA's director through three successive administrations. This one, he'd promised his wife and lively twins, would be his last. Until he walked out the door, however, he lived night and day with the knowledge that he put his agents' lives on the line every time he sent them into the field.

His eyes narrow and intent, Lightning studied the dual images projected onto the control center's wall-size screen. One was the face of the woman Wolf had captured in his crosshairs, digitized and transmitted back to OMEGA. The second image his people had pulled up after running the first through a highly sophisticated facial recognition program.

"Who is she?" he asked the tense operative standing next to him.

Deke Griffin, code name Ace, didn't hesitate. He'd acted as Wolf's controller from the start of this op, and he hadn't slept in almost forty-eight hours.

"Dr. Nina Nicole Grant," he replied, with no trace of his usual Texas twang. "Born Farmington, New Mexico. Graduated high school at sixteen. PhD in biology from University of New Mexico at twenty, followed three years later by an MBA from the same university."

A muscle ticked in the side of Lightning's jaw. "Smart woman."

"*Very* smart. She served as Director of Biomedical Research at Holbrook Laboratories. Left five years ago to start up Grant Medical Data Systems."

Ace paused, focusing intently on the left image. They'd pulled it from a *60 Minutes* segment on the latest crop of women to make the Fortune 500 list. The video still showed a slender businesswoman in a white blouse and neatly tailored black suit. Her light brown hair brushed her shoulders in a smooth, glossy sweep. Her caramel-colored eyes gazed at the camera with cool confidence.

"According to *60 Minutes*," he related tersely,

"Grant is well on her way to becoming one of the most successful entrepreneurs—male *or* female—under the age of thirty in this country."

"Smart and rich." The muscle in Lightning's jaw jumped again. "Just like DeWitt."

United States Senator Janice Dewitt, recently deceased. Victim or accomplice in a deadly, high-stakes game of espionage. It was OMEGA's job to find out which.

"What's Grant's connection to the target?"

"We haven't found one. We're still running her through the computers. If she and the target crossed paths anytime in the past, we'll smoke it out." Ace's eyes cut to the screen. "Maybe Wolf will have some luck on his end."

"He'd better," Lightning said, grimly. "We're fast running out of time. Tell him to make contact with Grant and nose out her game."

"Will do."

Ace flicked the switch on the console that put him in instant contact with Special Agent Rafe Blackstone, code name Wolf.

Wolf acknowledged Lightning's instructions, even as he kept the woman lined up in his scope. She'd lowered her oversize sunglasses just long enough for him to capture her image and transmit it instantly to OMEGA. The glasses were in place again, shielding her face, but he had her features imprinted on his brain. What he didn't have were answers to the questions her presence raised.

What the hell was she doing out here in the middle of nowhere? Alone. On foot. In the blazing sun. He tapped an impatient toe while a Hummer rattled down from the hacienda in answer to her call of a few moments ago.

"Paulo."

The figure stretched out beside Wolf cocked his head. "*Sí?*"

"Check the road from town. See if the woman has someone waiting for her."

With a nod, Special Agent Paulo Mendoza stuffed a pair of miniaturized but very high-powered binoculars into his shirt pocket and scuttled backward until he'd dropped below the line of sight of the hacienda's high-tech security cameras. Crouched low, he used the cover of prickly creosote and cactus to circle the base of the hill where he and Wolf had set up their surveillance. The only sound to mark his passage was a faint rattle of his boots on loose shale.

He returned mere moments later. "I spotted a car pulled over to the side of the road about a mile back. A rental, with the hood up."

Was it a ploy? A trick to gain entry to the heavily guarded hacienda? If so, it had worked. Wolf's stomach tightened as Grant climbed into the backseat of the dusty Hummer.

This had to be the rottenest vacation ever!

Forcing a smile, Nina declined her host's invitation to stay for tea on the tiled terrace overlooking the Sea of Cortez. She was hot and sweaty and in no mood for nice. Even with someone as urbane as the silver-maned expatriate whose men had just radioed in to say they'd reattached the fuel line that had shaken loose in Nina's rental.

"Thanks," she said with a smile, "but walking a mile in the sun took all the starch out of me. I'd better head back to town."

"Are you sure?" Sebastian Cordell's smile gleamed white against his deep tan. "It's not often such charming company is stranded almost at the gates of my hacienda."

"Some other time, perhaps."

"I shall hold you to that." Bowing, he kissed her hand with Old World graciousness. "My men will drive you to your car."

Nina winced as she traded the breeze-cooled shade of the portico for another blast of sun. With a nod to the muscled-up guard holding the Hummer's door, she climbed into the passenger seat.

Her escort's all-too-visible shoulder holster had sent her back a step when he'd first climbed out of his vehicle and asked her business. Tough Guy hadn't appeared the least bit sympathetic to her plight either. He'd checked inside her tote—for hidden weapons, she'd realized belatedly—then demanded to see some ID before he let her get anywhere close to the frigid air blasting from the Hummer interior. Sweat coursing between her breasts, Nina had handed over her wallet.

Not the smartest move, she admitted in retrospect, but this disaster was only the latest in a string of events that had thrown her off stride. The first was getting unengaged from the fiancé she'd discovered had tapped into her computer without her knowledge or consent and tried to milk the business connections she'd worked so hard to establish over the years. Connections that had helped transform her medical data digitization venture into a thriving enterprise with multimillion-dollar contracts.

You would think her employees would understand why she'd put her bruised heart into storage and devoted every waking hour to work. But no! Her entire staff, from her bossy executive assistant to the pimply adolescent who delivered the mail, had threatened to resign en masse if she didn't get out of the office and decompress, for God's sake!

So she *had* to fly down to Baja California. *Had* to check into an exclusive seaside resort. *Had* to twiddle her thumbs and force herself to vegetate by the pool for two days until a need to do something—anything—propelled her to jump in a rental car and drive out to view the remote seaside village her guidebook had touted as a "must see."

Then her rental car *had* to break down out there among the cactus and sun-baked hills. Where, she discovered, not a single bar popped up on her cell phone. Probably because she'd forgotten to charge the damn thing!

Thank God for the hacienda she'd spotted after a hot, dusty trek—and that the problem with her rental was so easily fixed. All she wanted now was a plunge in the pool at her resort, a frosty margarita, and some of that decompression time her staff insisted she needed.

Bracing herself for another blast of heat, Nina climbed out of the Hummer and thanked the two men who'd been sent to check the car. They sported shoulder holsters, too. Sebastian Cordell took his personal security seriously.

"Muchas gracias."

She fished a wad of pesos out of her straw tote, but the two men waved away the tip. Stuffing the pesos back in her bag, Nina thanked them again and slid behind the wheel. A dusty half hour later she hit the roundabout on the outskirts of Cabo San Lucas.

By then, a plunge in the pool had dropped well down her list of priorities. Her resort was another twenty minutes away. Her parched throat cried for something cold and wet—now! With that icy margarita in mind, she whipped the wheel and exited the roundabout. A screech of tires had her wincing and offering an apology to the vehicle that had pulled into the circle behind her.

"Sorry."

Luck was with her. She made only one wrong turn in Cabo's narrow streets before she found the multistory parking garage that served the inner harbor. The lower floors were full, but she zipped into an empty space on the fourth floor. Locking the rental car, she took the elevator down to the paved walkway leading to the marina.

According to her trusty guidebook, Cabo's protected inner harbor attracted sailboats and yachts from all over the world. A forest of tall silver masts validated that claim and acted as beacons to the restaurants, shops and bars lining the marina. Happy hour was in full swing Nina noted as she approached the crowded center. Lively salsa and mariachi music filled the air and souvenir hawkers had turned out en masse to capture the lucrative tourist trade.

She escaped most of the salesmen, but one particularly persistent youngster glued himself to her side. Flashing a grin, he flipped back a sleeve to display a skinny forearm banded with shiny bangles.

"*Hola, senorita!* You buy a bracelet from me, yes?"

"No, *gracias*."

"These very good quality silver. From Taxco."

Right. Uh-huh. If those bangles were products of Mexico's fabled silver mines, she was Angelina Jolie.

"They're very nice," she replied diplomatically, "but I don't wear silver."

"Very good quality," he chorused again, twisting off a braided band. "Here, you try."

"No. *Gracias*. No."

"You try! You try!"

He grabbed her arm and shoved the braided band at her clenched fist. Half suspecting a ploy to distract her while one of his cohorts lifted her wallet from the tote slung over her shoulder, she tried to pull her arm back.

"No! I don't—"

"You heard the lady. Beat it, kid."

The deep growl spun both Nina and the pint-size vendor around. She looked up—not a common occurrence for someone who measured five eight in her bare feet—and felt her stomach do a flip.

Whoa, momma! Not two minutes ago, she'd been thinking of Angelina Jolie. Now here was James McAvoy, Angelina's sexy costar in *Wanted*. Same dark hair, same blue bedroom eyes, same chiseled chin.

Only this version was tougher. Leaner. Definitely not into Hollywood chic. His boots had collected almost as much dust as Nina's sandals. His wrinkled khaki trousers and the gaudy tropical shirt he wore over a black T-shirt, looked as though he'd just pulled them out of a suitcase. And the man needed a shave. Badly.

Nina was no stickler for protocol. Well, maybe a little. Okay, a lot. She expected her employees to present a neat, businesslike appearance at all times. That applied equally to everyone, from her division heads to the medical data-entry clerks.

She was fair about it, though. She held herself to the same strict standards. She dressed well, if conservatively, and worked out regularly to maintain both her health and her trim figure. She was conservative in her makeup, too. A few swipes of mascara was all she needed to enhance her brown eyes. Peach lip gloss did the trick for her mouth—which she now forced into a polite smile.

"Thanks for the assistance," she said as the kid who'd dogged her footsteps scampered away. "The boy was nothing, if not persistent."

"You have to learn how to shake 'em off. Must be your first time in Cabo."

It was a statement, not a question, but she answered it anyway. "Yes, it is."

Those blue eyes made a slow descent from her wide-brimmed straw hat to her designer sunglasses to the lips her ex-fiancé had described as all too kissable.

That was before she'd handed the conniving rat his walking papers, of course. During their last, somewhat less than cordial meeting, Kevin had flung other descriptive phrases at her. "Hard" and "stubborn" and "a real ball-buster" came immediately to mind.

"I was just going to have a beer." The dark-haired stranger hooked a thumb at the open-air bar behind him. "Care to join me?"

Thirst battled with common sense. If Nina hadn't
been thinking of Kevin, odds were she would have
turned down this casual invitation, just as she had
that of the silver-maned hacienda owner. She *never*
cruised bars, much less let strange men pick her up.
But her parched throat and the remembered sting
of Kevin's insults overcame caution.

"Sure. Why not?"

The Purple Parrot looked much like the dozens
of other bars in the harbor area. Square tables
topped by chipped formica crowded its railed-in
veranda. Red and green-plastic chairs added a
colorful air, as did the plastic pennants strung from
corner to corner. Inside the bar itself were shelves
lined with a staggering array of bottles.

"Over there."

Grasping Nina's elbow, the stranger steered her
toward a just-vacated table with an unobstructed
view of the marina. The sudden and totally
unexpected sizzle that radiated up her bare arm
flustered her so much she barely took in the sea of
gleaming white sailboats.

"I'm Rafe," he said by way of introduction. "Rafe
Blackstone."

"Nina. Uh, Grant."

Oh, for pity's sake! The heat must have gotten
to her more than she'd realized. Bad enough she'd

given in to the impulse to have a drink with a man who looked like a cross between a movie stud and a hood. One touch, and said stud came close to finishing what the sun had started. She was practically melting under her linen sundress.

It had to be that dark stubble on his cheeks and chin. Or the way his black T-shirt stretched across a taut, flat belly when he leaned back in his chair and unfolded his long legs. Or the slow, considering look he gave her through a screen of ridiculously thick lashes that any woman would have killed for.

Whatever it was, Nina responded in a way she'd never responded before to any male, Kevin included. A delicious spark of heat licked at her veins, and she could feel the muscles low in her belly tighten. Surprised and not a little flustered by her reaction, she removed her sunglasses and tipped the man seated across from her another polite smile.

"Where's home, Rafe?"

"Here and there. Mostly San Diego these days. You?"

"Albuquerque."

"What do you do there?"

Before she could answer, a waiter materialized

at their table. She ordered a margarita on the rocks, her companion a Dos Equis.

"I own and operate a company that digitizes medical data," she said when the waiter retreated.

"That so?" He arched a brow. "Given the president's push to computerize the medical profession, your business must be thriving."

"It is…now. We had some lean years when we first started out," she admitted wryly. "Hospitals weren't exactly anxious to share patient data. Plus, we had to make sure we didn't violate privacy laws. We got our foot in the door by trending data from local sources and providing it to medical facilities and research facilities across the state." A touch of pride crept into her voice. "We now harvest information from more than three thousand sources, analyze the input, and supply trends to a host of private and governmental medical research centers across the U.S."

"Only the U.S.?"

His slouch was the epitome of lazy relaxation, but his obvious interest reassured Nina. She always worried about boring folks with her passion for what she did. Or worse, lapsing into so much technical jargon that she lost her listeners completely.

"We still have to work within privacy laws," she said, "but I'm hoping to go international soon."

The seemingly casual comment put a sudden kink in Wolf's gut. The woman wanted to go international, did she? With the help of Sebastian Cordell, aka Stephen Caulder, aka a half-dozen other aliases?

Or was she after the sensitive, top-secret information Cordell had stolen and intended to auction to the highest bidder? Had she staged her vehicle's breakdown? Used it as an entree into Cordell's heavily guarded compound? Was she that good?

Wolf was still trying to decide when the waiter delivered their drinks. The man placed two frosted glasses in front of Grant and earned a surprised look.

"I didn't order two drinks."

"This is happy hour, señorita. You order one, I bring two."

"But…"

"Same price. No problem."

She gave in with a shrug and a smile.

Wolf had to give her credit. She had that polite half smile down pat. Friendly, but with just enough reserve in it to keep a man at a proper distance.

Nina Grant didn't know it yet, he thought grimly, but the two of them were about to get up close and *very* personal.

The muscles low in his belly tightened at the prospect. This is what he did. What he'd done now for almost ten years. Why he kept to himself and trusted no one outside his immediate circle of friends and fellow agents. Over the years, he'd locked horns with too many men and women who'd crossed the line. In more than one instance, it was kill or be killed.

In this one…

He didn't have a fix on Nina Grant yet, and the uncertainty scraped on his nerves. Extracting the lime wedge from the neck of his beer, he tipped the bottle in her direction.

"Here's to international cooperation."

She clinked her frosted glass against the bottle. "I'll drink to that."

He let the lager slide down his throat, watching while she licked some salt from the rim before taking a sip of her drink. The small act was completely natural, the way most people tasted a margarita—and disturbingly provocative. Wolf's belly tightened another notch as he followed the movement of her tongue.

Come on, he urged silently. *Drink the damn thing.*

He knew from experience that two-for-one happy hour drinks at most Cabo San Lucas dives were usually so watered down you couldn't even taste the booze in them. The Purple Parrot, however, had a reputation to maintain. That's why he'd chosen it. Another double round, and he'd have Nina Grant singing like a tanked-up canary.

"How long have you lived in Albuquerque?" he asked to get the ball rolling.

"I got a job there after grad school and decided to stay. I love the climate. The people. The mountains. The incredible sunsets. Seems I've spent almost as much time traveling recently as I have at home, though. I almost cringe when I have to get on a plane these days."

Wolf pumped her for information, subtly, smoothly, and hid a smile of satisfaction when she took another taste of her drink.

"Whew! This is potent."

"Not that potent. It goes down easier after the first few sips."

"I'll bet." Her nose wrinkling, she set the glass aside. "It's hitting my empty stomach like a sledgehammer. I'd better stop with this one and head to my hotel."

So much for his plan to get her sloshed. No matter. He wasn't about to let her wiggle out of his net now.

"So let me buy you dinner."

Chapter 2

Nina blinked at Blackstone's unexpected invitation. An automatic refusal formed on her lips. Before she could voice it, his cell phone emitted a low, vibrating hum.

"'Scuse me." He slipped a sleek little jobbie out of his pocket and held it at an angle. "Sorry, I need to read this text message."

"No problem."

His face remained impassive as he scrolled the screen. She couldn't tell if the news was good or bad, but the brief interruption gave Nina time to reconsider his surprising offer of dinner.

She had to admit it was tempting. *Extremely*

tempting. She didn't need her string of degrees—or the intent look in this sexy stranger's eyes—to make the leap from drinks to dinner to a quick tumble into bed.

The mere thought made her throat go tight. It affected other parts of her, too. Parts that hadn't felt this sudden sizzle in way too long.

No surprise there. She was a biologist by training and a medical researcher by profession. She knew she possessed a normal, healthy sex drive. One that she and Kevin had made the most of. At first.

In the later stages of their engagement, their lovemaking had been less adventurous. It went decidedly flat when she began to suspect he'd courted her more for what she could do for him in the business arena than in the bedroom.

Maybe… Maybe this was just what she needed. An hour or two or three of hot, sweaty, completely mindless sex. What better way to get over the humiliation of Kevin's lies? How better to revalidate herself as a woman?

Ha! Who was she kidding? Inviting Blackstone back to her hotel had nothing whatsoever to do with validation, and a *whole* lot to do with his impact on her pulmonary system. The mere thought of peeling off his T-shirt and popping the snap on those wrinkled khaki's constricted her lungs and put a lump the size of Rhode Island in her throat.

Unfortunately, the biologist in her didn't have to delve very deep to compile a comprehensive list of diseases she could pick up by exchanging bodily fluids with a total stranger. Even one as hot as Rafe Blackstone. *Especially* one as hot as Blackstone. With a stab of real regret, she groped for the tote bag hooked over the back of her chair.

"Thanks, but I'll pass on dinner, too. Let me pay for the drinks."

"I'll get them."

"Really, I want to. I've enjoyed our—"

"I've got it covered."

Oooh-kay. She dropped her wallet back into her tote. That was twice today she'd stepped on it: first with the guys who'd fixed the fuel line on her rental, now with Blackstone. Guess she shouldn't have let his bristles and rumpled shirt mislead her into thinking he would appreciate a woman who preferred to pay her own way.

"I'll walk you to your car."

She started to decline the offer. The vendors milling outside the bar, waiting to pounce, changed her mind. With the sun gone down and the crowds of tourists thinning out, they would swarm all over her. Why not let this lean, tough-looking gringo deal with them?

Which he did, with a few well-chosen words. He also took her arm to weave a path for her through the grumbling souvenir hawkers. His hold was loose but oddly possessive. To Nina's consternation, the feel of his callused palm raised goose bumps over every exposed inch of skin.

She covered her involuntary reaction with a nod toward the rapidly darkening sky. "Cools off fast when the sun goes down, doesn't it?"

"It does," he replied, and promptly tucked her closer into his side.

His scent enveloped her. The seductive blend of sun-warmed skin and healthy male sweat retriggered the erotic sensations Nina was so determined to repress. Gulping, she tried to focus on the dramatic red-and-gold streaks in the dark sky, the raucous beat of music coming from the restaurants, anything but the man beside her.

She failed miserably and breathed a distinct sigh of relief when they reached the parking garage. Easing free of his hold, she punched the button for the fourth floor.

"Thanks again for the drinks."

"I'll ride up with you."

She turned to him with a polite but firm no

on her lips. He spiked it with a shrug and casual remark.

"This part of town is usually pretty safe, but a couple of tourists were mugged in this garage a few days ago."

Common sense prevailed. Parking garages in any part of the world could be risky. No sense tempting fate.

Which was exactly what she was doing by prolonging her brief association with Blackstone. She wasn't fooling anyone, herself included. The tingling awareness of his proximity, the delicious feeling of temptation rode all the way up to the fourth floor with her.

They stepped out into cavernous gloom. Their footsteps echoed as Nina led the way up the ramp, glad now that she'd accepted Blackstone's escort. The garage had emptied considerably since her arrival. Probably because most of the businesses in town that didn't cater exclusively to the tourist trade had closed for the day. Her rental now sat by itself at the end of the row.

Digging the keys out of her tote, she clicked the remote. The lights flashed, the locks popped, and she turned to her escort once more. He was close. A little too close. She put on a cool smile.

"Thanks again. I enjoyed—"

"Let me have the keys."

"Excuse me?"

"Give me the keys. I'll drive you back to your hotel."

Okay, enough is enough. Lifting her chin, Nina shook her head.

"Look, I don't know what signals you think I sent there at the bar, but you read them wrong."

"Give me the keys."

When he took a step closer, crowding her against the car, fright exploded in her chest. How stupid was this? How stupid was *she?*

She threw a wild glance down the ramp. Nothing moved. Not a single person walked to or from a car. No headlights stabbed through the gloom. She was on her own here.

Her throat clogged with fear, she tried to recall any of the moves from the self-defense courses she'd taken over the years. All she could remember, all she could think of was to yell her head off and gouge her attacker's eyes with her car keys.

She fumbled the pointed ends between her fingers, balled her fist, and screamed for help. Or tried to. She didn't emit much more than a squeak before Blackwater clapped a hard hand over her mouth. His other hand batted away the arm she'd brought up in a vicious arc.

She fought him, using every bit of her strength, but he was too big, too strong. Reaching behind her, he ripped open the car door and shoved her inside.

Her heart hammering in terror, Nina landed in a sprawl across the driver's seat. Pure instinct brought her knee up and her foot lashing out. Blackstone dodged the kick aimed at his groin, and took it on the outside of his thigh instead.

"Calm down!" he got out with a grunt of pain. "I'm not going to hurt you."

Right. Uh-huh. Sure.

She wasn't about to take his word for it. With his unyielding presence blocking the exit, she scrambled over the center console and made a desperate lunge for the passenger door. Cursing, he dropped into the driver's seat and wrapped fingers of steel around her upper arm. A swift yank jerked her back down.

"Listen to me. I'm not going to hurt you."

"Then let me go!"

"Not yet. And not here." He kept her in place with an iron fist. "We need to talk, Dr. Grant."

Dr. Grant?

The title penetrated her wild fear. She hadn't used the honorific in conversation. She was sure she hadn't. She rarely did, and then only in professional circles. So how did he know?

"Who are you?" she panted. "What do you want to talk to me about?"

"I'll tell you at the Mayan Princess."

Oh, Lord! He knew where she was staying. Had he followed her from the resort? Been following her the entire day?

He couldn't have! She would have spotted him out on that winding, dusty road before her rental broke down.

If it *had* broken down. What if he'd sabotaged her car? Anticipated that she'd be stranded out there in the middle of nowhere? Which she would have been, if she hadn't trudged a mile through the hot sun to Sebastian Cordell's hacienda. Or was that part of his diabolical plan, too?

The questions hammered at her as he eased his brutal grip, but she decided not to stick around for the answers. She made another grab for the door handle, only to hear the door locks snick.

"Child protective locks," he commented laconically as she tugged futilely on the handle.

Grinding her teeth in frustration, she sank back against the seat. Her cell phone was in her tote, she remembered. With a dead battery. Her last hope she thought as her abductor keyed the ignition, was the garage attendant.

Except there wasn't one. The booth where she'd forked over a fee when she'd entered was now empty. Apparently, anyone who drove in after the main businesses and shops closed got to park free.

Nor was there a police officer anywhere in sight when they pulled out of the garage and hit the streets. Nina seriously considered hammering on the window to attract the attention of the people out for a late evening stroll. A return of her common sense—and gradual subsiding of panic—subdued the impulse.

Blackstone said he didn't intend to hurt her. He also said he'd tell her what he wanted from her at the Mayan. That meant he had to pull up at the entrance to the posh resort, where the extremely well-trained parking valet, doorman and desk clerks all knew her by name. Blackstone could hardly waltz into the resort with her and waltz out again, leaving behind her dead and/or mutilated body and a small army of people who could ID him.

Could he?

She'd more or less reassured herself on that point by the time the resort appeared in the distance.

She'd also worked up as much reluctant curiosity as distrust. What the heck did this man want with her? She was pretty sure now it wasn't sex, and was shocked by the contradictory feelings that realization generated.

"Turn here," she muttered as they approached the long, winding drive that led up to the resort. When he flipped on the directionals, the lingering remnants of Nina's fear eased. He really *was* taking her back to the Mayan. She let out a low sigh of relief.

The resort was the latest in a string of San Cabo resorts that included Westin and Ritz Carlton and other high-priced escapes. Constructed to resemble a Mayan temple, the main building sat on a cliff overlooking the sea. Tall palms lined the drive leading up to it. Lit by floodlights, they provided an exotic approach to the stunningly dramatic pyramid gleaming against the night sky.

As Nina had anticipated, a valet came forward when the car rolled to a stop. He had to wait for Blackstone to hit the lock release to open her door. When he did, she scrambled out with considerably more haste than dignity.

"*Buenas tardes,* Dr. Grant. Did you have a good drive this afternoon?"

"I've had better, Ramon." Determined to

establish a record of events, Nina pointed to the driver rounding the front end of the car. "This is Señor Blackstone. Rafe Blackstone. He's visiting me. For a *short* time."

Ramon took the hint. "*Buenas tardes,* Señor. Will you need this car when you leave? If so, I will park it here by the entrance instead of taking it down to the lot."

"Here's good." Blackstone slipped him a folded bill with the car keys and took Nina's elbow. "Lead the way."

She did, making sure to repeat his name to the doorman and the clerks on duty in the breezeway that served as a reception area.

"There's a waiter over there by the pool," Blackstone drawled. "You want to introduce me to him, too?"

"You think this is funny?" she huffed. "Somehow, I don't find kidnapping amusing. Neither, I suspect, would the local police."

"Police down in these parts take a different view of things, but you can call them if you want. Ask for Chief Inspector Mannie Diaz. Tell him you're with me."

"Well, for…!"

Thoroughly indignant, Nina came to a dead stop. Hands on hips, she faced her tormentor.

"Why didn't you tell me you're a cop back there in town instead of scaring the crap out of me?"

"I'm not a cop."

"Oh. Well." That set her back a bit, but she recovered quickly. "So what are you?"

"We'll talk about that in your suite. Where is it?"

"You don't know?" she said snidely. "You seem to know everything else."

Ignoring the comment, he urged her through the open-air lobby to the pool beyond. It was one of four at the resort. Two catered to families, the other two to adults only. The one on this level was an infinity pool, its floodlit waters seeming to flow over the edge and drop straight into the sea far below.

Instead of booking her into the main hotel, Nina's superefficient assistant had reserved one of the casitas that clung to the cliffs behind the pyramid. They were quieter and more private— qualities Nina had very much appreciated until this moment.

Some of her nervousness returned as she led the way down several flights of steps and around bougainvillea-draped walls. The only sounds to disturb the evening quiet were the soft music emanating from hidden speakers along the walkways and the ever-present murmur of the sea.

By the time she'd reached her casita, however, her indignation had returned. Along with it came a healthy bout of anger. Fishing her key card out of her tote, she unlocked the door and marched inside. The spacious, beautifully decorated unit featured tile floors, a fully equipped kitchen, one bedroom with a master bath to die for and a small Jacuzzi tucked in a corner of the balcony that was suspended over the sea.

Nina didn't give her uninvited guest time to admire the ambience. Flinging her tote on a sofa covered in muted jungle print, she folded her arms across her chest.

"All right, Blackstone. If that's really your name. What's this all about?"

"It's really my name," he confirmed, glancing around. When those laser blue eyes came back to Nina, they sliced into her like a scalpel. "And this is about your friend, Sebastian Cordell."

"Huh?"

Of all the things she'd expected... Okay, she hadn't known *what* to expect. But this certainly wasn't it.

"Are you talking about the older gentleman I met this afternoon?"

"I'm talking about the man who invited you into his hacienda this afternoon." His jaw hardened. "As for whether or not he's a gentleman, you tell me."

This was getting way too bizarre. Frowning, Nina tapped a foot. "Before I tell you anything, *I* want some answers. Who are you and who do you work for?"

"I told you my name. Most of the time I run a marine construction company."

"Other times?"

"I do independent consulting. Hazard elimination. Debris removal. That sort of thing."

The sideline seemed legitimate. It was just the way he said it. As though there was more to removing debris than hauling it off in dump trucks or barges.

Nina's foot tapped again. "I want to see some ID."

With a sardonic shrug, he extracted a well-worn leather wallet from his back pocket and flipped it open to a California driver's license.

There he was. Rafael Conall Blackstone. Height, 6'2". Hair: black. Eyes: Blue. Weight: a really buff 180.

"'Conall'?"

"My grandmother's Irish." A gleam flickered in

his eyes, quickly come and just as quickly gone. "It translates to 'strong wolf'."

For some reason, the fact that he had a grandmother made him seem more human. Less dangerous. Which she knew was really absurd. Like murderers and rapists didn't?

"My turn." He slid the wallet back into his pocket. "What were…"

"Not so fast, Blackstone. I'm not finished yet."

Impatience rippled across his face. Making an obvious effort to contain it, he hooked one of the high stools from the marble counter separating the kitchen from the dining area and swung it around.

Nina gave a huff of disgust. "Make yourself comfortable, why don't you?"

He did, with one long leg braced against the floor tiles and the other propped on the stool's rung. "What else do you want to ask me?"

"Oh, just a few little things. Like how you knew I hold a PhD. And where I'm staying. And that I met Sebastian Cordell this afternoon. Oh, yes—one more. There's also the question of why in hell you didn't ask me about this guy in town instead of kidnapping and scaring the crap out of me!"

He had the grace to look a little ashamed. Not

much. Just enough to suggest he didn't go around abducting women every day of the week.

"Yeah, well, I'm sorry about that. To tell the truth, I planned to pour a couple more margaritas down you, get you loose, and pump you for information there at the Purple Parrot. When that didn't work, you forced me to resort to more direct measures."

"*What* information?"

"For starters, how you know Cordell."

"I don't know him! Or I didn't, before my car broke down this afternoon."

"Pretty convenient, how you arranged for it to break down so close to his compound."

"'Convenient'?" Nina echoed, incredulously. "'Arranged'?"

Thoroughly flummoxed, she groped for the other bar stool and yanked it closer so she could plop down. This whole thing was becoming more absurd by the moment.

"Why would I 'arrange' a breakdown?"

The rueful note disappeared from his voice. Hard and sharp-edged, it cut through the air between them.

"Maybe because Sebastian Cordell has some- thing to sell. Something you might want," he added, his eyes locked on hers. "You and a number of other *entrepreneurs.*"

The small sneer accompanying the last word brought Nina's chin up with a snap. She'd worked damn hard to establish her company. She'd sunk every penny of her savings into start-up costs, then borrowed heavily to purchase the building Grant Medical Data Systems now operated out of. The first months—the first years—had been scary as hell.

But she'd pulled it off. By sheer luck and perfect timing, she'd gotten in on the ground floor of a burgeoning and very necessary industry, and now turned an extremely healthy profit. One no one could sneer at!

Bristling, she poked a finger at Blackstone's chest. "You listen to me, fella. I'm going to say this one time and one time only. I did not arrange to have my car break down. I did not use it as a ploy to meet Sebastian Cordell. And I am *not* interested in whatever the man has for sale."

"Then why…"

The shrill ring of the phone sitting at the end of the counter cut him off.

"That," Nina announced, with fierce satisfaction, "is most likely Ramon, checking to see if he should move the car to the parking lot. I'll tell him to call you a taxi."

"Not yet."

"Yes, yet! This conversation is over." Glaring at him, she snatched up the receiver. *"Hola."*

The smooth, cultured voice that came through the earpiece made her swallow. Hard. With a helpless look in Blackstone's direction, she responded to the gracious inquiry.

"Yes, Mr. Cordell, I made it home safely."

Every muscle in Blackstone's body went taut. His narrowed gaze drilled into Nina as she clutched the receiver.

"What? Lunch tomorrow at your hacienda? I... Uh..."

Chapter 3

Wolf's gut twisted. Cordell! The prey he'd been sent to take down. The same bastard suspected of extracting top secret information from a United States senator. Now oozing his poisonous charm into Nina Grant's ear.

And here Wolf had come so close to believing the woman. Almost swallowed her tale of a breakdown. Damn near let her air of righteous indignation and melting, brown-sugar eyes convince him she'd flown down to Cabo on vacation as she claimed.

Yet…

The terse message Ace had texted a little while ago indicated they'd come up empty at their end.

OMEGA could access a host of databases, public, private and otherwise. Wolf knew damn well they'd run Nina Grant through every one. Yet none of the agency's wizards had been able to turn up a connection between Grant and Sebastian Cordell. As far as they could tell, she was clean.

Until this moment, everything in Wolf concurred with that assessment. He'd lived on the razor's edge so long he'd learned to trust his instincts where people were concerned. The short time he'd spent with her had him ninety-nine-percent convinced Nina Grant was the busy exec on vacation she claimed to be. The finger she'd poked in his chest moments ago had just about clinched the matter in his mind.

He had only a second to decide whether to go with his gut-level assessment. A mere heartbeat, while she looked at him, wide-eyed and stuttering, to come up with an answer to Cordell's invitation.

"Yes," Wolf hissed. "Tell him yes!"

He could see the doubt in her face, the distrust. Her knuckles were white on the receiver, her body taut with indecision. He was sure she would refuse his urgent request when she cleared her throat.

"Lunch sounds delightful, Mr. Cordell." Her eyes remained locked on Wolf's. "Twelve-thirty it is. No, no need to send someone to pick me up. I'll drive myself. What? Oh. Right. I guess I do need your phone number in case I get lost or stranded again. Let me get a pen."

Wolf had Cordell's numbers. All of them. But he kept silent while she hunted down a pencil and jotted a string of digits on a paper napkin.

"I've got it. Thanks. I'll...I'll see you tomorrow."

He was in! Or she was. Wolf contained his fierce elation as she hung up the receiver and stared at it blankly for a few seconds.

"I can't believe I just did that." Her eyes lifted to his. "*Why* did I just do that?"

"I can't speak to the why," he said slowly, "but I'll tell you this. A whole bunch of folks will be real happy that you did."

"At the risk of repeating myself...why?"

He sifted the details in his mind, sorting out what he could and couldn't tell her, and decided on the varying shades of the truth.

"I told you I freelance on occasion."

"Right." Her forehead crinkling, she repeated the line he'd given her. "At which time you specialize in eliminating hazards and removing debris."

"One of those hazards is Sebastian Cordell."

"Aha!"

Despite the seriousness of the situation, a grin

tugged at the corners of Wolf's mouth. "Aha"? Who said "aha" these days, outside of a slapstick comedy? Dr. Nina Grant, apparently.

She looked indignant again, like a tabby cat who'd been about to pounce and got its whiskers pulled instead.

"So that story about being into marine construction was just that?" she huffed. "A story?"

"No, that part's true. I do this as a sideline."

"Some sideline!" Frowning, she chewed on her lower lip for a few moments. "So why do you consider Sebastian Cordell a hazard?"

"We suspect he courted and seduced the senior senator from Maine."

"Janice DeWitt?" she gasped. "The senator who died in a car accident a few weeks ago?"

"There's some question," Wolf said carefully, "whether it was an accident or a suicide." Or something else.

So far the FBI and Secret Service had managed to suppress the evidence indicating that a member of the U.S. Congress had deliberately driven her vehicle through a guardrail and over a rocky cliff. Likewise the gut-wrenching e-mail she'd sent the President Pro Tem of the Senate, confessing that a disk encrypted with highly classified information might have been compromised by the man she'd taken as a lover.

"We also suspect," Wolf continued soberly, "Cordell may have used the senator to gain access to extremely sensitive top secret information."

Nina took a step back, and her shock that a popular, charismatic senator had indulged in an extramarital affair and possibly committed suicide took an instant and very personal turn. The information Kevin had downloaded from her personal computer certainly wasn't top secret, but it *had* been crucial to her business. She would have shared it with him if he'd asked. Not all of it, of course, just the nonproprietary data that might have been useful to his financial planning and investment operation. That he'd dug into her private files without her knowledge or consent had stunned her. That he'd leveraged the data he'd extracted to benefit one of her competitors had royally pissed her off.

"Bastard," she muttered.

"Yeah, he is."

Pulled back to the present, she blinked. "I was referring to the jerk who pulled almost the same thing on me."

Blackstone cocked his head. "How so?"

It embarrassed her to admit how blind she'd

been. She had to force herself to recap the sorry details.

"My fiancé stole proprietary information and sold it to a competitor. Correction, make that ex-fiancé."

She wasn't looking for sympathy. Good thing, because the man seated on the bar stool a few feet from her didn't display so much as a trace of it. Instead, a gleam of satisfaction leapt into his blue eyes.

"Then you understand why we're so anxious to nail Sebastian Cordell."

"I understand it," Nina replied cautiously, "but I don't see how my having lunch with him will help."

"We've been trying to get someone inside the compound. Unfortunately, Cordell's goon squad take their duties very seriously."

"I noticed."

"But Cordell just issued you an engraved invitation. We can fit you with a hidden camera, have you—"

"Whoa! Hold on there, Blackstone."

With the shoulder holsters strapped onto the goons he'd just mentioned all too vivid in her mind, Nina scrambled off her stool and backed away.

"I'm not into playing spy games."

"This isn't a game," he fired back.

"Yes, well, whatever it is, I'll leave it to the pros like you."

Blackstone vacated his stool and followed her into the living area. Like the rest of the casita, the room was elegantly furnished. A three-section sofa in muted colors formed a conversation pit, with a monster slab of white-veined black marble in the middle to serve as a coffee table. Facing the sofas was an entertainment center containing a sixty-inch flat screen TV, a DVD player, an assortment of recent movies and an iPod dock.

Nina's iPod and earbuds were still in her straw tote, so the only sound in the room, as she faced Blackstone was the restless murmur of the sea below the balcony, just off the living area.

"We need your cooperation, Dr. Grant. Cordell plans to auction the information he stole to the highest bidder. If it falls into the wrong hands—an unfriendly government or a terrorist organization, for instance—it could seriously jeopardize U.S. national security."

"Oh, sure. Lay the safety and security of the United States on my shoulders, why don't you?"

Nervously, Nina swiped her palms down the side seams of her linen sundress. She'd always considered herself a good citizen. She paid her taxes on time, donated to a number of charities, gave blood regularly and volunteered at a homeless shelter one weekend a month.

She did not, however, in any way, shape or form, see herself as a modern day Mata Hari. The prospect of entering Sebastian Cordell's heavily guarded compound with a camera hidden somewhere on her person made her break out in a cold sweat.

"Look, Blackstone, I'd like to help. I really would. This just isn't my area of expertise."

"We have from now until tomorrow noon. I'll make sure you know what you're doing before you go in."

Her palms froze in midswipe. "From now until tomorrow noon?" she echoed. "What are you planning to do? Camp out here tonight?"

"If that's what it will take to make you comfortable with the operation."

If anything, the prospect of spending the next twelve-plus hours in close quarters with Rafe Blackstone made her twice as nervous.

"It won't work," she told him firmly. "I'm the world's worst liar. Even a little social fib makes my face turn red, and I can't look people in the eye."

"Must be tough to conduct business negotiations," he drawled.

"Not particularly," she snapped, her chin coming up. "I conduct negotiations fairly and honestly."

The icy reply knifed through the air like a blade. Blackstone dipped his head in acknowledgment of the hit and hooked his thumbs in the pockets of his wrinkled khakis. The movement swung open the flaps of his jungle print shirt and gave Nina an unobstructed view of black cotton stretched across a muscled chest, but she was too miffed to appreciate the view.

"About those negotiations," he said, with a considering look. "Didn't you tell me earlier that your company supplies medical trend data to a host of private and governmental research centers?"

"Yes. So?"

"So I'm guessing government contracts must account for a sizable chunk of your business."

Nina drew in a swift breath. Government contracts accounted for more than a chunk. They constituted almost half of her business base.

"You'd better not be thinking what I think you're thinking, Blackstone!"

"If you're thinking those contracts can be cancelled with one phone call, I guess I am."

He didn't so much as blink. The bald-faced effrontery of it, the sheer gall, made Nina gasp.

"I don't believe this! You're actually trying to blackmail me into helping you?"

"Not trying, Dr. Grant."

He was dead serious. She could see it in his eyes, in the set of his jaw. She open her mouth to tell him go straight to hell. Then she remembered how many people she had on her payroll and snapped it shut again.

She'd worked so hard to build her business. Everyone at Grant Medical Systems had. Without their government contracts, she would have to cut back. Lay off a dozen or more employees. Grinding her teeth, she yielded.

"All right. I'll scout out Cordell's compound for you. Just so you know, though, he and my sleaze of an ex-fiancé aren't the only bastards I've encountered lately."

Wolf hid a wince. Exploiting snitches and useful contacts were part of *his* business. He'd never hesitated to strong-arm anyone into cooperating before. He wouldn't hesitate in the future. That didn't lessen the bite from the scorn in Nina Grant's brown eyes—or explain why it bothered him so much.

"I need to contact my people and have them send the equipment."

She waved a hand toward the phone on the

counter and treated him to a caustic smile. "Be my guest."

"I'll use my own."

He slid back the balcony doors and went outside. The triangular hot tub tucked into a corner of the deck drew a wry smile. Not a good spot for the acrophobic, suspended over the sea the way it was. But the bubbling water and the waves pounding against the rocky shore below provided an excellent sound buffer for a private conversation.

As he had at the Purple Parrot, Wolf angled the instrument so its built-in iris scanner instantly identified him. One click of a key connected him to OMEGA control. Ace's unshaven face filled the screen.

"What's happening, pardner?"

"A new development." His glance cut to the woman standing rigid with anger in the center of the living room. "Dr. Grant's having lunch at Cordell's hacienda tomorrow."

"Damn! We scrubbed her, Wolf. Up one side and down the other. We couldn't find a connection."

"She swears there isn't one, other than the chance meeting this afternoon."

"So what's with lunch?"

"I suspect Cordell researched her, too. As

we both know, the man has a taste for wealthy, attractive women."

His glance raked Nina Grant from head to foot. Attractive didn't really describe the doc. She wasn't what Hollywood types would label a classic beauty. Her chin was too stubborn and her mouth lacked the collagen pout that seemed to be the standard these day. Especially now, when she'd folded her lips into a tight, angry line and her eyes shot daggers at the man who'd invaded her luxury casita.

She had one hell of a body, though. Long and well toned and curved in all the right places. When he'd followed her along the pathway to the marina, Wolf had caught more than enough of her silhouette backlighted through her linen dress to know he'd give her his vote anytime, any place.

Ace's low whistle jerked his attention away from Nina Grant and back to the business at hand. "You think Cordell is planning to hit on her, the way he did DeWitt?"

"I think it's a distinct possibility."

"Does she know that?"

"No, but I'll make sure she does before she joins him for lunch tomorrow."

Ace lifted a brow. "She's cooperating with us?"

"She is, although she's not real happy about it."

Guilt bit at Wolf again as he explained about the government contracts. "I want her rigged out before she goes in, Ace. Tell Mac we need the best she's got in her bag of tricks."

"Will do."

Mackenzie Blair had served as guru of all things electronic for OMEGA and several other highly specialized government agencies until the birth of her twins. She was now on an extended leave of absence but still provided her expertise to OMEGA on request. Not surprising, since she was married to Nick Jensen.

"I'll take care of it," Ace promised. "You should have a delivery within the next couple hours."

"Have them deliver it to the Mayan Princess. Dr. Grant's casita."

"Roger that. And I'll update Lightning when I contact Mac."

"Thanks."

Flipping the phone shut, Rafe went back inside.

"Okay," he told the woman standing with her back stiff and her arms crossed, regarding him with all the warmth she would one of Mexico's spiny iguanas. "I've got some equipment on the way. It should be here in a few hours."

"What kind of equipment?"

"A special camera. It will be so small you won't even know you're wearing it. You can…"

"Good God!" Her arms dropped. "You were really serious? You want to rig me out with spy gadgets?"

"We'll rig you out with more than a gadget. The woman responsible for our electronic surveillance devices is the best in the business."

And diabolically clever. Mackenzie Blair had sent agents into the field equipped with everything from invisible skin patches with embedded satellite communication capability, to a translucent jade pendant that emitted silent and completely disabling ultrahigh-frequency sound waves.

"Count on whatever device she sends being completely invisible to the untrained eye," Wolf assured his extremely reluctant recruit.

"Untrained being the operative word."

Grant shook her head stubbornly, her soft brown hair swirling around her face.

"Cordell's goons, as you call them, almost did a strip search before they let me through the gate this afternoon. What if they do the same tomorrow?"

"Trust me, they won't detect whatever we equip you with."

"*Trust* you?" Scorn dripped from every word. "You expect me to trust a man who scares me half to death, then blackmails me into cooperating with him?"

Wolf bit back a sigh. He could tell it was going to be a long night.

"Sit down, Dr. Grant. I'll talk you through exactly what I want you to do, step by step."

As promised, Ace briefed Lightning when he contacted him and Mac at home that evening. He briefed the boss again at 11:00 a.m. DC time the next morning, following a terse update from Wolf.

After checking the status board to confirm Lightning was in his office, Ace took the titanium-shielded elevator that zipped individuals from the control center to the offices of the special envoy on the first floor. Before exiting, he checked the security screen displaying the entire first-floor reception area. Although Lightning's executive assistant had cleared him to see the boss, Chelsea Jackson was relatively new to OMEGA operations. She'd replaced silver-haired Elizabeth Wells, who'd retired a few months ago and waltzed off into the sunset with the orthopedic surgeon who'd done her hip replacement.

Jackson was brisk and efficient, but a number of OMEGA operatives—Ace included—had yet to warm up to her. Maybe because she *was* so brisk and efficient. In contrast to grandmotherly Elizabeth, Ms. Jackson kept her personal life private and maintained a polite but firm distance from the field agents.

The shield was in place when she greeted Ace. "I informed Lightning you were on your way down," she said in her cool, Boston brahman voice. "Go right in."

Ace stifled the impulse to linger beside her Louis XV desk and coax a smile out of the woman. What he had for Lightning was too urgent. He couldn't resist revving up his Texas twang, however.

"Thanks, darlin'."

She did her best to hide a flicker of annoyance while she pressed the hidden button that gave him access to Lightning's private office. Ace caught it though, and allowed himself a brief grin before he entered the inner sanctum.

As befitted the President's Special Envoy, the office contained enough polished mahogany to panel a medium-size castle. Bypassing the conference table that took up a good portion of the room, Ace took one of the high-backed chairs set in front of Lightning's desk.

"I just briefed the president an hour ago on our plan to infiltrate Cordell's compound," OMEGA's tawny-haired director said. "I hope you're not going to tell me there's been a change of direction."

"Sorry, Chief. There has."

Sighing, Nick loosened the knot of his red silk tie. He'd held this job long enough to know nothing ever went down as originally orchestrated. Given the stakes in this op, however, he'd hoped for the best.

"What's the glitch?"

"Dr. Grant."

"She's changed her mind about cooperating?" he asked, sharply.

"She hasn't changed her mind. Wolf has. He says Grant doesn't have the makings of an undercover operative. The mere prospect of going in wired gets her all nervous and flustered. If we send her in alone, he's convinced she'll tip Cordell we're on to him."

"Damn it!" Blowing out a frustrated breath, Lightning thrust a hand through his sun-streaked hair. "She was our best bet for getting inside the compound."

"She still is, but Wolf is going with her."

"How?"

"Turns out Grant recently dumped her fiancé." A wry grin creased Ace's bristly, unshaven cheeks. "Wolf intends to step into his shoes."

Chapter 4

"You're crazy! All of you!"

Completely wrung out by her long, frustrating night, Nina glared at the three men facing her across the coffee table. Cups ringed with the dregs of the countless pots of coffee they'd consumed were scattered on the polished slab of marble, as were the remnants of the breakfast her uninvited guests had ordered from room service.

"It's the only way, Dr. Grant."

That came from Chief Inspector Manuel Diaz. Sad-eyed and scarecrow thin, Diaz and one of his henchmen had rapped on the door to Nina's casita well past midnight. They'd brought with them an almost microscopic wireless device hidden inside a pearl button. Flown in by jet at the request of El Lobo, Diaz had advised her.

El Lobo. The Wolf. Otherwise known as Rafe Blackstone. If that was really his name. Nina wouldn't put it past him to have faked that California driver's license.

He stood across from her now, hands on hips and his face set with a frustration to match hers. Tough! It wasn't her fault she couldn't work the damn camera. She'd *told* this guy, Wolf, she was a terrible liar. Although he and Mannie Diaz had done their best to coax her out of her jitters, she'd fumbled every attempt to appear nonchalant while scanning the interior of her own casita. So how the heck was she supposed to pull off scanning Cordell's entire hacienda, much less hide the listening device they wanted her to plant.

She'd finally given up around 4:00 a.m., and announced she was going to take a break while they figured out an alternate solution. They'd waited to drop that solution on her until late midmorning, after she'd finished a late breakfast of bacon and eggs scrambled with salsa, delivered by room service.

"If I can't carry off a hidden scanner," she threw at the three men lined up like a firing squad, "how in God's name do you expect me to carry off a pretend fiancé?"

Sad-eyed Mannie Diaz replied for all three. "This man, this Kevin James, he breaks your heart, yes?"

Actually, a few weeks of time and distance had made Nina realize Kevin the Jerk had hurt her pride more than her heart. She wasn't about to admit that to these three characters, however.

"Now this *estúpido* appears without warning here in Cabo San Lucas," Mannie continued. "He tells you he's sorry. He pleads with you to take him back. Of course you are upset and very confused. But you have accepted Cordell's invitation to lunch. It would be most impolite to back out now. So you call him, yes? You ask him—no, you *tell* him you have a guest you wish to bring with you."

"It won't work," she insisted, with a glare in Señor Wolf's direction. "You don't know anything about me. Where I went to high school. What kind of music I like."

"Farmington Regional High School," he fired back. "Mostly jazz and easy rock, with a hefty dose of show tunes thrown in for flavoring."

When Nina gaped at him, he gestured to the iPod sitting in the dock in the entertainment center.

"The music part was easy. And you left your tote

on the counter," he said without a trace of apology. "Between that and the information the people at my headquarters dug up on you, I know more than enough to play your very contrite lover."

"It won't work," she repeated, with a touch of desperation. "You may have gleaned a few facts about me, but I know nothing about you."

"I'll tell you all you need to know during the drive out to Cordell's place. At the same time, you can tell me about this guy you were engaged to. Pick up the phone, Nina. Call Cordell. Remember, this lunch is as much in your interest as ours."

"You," she got out through clenched teeth, "are really despicable."

He shrugged aside the insult with the same ease he'd shrugged aside her objections. "Tell Cordell exactly what Mannie said. Your fiancé arrived in Cabo unexpectedly and you'd like to bring him to lunch. Put that way, he can hardly refuse."

Outgunned and outmaneuvered, Nina marched over to the counter and dialed the number Cordell had given her. To her profound dismay, he responded to her nervous request with urbane charm.

"But of course you must bring your friend. I look forward to meeting him."

He'd taken the bait, and now she was on the

hook! Hanging up the phone, she treated Blackstone to another glare.

"Okay. You're in."

"Good." He checked his watch. "We don't have much time. You'd better get cleaned up."

She managed not to slam the bedroom door behind her, but it took some effort. A hot shower and some judicious swipes of eye shadow and lip gloss erased most of the effects of her long night. Her hair presented a real challenge, however. She attacked it with a brush, tried a curling iron and finally decided to just twist up the heavy mass and anchor it with a clip.

What to wear presented another problem. The button-front linen sundress she'd worn yesterday—and most of the night, until she'd finally changed into shorts and a T-shirt—*looked* like she'd worn it all day and half the night.

She jammed the dress into a laundry bag with a slip requesting same-day service and reached for the multicolored, ankle-length cotton skirt she'd purchased her first day in Cabo. She teamed it with a red silk tank, added a rhinestone-studded belt that rode low on her hips, then slipped her feet into sandals.

"This is insane," she muttered to the image in the mirror. "Absolutely insane."

When she came out of the bedroom, Rafe was gripping a leather carryall. "One of Mannie's men retrieved my gear from my hotel. Won't take me long to clean up."

"We will leave now," the chief inspector said as Blackstone headed for the bedroom, "so we can be in position when you arrive."

"Position?" Nina echoed.

"El Lobo and I, we have had Cordell's hacienda under surveillance for several days. We listen, too, but Cordell is very cautious."

"You're not making me feel any better, Chief Inspector Diaz."

"You don't need to fear. We will be watching. And you will have El Lobo with you."

Somehow, that didn't exactly reassure her.

She was tapping a foot nervously when Wolf reappeared some fifteen minutes later. He'd showered and shaved and combed his damp black hair straight back.

Despite her jumpy nerves, Nina had to admit the man cleaned up *extremely* well. The wrinkled khakis had given way to pleated black slacks. The jungle print shirt was gone, thank goodness, replaced by a knit polo the same color as the sea at dusk. The deep color intensified the blue of his eyes. Not that they needed intensifying. Nina felt them on every inch of her body as he gave her a final once-over.

"Ready?"

"As I'll ever be."

"Did you call the desk and ask them to bring up your car?"

"Yes."

"Good girl. Let's get this show on the road."

Hot sun and blinding glare hit them the moment they walked out the door. Wincing, Nina slipped on her sunglasses. Rafe shielded his eyes with tinted aviator glasses. When they took the elevator up from the lower casita level and walked through the pyramid lobby, she saw Ramon was on duty again.

"*Buenos dias,* Dr. Grant."

"*Buenos dias.*"

The parking valet gave her a cheerful smile before shifting his glance to Rafe. He was too well trained to comment on the fact that the man Nina had insisted would only be visiting her for a short time had stayed the entire night.

Nor did he question the order of things when Rafe walked around to the driver's side. With another friendly smile, the valet opened the passenger door for Nina. He already had the air conditioner blasting, so she sank into a welcome bath of chilled air.

"I hope you have a pleasant day."

"Thanks, Ramon. I hope so, too!"

As soon as Rafe had the rental pointed down the resort's long, winding drive, he fleshed out his role as the would-be love of her life.

"We have to assume Cordell has looked for you on Google. He'll know about your business and that you're on your way to becoming one of the wealthiest women under thirty in the United States. He may also have checked out this clown you planned to marry. Was there a public announcement of your engagement?"

"There was," she said with a wry twist to her lips. "My mother made sure it hit all the papers."

"Did the breakup hit the papers, too?"

"It did. We were at a restaurant when I confronted Kevin about the files he filched from my computer. He tried to bluster his way out of it, then got all huffy and patronizing, which made me even angrier."

She squirmed, embarrassed by the memory of the events that had followed.

"I dumped my wine in his lap. You would think that would send a strong enough signal, but he tried to stop me from walking out of the place. So I, uh, sort of slugged him."

Rafe shot her a quick glance. "Sort of?"

"I went for his chin," she confessed, her face flaming, "but he ducked and I popped him in the eye instead. Kevin stumbled back and tripped over a passing waiter with a full tray of drinks. They both went down." She let out a sigh. "Of course, the *Albuquerque Journal* society page editor had to be sitting in the next booth."

A smile played at the corner of Blackstone's mouth. "Of course."

"That was *not* my finest moment."

Laughter rumbled up deep and rich from her companion's chest. "Sounds damn fine to me. I'm just glad you missed *my* eyes with those keys last night."

He should laugh more, Nina thought. *Or maybe not.* That wicked grin did things to her insides she had no business feeling.

"Tell me about this guy Kevin," he said, still chuckling. "Where's he from? What does he do?"

"He's an investment advisor and financial planner."

"Likes to play with other people's money, does he?"

"He does. He also likes to tool around in vintage sports cars."

She spent most of the drive into town detailing her former fiancé's background and wondering all over again how she could have fallen for such a wimp.

Not that Kevin was a lightweight. At six one, he packed as much muscle on his frame as Wolf did. It was just distributed differently. A little less at the shoulders, a little more at the waist. They both had dark hair, too, although Kevin's had already started to thin on top.

Yet despite their outward similarities, the two men possessed distinctly different personalities. Blackstone telegraphed a quiet assurance and an inbred toughness that Kevin couldn't achieve if he popped B-12 and pumped iron for the rest of his life.

"I've got the picture," Wolf said as they approached the roundabout and the turnoff for the road to Cordell's distant hacienda. "You got engaged to a glorified accountant with a taste for flashy cars, which he tried to pay for by stealing proprietary data from your computer."

She bristled but quickly deflated. Hard to argue with the truth. "That about sums it up."

"He's lucky he got off with a punch in the eye,"

Wolf commented as he slowed for the circle. He had to maneuver carefully to avoid the souvenir hawkers who darted out to flash trays of silver bracelets and rings at the tourists cruising by. "You could have... Well, hell!"

"What's the matter?"

"We forgot a ring."

"I don't need a ring. We're unengaged, remember?"

"Previously unengaged, currently reunited."

"Not reunited enough for me to be wearing your ring. Besides, if what you told me is true, a wedding band didn't stop Cordell from going after Senator DeWitt."

"True. But her husband stayed home in Maine, while she played with her lover in Washington. Cordell won't find it as easy to get around me."

With that dubious reassurance, he exited the traffic circle and took the road leading to Cordell's distance hacienda.

This talk about engagement rings and wedding bands left Nina prey to some very confused emotions. Frowning, she stared down at her naked ring finger and tried to come to grips with her thoughts.

Kevin had picked out the diamond he'd slipped on her finger. Round cut and mounted on a fussy, filigreed band, it wasn't a ring she would have chosen herself. Still, after he'd gone down on one knee and presented it with a goofy grin, she'd drifted for weeks on a tide of happy dreams of their life together.

Now, here she was—no Kevin, no ring. Certainly no happy dreams to follow. And she didn't care.

She really didn't care.

Relief washed through Nina in waves as she realized she'd put Kevin out of her life *and* out of her heart. The tumultuous events of the past twenty four hours—and a certain obnoxious special agent—had crowded Kevin completely aside.

She slanted Rafe Blackstone a quick glance. She still owed him for scaring her last night. Nor was she happy about the way he'd strong-armed her into taking this jaunt into the countryside. El Lobo had certainly injected more excitement than she'd anticipated or wanted into her enforced vacation.

Then there was the matter of his startling transformation. Despite his bristles and gaudy tropical shirt, he'd looked hot as hell last might. Minus the bristles, he was smokin'. Far too sexy for any woman's peace of mind.

She shifted in her seat and sternly suppressed a ridiculous little twinge of regret that their pretend engagement would end the moment they departed Cordell's hacienda.

Assuming they got in, that is. She knew Rafe planned to plant some kind of listening device. Maybe more than one. He had the bugs with him. Somewhere. God knew what else he had on him.

Nina grew more anxious about that with each mile. Those armed guards with holsters tucked into their armpits had made a distinct impression on her yesterday. She tried not to obsess over the guns. Tried *very* hard.

In desperation, she focused on the passing countryside. It looked the same as it had when she'd driven through it the first time. Tall cactus, spiny creosote, a scattering of green-leafed trees hugging the few streams and creeks that cut through the otherwise parched hills.

Along one stretch of the road, the trees dripped with vines sprouting bright yellow flowers. She hadn't noticed the showy blossoms yesterday. Then again, she'd been more concerned with the coughing coming from her car engine than the local flora and fauna.

Despite her determined search for distraction, Nina had worked up a bad case of the jitters by the time Cordell's compound appeared on a distant hill. With its red tile roof and cream-colored adobe, the sprawling hacienda looked so inviting, so enticing, set on its cliff above the sea.

Their host was expecting them, she reminded herself nervously. Surely the guards would escort them right to the house. Or would they? Remembering how they'd searched her tote, she glanced uneasily toward Wolf.

"You're not armed, are you?"

He shrugged. "Not with anything Cordell's thugs will discover if they pat me down."

Chapter 5

Great. Wonderful. Marvelous.

Here she was—neat, precise, always-in-control Nina Grant—at this very moment pulling up to the gates of a compound with a man packing some sort of lethal weapon that couldn't be discovered by a pat-down.

Never, ever, in her wildest imagination would she have pictured herself in this situation. Her employees wouldn't believe when she told them about it. *If* she lived to tell them about it.

For several panicky moments Nina seriously considered informing Blackstone that she'd changed her mind. No government contract was worth either life or limb. His terse assertion last night that this was a matter of national security made her hesitate.

Then it was too late. The security cameras mounted at strategic angles above the gates blinked red and Rafe leaned out the window to hit the call button.

"*Sí?*"

He responded to the gruff query. "Dr. Nina Grant and Mr. Kevin James to see Mr. Cordell."

"Wait there. Someone comes."

The window whirred up again, enclosing them in a cool cocoon that did little to soothe Nina's increasingly frazzled nerves.

"I bet they're going to search my bag again. They'll check you, too."

Twisting in her seat, she skimmed a nervous glance over his knit shirt and pleated slacks. She couldn't spot any bulges. Except one, and that was right where it should be. Hastily, she raised her eyes.

"Are you sure they won't find anything?"

"I'm sure."

The reply was calm and reassuring. Until a very belated thought hit her.

"Oh, Lord! They asked me for some identification the first time. What if they ask to see *your* ID?"

"Not a problem. The people I work with took care of that while you were in the shower."

"How in the world...?" She shook her head. "Never mind! I don't want to know!"

"Relax, Nina." He flicked a casual glance at the cameras still aimed in their direction. "We're being watched, remember?"

"Like I could forget?"

He shifted in his seat and stretched an arm along the back of hers. Those blue eyes lanced into her. "You're wound tight, aren't you? You need a distraction."

"You think?"

"Let's try this."

With calm deliberation, he curled his arm around her shoulders. Nina had a moment, just a moment, to grasp his purpose as he angled her as far as her seat belt would allow and leaned across the console.

She could have pulled back. His hold was loose enough, his intention clear. Sheer surprise held her still—coupled with a overwhelming and completely irrational hunger to feel his mouth on hers.

She got her wish. The kiss started light, casual, a leisurely exploration of her mouth with his. She had no idea whether he deepened it or she did, but someone certainly upped the stakes. Next thing she knew, her palms were splayed against the muscled contours of his chest and the lips that had merely toyed with hers suddenly came down hard. Demanding instead of coaxing. Taking as much as they gave.

Swift and unexpected, a searing heat shot through her. It came in a short, intense burst that curled her toes against the soles of her sandals. Her rational mind said this was crazy, that Rafe Blackstone was a stranger, and a dangerous one at that. The rest of her thrilled to the taste and the feel and the scent of him.

He was the first to draw back. Fighting for breath, Nina was happy to see that the kiss had disconcerted him as much as it had her. The skin across his cheeks was stretched tight. A deep groove creased his forehead.

"Mission accomplished," she got out on a shaky breath. "Consider me officially distracted."

The crease carved deeper into his brow. "Christ, Nina, I'm…"

The rattle of the electronic gate swinging back on its hinges cut him off. Muttering a curse, he withdrew his arm and shifted to face front.

The driver of the Hummer that pulled up beside them was the same guard who'd driven Nina back to her rental car yesterday. He leaned out the window, his dark eyes raking over them. Despite Rafe's assurances—and very potent distraction—Nina gouged her nails into her palms while the guard in the passenger seat climbed out.

"You will step out of the car, please, so I may look inside."

The searing heat sucked away what little air Nina had left in her lungs, but her hands got cold and clammy as the guard checked the rental's interior and bent to look under the seats before popping the trunk. When he extracted a long pole with a mirror attached from the back of the Hummer and examined the rental's undercarriage, Wolf shook his head in a very credible show of disbelief and amusement.

"What's with all this? Does your boss think my fiancée and I are terrorists or something?"

"Señor Cordell is a very powerful man. He has many friends, and many who envy him his possessions. He takes no chances."

"Yeah, I see that."

"Dr. Grant, I must check your bag."

"Okay."

The guy pawed through her tote, then set it aside. Nina thought her heart would stop when he turned to Wolf and asked him to hold out his arms.

"You're kidding, right?"

"No, *señor*."

With a shrug, Blackstone extended his arms. Nina didn't draw a single breath until the guard finished with him and gestured them back to their vehicle.

"Please follow us up to the hacienda."

She dropped into her seat. This was *not* her idea of a restful vacation.

"Are you going to tell me what kind of supersecret weapon you're carrying? It would be nice to know, if you whip it out and I need to duck or something."

"I'm not carrying anything. You might want to give me the little plastic bottle I slipped in your tote, though. Looks like ordinary hand sanitizer," he added helpfully.

Her jaw dropped. She had to struggle for words. "You...you used me? As a *mule?*"

"We didn't have a whole lot of time to improvise this morning. I figured you're more the hand sanitizer type than I am."

Flabbergasted, Nina could only gape at him. In a few short hours, Rafe Blackstone had turned her world upside down. Not to mention putting her on an emotional roller coaster. In rapid succession, she'd progressed from lusting for him to fearing him to loathing him to wishing the kiss a few seconds ago lasted a whole lot longer.

Now anger topped the list again. A nice, cleansing rage, that had her diving into her tote and winding up to fling the plastic bottle at his head.

"Careful! That stuff can be volatile."

Her hand jerked to a stop. Carefully, very carefully, she deposited the container on his outstretched palm.

"What *is* that?" she demanded as he slipped it into his shirt pocket.

"Nothing you need to worry about right now. We're almost there."

Wild thoughts of explosive gels and/or nerve-paralyzing agents rushed through her mind as El Lobo brought the rental to a stop inside the flower-filled courtyard.

Cordell had come out to greet them. Elegant in white slacks, a slim belt, and a pale blue silk shirt with his monogram on the pocket, he strolled forward to open Nina's door. She had to dig deep for a smile when he helped her out and raised her hand to his lips.

"I'm so pleased you could join me, Dr. Grant. And you, Mr. James," he added when Blackstone exited the rental.

"Thanks for including me in the invitation."

The two men engaged in that time-honored male ritual of crunching each other's digital phalanges while sizing up the competition.

"I gather from Nina's call this morning that your trip to Cabo was somewhat spur of the moment."

Nodding, her pretend fiancé looped an arm around her shoulders. She didn't have to feign unease or nervousness. Or the residual temper that made her shrug out of his loose embrace. She'd be a long time forgetting that plastic bottle of whatever he'd slipped into her tote.

If Sebastian Cordell noted the deliberate disengagement, he didn't comment on it. Instead, he ushered them through a vine-draped breezeway and into the wide, double-doored entrance to the main building.

Nina had only seen portions of the interior on her previous visit, but that was enough to prepare her for Cordell's masterful blend of contemporary and antique. Despite her nervousness, she drank in the beauty of his book-lined study, which showcased an Italian Rococo desk topped by a sleek computer with a twenty-inch monitor. In a sunken living room the size of a football field, an Italian rococo armoire housed a state-of-the art sound system. The white leather-and-chrome sectional sofa was positioned opposite a glass wall with a spectacular view of the sea.

But it was the man's art collection that once again stopped the breath in Nina's throat. She'd always been more into science than art, but even her untrained eyes recognized masterpieces when she saw them. Sculptures in bronze and marble held places of honor on pedestals and in subtly lit niches. Paintings—some small and exquisitely framed, some wall size—ran the gamut from soft, dreamy impressionist landscapes to bold, almost violent slashes of color.

"I told the staff to serve lunch on the terrace." Their host gestured toward a set of sliding glass doors that framed a vista of sparkling fountains, marble statues and colorful bougainvillea. "It's shaded and cooled by the sea breeze, but we can eat inside if you prefer."

"No," Nina breathed awed in spite of herself by the glorious setting, "the terrace looks perfect."

Wolf made a slight movement on her other side. She threw him a quick look and remembered belatedly that the whole reason for this visit was to give him a chance to scope out the inside of the hacienda.

Well, hell! Five minutes into her role as a

modern day Mata Hari and she'd already flubbed it. Kicking herself, Nina tried to recover.

"Unless… Uh… Kevin hasn't had time to acclimate to the Cabo sun. Maybe we should eat inside."

"Kevin" shook his head. "Outside is fine."

"Are you sure?" Cordell asked graciously. "The enclosed portion of the terrace has an equally fine view."

"I'm sure."

"Very well." He slid back one of the glass doors and took Nina's elbow. "Shall we have an aperitif first? Since moving to Mexico, I've invented a most refreshing drink that consists of equal parts lime juice and *Pasión Azteca*."

"*Pasión Azteca*," she murmured, fighting not to flinch away from his touch. "That sounds very exotic."

"It is. Quite exotic, I assure you."

He ushered them along a passage shaded by vines woven through white latticework.

"Most aficionados believe *Pasión Azteca* is the world's finest tequila. It's made from the pure sap of the blue agave plant that's been fermented, distilled, and aged for more than six years. The bottles themselves are limited edition works of art, done in silver, gold or platinum."

"Platinum? You're kidding!"

"Not at all. Each bottle is individually designed and engraved by Alejandro Gomez Oropeza, one of Mexico's greatest artists."

The husky note in his voice told Nina he really got off on this stuff. That, and the slow up-and-down stroke he gave her arm.

"A platinum edition of *Pasión Azteca* sold at auction last month for well over two hundred thousand dollars. I foolishly let myself be outbid on that one but I have my people looking for another. Today, I'm sad to say, we must make do with a silver edition."

His "make do" bottle sat in splendor on a wheeled bar cart tended by a servant in a white jacket and gloves. Shaped like a spiked sea shell, the bottle gleamed in the few rays that managed to sneak past the vines shading the terrace.

"Three glasses with ice, Enrique. I shall mix the drinks myself."

"*Sí,* Señor."

With Wolf beside her, Nina watched a master at work. Thankfully, it looked as though he added more fresh squeezed lime juice than tequila to the crystal martini shaker. The last thing she needed was to get a buzz on and say or do something stupid.

She realized the error of her thinking as soon as she took the first sip from a long-stemmed glass. This baby tasted nothing like the drinks at the Purple Parrot. Or anywhere else, for that matter.

Marvelously smooth and deceptively gentle, the tequila-tini glided down her throat. She didn't feel its lethal bite until a few moments later, when they were seated at a vine-shaded table and had the Sea of Cortez in all its mesmerizing beauty laid out before them.

"I have a confession to make, Dr. Grant," Cordell said with a smile. "Or may I call you Nina?"

"Yes, of course."

"And you must call me Sebastian." He twirled his glass, his pale blue eyes drifting from her to Wolf and back again. "After you appeared at my gates yesterday and gave me your card, I looked for you on Google."

Oh, God! Here it comes.

Her stomach lurching, Nina was sure she and El Lobo were about to be exposed as complete frauds. She had visions of her companion whipping out his hand sanitizer and squirting their way out of the compound when Cordell gave her an approving smile.

"I'm quite impressed by your business acumen, my dear. Grant Medical Data Systems is perfectly positioned to ride what most experts predict will be the wave of the future in health care data sharing."

"I certainly hope so."

Cordell's beautifully manicured hand twirled the glass stem again. "From what I read, less than half your funding derives from private sources, with the majority coming from government contracts."

Heroically, Nina managed to refrain from shooting El Lobo an evil glare. "That's true."

"I may be able to help you increase your slice of the government pie. Although I now reside in Mexico, I still have a good many friends in Washington."

One of whom was now extremely dead.

Hastily, Nina masked the grim reminder of Senator DeWitt behind another sip of tequila.

"Perhaps you should provide me with a complete company prospectus and five-year plan," Cordell said smoothly. "I'll make sure it gets in the hands of people who can make things happen."

Sure he would. The man had to be drinking something a whole lot more potent than blue agave sap if he thought she was going to give him access to her company's finances. She was framing a polite refusal when Blackstone laid a possessive arm across the back of her chair.

"That's exactly what I've been telling Nina. She needs to exploit any and all business contacts. I sure would."

This time she couldn't restrain a glare. He was cutting his role as her scumbag ex-fiancé a little too close to the bone.

"Yes," their host agreed, "I imagine you would. You're in the investment and financial planning arena, aren't you?"

"Did you get that off Google, too?"

"I did." A smile flitted across Cordell's tanned face. "Along with a rather descriptive account of the termination of your engagement to Nina. How fortunate for you she took you back."

"She says she's still thinking about it," Wolf replied with a wink, "but I'm ninety-nine-point-nine-percent sure of the outcome."

When he gave her shoulder a squeeze, Cordell dipped his head in a benign nod. "I wish you luck."

It was all so civilized, so polite. Yet Nina couldn't shake the nasty feeling she was a small, brown mouse being batted between the paws of two very powerful and very predatory jungle cats.

"It was a long ride out here," Rafe said, interrupting her uneasy thoughts. "Guess you'd better point me in the direction of a bathroom."

"Of course. There's one in the pool cabana at the other end of the terrace. Or you may go back inside the house and to your left."

"Thanks. Mind if I take a look at some of your bronzes while I'm at it? I'm something of a collector myself."

"Are you? Then I must give you a guided tour after lunch."

"Great."

When Wolf headed for the sliding glass doors, Nina had to swallow a panicky urge to call him back. This was what he'd come for, why he'd coerced her into acting as his entree into Cordell's compound. Now that she knew about her smooth-talking host's dark past, however, she didn't particularly relish being left alone with him. She did her best to hide her unease as he leaned back in his chair and regarded her with slow consideration.

"I hope I didn't embarrass you by bringing up that article about the termination of your engagement."

"I'm well past being embarrassed by it."

"Yet I sense… Forgive me if I'm getting too personal." His gaze dropped to her ringless left hand and lingered a moment before lifting to her face. "I sense you and Kevin haven't quite repaired the, shall we say, cracks in the road that led to your breakup."

"We're working on them."

"I see." He drummed his fingers on the tabletop, the picture of friendly concern. "Would you like a word of advice from one who's tasted great passion a few times in his life?"

At her cautious nod, he stretched out an arm and laid his hand over hers.

"Someone as young and beautiful as you shouldn't have to work at love."

Right, she thought scornfully, *for "young", read "gullible". For "beautiful", try "well off".* In a patently obvious attempt to change the subject, she eased her hand from under his and gestured to a gleaming yacht anchored a few hundred feet from the rock cliffs.

"Is that your boat?"

"It is. Would you like to take a cruise aboard her?"

"Well… I…"

"And Kevin, of course. Assuming he's going to remain here in Cabo with you."

"I don't know. We, uh, need to work on those cracks you mentioned."

"I have commitments tomorrow, but I could take you out Thursday morning. I've already instructed my crew to have the boat ready for a sea voyage later in the day. How does that work for you?"

"Let me think about it."

Desperate, she resorted to polite chitchat about the weather and the crowds in Cabo until Wolf reappeared. She greeted his return with relief. Let him get us out of this entanglement!

"Sebastian has offered to take us out for a spin in his boat."

His glance shot to the yacht anchored offshore. "By boat, I hope you mean that beauty."

"She does, indeed," Sebastian answered. "As I told Nina, however, I couldn't do it until Thursday afternoon." His hooded gaze locked with Wolf's. "Will you be staying in Cabo until then?"

Even Nina, as jittery as she was, sensed Cordell had thrown down a gauntlet. His opponent picked it up without missing a beat.

"Damn straight I will."

Oh, Lord! He wanted to take Cordell up on his offer! She could see it in his eyes, read it in the speculative glance he gave the gleaming white yacht.

There was absolutely no way she was heading out to sea on that monster, pretty as it was. She got seasick in the bathtub, for pity's sake. She leaned back, out of Cordell's line of sight, and telegraphed a silent but unmistakable *no!*

Her "fiancé" acknowledged the frantic signal with a small nod and proceed to completely ignore it.

"Thursday works great for us, doesn't it, Pumpkin? We didn't have anything heavier on the agenda than soaking up some rays at the pool. What time do you want us here, Sebastian?"

Chapter 6

Riding a wave of fierce elation, Wolf took a last look at the cliffside compound in the rearview mirror.

He'd managed to plant two listening devices— one in Cordell's study and one behind a painting of what looked like rotting fruit. In the process, he'd burned the layout and dimensions of each room he'd passed through into his brain. He'd also scouted the grounds. If he had to go back into the compound, he knew exactly how he would do it.

That was looking more and more necessary. All indications were Cordell intended to move the technology he'd stolen from Senator DeWitt's office within the next few days. Interpol, the CIA, and military listening posts all over the world had picked up increasing chatter about interested buyers. Everyone from hostile heads of state to drug czars would kill to get their hands on the design for a new generation of ultrasmall, ultrasophisticated Unmanned Aerial Vehicles.

Compared to the UAV's currently flying combat missions in Iraq and Afghanistan, the new generation of drones would cost next to nothing. They would also be almost invisible in flight. If they performed even half as well as advertised, the fifteen-inch-long vehicles could weave through a jungle of skyscrapers, zoom under bridges and land on the balcony of a twenty-story apartment building.

They would also be so simple to operate, any pimply preteen could fly one loaded with, say, fifty kilos of cocaine from a jungle processing center in Colombia to the backyard of a dealer anywhere in the world. Wolf didn't even want to *think* about the lethal virus some nutcase could send through a window of the Oval Office.

"Pumpkin?"

Nina's sarcastic drawl cut through his swirling thoughts.

"Do I really strike you as the 'Pumpkin' type?"

Wolf shot her an incredulous look. Of all the lies and half-truths they'd just spun for Cordell, that was the one playing heaviest on her mind?

"It was kind of the spur of the moment," he admitted. "But now that you mention it…"

He made a quick visual sweep, from the strands of soft brown hair that had slipped free of her clip to the chili-pepper-red silk top shaping her breasts. After letting his gaze linger there a second or two longer than it should, Wolf brought his eyes back to hers.

"'Pumpkin' suits you. You're all soft and smooth, like a slice of Thanksgiving pie, but you pack enough spice to face Cordell down in his own lair."

"Thanks. I think."

She thinned her lips and gave him a taste of the spice he'd just mentioned.

"Incidentally, I don't appreciate the way you ignored my very obvious lack of desire to sail off into the sunset with Cordell."

"Sorry. I thought it best to keep all options open."

"I hope you don't think I intend to continue our charade until Thursday!"

"With any luck, this will be over before then."

By tonight, Wolf thought, if the devices he'd planted picked up any clues to where, when and how Cordell intended to dispose of his pilfered technology. Wire-tight with anticipation, he forced a smile.

"You did good today, Grant. Very good."

Oooh, boy, Nina thought. *There it was again.* The crooked grin that crinkled the skin at the corners of his eyes and almost made her forget Rafe had blackmailed her into acting as his entree into a viper's den. Steeling herself to resist its pull, she demanded clarification.

"So we're square? No more heavy-handed pressure about my government contracts?"

"We're square."

His reply should have satisfied her. She was off the hook. Done. Finito. She could go back to being merely a stressed-out exec on vacation.

So what the heck was with this sudden flat feeling? She wasn't Lara Croft, Tomb Raider, for Pete's sake! She'd just about wet herself when Cordell laid his hand over hers. All through lunch her stomach had been so knotted with tension she'd eaten maybe two bites of the *coquille St. Jacques* his chef had dished up. The entire time, she couldn't *wait* to get out of the hacienda. Out of this whole, weird scene Rafe Blackstone had dragged her into, kicking and screaming.

This sudden letdown was a natural reaction, she decided. Her system was readjusting itself, as did every stressed biological organism. Plants faced with drought conditions increased a key hormone called abscisic acid. Animals in tight situations reacted with abrupt changes in neurohormone levels. Their catecholamines and corticosteroids shot off the charts. Serotonin was suppressed.

She was just coming down after the pressure high of the past few hours, she told herself firmly. All she had to do was sit back and breathe. In. Out. In.

Unfortunately, every deep breath ratcheted up her awareness of the man beside her. Each whiff of the sun-warmed scent of his skin or the faint tang of his aftershave threw her neurohormones out of whack again.

She had them more or less under control by the time they approached the roundabout with the spin-off road leading to her resort. Then she noticed El Lobo spearing intent glances at the rearview mirror.

"What's the matter?"

"We've picked up a tail."

A tail! Good grief. Had she dropped into some alternate universe?

"He's been following us since we hit the outskirts of town," Wolf said calmly.

Her nervous system going berserk once more, Nina twisted around. The traffic in the circle was as chaotic as usual, with cars weaving in and out and trucks belching diesel fumes as they shifted gears.

"Which one is it?"

"Gray Chevy Aveo, three cars back, right lane."

While she searched the stream of traffic, her companion reached into his shirt pocket and flipped open his cell phone.

"Mannie, this is Wolf. I've got a Chevy Aveo on my ass. Is it one of your men?"

The response didn't appear to please him. He listened for another moment, keeping one hand on the wheel and one eye on the mirror.

"*Gracias, amigo.* I'll get back to you."

"Who is it?" Nina asked anxiously.

"Hang on a sec."

Holding his phone at eye level, he punched one button. A second later, he had the phone to his ear.

"Ace, this is Wolf. I need you to run a check on license number…"

He squinted into the mirror and reeled off the digits. Nina dug her nails into her palms until he flipped the phone shut again.

"What's going on? Who's Ace?"

"My controller. Same guy who arranged my new identity as your fiancé. Speaking of which…" He shot her a rueful grin. "We have a slight change in plans."

"*How* slight?"

"Mannie got a report of a repair order being called in for the flat screen TV in your suite at the Mayan Princess. A technician worked on it while we were at lunch."

"There wasn't…"

Her voice trailed off, then came back much weaker.

"There wasn't anything wrong with the TV last time I checked."

"Exactly."

He sounded so blasé! As if the possibility that a person or persons unknown had planted a bug in her hotel room was no more than a minor inconvenience.

Swallowing, she tried to grasp the implications. "Do you think Sebastian is behind this?"

"Probably. You're just his type. Smart. Beautiful. A power player."

She blinked, shaken out of her renewed bout of nerves. Smart and beautiful was better than soft and smooth. *Much* better. She basked in the compliment until Wolf added a casual kicker.

"I'm guessing Cordell wants to get a better picture of how things stand between you and me before he moves in for the kill."

"When you say kill, you *are* speaking metaphorically, aren't you?"

"Of course."

She might have believed him if not for a certain dead senator.

"Until we find out for sure what's going down," he continued with a sideways glance, "I'm afraid you're stuck with me. Think you can handle a few more hours?"

"I'll give it my best shot."

Her dry response in no way mirrored the quick flutter just under her ribs. Her thoughts zinged back to El Lobo's "distraction" just outside the gates of Cordell's compound. Then ahead, to the possibility he might have to distract her again. Her neurohormones skittering all over the place, Nina contemplated that possibility for the rest of the drive to the Mayan Princess.

* * *

Late afternoon had brought the resort to life. New arrivals waited in the open-air lobby to check in. Laughter and noisy splashes echoed from the crowded family pool on the lower level. Smiling waiters served tall, frosted drinks to couples lazing on double-wide lounges at the adult-only infinity pool on the upper level.

Just yesterday she'd been stretched out on one of those loungers and so bored she'd decided to drive out to see the countryside. In the twenty-four hours since, she'd stumbled into something right out of a James Bond movie. She couldn't quite believe she was now returning to her casita with an undercover operative to check it for bugs.

Unreal. Absolutely unreal.

"Act naturally," Wolf warned as they approached her unit. "If this TV repairman worked on anything besides the flat screen, we'll know soon enough."

"How?"

"Remember the woman I told you about? Our communications chief? Mackenzie Blair can pack more technology into a cell phone than NASA did into the Hubble telescope."

He proved his point once they were inside. While Nina made straight for the fridge and a bottle of chilled water, he flipped up his phone.

"I need to check my voice mail," he said casually.

He kept his jazzed-up Hubble telescope at his ear and appeared to be listening intently while he paced the living area before strolling out onto the balcony. Nervous as a cat, Nina watched him lean a hip against the railing that framed the triangular hot tub. A sudden and very explicit vision grabbed her by the throat.

El Lobo. Her. In the hot tub. Naked. With a full moon reflected in a dark, shimmering sea.

She chugged down her water, half scared, half hoping he would find a bug that would force him to play her would-be lover just a *little* bit longer.

He did. Two, in fact. One in the living room, one in the bedroom. Both very sophisticated and high tech, but no match for the gizmo Wolf aimed at them.

Signaling Nina to join him in the bedroom, he gave her a status report. "I left the one in the living room active," he said in a low voice, "but scrambled the signal on this one. Whoever is listening will think it malfunctioned."

"Who *is* listening?"

"I should have the answer to that shortly. I've requested a signal intercept. Until we get a fix on it…"

Her heart skipped a beat.

"…we need to continue our respective roles."

She gathered the folds of her colorful broom skirt in her fists, bombarded once again by the image of the two of them in the hot tub. Naked. Etc.

"Relax," he said with a smile that produced the exact opposite of its intended effect. "I don't expect you to perform for the cameras."

"That's a relief."

Damn! Why couldn't she lie with a straight face like everyone else? She could feel the heat coloring her cheeks as Blackstone outlined his plan of attack.

"Here's the deal. We amble back into the living room. I comment on the long drive back from Cordell's and suggest a drink up at the pool. You counter with that old stand-by 'we need to talk'. I agree, but insist we can do that poolside as easily as we can here. We change, slather on some sunscreen, and move out of listening range."

The plan was simple enough. Nina even managed to inject a note of authenticity into her assigned line of dialogue. If Wolf were Kevin, they certainly would have to talk.

The first glitch occurred when he walked out of the bedroom wearing a pair of low-riding gym shorts and not much else. The second, when he took the bottle of sun lotion from her suddenly nerveless hand.

"I'll do your back."

He did her back *and* neck *and* arms *and* thighs. Nina wasn't sure her knees would keep her upright when it was her turn to perform the same service.

"Turn around."

He obliged and presented a broad back that tapered to a lean waist and a very tight, very trim butt. Eyeing it appreciatively, she oozed lotion into her palm. The sunscreen was cool and creamy, in direct contrast to her throat, which got hotter and drier with every swipe of her hands over his back and shoulders.

She tried to remind herself this was all for show, that Blackstone's only intention was to keep up the pretense. The stern reminder didn't prevent her fingers from gliding over his back longer than was absolutely necessary to work in the sunscreen.

"There." Swallowing to lubricate her bone-dry throat, she capped the bottle. "That should do you."

"Thanks."

He didn't turn around, just stared at the doors to

the balcony. "Why don't you go on up to the pool? I'll follow in a minute."

Oh, God! Now what? Imagining all kinds of disasters, she grabbed her tote and cover-up and fled the scene.

Wolf heard the door shut behind her but didn't move. He couldn't. The woman's slow, sensual strokes had damn near paralyzed him. Half of him, anyway.

Above the waist his lungs were so tight and frozen he had to fight to suck in air. Below the waist…

He was tight there, too, but certainly not frozen. Hunger burned hot and fierce in his belly. Swearing, he gritted his teeth and glared at the endless expanse of ocean beyond the balcony.

As if he didn't have enough to contend with. One dead United States senator. Stolen technology up for grabs to the highest bidder. A disaster in the making for U.S. national security. Now he had to go and develop a serious case of lust for Dr. Nina Grant.

She wasn't even his type, for God's sake! Too nice. Too damn gullible. Wolf had always gone for the kind of woman who didn't expect—or particularly want—him to hang around. The kind he could kiss goodbye and forget, once he'd completed an op. Nina, he suspected, wasn't the forgetting kind.

More to the point, she represented everything he'd deliberately avoided during his years with OMEGA. Ties. Commitments. Responsibilities that might shade his judgment when he went into dangerous situations. Although Wolf had seen many of his fellow agents successfully combine undercover work and marriage, the effort took its toll. Most left the business eventually. He just hadn't met the woman he wanted to make the switch for.

This one, though, stirred all kinds of thoughts he had no business thinking. Setting his jaw, Wolf willed his body into submission. He had to remember where he was. Had to stay focused on the mission. There was too much at stake to indulge in his ferocious urge to drag Ms. Grant back down to her suite, peel off her bathing suit, and bury himself between her lotion-slick thighs.

With another smothered curse, Wolf stalked out of the casita. His phone buzzed just as the door slammed behind him. He glanced at the coded ID on the display, flipped up the lid, and snarled into the mouthpiece.

"What?"

"Wolf?" Ace asked sharply. "You okay?"

"Yeah." Gritting his teeth, he moderated his tone. "What have you got?"

"The tag on the Chevy Aveo checks to Economy Rentals at the Cabo airport. They leased it this morning to one Anton Hdrovski. The name's fake. Ditto the passport he registered with them."

"Did you get a visual from airport surveillance?"

"We did. No positive ID yet, but this character sure looks like Ivan Alekseev. Heavier build. Less hair. Same ugly sneer."

Wolf's gut took another twist. A suspected lieutenant in the Russian mafia, Alekseev reportedly ran a host of illegal activities. Everything from drugs and black market military weaponry to white slavery.

So far, Interpol hadn't been able to nail him. Wolf had never worked in his area of operations, but he knew at least two Interpol agents had died trying to infiltrate the Russian's tight inner circle. The fact that Alekseev had appeared on the scene upped the stakes considerably.

"How did Alekseev pick up my tail?" he asked, grimly.

"Actually, we think he was tailing Dr. Grant. Once we ID'ed him, Mannie Diaz shook down some of his sources. They confirm the Russian heard from *his* sources here in Cabo that Cordell invited an American woman to his compound for lunch. Alekseev was too late to follow her to the hacienda, but he caught her on the way back into town."

"Hell!" Wolf considered a dozen possibilities, none of them good. "Sounds like Alekseev thinks she might be another potential buyer, or acting for one."

"Sounds like."

His jaw locked. He didn't need Ace to spell it out for him. If Alekseev and company believed Nina was a player in Cordell's auction, they could well decide to eliminate the competition.

"What about the signals emanating from the bug in Dr. Grant's suite? Did you run the intercept?"

"We did. They're low frequency, with a limited range."

Which meant whoever was listening could be close enough to have his ear to the wall. His spine crawling, Wolf made a slow three sixty.

"Mac's still working the intercept," Ace told him. "She said to give her a few more hours. She's confident she'll be able to lock in on the listening post."

He hoped to hell she did. The ultraluxurious

casitas were stacked one on top of the other, clinging to the cliff face below the towering pyramid of the main building. There must be close to a hundred of them. One-, two- and three-bedroom units, in shades of umber and ochre that blended in with the cliffs themselves.

He could help at this end, he decided. He'd get with hotel management. Find out who checked into which units in the past twenty-four hours. In the meantime...

"Lightning wants you to stick close to Dr. Grant," Ace reported. "Intentionally or not, she's becoming a key player in this op."

And he'd forced her into it.

Wolf had never hesitated to employ whatever tools necessary to accomplish a mission, but this particular tool was starting to play on his conscience, big time. He didn't need Lightning's instructions. He intended to stick *extremely* close to Nina Grant. Day and night.

Chapter 7

Infiltrating Sebastian Cordell's compound with a fake fiancé in tow had pretty well maxed out Nina's fun meter. That exercise was a stroll on the beach, however, compared to having her fake fiancé stretched out next to her on a double-wide lounger.

An absorbent, cloth-covered mattress at least four inches thick cushioned the lounger. A roll made of the same cushiony material served as a pillow. With her head propped on the roll, Nina had an unobstructed view across a seamless blend of turquoise pool and achingly blue ocean.

Unobstructed, that is, except for a bent knee.

Which connected to a hard, muscled thigh. Which connected to the hip that bumped hers as Wolf settled in beside her.

"I just talked to my people. They—and I—think it's best if we remain engaged until Cordell makes his move. Or at least for the duration of your stay in Cabo. When are you supposed to head home?"

"My assistant booked me for an entire week."

Very much against her will.

Talk about irony. When her staff had threatened to resign en mass if she didn't take some time off, Nina had reminded them of all the hot projects they had in the works and insisted she couldn't drop everything and jet off to Mexico. Even after she'd caved and arrived here at the Mayan Princess, she hadn't been able to relax. Too many things on her mind, too much restless energy.

Rafe Blackstone had certainly tapped into that energy. And something deeper. More urgent. She wanted to believe it was a sense of outrage over Cordell's alleged role in Senator DeWitt's death, but she knew darn well the naked chest just inches from her nose factored heavily into the equation.

"I don't fly home until Saturday," she told him. "I, uh, could stay longer if you need me."

The cushion dipped as he propped himself up on an elbow and tipped his mirrored sunglasses.

Surprise and a touch of amusement played in his blue eyes.

"Is this the same Nina Grant who made me swear not more than a half hour ago that we're all square?"

"It is," she said loftily. "Just because I dislike being blackmailed doesn't mean I won't do whatever I can to help expose a traitor."

"I appreciate the offer, but as I told you in the car, this should be over soon."

"What if it's not?" It was Nina's turn to tip her sunglasses. "Don't you think it's about time to tell me what, exactly, Sebastian intends to auction off to the highest bidder?"

Wolf had to make a split-second decision. Grant wasn't cleared for the level of detail she now demanded. He could stonewall her—or bring her fully into the op. He went with his instinct.

First, though, he speared a quick glance around the pool. They weren't the only couple soaking up the late afternoon rays but none of the others were anywhere close enough to overhear. Nevertheless, Wolf kept his voice low as he described the new generation Unmanned Aerial Vehicles at risk because Janice DeWitt hiked up her skirt, shimmied out of her thong panties, and had sex with the man she knew as Stephen Caulder atop her desk in the Russell Senate Office Building.

With her PhD in biology, Nina grasped the devastating potential of the stolen technology immediately. Her eyes went wide with dismay.

"If these UAVs are as inexpensive to build and easy to fly as you say, some wild-eyed terrorist could deliver a deadly strain of anthrax or ebola anywhere on the planet."

"Just about."

"No wonder you resorted to kidnapping and blackmail to gain entree into Cordell's compound!"

She swiped her tongue across her lips, clearly trying to take it all in. Wolf half expected her to reneg on her offer at that point. As he'd related to Ace after the frustrating prep session, Dr. Nina Grant didn't have the temperament for undercover work. So her angled chin and terse reply took him by surprise.

"Count me in, Blackstone. I'll do whatever I can to help put Cordell behind bars where he belongs."

"You sure?" Now that he'd secured her willing cooperation, Wolf was hit with a fierce need to talk her out. "We're playing for extremely high stakes, Nina. People could get hurt."

She paled, but nodded. "I'm sure."

Her declaration shifted something inside Wolf. He couldn't quite identify the odd sensation. Probably because he'd never felt this combination of respect, admiration, guilt and fierce protectiveness before. All he knew at that moment was that he had to make her understand what she was up against.

Digging his elbow into the mattress, he leaned closer. She tilted into the crease and almost slid under him. His pelvis pressed into hers. His chest flatted her right breast. To any interested observer, they would project the image of a couple caught up in a very intimate conversation.

"You and I and Cordell aren't the only players in this game. My controller contacted me right before I came up to the pool. That tail we picked up...?"

Some of the bravado seeped out of her, replaced by a wary caution. "What about it?"

"From all indications, it was a real badass by the name of Ivan Alekseev. He's a major player in the Russian mafia."

Wolf saw her eyes widen behind her tinted lenses. She swallowed and said very carefully, "The Russians are following you?"

"Not me. You."

Her jaw dropped. *"Me?"*

"You." With brutal honesty, he laid the cards on

the table. "Mannie says Alekseev arrived in town just in time to hear from his sources that Cordell had invited a special guest to lunch. He's going to want to know who you are and what interest Cordell has in you."

The incredible news that she'd now become the focus of the Russian mafia shook Nina almost as much as lying chest to chest with Rafe.

"Wh…?" She struggled to sound coherent. "What do we do now?"

"Until I say otherwise, we do just what Nina and Kevin would do. We lie in the sun, we cool off in the pool, we have dinner, we take a moonlight strolls along the beach. In the process, we work out the kinks in our relationship."

Nina went into the pool several times in the hours that followed, but the cool turquoise water did little to soothe her frazzled nerves.

Particularly when Wolf rested his elbows beside hers on the pool's curved ledge. They floated side-by-side, massaged by the thin stream of water cascading over the lip. With nothing but that lip between them and the endless blue of the Pacific, they could have been alone in the universe.

Except, of course, for whoever might be watching. Or listening. Or trying to figure out if she was a player in Sebastian Cordell's dangerous game. The notion was absurd, and scary as hell. So scary that goose bumps popped out on her arms when she and Wolf abandoned the pool and went down to her casita to change for dinner.

The air-conditioned chill inside the casita piled another layer of goose bumps on top of the first. Shivering, Nina deposited her tote and wide-brimmed hat on the counter.

"I need to shower off the chlorine before dinner," she told him.

"Me, too."

"You want first crack at the bathroom?"

"No reason to take turns. I'll scrub your back, you scrub mine."

He delivered the suggestion in a caressing tone that squeezed the air from Nina's lungs. It took her several heart-stopping seconds to remember the bug behind the flat screen TV. Scrambling for a reason to decline the seductive offer, she shook her head.

"As tempting as that sounds, we'd better forego the back-scrubbing. We'll have to rush to make our dinner reservations as it is."

Was that a glint of approval for her quick thinking in his eyes? She couldn't quite decide, as he curled a knuckle under her chin.

"You wouldn't turn down a back scrub if you were really ready to forgive me."

"I'm still working on that," she said, fighting to remember her role as his thumb glided along her lower lip.

"Work harder. I'll do anything to get back into your heart, Pumpkin."

Oh, gag!

She didn't have any trouble interpreting the gleam in his eyes now. He was laughing at her.

Indignant, she fired back with a quick retort. "My heart, Kevin, or my bed?"

His thumb stilled. She had the satisfaction of seeing his amusement fade before she issued a tart warning.

"Don't push me, fella. I haven't had time to adjust to your unexpected appearance here in Cabo, much less your insistence we put the past behind us and start over. Let's just take this a day at a time."

"Guess we'll have to," he said after a moment. "You're calling the shots on this one."

His thumb glided over her lip one last time before he issued a warning of his own.

"Just don't expect me to roll over and play dead while you try to make up your mind about us. I want you, Nina. I didn't know how much until I lost you. I intend to do everything in my power to make you want me again, too."

Whoa! Playacting was one thing. Making her legs start to buckle and her heart thunder like the opening stanzas of Beethoven's Fifth was another. Scarcely able to breathe, Nina beat a hasty retreat to the bedroom.

Wolf let her go. Their hours at the pool had damn near shredded his concentration. Touching her, breathing in her chlorine-scented hair and skin had just about sent him over the edge.

Suppressing a savage oath, he hit the Play button on Nina's iPod and spun it to full volume before stalking out on the balcony. Another vicious spin brought the hot tub jets to noisy, bubbling life. His jaw locked, he contacted his controller.

"Ace, this is Wolf. Speak to me."

A cool shower and a change into the sleeveless sundress she'd had laundered and pressed helped Nina regain a semblance of her composure.

It slipped again when Wolf suggested they cancel their reservations at the resort's elegant dining room and eat at the open-air restaurant clinging to the cliff, just a hundred feet above the crashing waves.

"Good atmosphere," he murmured in her

ear, when he waved the hostess away to seat her himself, "and great cover. Still, it might be best to wait until we take that walk along the beach to shed our respective roles."

Good God! Did they have unseen observers watching them even here? Aiming some superbionic electronic ear their way from the top of the cliff or the balcony of one of the casitas?

Feeling hunted, Nina almost jumped out of her skin when Wolf bent lower and dropped a kiss just under her ear. Pure reflex had her hunching a shoulder and jerking quickly to one side.

"What are you doing?"

"Initiating the next phase of my campaign to make you forget the past and concentrate on our future."

Wolf reeled off the answer easily enough. Shaking off the lingering effect of that brief taste took considerably more effort.

It didn't help that Mackenzie had completed the signal intercept. According to Ace, the transmissions from the device behind the flat screen TV in Nina's living room traced to a receiver aboard one of the boats anchored in the Mayan Princess's protected cove.

Wolf could see it from where he sat. The twenty-foot runabout bobbed on the slowly darkening sea.

Who manned her? Who was listening? Cordell's henchmen? Alekseev's contacts? Or an unidentified third party? The uncertainty scraped at Wolf's nerves.

He'd find the answer. Later.

Right now he was still processing Ace's second bit of news. Turns out Cordell had taken a very interesting phone call in his study late this afternoon. The listening device Wolf had planted picked up every word. Slick as ever, Cordell couched his conversation to sound as though he was auctioning off one of his sculptures and indicated he was waiting to hear from one last buyer. The buyer had until noon tomorrow to put in his offer, then Cordell would close the deal and advise the successful bidder where and how to take delivery of the merchandise.

The clock was winding down, and with every second that ticked off Wolf's tension mounted. He was sick of waiting, tired of watching.

Putting a hard clamp on his impatience, he slipped back into the role of Nina's fiancé and scooted his chair over a few inches. His arm stretched across the back of hers. He kept his gaze on the spectacular sunset until a waiter materialized at their table.

"Would you like a drink before dinner?"

"We would." He gave Nina's shoulders an affectionate squeeze. "Let's have Champagne, Pumpkin, to celebrate our new beginning."

She didn't roll her eyes, but she came close. Despite the simmering tension, Wolf had to hide a grin as he placed the order.

"Cristal brut, 2002."

"Excellent choice, *señor*."

"And very expensive," Nina commented as the waiter left to put in the order.

"You're worth it."

Nina would always blame the Champagne for what happened next. She didn't drink that much. A glass and a half. Two at most.

But those glasses hit hard. Probably because she'd taken only a few bites of breakfast and been too nervous to do more than sample the *coquilles St. Jacques* Cordell's chef had prepared for lunch. She tried to blunt the bubbly's impact with a Caesar salad mixed table side and succulent tilapia with angel hair pasta, but the heady sensation stayed with her right through a caramel crème brûlée to die for.

Wolf, damn him, exacerbated her tingly feeling at regular intervals with oh-so-casual touches. She knew he was merely performing his self-assigned role. That didn't stop the nerves just under her skin from dancing every time he touched her. Or keep her from quivering with anticipation at the idea of a moonlight stroll on the shore. Alone. Away from prying eyes or hidden devices.

Her anticipation mounted when they left the restaurant and approached the elevators. One bank ferried guests up to the resort's main lobby. Another whizzed them down the beach beyond the cliffs.

Wolf paused and gave her a choice. "You've had a helluva day. Are you too tired to take a walk?"

Nina prided herself on her common sense. She always thought things through, studied every option, made decisions only after considering all the facts. Every way she looked at the idea of a stroll along the beach with Wolf suggested she would be wise to take the out he offered. Wise, but dull, dull, dull. Tucking rational, deliberate Nina away for another day, she shrugged.

"After that sinful crème brûlée, I need a walk."

Ha! Who was she kidding? What she wanted was to lock her arms around Wolf's neck and drag him down into the surf, to make wild, passionate love à la Burt Lancaster and Deborah Kerr in *From Here To Eternity*.

All too vivid images of his naked body sprawled

atop hers haunted Nina as she and Wolf left a trail
of footprints in the damp sand. Not until they
reached a small cove some distance from the hotel
and she'd kicked off her shoes to wade into the
shallows did the images evaporate. The shock of
a cold wave slapping her calves banished them
instantly. No way she was dragging *anyone* into
this chilly water to have her evil way with him!

With the surf foaming around her ankles, she
headed for the shelter of the cove, but the now
retreating wave cut the sand out from under her
feet. She windmilled wildly and would have gone
down if not for Wolf's quick reaction.

"Careful." He swept her up, out of the sucking
sand and water. "The undertow can be treacherous
along this stretch of coast."

Not just the undertow, she realized when he
hefted her higher against his chest. The combination
of moonlight, the relentless song of the sea and
the feel of his arms around her was every bit as
dangerous.

The skirt of her linen dress trailed in the surf as
he carried her out of the water. She expected him
to put her down once they'd gained higher ground.
Instead, he stopped at the water's edge and stood
there with her in his arms.

Surprised, Nina glanced up. The moon's glow

cast his features into sharp planes and angles. His jaw had locked, she saw, and the look in his eyes sent her already heightened senses into a joyous leap.

He wanted to kiss her, she saw with fierce elation, and not merely as a distraction this time! The desire was there, sudden and raw, more than matching her own.

As he had this morning outside Cordell's hacienda, Wolf gave her time to cry foul. One word, and he would have put her down. One slight tilt of her head away from his, and he would have ended it.

Nina had no intention of letting him end anything. She made that clear when she slid her free arm up to join the one she'd looped around his neck. He reacted to the glide of her palm over his chest and shoulder with a gruff warning.

"We're playing with fire here."

"I know."

When she tightened her arm, brought her mouth within an inch of his, he issued one last warning.

"This wouldn't be for show, Nina."

"God, I hope not!"

Chapter 8

With all due respect to Burt Lancaster and Deborah Kerr, making love on a moon- and sea-swept beach lacked certain basic amenities.

Like the assurance of privacy, for one thing. Although Nina estimated they'd walked a half mile or more from the Mayan's floodlit grounds, another couple might decide to take the same moonlight stroll. Or worse, the Russians Wolf said were scoping her out.

Then there was the small matter of sand fleas. Nina didn't notice them nipping at her bare toes right away. She was too aroused, too eager to touch and be touched.

Wolf didn't appear to notice them, either. Burying a hand in her hair, he anchored her head for his kiss. His other hand slid down her back to cup her bottom and urge her closer. They stood chest to chest, pelvis to pelvis, straining against each other while his hand roamed her derriere.

"I was right," he murmured against her lips. "You're as soft and smooth as—"

She interrupted him with an indignant huff. "You'd better not be going where I think you're going with that!"

Laughing, he avoided any further reference to pumpkins and dipped his head to kiss the slopes of her breasts above the neckline of her sundress. When he eased open the top few buttons for greater access, Nina sucked in a swift breath. Her stomach hollowed at the rasp of his tongue on her bare skin. The sensation was so erotic she had to dig her fingers into his shoulders to steady herself.

Her shaky legs gave out a few moments later, right along with her ability to withstand his assault on her senses. She sank to her knees in the soft sand. He followed, holding her close. She could feel him rock hard and jutting against her stomach. The sensual pressure tightened her own belly and sent spirals of dark, hot pleasure spinning through her.

She was panting when he tumbled her down to

the sand. Her dress flared out like a beach blanket and should have protected her more from most uninvited guests. Four wiggles and a hard slap later, she recognize the error of her thinking.

"I'm being eaten alive."

"That's the plan," Wolf said with a look that curled her toes into the sand. "But maybe we should adjourn to the resort first."

They made the twenty-minute walk back to the Mayan Princess in ten. As swift as the hike was, it gave Wolf the time he need to recirculate the blood that had emptied out ofhis brain and pooled below his waist.

He had to be out of his mind. He'd had a taste of what this woman could do to him earlier this afternoon. He knew better than to play with fire like this. Letting down his guard for even a few minutes was a good way to get real dead, real fast.

He was in the midst of an op, for God's sake. He had a boat anchored less than a hundred yards off shore. Men hunched over a receiver, tuned in to any sounds emanating from Nina's casita. Yet all Wolf could think of was hauling her back to the suite and getting her naked.

Nina Grant had him tied in knots like none he'd

ever learned in the navy. He'd damn well better take control of the situation. Rein in his raging hunger and in the process bring her down carefully, gently.

He had every intention of doing exactly that. Even when they reached the lighted pathway leading from the beach to the resort and he glanced down at her. Silvery sand dusted almost every inch of her skin. Her hair had tumbled around her shoulders in a wild tangle of honey brown. The lower half of her dress was soaked from the surf, the upper half buttoned haphazardly. But it was the smile she flashed him that got Wolf so hard and tight again he almost doubled over.

If he worked at it, he could rationalize making love to her. He was almost ninety-nine-percent sure those were Cordell's goons out on that boat, listening in. By making an obvious show of taking Nina to bed, Wolf would mark her as his and send a signal to Cordell to back off.

It was that one percent that gnawed at him. So much, that his head was still waging a fierce battle with his body when the door closed behind them.

Nina had no such reservations. The moment they were inside she dropped her sandals, turned and tugged his shirt free of his slacks. With the tails came a shower of sand.

"We must have brought half the beach back with us," she said between quick, nipping kisses. "I hope we didn't bring anything else, Wo... Kevin."

She caught herself in time, but the near miss reinforced his decision to call a halt. Now. Before he let down his guard again and put her at even more risk.

"I'm sorry, Nina." He didn't have to feign a show of reluctance when he reached up and eased her arms from around his neck. "You were right earlier."

Confusion worked its way through the hot desire in her eyes. "About...?"

"I came down to Cabo thinking all I had to do was finesse you into bed to make things right between us. I see now that's not the way to win you back."

He had to touch her, if for no other reason than to blunt her dawning comprehension and dismay. He brushed a knuckle over her cheek and gave a small, almost imperceptible nod toward the flat screen TV.

"I still want you." God, he wanted her! "I'm willing to wait until you trust me again, though."

"You are, huh?" Shooting daggers at him, she played to their unseen audience. "We've got a long way to go before that happens, *Kevin*."

"I know."

"I'm glad you recognize that." She tossed her tangled hair and left him to stew in his own juices. "You know where the spare pillows and blankets are. Good night."

She didn't exactly slam the bedroom door, but the solid thud spoke volumes. Wolf thought about following her to explain his sudden about-face. The fact that he was afraid to test his tenuous control took everything he knew about himself and turned it upside down.

With a smothered curse, he went to the kitchenette to make a pot of coffee. It was going to be a long night. Even longer now that the brown-eyed doc had tied him in knots!

He waited until 2:00 a.m. to make his move.

Moving silently on bare feet, Wolf cracked the bedroom door. Nina's steady breathing assured him she was out for the count. The sheets tangled around her hips and legs suggested she hadn't gone down without a fight.

Guilt and regret nagged at him as he retrieved his gear bag from the closet where he'd stashed it earlier. He'd had plenty of time in the past few hours to acknowledge how badly he'd handled the situation down on the beach.

He should have called a halt after the first kiss. He was supposed to be the trained agent, the one with the cool head and iron nerves. Instead, he'd let his body call the shots. Like some overeager teen fumbling around with his girlfriend in the backseat of his daddy's car, for God's sake! He suspected Nina would take a long time forgiving that bit of idiocy.

With a silent apology, he clicked the door shut and went into the bathroom. He emerged a few minutes later in the wet suit he wore so often in his work that it felt like a second skin. A waterproof waist pack held his phone and the kit he'd put together for situations like this one. He'd left his scuba gear and air tanks in the trunk of Mannie's car, but he wouldn't need them for this job. Not with the roundabout anchored so close to shore.

Before exiting the casita, Wolf rigged one of Mac's low-tech but extremely effective alarms. If anyone tried the door while he was gone, a siren-like wail would wake Nina and everyone else within a half-mile radius.

A murmur of subdued voices drifted from the adult pool, but the rest of the resort had shut down for the night. Still, Wolf avoided the elevators and stuck to the shadow of the stairs that wound down to the beach. Once there, he turned left, away from

the moon-washed stretch of shore he'd walked with
Nina. His goal this time was the protected cove
sheltering the resort's water sports marina—and
the pleasure craft riding at the ends of their anchor
chains. There were four. Two sailboats with their
sails furled, one cabin cruiser showing only its
safety lights, and the twenty-two-foot runabout.

Before going into the water, Wolf extracted a
camo stick from his waist pack. A few quick strokes
blackened his face and hands. Then he entered
the sea at an angle that would allow him to take
advantage of the strong undercurrents to carry him
toward the runabout.

Cutting through the dark water felt as natural
to Wolf as breathing. It should. He'd spent half his
life in this dimension. All those years of training
and experience as a naval underwater demolition
specialist had led naturally to a follow-on career
in the same field. It was a dangerous and highly
specialized profession, but one he and the men he
employed excelled at.

This was what he knew, what he did. Instead of
tiring, Wolf felt his strength and stamina build a
little more with each stroke. And with each clean,
silent stroke, the runabout got a little closer.

Even in the darkness he could see the boat
was new and well maintained. Its fiberglass hull

gleamed. Its eco-friendly, air-cooled electric engine would ensure it entree into marinas trending away from traditional gas-powered boats.

Admiring the boat's sleek lines, Wolf slipped under the water and swam submerged until the hull loomed directly ahead. He surfaced portside, nothing more than a shadow on the dark water, and listened intently. The only sounds he picked up were the wash of waves against the hull and the creak of the anchor chain as the runabout rode the low swells.

As silent as an eel, Wolf swam to the stern and hauled himself over the side so carefully the gunwale hardly rocked. He crouched in the deck well, listening, waiting, his gaze locked on the dim light that speared through the cabin's half-closed hatch. Only when he was satisfied that he'd come aboard undetected did he approach the cabin.

The two-man crew was inside. One snored loudly in the runabout's bunk. The other sat slumped over the built-in table next to the bank of navigational equipment, his head on his crossed arms and a set of earphones on the table beside him.

With a grim smile, Wolf eased into the cabin, reached into his waist pack for two plastic capsules and pinched them under each man's nose. One whiff of the colorless, nonlethal gas would keep them both out cold for a good hour.

He needed less than a fraction of that to find what he'd come looking for. A handwritten log sat next to the ship-to-shore radio. The watchers had made annotations indicating each time Wolf and Nina had entered and exited the casita since noon. Ditto the times they'd engaged in conversations.

Two separate log entries indicated a radio report to "base," the latest one just after midnight. Beside the last entry was a note relaying instructions from Señor Cordell to maintain their position.

Well, that answered that question. It also confirmed Wolf's guess that Cordell had Nina lined up in his sights as a potential mark. Dollar signs must have flashed in front of the bastard's eyes when he discovered Dr. Grant was leading the charge in medical data collection, analysis and exchange. The possibilities for profit—and fraud— probably had him salivating.

The unexpected arrival of Nina's fiancé would have thrown a monkey wrench into whatever tentative plans Cordell had formed for her. If so, the fact that Kevin was still relegated to the living room sofa must have put a smile on the snake's face. He'd be eating that grin before too long, Wolf vowed silently.

Still restless, he prowled the small cabin. On a hunch, he sat down in front of the runabout's marine navigation system. It was state of the art, like everything else on the craft. Housed in a waterproof, shockproof case with an IP66 rating that ensured it would withstand the heaviest seas, the system connected wirelessly via Bluetooth to a GPS, a wind meter, a knot log, and depth-sounder fish-finder. All viewable on a fifteen-inch touch screen LCD with a sunlight readable display, no less.

Damn, Wolf thought wryly. Stealing government secrets obviously paid better than retrieving them. Lusting for a system like this one, he fingered the chart plotter icon and squinted at the long list that painted down the screen.

Another touch of the screen highlighted the three courses plotted in the past twenty-four hours. As each came up, Wolf studied them intently. The first charted the runabout's course from Sebastian Cordell's seaside villa to the Mayan Princess. The second would take the runabout home again.

The third, he saw with a leap of excitement, integrated the weather forecast and tides for 11:00 p.m. Thursday. This course led to a point off the tip of the Baja peninsula some seventeen nautical miles out to sea.

Cordell had invited Nina and Wolf for a short cruise on Thursday afternoon before he took his yacht out for a longer voyage that evening. Made sense that he'd have the runabout shadow the yacht and stay within hailing distance. Just in case.

Reenergized, Wolf went into the water and swam back to shore with clean, strong strokes. His phone came out the moment he cleared the surf.

"Yo, Wolfman. You're up early."

"So are you, Ace. Any news?"

"It's going down just as we anticipated. Cordell received a final bid for the merchandise just before his midnight deadline."

"Did he accept it?"

"Negative. But he did contact your pal, Alekseev, right after that call to advise him the bidding had closed. Alekseev wanted to know when he would designate a time and place for delivery."

"I think I know the time and place."

"No kidding?"

"No kidding. D-day is Thursday. H-hour is twenty-three hundred local, give or take."

"And the coordinates?"

Wolf relayed them, then waited while Ace pulled the location up on the control center's wall-size digital map.

"Looks like Cordell intends to make the exchange outside Mexico's territorial waters."

"Looks like. Mannie will want in on the take-down, though."

"Not a problem. I'll work the coordination at this end. We'll put eyes in the skies, buddy, and have an assault team hovering just over the horizon. What else can I do for you?"

"Arrange an extraction for Nina—Dr. Grant—before the assault Thursday evening. I want her safe and out of the picture."

"Roger that. I may just fly down there and extract her myself. I'm getting saddle sores from all this sitting around. I need some action."

Wolf's reaction was instant and visceral. He knew damn well that Ace's code name didn't refer solely to his ability to throw a jet around the sky at Mach 2. The cocky pilot scored as many hits on the ground as he did in the air.

"Fly down if you want," Wolf told his friend, "but understand this. Dr. Grant is off-limits."

His controller didn't pretend to misunderstand. A low whistle drifted through the phone.

"Like that, is it, Seabiscuit?"

"Yeah, Flyboy, it's like that."

It was most definitely like that.

The realization shook Wolf. It also made him

feel as predatory and territorial as the gray wolves re-introduced into Yellowstone National Park the last summer he worked there. He was just a kid. A long, lanky seventeen-year old about to enter his senior year.

Controversy over the proposed plan had been raging forever. Despite years of objections and a series of lawsuits by ranchers and hunters, the U.S. Fish and Wildlife Service finally brought in thirty-three breeding pairs to counter the out-of-control elk population. Wolf had never forgotten his first glimpse of the animals in their acclimation pens a few days before they were released into the wild. Those bared fangs and black, quivering gums made an indelible impression on a seventeen-year-old kid. So indelible, he had no trouble choosing a code name when he signed on with OMEGA.

Of course, Ace would tell it differently. *He* claimed Rafe had earned his handle by cutting love 'em and leave 'em women out of the pack, then doing precisely that.

Wolf should have listened to his instincts when they warned him Dr. Nina Grant wasn't the love 'em and leave 'em type. In less than forty-eight hours she'd gotten under his skin more than any woman he'd ever known. It wasn't just lust, although the prospect of sliding into bed and losing himself in her severely impacted his ability to walk upright.

The truth broadsided him while he made his way back to the pyramid illuminated dramatically against the night sky. For the first time in his life he wanted more than casual sex.

Damn if he didn't feel the most ridiculous need to brush the soft brown hair back from her cheek and nuzzle the skin behind her ear. To chuckle at her grimace when he laid that Pumpkin tag on her. Hear her gasp with surprise and delight as the surf swirled around her ankles.

He'd like to see her in her own world, too. She had to be one savvy business exec, more than able to hold her own in the boardroom. Throw in her expertise in the area of biomedical systems...

Wolf jerked to a halt in the shadow of a leafy jacaranda, as disgusted with himself as he was disconcerted. Christ! He had it bad. Much worse than he thought. Good thing he'd arranged to get Nina out of Cabo. He needed a clear head and the absolute assurance she was safe when he faced down Cordell and/or Alekseev.

He'd get her out now, he thought grimly, if he didn't need to maintain cover until Thursday. After that all bets were off.

Chapter 9

Nina woke Wednesday morning feeling sluggish and disgruntled and bitchy as hell.

Part of her pissy mood she could blame on the heat pouring through the sliding glass doors she'd left open last night. With the screen latched and the fan turning lazily overhead, she'd counted on the sea breeze and the murmur of the waves to help her get over being left high and dry by a certain rat fink undercover agent.

The ploy didn't work. Sticky with sweat, she rolled out of bed almost as uptight as when she'd flopped into it.

"Some vacation," she said, grousing to the

tangle-haired woman in the mirror before she padded across the room to close the sliding glass doors and flip on the air conditioning.

The sound of the shower going full blast didn't improve her mood. She urgently had to use the bathroom.

Still grousing, she went into the kitchenette and dumped the cold dregs from the coffee pot, then tapped an impatient foot while the fresh brew bubbled and her need to hit the bathroom mounted. Jaw set, she tried to think about what she would order for breakfast, about what she'd wear today, about *anything* except Rafe Blackstone wet and naked under those gushing jets.

That ploy didn't work either. Consequently, she greeted him with something less than friendliness when he finally emerged with a towel slung around his neck and his unsnapped jeans riding low on his hips.

"About time," she said, huffing. "I thought you were going to spend all day in there."

With a crooked smile, he zeroed right in on her problem. "Rough night?"

"Not at all. I slept like a baby."

Damn it! Why couldn't she lie better? She could feel her cheeks heating even as his smile took a wry twist.

"Sure glad someone did."

She started to remind him that sleeping on the couch was his idea, but settled for an airy wave in the direction of the kitchen. "I made a fresh pot of coffee. Help yourself while I hit the bathroom."

One more day, she reminded herself, as she twisted the jets to full power. Two at the most. That's all she and Wolf had to get through before they ended this farce.

After last night, the end couldn't come soon enough for Nina. She'd thought Kevin had put her through the mother of all emotional upheavals. This was fifty times worse. At least her former fiancé hadn't left her so sexually frustrated she wanted to hurl a lamp at his head.

Still simmering, she toweled off and clamped her wet hair on top of her head before examining the meager contents of the bedroom closet. There wasn't much to choose from. She hadn't packed for cruises with smarmy expatriates or lounging around with fake fiancés.

Since Wolf was in jeans, she went with white slacks, a turquoise T-shirt and a pair of flip-flops. Her soles slapped the tiles as she marched into the living room.

"What's on the agenda today?"

He hiked a brow at her tone, but shrugged and

handed her a fresh cup of coffee. "This is your vacation. I'm just along for the ride. What are you up for, Pumpkin?"

Enough was enough.

"Grinding your head into the sand if you call me that again. You know I hate it, *Kevin*."

"Right. Sorry." He looked anything but contrite as he leaned his hips against the kitchen counter. "What do you want to do today?"

She knew several things she *didn't* want to do. Floating hip to hip in the pool for one. Sipping Champagne under a starlit sky for another.

"Let's start with breakfast," she said, sounding tart even to her own ears. "We can decide what to do or where to go from there."

When they stepped into the elevator that would zing them up to the main section of the resort, Rafe tried to soothe her ruffled feathers.

"I need to explain about last night."

"No explanations necessary." Chin held high, she stared straight ahead. "I got the message."

"Not the message I intended to convey."

"Really?" She turned and slid her sunglasses down to the tip of her nose. "You'd better clue me in then. I obviously misinterpreted those hot-and-heavy kisses down on the beach."

"No, that part was real enough."

"So, which part wasn't? The part where we hustled back to the resort? Or the part where you backed away like a frightened virgin?"

Wolf couldn't help it. He had to laugh, even though he knew Nina would take it the wrong way. Which of course she did.

"You think last night was funny?" she fumed.

"Not hardly. It's just—"

"What?" she demanded when he tried unsuccessfully to smother another chuckle.

"I've been accused of a lot of things over the years, but this is the first time anyone's ever thrown 'frightened' and 'virgin' at me in the same sentence."

Her mouth opened then snapped shut again.

"Okay," she said after a silence. "I'll concede that being nervous about your ability to perform last night may not have been the issue."

"Thanks."

"Then what was?"

His grin fading, Wolf tucked a loose strand behind her ear. The truth was harder to admit than he would have thought possible two days ago.

"Okay, here's the problem in a nutshell. I almost forgot where we were last night. Worse, I came close to forgetting the situation I've dragged you into."

Nina scowled, but before she could reply the elevator glided to a halt at the resort's terraced café.

"We're not done with this conversation," she warned before she stepped out.

Wolf suspected as much, and used the time that it took the hostess to show them to a table by the window and a waitress to supply them with a pot of coffee to gather his thoughts.

"I'm sorry," he said quietly. "Last night was all my fault. I shouldn't have let things get so out of hand down there on the beach."

"*Let* them get out of hand?" She sat back, studying him with another frown. "Are you usually so in control that you can turn your feelings on and off?"

Pretty much, Wolf admitted silently. *Until last night.*

"I dragged you into this mess," he reminded her. "It's my responsibility to get you out again safely. To do that I need to stay focused."

"Focused," she echoed stiffly as she buried her face behind the menu. "Right."

Hell! He was handling this all wrong. Wolf tried another tack.

"Listen to me, Pum...Nina. I don't want you hurt. If it wouldn't rouse Cordell's suspicions, I'd put you on a plane out of Cabo this morning. I may yet, if the situation gets any dicier."

The menu came down again and hit the table with a silverware-rattling thud.

"Now you listen to me. I'm in this as deep as you are. More to the point, I make my own decisions."

"Granted, but—"

"No buts." Temper flaring in her brown eyes, she leaned forward and stabbed the air with a forefinger for emphasis. "Get this straight, Blackstone. You are not 'putting' me anywhere."

She jerked the menu up again, leaving Wolf to contemplate the gold-embossed Mayan pyramid on its front cover...along with the possibility he might have to break another capsule, hold it under Dr. Grant's nose and call in Ace to make the extraction after all.

They spent the rest of the morning in what Nina would term a state of armed neutrality.

Conditions started to thaw when they went up for a late lunch. Nina found it difficult to remain hostile to a man with Rafe's quick, slashing grin and complete imperviousness to her snubs.

By early afternoon, she was ready to declare a truce. Especially since Rafe had cranked up her iPod and made several trips out to the balcony to take or return calls on his juiced-up phone. Each time he came back in, his leashed tension was almost palpable.

The call he'd obviously been waiting for came a little past three. He beckoned Nina out to the balcony and broke the news while she sat on the edge of the hot tub and swirled her feet in the bubbling water.

"Cordell's accepted the Russians' bid for his merchandise."

She shook her head in disgust. "How much is he getting to sell out his country?"

"Six million. Half to be wired to his account by the close of business today, the rest when he makes delivery."

"Which you think he's going to do by boat? Tomorrow? Somewhere off the Baja coast?"

"That's our best guess. We'll know for certain soon enough. Cordell told the Russians he would let them know when and where to rendezvous. If he sets up an exchange at sea, they'll need time to charter a boat and crew."

Nina shook her head in disbelief. Less than a week ago work had constituted her whole world. She went in to the office at 5:00 or 6:00 a.m. and didn't leave until late in the evening. The long hours and thrill of bringing in major new customers for her company's medical trending data had gone a long way toward blunting the sting of Kevin's betrayal.

Now here she was, sitting on the balcony of her luxurious casita, looking out over the sparkling blue Pacific. With this sexy hunk standing just a few feet away, no less. And instead of enjoying the view—or each other—they were calmly discussing a traitorous act of piracy that had already led directly or indirectly to the death of a United States senator.

"I don't understand why they're rendezvousing at all," she said, struggling to wrap her mind around the bizarre situation. "Why doesn't Cordell just transfer his 'merchandise' electronically?"

"The disk that disappeared from Senator Dewitt's office is encrypted. Its contents can't be copied or e-mailed."

"If it's encrypted, wouldn't Cordell need a special password or code to access it?"

"We have to assume he got the code from Senator DeWitt. Otherwise he'd have nothing to sell."

Ouch! That hit a little too close to home.

Before the Kevin fiasco, Nina would have scoffed at the idea of Sebastian Cordell duping a smart, savvy woman like Joyce DeWitt into allowing him access to highly classified technology. Now she felt only sympathy for the woman.

"Our boy is now in a classic standoff," Wolf said with a predatory smile. "He can't let the merchandise out of his hands until he sees the final payment, but he doesn't receive that payment until the customer sees the merchandise."

Nina shifted her gaze to the shimmering Pacific. Incredible to think Sebastian Cordell planned to take them aboard his gleaming yacht for the promised cruise along the Baja Peninsula a few hours before setting out on a far more dangerous voyage.

The silver-maned traitor had nerves of steel. She had to give him that. Not many men could play the gracious host simply to kill some time before rendezvousing with a badass lieutenant in the Russian mafia.

No, not simply to kill some time. If Wolf was right, Cordell had her lined up as a potential mark. The prospect gave Nina a creepy feeling that crawled along her nerves more with each passing hour.

Sheer desperation finally prompted her to suggest a temporary distraction. She waylaid Wolf in the living room and was careful to play for Cordell's listeners.

"You haven't seen much of Cabo San Lucas yet,

Kevin. Why don't we walk around town, then have an early dinner at the marina?"

"Sounds good," he replied, his eyes glinting. "One of the waiters at the pool yesterday mentioned a great place for margaritas and shrimp fajitas. The Pink Parrot, or something like that."

Incredible. She was a twittering bundle of nerves, and he was yanking her chain.

"I saw that place when I was downtown," she tossed back. "The parrot's purple, not pink."

"Whatever. I'd better slather another layer of sunscreen on you first. The backs of your legs are looking a little red." He scooped the lotion off the coffee table. "Turn around."

"I'll do it."

She snatched the lotion out of his hand and backed away. No way she was letting him slide his hands between her thighs again.

Duly slathered and smelling strongly of coconut, she called to have the rental car delivered from the parking area. The cheerful, smiling parking valet had it idling at the curb when they emerged from the open air lobby.

"*Buenos dias,* Dr. Grant, Señor James."

"*Buenos dias,* Ramon."

"I'd better drive," Wolf said as they approached the vehicle.

He'd taken the wheel of the rental before his too-casual comment registered with Nina.

"Why do you need to drive?"

"I know the town better than you do."

Also too casual. As he adjusted the rearview mirror, she bit her lip and wondered if she'd made a mistake by suggesting they get out for a few hours.

She got her answer less than thirty minutes later.

They'd just parked the rental and were strolling through the plaza in Cabo's open-air mall. A gallery with arched windows showcasing exquisitely painted pottery caught Nina's gaze, but Wolf spotted something entirely different in the windows.

"Hell!"

She glanced up and saw he'd locked on a wavy image reflected in the window. It showed the shop across the plaza, with two men standing just outside the front entrance.

Nina threw a startled glance over her shoulder. She had time to note only sketchy details—the shop was a tobacco store and the taller of the two men was rolling a fat black cigar between his thumb and forefinger—before Wolf thrust her at the gallery entrance.

"Get inside! Now!"

Her heart pounding, she reached for the elaborate brass latch and stumbled over the threshold.

"Who is it?" she asked when Wolf whipped in behind her.

"I don't know the one on the left. The tall one on the right is the Albanian sewer rat who pumped two rounds into me before I shot him."

"Please tell me you're kidding!"

"I wish."

Wolf used the pottery display as a screen and kept his eyes on the men across the plaza. "The hits must have thrown off my aim," he muttered in disgust. "I was sure I put one dead center before the whole friggin' warehouse blew."

"Your sewer rat," Nina gasped. "Do you think he's working for the Russians?"

"That would be my guess. Alekseev is probably inside the tobacco shop now, stocking up on hand-rolled Hobanas."

Albanians. Russians. Lying, stealing, scum-sucking Americans. The whole alternate universe thing was now officially freaking Nina out!

Scarcely able to breath, she peeked around Wolf. Her chest cramped when she spotted the taller of the two men frozen in place, staring at the gallery entrance. The cramp doubled in intensity when he said something to his pal and they started across the plaza.

"May I help you?"

The polite query almost brought Nina out of her skin. Close to hyperventilating, she slewed around to face a smiling salesperson.

"No, uh, thanks. We're just, um, looking."

She'd barely gasped out the reply before Wolf wrapped a hand around her upper arm. Hustling her past the startled saleswoman, he hauled her toward the rear of the gallery.

"Señor! You cannot go out that way!"

He ignored the woman's shout and hit the emergency release bar on the back door. The action triggered an ear-splitting alarm. Wincing, Nina hunched her shoulders against the vicious assault. She winced again when she caught a whiff of the garbage bins that lined the back alley, their contents steaming in the heat.

Wolf didn't give her time to adjust to the screaming siren or the stink. He shoved the rental's keys into her hand and rapped out instructions.

"Take the car. Drive straight back to the resort. Don't open the door for anyone except me or Mannie. Or Ace, my controller," he reminded her as he hiked up his pant leg. Ripping up the Velcro strap on his ankle holster, he straightened again in one fluid move.

"Wolf! What are you—"

"Go, Nina."

He spun her toward the north end of the alleyway and shoved. She took a few stumbling steps, then started to run.

Instinct told her she would only get in his way if she didn't do as he instructed. Or force him to take stupid risks to protect her. Or…

Oh, God!

She skidded to a stop and ducked behind a garbage can. One glance back down the alley twisted her insides in knots. Wolf stood at the far end of the alley. Clearly silhouetted against a bright shaft of sunlight, Nina saw as terror closed her throat.

He'd set himself up as a target to give her time to get away!

She wanted to scream at him to take cover, but she knew he wouldn't hear her over the screeching alarm. Then the sewer rat and his friend burst through the gallery's back door and she realized in a blinding flash that they couldn't hear her, either. Not with their entire attention fixed on the figure at the far entrance to the dank passageway.

Careful, precise, cautious Nina didn't stop to think. Snatching a lid off the garbage can, she charged down the alley.

Chapter 10

"She took the Albanian down with the lid from a *garbage can?*"

The stunned response coming through Wolf's cell phone might have made him grin if he wasn't still trying to recover. Even now, almost an hour after the fact, the image of Nina tearing down the alleyway had him leaning an elbow against the wall outside Mannie's office for support.

"She came at him from behind," he confirmed, "and whacked the hell out of him."

"Are you sure we're talking about the same woman?" Ace asked incredulously. "Isn't this the one who was so twittery and nervous about wearing a bug that you had to jump into the picture as her fiancé?"

"That's the one."

"Damn!"

"Yeah," Wolf drawled, "that was pretty much my reaction, too."

"Wait until I tell Lightning about this," Ace said, his voice filled with unholy glee. "One of OMEGA's crack agents creases the Albanian's skull in Paris a few years ago, and he walks away. Dr. Grant whacks him with the lid from a garbage can and he goes down for the count."

"Can we get serious here?"

"Sorry, Wolfman. You said two men came after you. I assume you took care of the second."

"I did. Mannie's got them both in holding cells. They're not talking, and he's not letting them make any calls. For the time being, anyway."

Wolf shifted just enough to peer inside the office Mannie and his elite federal task force had commandeered in Cabo San Lucas's central police station. Nina sat on the edge of a battered desk, her eyes huge, as Wolf's counterpart for this op regaled her with God knew what stories from their checkered past.

"What about their boss?" Ace wanted to know, reclaiming Wolf's attention.

"Alekseev was in a tobacco store across the plaza. Mannie's people grilled the shop owner. He swears he and his customer didn't hear the alarm go off in the alley behind the gallery, but realized something had happened when the police arrived on the plaza with sirens screaming. Reportedly, Alekseev rushed to the front entrance, saw his two watchdogs had gone missing, then cursed and tore back through the shop."

"So the Russian doesn't know what went down?"

"Not yet. He's got sources. He'll find out eventually. So will Cordell. The question now is whether this will spook them into calling off the deal."

The possibility ate at Wolf like battery acid. They were so close to nailing the traitorous bastard. So damn close. He hated the possibility they'd have to reinitiate surveillance and start all over again.

"My guess is they'll press ahead," Ace said. "The wire transfer for the first three million went through a half hour ago."

That should have been enough to take Cordell down. If the man hadn't been so careful, if he'd made an actual reference to the stolen technology during his so-called negotiations, Wolf and Mannie could move on him now. But all they had on tape were vague references to "merchandise." They had to nail him with the disk in his possession. Preferably at the time of hand-off, so they could catch the buyers in the same net.

Which would have happened tomorrow night, some seventeen miles out to sea.

Wolf gripped the phone in a white-knuckled fist. Every job he did for OMEGA involved uncertainties. The unexpected had to be anticipated. Things could—and often did—go wrong. He suspected that in other circumstances he would have assessed the implications of his encounter with the Albanian, calculated the risks and pressed ahead with the op as originally planned.

A sudden outburst of laughter brought Wolf around again. Nina had her head and shoulders back, chortling in delight. Despite her present merriment, she displayed ample evidence of their grim back-alley confrontation. The hair that spilled over her shoulders was damp with sweat. Dirt streaked one cheek. A variety of stains discolored her once-pristine white pants.

Slammed once again with the mental image of her charging down the alley, swinging that damn lid, Wolf opted instantly for Plan B.

"I want Dr. Grant out of Cabo this evening. Although we have the Albanian and his pal on ice,

I can't take the chance they'll get word to Alekseev, or tip Cordell to the fact that I'm not really her fiancé."

Ace had spent too many years in the field to question an operative's on-scene assessment. "Your call, Wolfman. I can set up an extraction and have her out of there in an hour."

"Make it two. There's a chance Cordell won't connect her—or me—to the incident with Alekseev's boys, so we need to make her departure look legit. I'll drive her back to the resort to pack her things and check out. That way, when she calls Cordell to tell him there's been an emergency at home and she has to leave Mexico, the hotel can verify that she's checked out and departed."

"Two hours works perfectly," Ace replied. "Diamond's in Scottsdale at a showing of her new line. T.J.'s with her. I'll set up a private jet and have one of them in Cabo by the time you get Dr. Grant to the airport."

Wolf felt the tight knot of tension at the base of his skull ease a fraction. Jordan Colby, code name Diamond, designed a line of high-fashion eyeware coveted by queens and teenagers alike. Only a few insiders knew that she donated all proceeds from her business to charities that cared for abused or abandoned children.

In her other life, Diamond was the one of the coolest agents under fire Wolf had ever worked with. Her husband, former NYC cop, T. J. Scott, was no slouch, either. T.J. could talk down, stare down or take down all comers. Wolf could trust either of them to keep Nina safe until he tied things up at this end and rejoined her.

Whoa! Where had that come from?

Until this moment, he hadn't thought beyond nailing Cordell and recovering the stolen technology. Now he was projecting ahead to more days with Nina. And nights. Like last night, he thought, with a sudden tightening in his belly, but with a *very* different ending.

Wolf waited until they were in the rental car and headed back to the Mayan Princess to inform Nina about the change in plans.

"The encounter with the Albanian upped the stakes." He kept an eye on the rearview mirror, as much from instinct as from nerves. "Mannie's promised to hold him incommunicado for the next twenty-four hours."

"Until after the exchange."

"Right. But there's no guarantee Alekseev won't nose out what happened, maybe finger me as the agent who tangled with his boy in Paris a few years back. If he does, he'll want to know what I was doing at Cordell's hacienda with you."

"Cordell will want to know the same thing," she said, with a catch in her voice. "This just keeps getting hairier and hairier."

"Which is why we need to get you out of it. This evening, Nina."

He braced himself for a spurt of angry protests. She'd made her feelings about staying in the game clear enough at breakfast. And he had to admit she'd more than held her own back there in the alley. To Wolf's surprise, she merely gave a small nod.

He should have let it go at that. He'd made his point. Had her unspoken acquiescence. No need to muddy the waters with a fumbling explanation.

"It's not just your confrontation with the Albanian," he heard himself say. "It's how I felt when I saw you charging down the alley."

That caught her attention. She cocked her head and studied him with an arrested expression. "How did you feel?"

Wolf hesitated. This was tougher than he'd imagined. He'd never told a woman he loved her before. He couldn't tell this one, either. The standard, hackneyed phrases just wouldn't come.

"Like the ground dropped out from under my feet."

"I felt pretty much the same way when I realized you were setting yourself up as a target to lead your Albanian pal away from me," she said slowly.

Wolf shot her a quick glance. So she'd tumbled to that, had she? He'd figured she'd just reacted instinctively back there in the alley. The realization that she'd put herself in the line of fire to save *him* reinforced Wolf's decision to get her out of Cabo.

"Then you understand why I need to know you're safe, Pumpkin. Otherwise I won't be able to concentrate on my job, and that doubles the risk to both of us."

Nina understood all right. She didn't like it, but she understood.

These days and nights with Rafe Blackstone had triggered something inside her. Some craving for adventure and excitement she'd never realized she possessed. It was as though he'd flicked a switch and turned on a hidden Nina. Bolder, braver, more reckless.

Everything in her resisted the idea of flicking the switch to Off again and going back to her safe, secure world. But the possibility that her continued presence in Cabo could get Wolf killed overrode every other consideration.

She took heart from the unspoken message buried in his gruff admission, however. Even more from that ridiculous nickname. Suddenly being compared to a slice of Thanksgiving pie didn't seem quite as obnoxious as it had before.

"Don't worry," she told him. "I'll go quietly, sheriff."

The smile he flashed her almost made up for being hustled out of Cabo. Almost.

"Here's the deal. Ace is sending a private jet to pick you up, along with another OMEGA agent to act as your escort. She, or he, will stay with you until this op terminates and I can join you in Albuquerque."

Nothing hidden in that message! The excitement started to trickle back.

"You're coming to Albuquerque?"

"That's the plan." He slanted her an inquiring glance. "Unless you say otherwise."

Was he kidding? Delight curled in her belly, but she was darned if she'd make it that easy for him.

"So now I get a vote?"

His smile turned wicked. "Not really. I was just being polite. You and I have some unfinished business to take care of, Dr. Grant."

She wanted to follow up on that interesting comment, but Wolf insisted they use the remaining five or ten minutes until they reached the casita to rehearse the exit lines they'd feed to Cordell's listeners.

They assumed their respective roles as soon as he'd keyed the front door and done a quick sweep of the interior. Ushering Nina inside, he tossed the key card on the counter and did his best to project a disgruntled lover.

"I can't believe your biggest customer calls you and insists he *has* to meet with you tomorrow morning. This is your first vacation in years. What's so serious it can't wait until next week?"

"I told you. Mike has a good shot at fifteen million in medical-reform dollars. He needs sanitized data from us, like yesterday, to demonstrate the viability of the med-chip he proposes to imbed under patients' skin."

"Well at least he's sending his private jet for us. Sure hate to miss going out on your friend Cordell's boat, though. You'd better call him and cancel."

"I'll do that right now."

Much to Nina's relief, Cordell's answering machine clicked on. She might have discovered a newfound bravado in herself, but she was still the world's worst liar.

"Hi, Sebastian. This is Nina Grant. I'm so sorry,

but Kevin and I have to bow out of the cruise tomorrow afternoon. Something's come up at work and I need to get back to Albuquerque. We're flying home in a few hours."

She had to force herself to fumble through her last few lines.

"I, uh, enjoyed meeting you. I hope I'll see you again sometime."

Like in the newspapers, when she read that he'd been sentenced to ten to twenty years.

"Thanks again for your hospitality."

Despite her newfound craving for excitement, she felt only a sense of relief when she hung up. This undercover business did a real job on the nerves.

"Need help getting packed?" Wolf asked casually.

"No thanks. I'm good. Or maybe not," she amended as he followed her into the bedroom.

She thought he wanted to add some last-minute instructions or make sure she gathered all her belongings. She did *not* expect him to shut the door, catch her arm and spin her against the wall.

"About that unfinished business…"

Her breath caught. "Yes?"

He planted an arm beside her head and smiled down at her. Nina could see herself reflected in his eyes. She saw something else as well. Something that made her heart thud against her ribs.

"I thought maybe you should take this home with you."

"This" was a slow, sensual kiss. An erotic blend of touch and taste and tongue.

Slow was good. Great, in fact. But Nina needed more. Hooking her arms around his neck, she made that abundantly clear. Her mouth locked on to his. Angling, she canted her hips into his lower body. The effect was instantaneous and everything she'd hoped for.

With a low grunt, Wolf wrapped an arm around her waist and pulled her against him. His kiss got harder, hotter. So did Nina. Consumed by the searing heat, she fanned the flames even more by hooking an ankle around his calf and grinding her hips into his. She could feel him harden, thicken, until his entire length pushed at her through the zipper of his jeans.

"How...?" She jerked her head back, gasping. "How long before we have to leave for the airport?"

He stared down at her, his blue eyes smoky. He wanted more, too, she saw on a wave of reckless exhilaration.

"How long, Wolf?"

A muscle ticked in his jaw. He didn't answer for five seconds, ten. Nina was ready to drag him bodily to the bed when he growled down at her.

"Long enough."

The first time was frenzied. Frantic. Right there, against the wall.

She tore at the buttons of his shirt and ripped it down his arms, needing to touch him, taste him. He shed the shirt without breaking contact. His mouth was locked on hers and his hands rough as he hiked up her T-shirt. She had to pull away to get it over her head.

That gave Wolf the perfect opening. Contorting, he dropped nipping kisses across the slopes of her breasts. By the time she shimmied out of her bra, he'd tugged down her slacks and had a hand between her thighs.

She was ready for him—hot and wet and so ready she almost came right then. But when he yanked down her briefs, safe, cautious Nina surfaced with a small shriek.

"Wolf! Please tell me you've got a condom in your wallet!"

"Sorry, sweetheart."

She groaned, and he grinned.

"But I do have several in my gear bag. Don't move. Do *not* move!"

"Like I could?"

She splayed both hands against the plaster and almost quivered with need. Wolf wasn't in much better shape. He'd never wanted any woman as badly as he did this one. Hunger for her burned in his belly, so fierce and primitive it took him three tries to tear open the damn condom.

The delay was brief, only a few seconds. Just long enough for a thin thread of sanity to snake through the red haze in his head. He'd called a halt last night to keep from losing his focus. The situation hadn't changed. If anything, it had grown more serious. What was he doing, slamming Nina up against the wall and going at her like some drunken sailor?

He turned with the condom in his hand. His second thoughts must have shown in his face, because Nina drew in a swift breath, reached out and hooked a hand in his waistband.

"Oh no," she breathed, hauling him against her. "Not this time, Blackstone."

Their second round lasted longer. Probably because their first orgasm was so explosive Wolf had to brace one hand against the wall and hold

Nina up with the other while his chest heaved and the blood slowly returned to his extremities. Or maybe because he wanted to explore the curves and hollows he'd missed the first time around.

Whatever the reason, he took sensual delight in leading her to the king-size bed. She arched like a cat on the clean sheets, one arm over her head, a smile curving her lips.

"Again?"

"Again," he replied, with a grin. "As soon as I get my wind back. In the meantime…"

He stretched out beside her and propped his head on a hand. The other he skimmed over her belly and breasts. The damp, silky texture of her skin combined with the yeasty scent of their lovemaking to get him hard again. Much quicker than Wolf would have believed possible.

Despite the sudden rush of blood and the clock ticking away at the back of his mind he forced a deliberation he was far from feeling. He made every kiss a new discovery, each touch a sensual invitation.

Nina responded slowly at first. Limp and languid, she let him explore at will. Gradually, her breathing quickened and the body he'd teased back to life took on a coiled tension that matched his own.

Wolf hated to end it but the damn clock kept

ticking. Burying his hands in her hair, he slid in, pulled back, thrust home. Her eyes flew open. Wolf looked down at them and knew he'd met the one woman who could change his world. Had changed his world. For the first time in all his years with OMEGA, his mission took second priority.

He should have told her then. Should have said the words that wanted to come so badly he had to bite them back.

Wolf *thought* he was doing the right thing by covering her mouth with his and thrusting in again. *Thought* he had all bases covered when Ace called to confirm that Diamond would touch down at the airport in a little less than thirty minutes. *Thought* all he had to do was hustle Nina aboard the private jet and finish his job down here in Cabo.

He should have known it wouldn't be that easy.

Chapter 11

The attack came on the way to the airport. Wolf spotted the car following them just moments after they'd pulled out of the Mayah Princess' long, curving drive.

"We've got company," he said with a glance in the rearview mirror.

"Again!"

With a weird sense of déjà vu, Nina twisted to peer out the back window. She'd dressed comfortably for travel in drawstring slacks and her red silk tank. They moved easily with her as she searched the early evening haze and tried to pick out their tail.

"Who do you think…?"

"Hell!"

Wolf's curse brought her slewing back around in time to see a Hummer shoot out of a side street and screech to a halt just yards ahead.

"Omigod!"

Yelping, Nina braced both arms on the dash. Wolf cursed again, stood on the brakes and fought the wheel. Their car made almost one-eighty before coming to a squealing, shuddering stop on the dirt shoulder.

The Hummer's passenger had leaped out before the rental's tires stopped spinning. Nina's stomach did a somersault when she recognized the same muscled-up thug who'd searched her bag the afternoon her car broke down. But before she could so much as shout a warning to Wolf, the man smashed her window with his gun butt and screwed the barrel into her temple.

"Señor Cordell wants to see you," he sneered. "You, too, gringo. Get out of the car slowly. Very slowly. Do not force me to blow your woman's brains all over you."

Nina couldn't flick Wolf even a single glance. The barrel jammed so brutally against her temple prevented her from turning her head. She heard a door snick open though, and saw his jean-clad leg swing out.

"Now you," Cordell's thug instructed.

The vicious pressure eased for a fraction of a second. Just long enough for him to yank open the car door, ram the barrel against Nina's neck, and haul her out onto the dirt shoulder. Silvers of broken glass fell from her lap like teardrops. Her sandals crunched on the shards as the muscle-bound creep propelled her toward the Hummer.

"Get in. And you, gringo."

Wolf didn't move. Nina could see him only out of the corner of one eye. That glimpse was enough to stop her heart. His face could have been carved from stone, but his eyes were lethal.

He was going to do something stupid! Make some ridiculously heroic self-sacrifice to save her!

"Just go along with them," she pleaded desperately. "Please!"

"You'd better listen to your woman, gringo."

A screech of tires underscored his warning. The car tailing them, Nina realized, as two more men jumped out and approached Wolf with guns in hand.

Other traffic whizzed by. She saw a shocked face or two pressed against a window, but no one stopped. She had time for only a short, fervent prayer that someone would call the police before Cordell's thug shoved her into the rear door of the Hummer.

Sprawled half-across the seat, she tried to push up. Then the driver reached back, clamped a hand on her neck and mashed her face into the leather.

"Hey!"

Half smothered, she barely felt the tiny prick in her bare arm. When she realized she'd been stuck, she bucked frantically. Every horror story she'd ever heard or read about contaminated needles and infectious diseases rose up to choke her. Fear consumed her as an icy heat raced from her arm to her neck to her chest.

"What...?" Her tongue felt thick. Her lungs had to fight to pull in air. "What did...you...give me?"

"Something to keep you quiet."

As if from a distance, she heard Wolf's vicious snarl.

"You filthy bastards!"

Something hit with a sickening crunch. Bone on bone? Steel on bone? Nina couldn't drag the answer from the gray mist swirling across her mind. She had one last, coherent thought before the mist closed in.

This can't be happening!

* * *

She came awake to the sour taste of bile.

Nausea churned in her stomach. The bed she was lying on rolled. The darkened room spun. A low, constant thump repeated over and over inside her head. Groaning, Nina squeezed her eyes shut again.

She woke a second time moments later. Or was it hours? She had no clue. Breathing through her nose, she tried desperately to control her queasy stomach while her eyes became accustomed to the gloom. She was in a bedroom, she saw. A large and very elegant bedroom, boasting teak built-ins, subdued lighting, and small, square windows curtained in straw-colored silk.

Frowning, Nina focused on the curtains. Were they swaying, or was she? They were *both* moving, she realized, when the bed dipped gently beneath her. She pushed up on one hand, shoved back her tangled hair with the other and took a closer look at her surroundings.

Okay. All right. She had the picture now. The bedroom was actually a luxuriously outfitted cabin. Aboard Sebastian Cordell's monster yacht, if those sculptures in recessed niches were any indication. The swaying—and the sound she now recognized as the gentle thump of waves against the hull—meant the boat was out to sea.

The realization produced a spurt of profound relief. Maybe, just maybe, the churning in her stomach wasn't a residual effect of whatever Sebastian's goons had given her. The biologist in her cringed at the thought that some unknown toxin might be lingering in her system. With any luck, she was just feeling incipient motion sickness.

She sat still for a moment, her legs dangling over the side of the bed, and tested her theory. Another slow roll confirmed it. Thank God! She could handle seasickness. She *had* to handle it.

Pushing off the silk coverlet, she thrust her feet into the sandals someone had aligned neatly beside the bed. She didn't see her tote or anything she could use as a weapon. Except...

Her jaw set, Nina marched over to one of the recessed niches and wrapped her fist around the neck of a slender marble nymph. The sculpture was either glued or plastered to its pedestal but came off after several hard tugs. She took a few experimental swings, deriving fierce satisfaction from the heavy weight of the nymph's base.

All right, Cordell, she thought, as she headed for the door. Prepare to meet one pissed woman.

She fully expected to find the door locked,

and almost fell through when it swung open on well-oiled hinges. Stumbling, she came face to face with an equally startled steward in a starched white jacket. He jumped back and barely avoided tipping his tray of crystal wine glasses.

"Hey!" Nina gasped. "I know you!"

"*Sí,* Dr. Grant. I am Enrique, Señor Cordell's chief steward. I served you drinks at his hacienda when you…*Madre de Dios!*"

His eyes widened with horror, and Nina swung around. She had the nymph hefted, ready to come crashing down on an attacker, when Enrique gasped out an urgent plea.

"That statue, Dr. Grant! It is one of Señor Cordell's most cherished. You must—"

"The man I was with," she interrupted fiercely, spinning back around. "My fiancé. Where is he?"

"With Señor Cordell in the main salon. I will take you there. But first," he entreated, "you will return the statute to its place, yes?"

"No way. Let's go."

He gave her another pleading look. Nina ignored it and kept the marble nymph at the ready as he edged past her. It stayed ready while she followed him down a wood-paneled corridor.

She couldn't quite believe he'd agreed to take her

to Sebastian so readily. Was it a ruse? Would one of Cordell's goons jump out of a side passageway when she passed and poke another needle in her arm? The very real possibility kept Nina so tense she forgot all about her propensity to upchuck every time she left dry land.

"Up here, Doctor."

Wine glasses tinkling, Enrique stood aside so she could precede him up a shallow flight of stairs. Nina gripped the statue in a white-knuckled fist and mounted the steps. She paused three stairs from the top to survey a room that seemed to stretch the entire length of the yacht.

The first thing she noticed were the floor-to-ceiling windows running half the length of the salon. On one side, the bank of windows showcased only pitch blackness. On the other, lights twinkled in the far distance. They were miles and miles off the coast, she realized with a gulp of dismay.

She took another hesitant step and saw that the vast salon included three different seating areas, each with its own entertainment center and flat screen TVs. Stock quotes scrolled across one, headline news across another. The third screen was blank. Probably because the two men seated across from each other on opposite sides of the TV had other matters on their mind than news or stock quotes.

So, apparently, did the man perched on a barstool in front of a gleaming teak bar. It was fitted with recessed lighting and railed shelves, with Cordell's two-thousand-dollar bottle of tequila holding the place of honor on the middle shelf. Nina barely registered the shell-shaped bottle. Her focus was all on the gun the individual at the bar held level and aimed at Wolf.

The gunman spotted her first and called out a soft warning. "Señor Cordell!"

Sebastian turned and when he saw Nina, he rose from his white leather captain's chair with every evidence of delight. Looking the essence of the nautical male in tan slacks, a navy blazer and white silk ascot, he held out a hand.

"So you're awake at last, my dear. We've been waiting for you. Please, come and join us."

She refused to take another step until Wolf added a gruff endorsement.

"It's okay. Come on up."

She guessed it was as far from okay as it could get, but mounted the last step anyway. Enrique followed and made for the bar with his tray of glasses. Sebastian, unbelievably, played the gracious host.

"I'm so pleased to see you up and about, my dear. You must be thirsty. Shall I pour you a drink?"

"No."

"Are you sure?"

When she simply stared at him stonily, he spread his hands in a graceful gesture.

"I really must apologize for the distress my men caused you. It was necessary, as I'm sure you'll agree when I…"

He broke off, his gaze dropping to the object gripped in her hand. His face took on the same horrified expression his steward's had a few moments ago.

"My dear! That's a priceless work of art you're wielding like a club."

"Is that so?"

"It's a Greek water naiad," he said with a touch of desperation, "sculpted by an unknown artist in the second century B.C."

"Yeah, well, this little naiad is going to hit the bulkhead in about two seconds if a certain twenty-first-century piece of slime doesn't order his friend at the bar to hand Wolf that gun."

She hoisted the statue, fully prepared to carry out what she knew in her heart was an empty threat.

"Nina! I implore you. That piece is irre-placeable."

And she and Wolf weren't? The implication made her ache to bring Cordell's nymph crashing down on his head.

"Destroying the statue will cause me considerable grief," he admitted, keeping a wary eye on his precious marble, "but I promise it will gain you nothing."

He'd called her bluff, damn it! She ought to smash the thing just for spite. She might yet, she thought, as she lowered her arm.

Cordell gave an audible sigh of relief. So did Enrique. Wine glasses rattling, the steward set the tray on the end of the bar.

"Thank you, Enrique." Recovering his poise, the master dismissed his servant. "We'll serve ourselves."

The white-jacketed steward avoided Nina's gaze as he passed her en route to the stairs.

"Thanks a lot," she muttered to his retreating back.

Skirting a cream-colored sofa, she moved to Wolf's side and got her first look at the ugly bruise on his right temple. So that bone-crunching thud she thought she'd heard hadn't been some drug-induced hallucination! Cordell's thugs had put Wolf to sleep the hard way.

Furious, she tightened her fist on the statue and

swung on Sebastian again. "You think you can get away with drugging and beating and kidnapping people?"

"I regret having to resort to such extremes, my dear. I prefer to avoid violence when possible but as you can see, my men had to take rather direct action with your friend here. I assure you, however, the agent they administered to you will leave no lasting effects."

"What was it, Sebastian? What did they inject me with?"

"Of course you would want to know. It's your profession, isn't it?"

The condescending comment made Nina seriously consider knocking his capped teeth down his throat.

"I have the mixture prepared at a lab in Dallas. It's extracted from castor beans and…"

"Ricin!" The sudden lurch her stomach made had nothing to do with the boat's motion. "You had your people pump ricin into my veins!"

"In a very small, very controlled amount, I assure you."

"I certainly hope so!"

The military had developed ricin for use in biological warfare. The toxic agent could be dispensed as a cloud, enveloping whole cities, and caused permanent paralysis if inhaled in significant quantities. Swallowed or injected, it could precipitate a slow, agonizing death.

The fact that she'd survived the injection substantiated Cordell's claim that she'd received a carefully calibrated dosage. Enough to incapacitate but not completely shut down all bodily functions. Still, the mere idea that she'd had the deadly toxin swimming through her veins made her throat go tight.

"I can't believe you would let your people play around with that stuff, much less inject it."

"Only into those who show up at my gates and gain entrance to my hacienda under false pretenses," Cordell returned. "Like you and the gentleman posing as your fiancé."

She threw Wolf a helpless glance, but tried to brazen it out. "Who says he's posing?"

"No need to continue the pretense, my dear. From what I read about your fiancé when I researched *you*, the real Kevin James isn't the type to strap a snub-nosed police special to his ankle."

She couldn't argue with that. Wolf didn't bother to try.

"Let's all cut the act, Cordell or Caulder or whatever the hell you want us to call you. Nina knows who you are. You know—or think you do—who I am. The only question left to answer is whether you'll make it easy on yourself and surrender voluntarily."

"And if I choose not to?" he inquired with silky menace.

The two men measured each other. Stripped of every semblance of civility, they emanated a dangerous aura that raised the hairs on the back of Nina's neck.

"You're going down, Cordell. One way or another."

"If I do, I'll take you and Dr. Grant with me."

The threat was real—*very* real, considering the gun still leveled at them by the man at the bar.

Gulping, Nina tightened her grip on the marble nymph. She'd played some sports in high school and college but would never claim to have much of a throwing arm. Maybe if she got closer…

She didn't have to feign a case of the jitters as she paced nervously. Her throat tight, she responded to Cordell's lethal promise to take her and Wolf down with him.

"Like you did Senator DeWitt?" she asked.

"Ah, yes. Beautiful, clever Janice." What looked like genuine regret crossed the man's face. "So tragic, her suicide, and so completely unnecessary."

"If it *was* suicide," Wolf countered grimly.

"It was, I assure you. I certainly had no reason to dispose of her. She gave me what I wanted."

"Let's talk about that, Cordell. You have to know we're not going to let you hand the disk you stole over to the Russians. Or anyone else, for that matter."

"Aren't you? Well, we'll see soon enough. Are you sure I can't pour either of you a drink? I brought the Azteca with me. We have time to indulge before Alekseev arrives."

Wolf didn't bat an eye, but Nina wasn't as skilled at masking her emotions. Cordell read her dismay like an open book.

"Yes, my dear. After the incident in the plaza this afternoon, the purchaser and I decided to move up delivery of the merchandise. We'll make the exchange tonight, not tomorrow night as planned. Then Sebastian Cordell will disappear, just as Stephen Caulder did. So, I'm afraid, will you and your companion."

Oh, God! Did Wolf's people know about the schedule change? Had he managed to get word to them, or to Mannie Diaz? Or the people who were supposed to have met her at the airport? They must have suspected the worst when she and Wolf didn't show. They had to be trying to locate them. If not…

Nausea churned in her stomach again. Swallowing hard, she forced herself to take a few more paces.

"I think I'll take that drink after all."

"Very good, my dear. Let's have the Azteca, shall we?"

Cordell went to the bar, taking care not to block his underling's line of fire. With great deliberation he lifted the shell-shaped bottle from its shelf.

"Alekseev was the one who tipped me to the incident in the plaza, by the way. He didn't have all the details. Only that a *Norte Americana* and her companion had tangled with two of his men."

He ran a fond glance over the spikes of the shell-shaped bottle. Almost like a lover admiring his mistress. Or, Nina thought with a sudden kick to her pulse, a man with a fortune in his hands.

"Alekseev was unable to speak with his men, but he did obtain a description of the American woman and her companion from the sales clerk who witnessed the event. When Alekseev relayed that description to me, I knew immediately it had to be you two."

Nina barely heard him. The medallion in the bottle's center had her full attention. She'd thought it was bronze when Cordell had flashed his precious Azteca in the bright sunlight, but the fluorescent lighting gave it a different hue. More slate colored, and smooth. Very smooth. Much like…

"Señor Cordell?"

The sudden appearance of a crewmember jerked Nina's attention away from the medallion.

"Yes?"

"We're approaching the rendezvous point."

Chapter 12

The rendezvous! Dear God!

Her heart in her throat, Nina whipped her horrified gaze from the crewman to Wolf. He'd pushed to his feet, his muscles coiled and his eyes dangerous.

"If he takes a single step," Cordell instructed the gun-toting henchman still seated at the bar, "shoot the woman."

The threat rooted Wolf to the polished teak flooring.

"Yes, I thought that would stop you," Cordell mused before giving Nina an appraising glance. "You're quite a surprise, my dear. When we first met, my instincts told me you were ripe for the plucking. The research I did on you confirmed those instincts. Even after you brought your so-called fiancé for a visit, I sensed a fire in you that had yet to be tapped. Now…"

"Now?" she echoed, her jaw tight.

"Now," he said with a knowing smile, "it appears our friend here has done some serious tapping."

She certainly couldn't argue with that. The stolen hour with Wolf before they'd left for the airport had rocked her world. In a blinding flash of insight, she knew that whatever happened in the *next* moments or hours, she'd tasted more of life and love with Rafe Blackstone during the past few days than she ever had before.

"You're quite magnificent," Cordell continued with mingled admiration and regret, "prepared to do battle for your man, armed only with my water naiad."

She'd forgotten all about the damn statue still clutched in her hand. It took everything she had not to fling it at Sebastian's head as he replaced his precious bottle of Azteca in its protective rack.

"I'm sorry, but I must ask you both to sit down and wait quietly while I greet my business associate."

With the small, round barrel aimed at her

midsection, Nina gave up all hope of getting close enough to disable the gunman. Sebastian sighed with audible relief when she retreated to the leather sectional. She eased down beside Wolf and placed the water nymph on the brass-trimmed coffee table.

"When my business is concluded," Sebastian promised, "we'll have our drink."

"You know what you can do with that drink."

Ignoring her sarcasm, he issued a final admonition to his henchman to keep a close eye on them and mounted the polished teak stairs to the upper deck. The tension he left behind was so thick that Nina jumped when Wolf covered her hand to give it a squeeze.

"That stuff Cordell's men pumped into you?" he asked in a murmur. "It didn't leave any residual effects?"

"Not that I can feel."

This is so surreal, she thought wildly, as she gripped Wolf's hand. Almost like an out-of-body experience. Here they were, ensconced on a cloud-soft leather sofa in a luxurious salon fit for a Saudi prince. With a gun pointed in their direction. After a murderous bastard calmly announced he intended to dispose of them. Yet Wolf's primary concern at the moment appeared to be her health.

Fighting a rising panic, Nina kept her voice low and one eye on their watchdog. "What's the plan? What're we going to do?"

"Sit tight, for the moment."

That wasn't exactly what she wanted to hear.

"What about your contacts? Mannie Diaz? The people who were supposed to meet us at the airport? Were you able to signal any of them?"

"No, but we've had Cordell under surveillance since the start of this op. They know what's happening."

"So why…?" She stopped and took a deep breath to contain the hysteria that threatened to spiral out of control. "So why aren't they here?"

"They will be."

His utter confidence should have reassured her. Unfortunately it contrasted dramatically with the lethal calculation that leapt into his eyes when the deck beneath their feet gave a delicate shudder and the boat began to slow.

Wolf ignored the grinding pain from the blow to his temple, ignored the tension that had been gnawing at his insides from the moment he'd come awake, ignored everything but the woman he'd dragged into this mess.

"Listen to me, Nina."

He'd been waiting for this moment. The crew

would be absorbed with maneuvering their luxury craft into position alongside whatever boat Alekseev had chartered. Cordell was on deck, overseeing operations.

"We don't have much time now. Here's what I want you to do. Jump up, cross your arms over your middle and act scared, real scared."

"*Act?*" she squeaked.

With another shudder, the yacht came to a dead stop. It was now or never.

"Jump up," Wolf murmured without showing any hint of the urgency knotting his gut. "Grab your middle, then keel over in a dead faint. Got that?"

"I…"

"Now, Pumpkin."

"Oh, God!"

The wild panic in her eyes when she lunged off the sofa was so vivid it startled even Wolf for a second. More to the point, it brought their watchdog's gun up with a jerk.

"I can't take this! I can't!"

Wolf rose as well and reached out as if to soothe her.

"No! Don't touch me! I'm—" she gripped her middle and bent over, moaning "—I'm going to be sick."

"Christ! She needs water," he snarled at their heavy-set guard. "*Agua!*"

Nina sank to her knees between the sofa and coffee table, retching with such realism that Wolf knew in that instant she wasn't acting. He angled his body between her and the guard and shouted over his shoulder.

"*Agua!*"

The guard hesitated for two or three agonizing seconds before sliding off his stool and moving behind the counter. As he yanked at the door of the bar fridge, his gun never wavered and his eyes didn't leave the two of them for a second. The only opportunity that arose, the only opportunity Wolf knew he'd get, came when the guard rounded the counter again and moved just close enough to toss a plastic water bottle across the intervening space.

He shoved Nina down with one hand. The other swept the marble nymph off the table. The statue passed the water bottle in midfight. It caught the guard right between the eyes before crashing to the deck and splintering into a hundred pieces.

Wolf came right behind it. He lunged low and fast as the guard stumbled back, firing wildly. The first shot whizzed past Wolf's ear and thudded into the bulkhead behind him. The second tore through his upper arm. He didn't feel the hit, never noticed the pain, as he slammed his fist into the man's face.

Bone crunched on bone. Blood spurted from the thug's pulped nose, adding to the torrent gushing from the cut in his forehead. His eyes rolled back in his head. With a strangled grunt, he slumped to the deck.

Wolf wrenched away the man's weapon and spun on one heel. "Let's go!"

"Go where?" Nina gasped, scrambling up from her crouch.

"Back to the fantail." He grabbed her arm to haul her with him. "I want you over the side and in the water before the real fireworks start."

"In the water?" Her feet dragged. "With sharks and barracuda and stingrays?"

"I'll put you in a launch." He listened for the thud of feet running on the deck above them. Cordell and company had to have heard the shots, had to be on their way...

Wolf broke off as the sounds he'd been expecting exploded. Footsteps pounded on the deck above. Shouts rang out. A scuffle sounded at the top of the forward stairs.

He shoved Nina toward the salon's aft exit. They catapulted into the narrow corridor bordered by staterooms and ran like hell. Behind them, a shrill, agonized cry rose above the general tumult.

"My naiad!"

With Nina in the lead, they rounded a corner and smacked into Cordell's white-coated steward. Enrique stumbled back, his eyes bugging, but before he could let out more than a gasp, Wolf clipped him with the gun butt. Enrique went down like a felled ox.

"This way."

Another turn, and they sprinted the last few yards to the stairs leading up to the aft lounge and deck. Nina was panting when they burst out onto the deck, with its sweeping views. As far as she could see, the Pacific undulated in shades of deep purple and the darkest green. Squinting, she made out faint lights in the distance.

Very faint lights!

In the *very* far distance!

"Wolf, I don't think…"

"Quiet!"

He thrust out an arm, shielding her behind him while he skimmed a quick glance along the yacht's starboard side. Nina peered over his shoulder and gulped when she spotted a deep-sea fishing boat tethered to Cordell's craft by mooring lines. Two individuals with obvious Slavic features stood with Uzis at the ready in the boat's open deck. The Russians had most definitely arrived!

"Over here."

Wolf propelled her toward the small launch hoisted on davits on the portside. She could hear men shouting below, doors slamming one after another. Cordell and his crew, checking the staterooms and galley, she guessed. Her heart in her throat, she watched while Wolf ripped off the launch's cover and released the winch to let it splash down into the sea. It bobbed just a few feet below the rail.

"Here you go," Wolf said urgently as he unlatched the rail gate.

She approached the opening, feeling ridiculously helpless. "I don't know how to start the engine."

With a muttered oath, he dropped into the launch and pumped a button a few times. When the engine kicked to life he held up a hand.

"Now, Nina."

She swallowed—hard—and stepped down. The small boat lurched under her feet.

Don't think about the motion!

Do not think about it!

Fighting fear and incipient nausea, she let Wolf position her at the wheel. He dropped a quick, hard kiss on her lips.

"Now go."

"Come with me," she begged.

Too late. He'd already swung back aboard. Her last sight of his broad back was as he raced over to the port side. To show himself to the Russians, she guessed, with a sick feeling in her heart, and direct pursuit away from her.

Only this time, she couldn't charge back to help him. She was puttering through dark, rolling swells in this friggin' boat. She could barely steer the thing, much less use it as battering ram.

Where were his friends? What were they waiting for? Why in hell didn't they...?

The answer to her frantic questions blazed out of the night with sudden, blinding potency. One after another, high-intensity spotlights stabbed through the darkness. Five. Eight. Ten or more! Completely surrounding the tethered yacht and fishing boat.

The spots came from rubber rafts, she saw before she threw up an arm to block the eye-searing glare. Small, silent rubber rafts that had come in under the yacht's sophisticated radars! With machine guns mounted in their bows! Blinded but gleeful, Nina did a mental happy dance while a voice blasted through a bullhorn.

"Ahoy! Yo soy teniente Escobar, Marina de Guerra de México. Estamos veniendo a bordo."

Her glee turned to acid in the next second. She was sure she would hear the stutter of machine gun fire, braced herself for a sea battle of epic proportions. Her knuckles went bone white where she gripped the wheel. She didn't move, didn't breathe until an answering shout rang out from the yacht.

"Ahoy, Lieutenant Escobar. Come aboard."

It took three fumbling tries, but she finally figured out how to cut the engine. Then there was nothing to do but hunker down, watch black-suited, heavily armed Navy SEALS scramble aboard the yacht and wait for rescue.

Not until Nina had clambered back aboard the yacht did she discover the reason Cordell and the Russians had given up without a battle.

"Has Cordell surrendered the disk?" she asked Wolf as he helped her from the bobbing launch.

"No." His jaw worked. "We seem to have a classic Mexican standoff."

"Huh?"

"You'll see."

He escorted her back to the main salon, where she found Cordell and a tall, wiry individual she guessed was Alekseev. They faced a black-suited and black-faced Mannie, a willowy blonde in a wet suit that fit her like a second skin, and an array of heavily armed Navy personnel. The tension was so heavy it almost hit Nina in the face, but—unbelievably!—Sebastian greeted her with a smile.

"Ah, there you are, my dear. I wondered where you'd hidden yourself." His smile grew somewhat strained. "I'm not surprised you were reluctant to face me after smashing my little nymph. How unfortunate that you injured one of my men in the process."

"*Most* unfortunate," she retorted. "I would have much preferred it had injured you."

"But why?" Sorrowfully, he shook his silver-maned head. "I offered you nothing but the hospitality of my home and my boat, which any number of witnesses will attest you accepted."

Incredulous, she gaped at him, at Wolf, at him again.

"You're kidding, right?"

"Not at all."

"This is the line you're taking?" She couldn't believe it! The man's gall was incredible. "You're suggesting we were *guests* aboard your little floating pleasure palace?"

"Not suggesting."

"You're crazy! You can't just shrug away the

bruise on Wolf's temple or the drug you pumped into me."

Sebastian shot his cuffs, looking coolly unperturbed. "Again, I can produce any number of witnesses who will confirm the man you introduced to me as your fiancé came aboard with that bruise. And if there are residual drugs in your system, I can only hope most sincerely that you kick whatever habit you've developed."

"Oh, for...!" Wolf slammed the handgun he'd taken from the downed henchman onto the bar counter. "Cut the crap, Cordell. You're not wiggling out of this one. You know damn well we've got the goods on you."

"Do you?" Calmly, he adjusted his cuff. "What goods, may I ask?"

"The encrypted disk you lifted from Senator DeWitt's office and sold to our friend here."

"Indeed? And where, precisely, is this disk?"

A muscle twitched in Wolf's jaw. Spotting it, Nina felt a sudden, hollow sensation in the pit of her stomach. He'd jumped back aboard the yacht, not just to cover her escape, she realized. He'd wanted—no, needed—to be in on the handover of the disk.

That, obviously, hadn't happened. And without the hard evidence linking Cordell to the stolen technology, the bastard might just wiggle off the hook after all.

"You're going to tell us where that disk is," Wolf warned, emanating promise and menace in equal measure.

"I can hardly tell you what I don't know."

The sheer arrogance of the man took Nina's breath away. Fist clenched, she stomped across the salon.

"Nina?"

Ignoring Wolf's questioning glance, she rounded the end of the bar.

"My dear!"

The wary note that leaped into Cordell's voice gave her a vicious satisfaction.

"What are you doing?"

"Treating myself to that drink you promised me. I think I've earned it, don't you?"

"Let me pour it for you."

Before he could take a step, she snatched the silver encrusted tequila bottle from its protective rack and whipped around.

"That's okay." She held the bottle up by its neck. "I'll pour my own."

Her eyes locked with Cordell's. She saw realization flare in his, felt triumph flood her own. Deliberately, Nina opened her fist.

"Ooops."

The two-thousand-dollar bottle shattered against the gleaming teak counter. Glass splintered and liquid spilled out, but the spiny silver plating held its shape. So did the medallion at its center. Which, Nina confirmed, with a blaze of satisfaction, was *not* made of bronze.

"Well, lookee here."

She poked carefully among the gooey shards and used a finger and thumbnail to lift the round, gray-colored object. Her glance swept the salon full of stunned personnel. She took almost as much pleasure from Alekseev's fierce scowl as from the red that now mottled Cordell's cheeks. The gleam of respect in the tall, slender blonde's eyes wasn't bad, either. But it was Wolf's crooked grin that put a silly smile on her face.

"I think this might be what you're looking for," she told him.

"I think it might."

Chapter 13

"I'm glad T.J. and I arrived in time to get in on the action," the long-legged blonde mused as she and Nina downed mugs of hot coffee and watched the sun come up from the forward deck of Cordell's yacht. "Been a while since we had this much fun."

The boat was on its way back to shore, minus its owner and about half the crew. They'd been hustled aboard the navy cutter that had come alongside several hours ago. Mannie had hauled Alekseev and his pals onto the cutter, too, citing violations to Mexico's gun laws and suspicious activity involving transfer of funds. A small contingent from Mexico's elite marine ops squad had remained aboard the yacht to bring it to safe anchorage at the police impound marina.

Wolf had gone with Mannie, along with a tall, well-muscled male in a black wetsuit. He'd turned out to be the husband of Nina's present companion, Jordan Colby, aka Diamond.

Diamond had traded her own wetsuit for a cool, cotton-weave robe appropriated from one of the yacht's well-supplied guest cabins. Beneath it she wore only the two-piece bathing suit she'd had on under the wetsuit. Nina had caught glimpses of the mile-long legs and slender body that had made the woman one of the highest-paid models in the world before she'd quit to begin designing her line of signature eyewear.

A pair of her sunglasses, with their distinctive butterfly logo, picked out in small diamonds in the corner of the left lens, rested on the bridge of her nose now. The sophisticated shades imbued Nina with intense envy and a firm resolve to order a pair as soon as she got home.

Home.

The very thought of it reverberated in her head. After last night, her condo nestled in the foothills of the Sandia Mountains beckoned like a shimmering oasis of peace and calm in an otherwise insane world. Sebastian Cordell and friends had maxed out Nina's newly awakened craving for excitement and danger. No way she could ever classify last night's terror "fun," the way Diamond just had.

"Tell me something." Cradling her coffee mug in both hands, she turned to the cool blonde. "You and T.J. work for the same agency that Wolf does. How often do you get tapped for assignments like this one?"

"It varies. Sometimes we go for months between ops. Other times, we might hop from one right into another."

"And you like living on the edge like that?"

"It certainly keeps life interesting." She slid her glasses down and tipped Nina a glance. "It's not for everyone, though."

"No kidding!"

Diamond hesitated, obviously choosing her words with care. "Look, it's obvious you and Wolf have something going on. If you're worried about getting in too deep, you might want to ask him how he came by his code name sometime."

"Thanks. I will."

Nina didn't tell her she was already in way over her head, but she couldn't help wondering what it would be like to live with a man who jumped into danger on a more or less regular basis. Could she lie awake night after night, wondering and worrying?

Not that Wolf asked her to do either. She was putting her own spin on his casual promise to come to Albuquerque when he'd wrapped things up down here.

Then again, Nina reminded herself, he'd made that promise while they still had some "unfinished business" from the beach to take care of. Maybe those two wild sessions at the Mayan Princess, before they'd left for the airport yesterday afternoon, had settled that score.

She didn't *think* so, but the uncertainty gnawed at her so much that she was only marginally grateful, once back on dry land, to find that Mannie's people had recovered her luggage from the hijacked rental car. They had no idea what had happened to her straw tote, however. So her first act was to borrow Diamond's cell phone to cancel her credit cards and notify the on-call duty officer at the U.S. Consulate in Cabo San Lucas that she'd lost her passport.

"They want me to come by and fill out an application for a replacement passport."

"Not a problem," Diamond assured her. "Let's get changed. We can swing by the consulate on our way to rendezvous with the guys."

Diamond and her husband had left their gear

at Wolf's hotel. They'd checked his room after verifying that he and Nina had departed the Mayan, then failed to show at the airport. At that point, she and T.J. had contacted Mannie Diaz and joined the naval assault team.

"How did you get in?" Nina wanted to know as she and Diamond swept past the front desk of the hotel overlooking the sea. The Pacifica was several steps down from the ultra-fashionable Mayan Princess, but bursting with color and fragrant with the scent of bougainvillea.

"OMEGA operatives have their ways of accessing hotel rooms," Diamond said with a smile as she zapped the key code on the door to Wolf's.

Once inside the functional one-bedroom minisuite, Nina looked around with interest. Rafe Blackstone certainly wasn't the neatest person in the world. The desk chair sported the wrinkled and very gaudy tropical shirt he'd had on the night they'd met at the marina. The knit polo he'd worn to lunch with Cordell lay crumpled at the foot of the bed. A beat-up leather carryall spilling a variety of electronic implements sat atop a dresser.

Diamond set her small overnighter on the desk. "You want first dibs on the shower?"

Nina wanted out of her wrinkled linen slacks and red tank in the worst way, but another urgent priority had surfaced. She tried to remember when she'd last eaten and came up blank.

"You go ahead. I'm famished. While you do your thing, I'll hit the café and order two breakfasts to go."

"Sounds good." Diamond fished a wad of pesos out of her sleek designer handbag. "Better take these, since you're cash- and credit-cardless."

Nina felt a little weird as she strolled the palm-shaded walk that wound between the detached units. After days of looking over her shoulder and playing to a listening device and getting kidnapped not once, but twice, she experienced a relieved, if slightly nervous, sense of freedom. Her stomach provided a distraction as she approached the crowded café and caught her first whiff of sizzling sausage and spicy huevos rancheros. Unfortunately, she'd timed her expedition at the height of the breakfast hour. It took almost a half hour to get a carry-out order.

Balancing a heavy sack and two tall cups of coffee, she made her way back along the palm-shaded walk. With both hands full, she had to kick the door panel to get Diamond's attention. But when the door swung open a few seconds later, the individual on the other side was neither blonde nor freshly showered.

"Wolf!"

He looked rumpled and red-eyed from lack of sleep, with dark bristles shading his cheeks and chin. The bruise on his temple had turned an ugly purplish green. Yet the grin he gave her was all male, and so potent that Nina's heart skipped several beats.

"Diamond indicated we would rendezvous with you and her husband downtown," she said a little breathlessly.

"That was the plan." He relieved her of the precariously balanced coffees. "But it looks like the wrap-up will take longer than expected. So we decided to take a break, clean up, and start fresh later this afternoon."

She trailed him into the minisuite and looked around. "Where are your friends?"

"They went to the front desk to get their own room." He set the cups on the desk and reached for the paper sack. His blue eyes held hers. "They have to stay for wrap-up, but they plan to fly back tonight, if possible. Diamond offered to take you to the consulate to get a replacement passport so you could leave with them. I told them I'd take care of all that. Later."

Oooh-kay.

"If that's all right by you," he added with a

totally unconvincing show of willingness to defer to her wishes in the matter.

"Well…"

"Good. That's settled. Let's eat. I'm starving."

They took their breakfast to the suite's small balcony and ate from the cartons. The double order of beans and huevos rancheros disappeared in quick, hungry forkfuls. So did the warm, sugar-dusted *sopapillas* slathered with butter and honey. Washed down by gulps of coffee, it was hands-down the best meal Nina had ever consumed.

The absence of nerve-crawling tension added to her enjoyment, of course. Then there was the company. He sat across from her, still rumpled and red-eyed and unshaven, but looking totally relaxed…until he caught her gaze.

Eyes narrowed, he searched her face. "You sure you're all right? No lingering aftereffects from the stuff Cordell's goons pumped into you?"

"Not that I can tell."

"I was ready to kill him when I came to. I came close, very close, just before you showed up in the salon."

A shudder rippled down Nina's spine. Sitting here in the bright sunlight made the terror of the night before seem even darker and more desperate.

"The worst of it is that I didn't tell you…"

Scowling, Wolf scraped a palm across his chin. "That is, I didn't let you know…"

"What?"

His frown deepened. "Do you remember me telling you how I felt when I saw you charging down the alleyway?"

Like she could forget it? "As if the ground had dropped out from under you."

"Right. Well, take that feeling and multiply it by a thousand," he said with grim emphasis, "and you might come close to how I felt last night."

She caught her breath. Was he trying to say what she thought he was?

"I'm sorry I dragged you into this mess, Nina."

The air left her lungs with a whoosh. "That's what you've been leading up to? An apology?"

Shoving back his chair, he took her hand and tugged her up to stand beside him on the narrow balcony.

"I'm *trying* to say I love you."

Well! That was better.

"I know it's too soon," he said gruffly, sliding his arms around her waist. "We haven't really had time to get to know each other and you're still getting over the hurt from your jerk of a fiancé."

"What fiancé?"

A sense of absolute rightness filled her heart as she framed his bristly cheeks with both hands.

"I dated Kevin for almost a year before we got engaged, and look what a disaster that turned out to be. I've known you for, what? Five days? Yet I know all I need to about you. No, wait! There is one thing."

"What's that?"

"Diamond told me to ask you how you came by your code name."

A rueful smile tipped his lips. "She did, huh?"

"She did. What's that all about?"

"Most wolves run in packs, but I've always preferred to operate independently. No ties, no entanglements."

"I assume that includes women."

"It did." His arms tightened, pulling her closer. "Until now."

She could feel him hardening against her belly. Her pulse leaped in response, but the doubts that had pinged her earlier came creeping back.

"We need to talk about those ties, Wolf. I'm not sure how well I would do, sitting home and chewing on my fingernails while you go off to battle the Cordells and Alekseevs of the world."

He brushed back a strand of tangled hair. "Someone has to do it."

"True."

"But I've been thinking about that, too. Even lone wolves need to come in from the cold eventually. I've been with OMEGA ten years now. It may be time to take a break, work on other interests. See what new directions life takes."

"That," she breathed, sliding her arms around his neck, "sounds like an excellent idea."

"And in the meantime…" He dropped a fierce kiss on her mouth. "A quick shower and a good three or four hours of sack time might be in order."

"Might, hell!"

Their shower turned out to be anything but quick. Wolf soaped her down, up, and down again. Nina returned the favor, deriving intensely erotic pleasure from the glide of her hand over his taut muscles and slick skin.

And when he lifted her, hooked her legs around his waist, and thrust into her, she knew most definitely her wolf had come in from the cold.

* * * * *

INTRIGUE.

2-IN-1 ANTHOLOGY
TWELVE-GAUGE GUARDIAN
by B.J. Daniels

Journalist Raine is on the run from a killer, but her luck
could be about to change when she catches the eye of
sexy cowboy Cordell Winchester.

SHOTGUN SHERIFF
by Delores Fossen

Texas Ranger Livvy's been sent to Comanche Creek as a
forensic expert, horning in on Sheriff Reed's investigation
and getting him hot under the collar!

•••

2-IN-1 ANTHOLOGY
GUARDING GRACE
by Rebecca York

Grace was haunted by a sinister secret tied to her broodin
bodyguard Brady's brother's murder—a secret that
could tear them apart forever...

SAVING GRACE
by Patricia Rosemoor

Grace never thought she'd trust a man again...until she
met Declan, her gorgeous P.I. protector. He's duty bound
to safeguard her, but could she capture his heart?

On sale from 17th June 2011
Don't miss out!

0611/46a

INTRIGUE...

VAMPIRE SHEIKH
BY NINA BRUHNS

Powerful Seth is enraged. The recent defections of his two favourite lieutenants inspires a bitter need for vengeance. And he's determined to take down mortal enemy Josslyn, despite the passion she arouses in him!

TAKEN
BY LILITH SAINTCROW

Sophie never believed she was special. Then vampires murder her best friend and Sophie's kidnapped by sexy shape-shifter, Zach, who insists she's a Shaman— someone with a rare gift for taming his savage side!

ON SALE 17TH JUNE 2011

THE WOLVEN
BY DEBORAH LeBLANC

Someone is systematically murdering the members of Danyon's werewolf pack. As Alpha, he knows that finding and punishing the murderous entity is his responsibility. But to stop the slayings he'll have to accept the help of wickedly sensual *mortal* Shauna.

ON SALE 1ST JULY 2011

Don't miss out!

Available at WHSmith, Tesco, ASDA, Eason and all good bookshops
www.millsandboon.co.uk

& NOCTURNE

...ting and Other Dangers
Natalie Anderson

...er being trashed on Nadia Keenan's dating website, Ethan ...sh faces three dates with her! *He's* determined to clear his ...me. *She's* determined to prove him for the cad he is...

...e S Before Ex
Mira Lyn Kelly

...orld famous celebrity Ryan Brady's secret wife is filing for ...vorce! Unfortunately for Claire Brady, her soon-to-be-ex is ...l the only man her body wants...

...rl in a Vintage Dress
Nicola Marsh

...a Lombard, 1950s style siren, is petrified: she's got to ...ganise a terrifyingly glam hen do! Worse still, the bride's ...orgeous brother seems interested in the shy woman behind ...e red lipstick...

...punzel in New York
Nikki Logan

...hen a knight in pinstripe rushed to the aid of this damsel, ...e declared she didn't want saving, even by a billionaire! ...t sometimes even *modern Maidens secretly need* ...scuing...

...n sale from 1st July 2011
...on't miss out!

...ailable at WHSmith, Tesco, ASDA, Eason
...d all good bookshops

...ww.millsandboon.co.uk

BAD BLOOD

A POWERFUL
DYNASTY,
WHERE SECRETS
AND SCANDAL
NEVER SLEEP!

VOLUME 1 – 15th April 2011
TORTURED RAKE
by Sarah Morgan

VOLUME 2 – 6th May 2011
SHAMELESS PLAYBOY
by Caitlin Crews

VOLUME 3 – 20th May 2011
RESTLESS BILLIONAIRE
by Abby Green

VOLUME 4 – 3rd June 2011
FEARLESS MAVERICK
by Robyn Grady

8 VOLUMES IN ALL TO COLLECT!

BAD BLOOD

A POWERFUL DYNASTY, WHERE SECRETS AND SCANDAL NEVER SLEEP!

VOLUME 5 – 17th June 2011
HEARTLESS REBEL
by Lynn Raye Harris

VOLUME 6 – 1st July 2011
ILLEGITIMATE TYCOON
by Janette Kenny

VOLUME 7 – 15th July 2011
FORGOTTEN DAUGHTER
by Jennie Lucas

VOLUME 8 – 5th August 2011
LONE WOLFE
by Kate Hewitt

8 VOLUMES IN ALL TO COLLECT!

www.millsandboon.co.uk

2 FREE BOOKS
AND A SURPRISE GIFT

We would like to take this opportunity to thank you for reading this Mills & Boon® book by offering you the chance to take TWO more specially selected books from the Intrigue series absolutely FREE! We're also making this offer to introduce you to the benefits of the Mills & Boon® Book Club™—

- **FREE home delivery**
- **FREE gifts and competitions**
- **FREE monthly Newsletter**
- **Exclusive Mills & Boon Book Club offers**
- **Books available before they're in the shops**

Accepting these FREE books and gift places you under no obligation to buy, you may cancel at any time, even after receiving your free books. Simply complete your details below and return the entire page to the address below. You don't even need a stamp!

YES Please send me 2 free Intrigue books and a surprise gift. I understand that unless you hear from me, I will receive 5 superb new stories every month, including two 2-in-1 books priced at £5.30 each and a single book priced at £3.30, postage and packing free. I am under no obligation to purchase any books and may cancel my subscription at any time. The free books and gift will be mine to keep in any case.

Ms/Mrs/Miss/Mr _____ Initials _____

Surname _____

Address _____

_____ Postcode _____

E-mail _____

Send this whole page to: Mills & Boon Book Club, Free Book Offer, FREEPOST NAT 10298, Richmond, TW9 1BR